Puppeteer

Bryan Seaton: Publisher/ CEO
Shawn Gabborin: Editor In Chief
Jason Martin: Publisher-Danger Zone
Nicole D'Andria: Marketing Director/Editor
Danielle Davison: Executive Administrator
Chad Cicconi: Akumatized
Shawn Pryor: President of Creator Relations

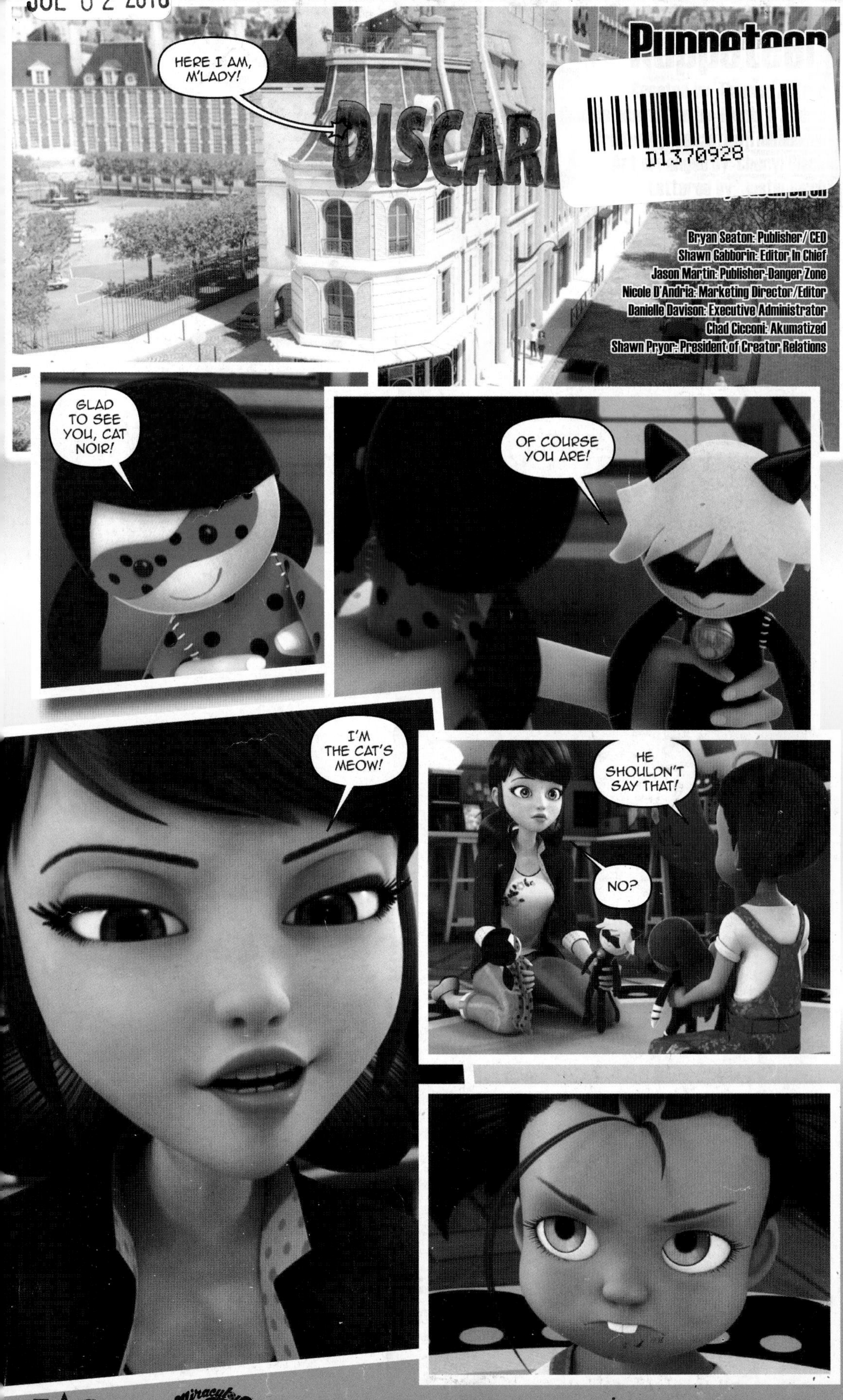
HERE I AM, M'LADY!
GLAD TO SEE YOU, CAT NOIR!
OF COURSE YOU ARE!
I'M THE CAT'S MEOW!
HE SHOULDN'T SAY THAT!
NO?

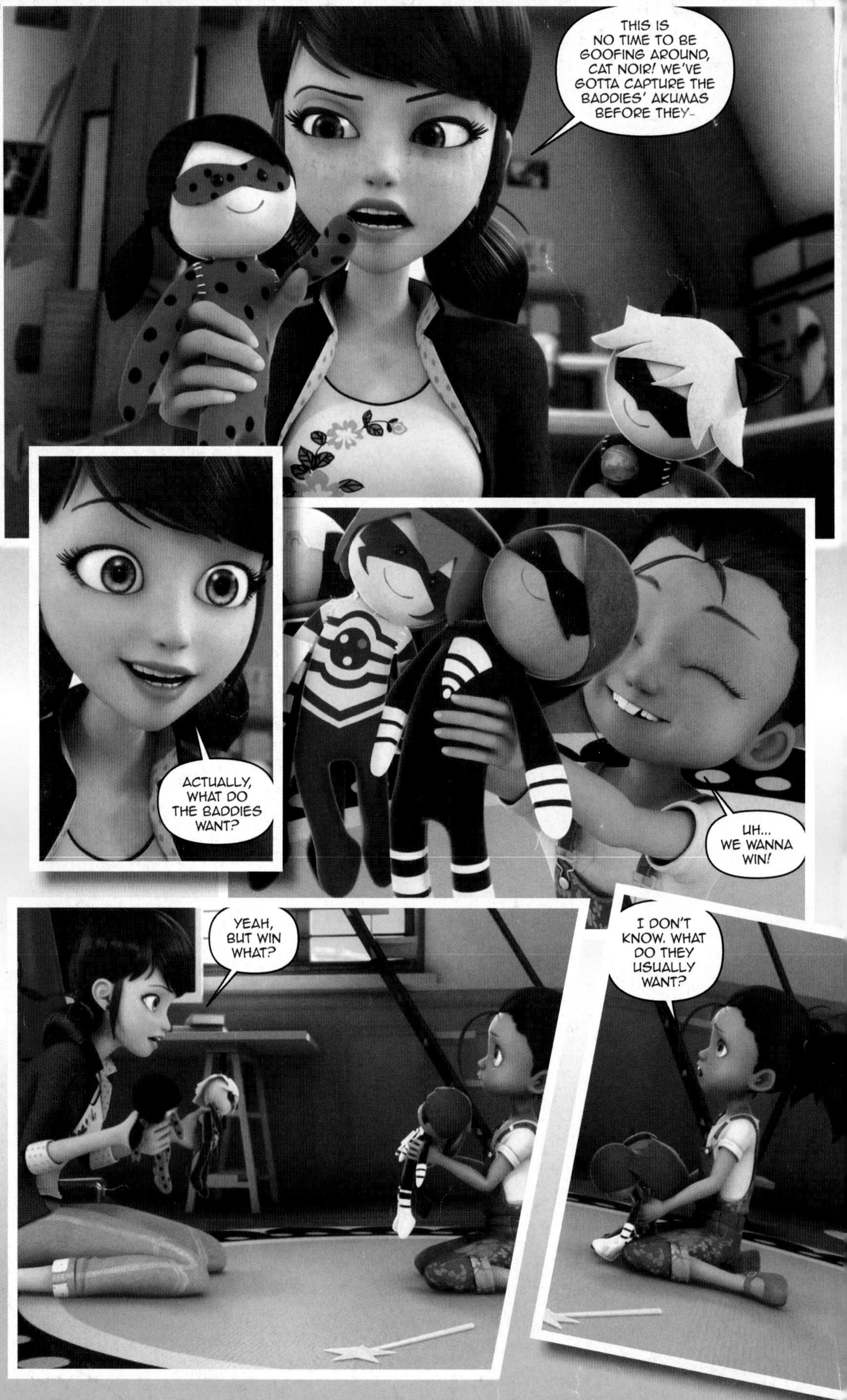
THIS IS NO TIME TO BE GOOFING AROUND, CAT NOIR! WE'VE GOTTA CAPTURE THE BADDIES' AKUMAS BEFORE THEY-
ACTUALLY, WHAT DO THE BADDIES WANT?
UH... WE WANNA WIN!
YEAH, BUT WIN WHAT?
I DON'T KNOW. WHAT DO THEY USUALLY WANT?

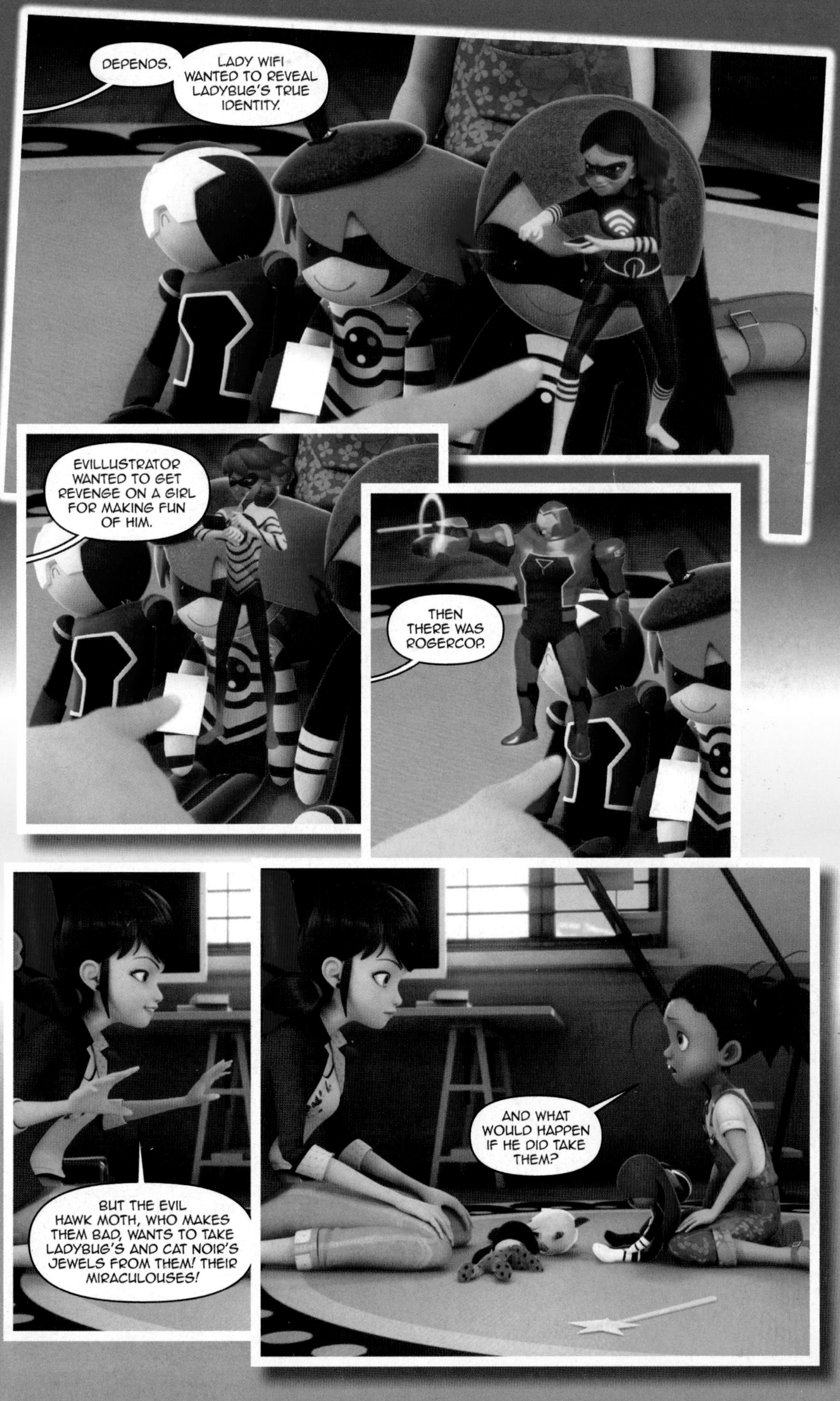
DEPENDS.
LADY WIFI WANTED TO REVEAL LADYBUG'S TRUE IDENTITY.
EVILLUSTRATOR WANTED TO GET REVENGE ON A GIRL FOR MAKING FUN OF HIM.
THEN THERE WAS ROGERCOP.
BUT THE EVIL HAWK MOTH, WHO MAKES THEM BAD, WANTS TO TAKE LADYBUG'S AND CAT NOIR'S JEWELS FROM THEM! THEIR MIRACULOUSES!
AND WHAT WOULD HAPPEN IF HE DID TAKE THEM?

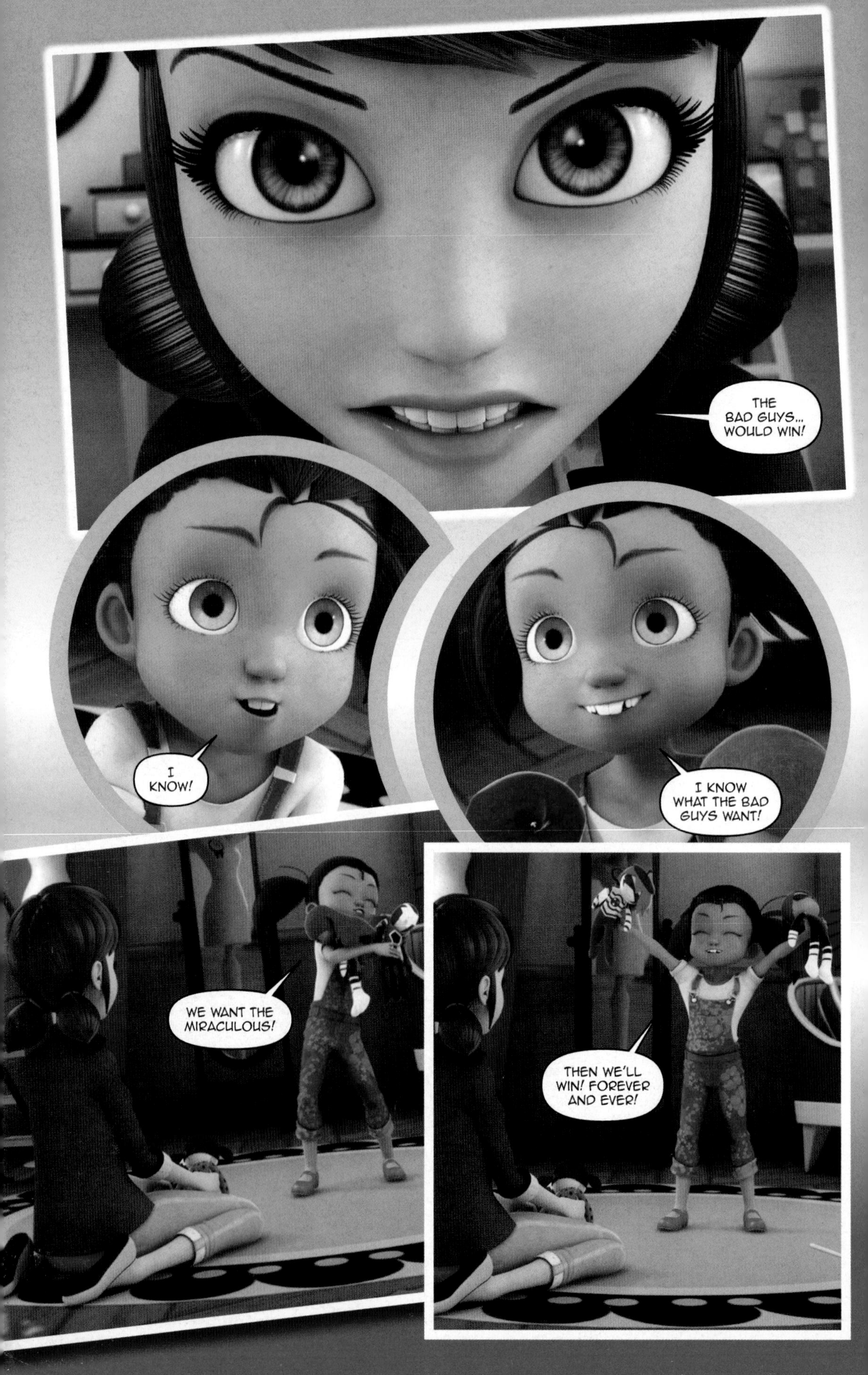
THE BAD GUYS... WOULD WIN!
I KNOW!
I KNOW WHAT THE BAD GUYS WANT!
WE WANT THE MIRACULOUS!
THEN WE'LL WIN! FOREVER AND EVER!

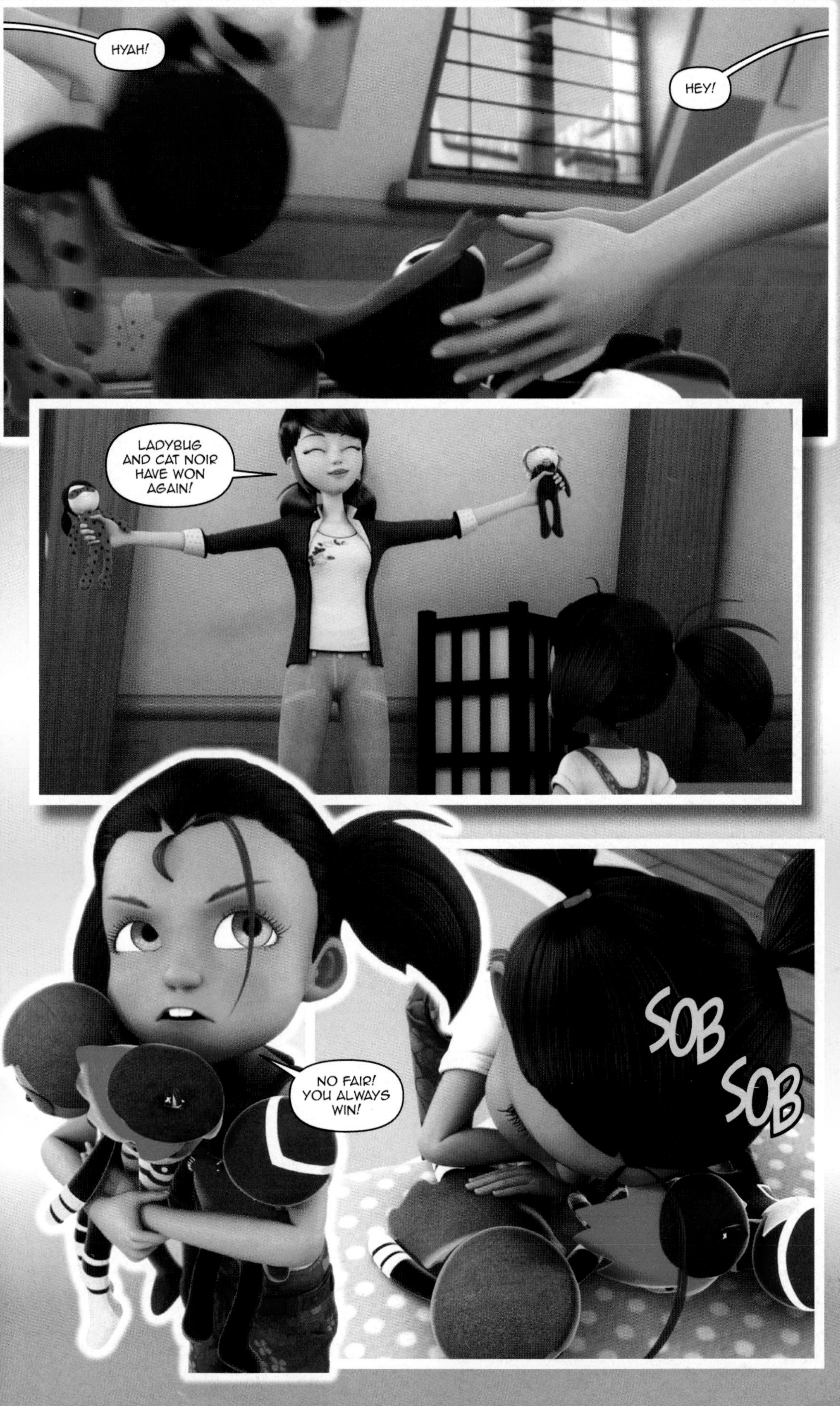
HYAH!
HEY!
LADYBUG AND CAT NOIR HAVE WON AGAIN!
NO FAIR! YOU ALWAYS WIN!
SOB SOB

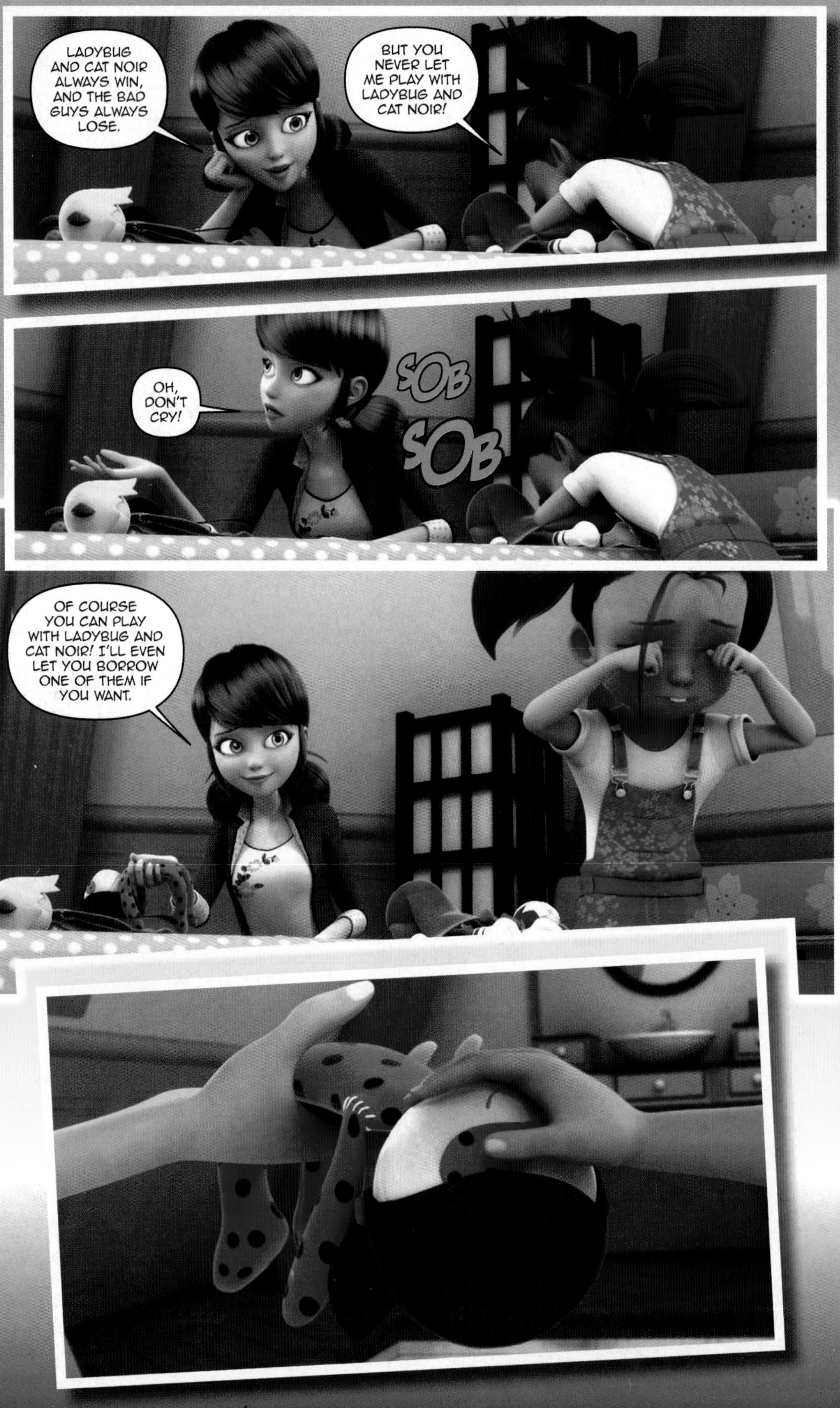
LADYBUG AND CAT NOIR ALWAYS WIN, AND THE BAD GUYS ALWAYS LOSE.
BUT YOU NEVER LET ME PLAY WITH LADYBUG AND CAT NOIR!
SOB
SOB
OH, DON'T CRY!
OF COURSE YOU CAN PLAY WITH LADYBUG AND CAT NOIR! I'LL EVEN LET YOU BORROW ONE OF THEM IF YOU WANT.

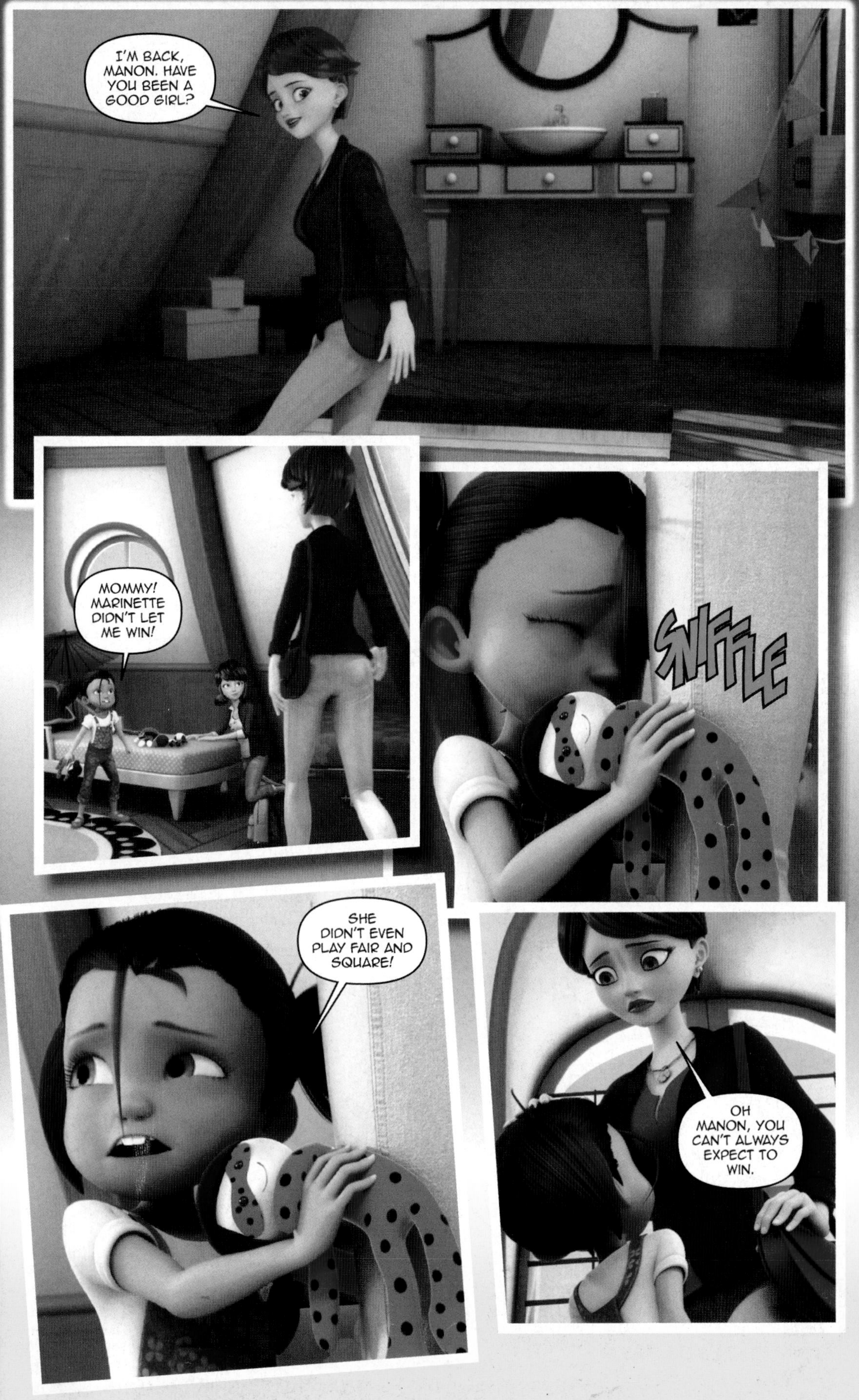
I'M BACK, MANON. HAVE YOU BEEN A GOOD GIRL?
MOMMY! MARINETTE DIDN'T LET ME WIN!
SNIFFLE
SHE DIDN'T EVEN PLAY FAIR AND SQUARE!
OH MANON, YOU CAN'T ALWAYS EXPECT TO WIN.

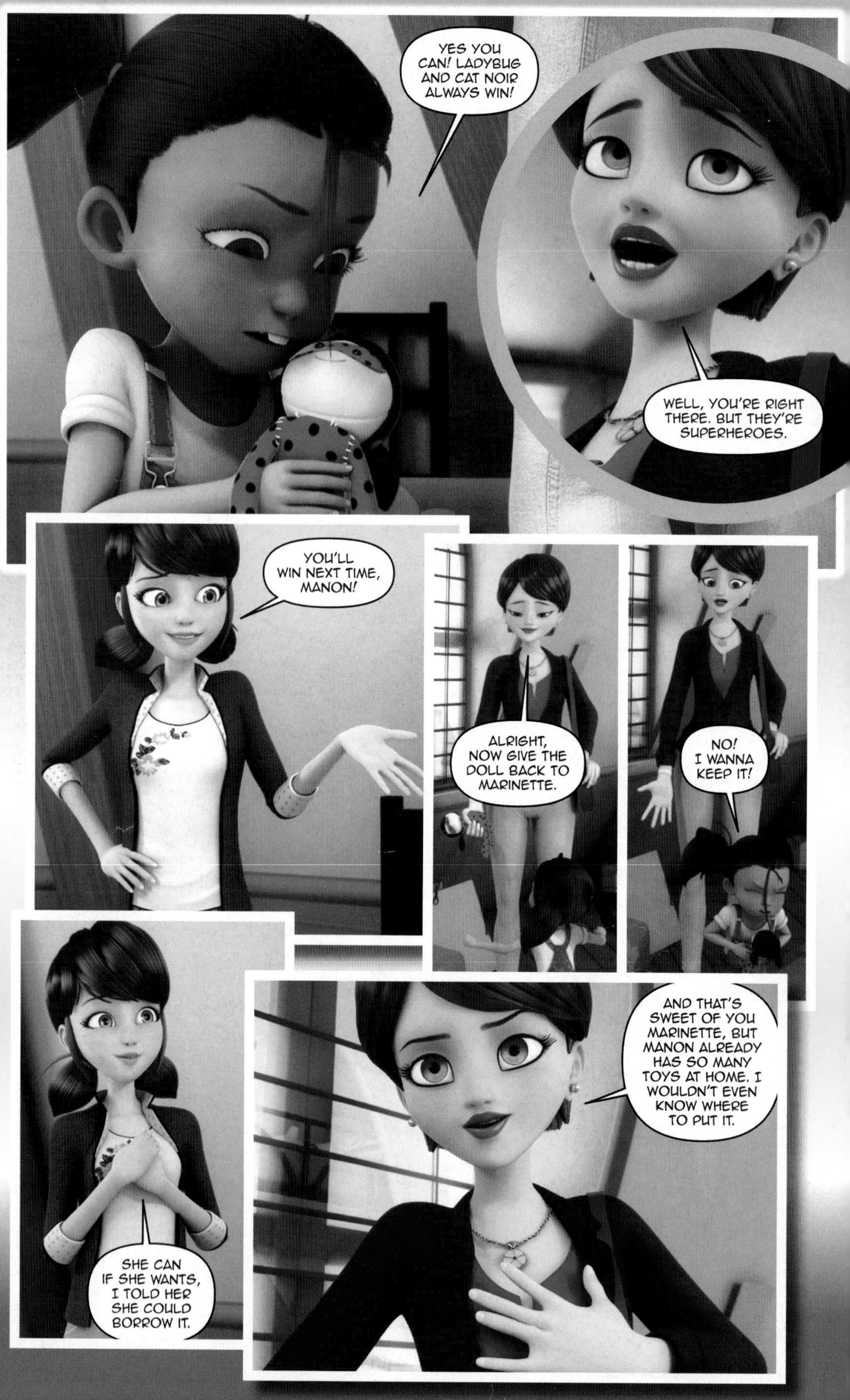
YES YOU CAN! LADYBUG AND CAT NOIR ALWAYS WIN!
WELL, YOU'RE RIGHT THERE. BUT THEY'RE SUPERHEROES.
YOU'LL WIN NEXT TIME, MANON!
ALRIGHT, NOW GIVE THE DOLL BACK TO MARINETTE.
NO! I WANNA KEEP IT!
SHE CAN IF SHE WANTS, I TOLD HER SHE COULD BORROW IT.
AND THAT'S SWEET OF YOU MARINETTE, BUT MANON ALREADY HAS SO MANY TOYS AT HOME. I WOULDN'T EVEN KNOW WHERE TO PUT IT.

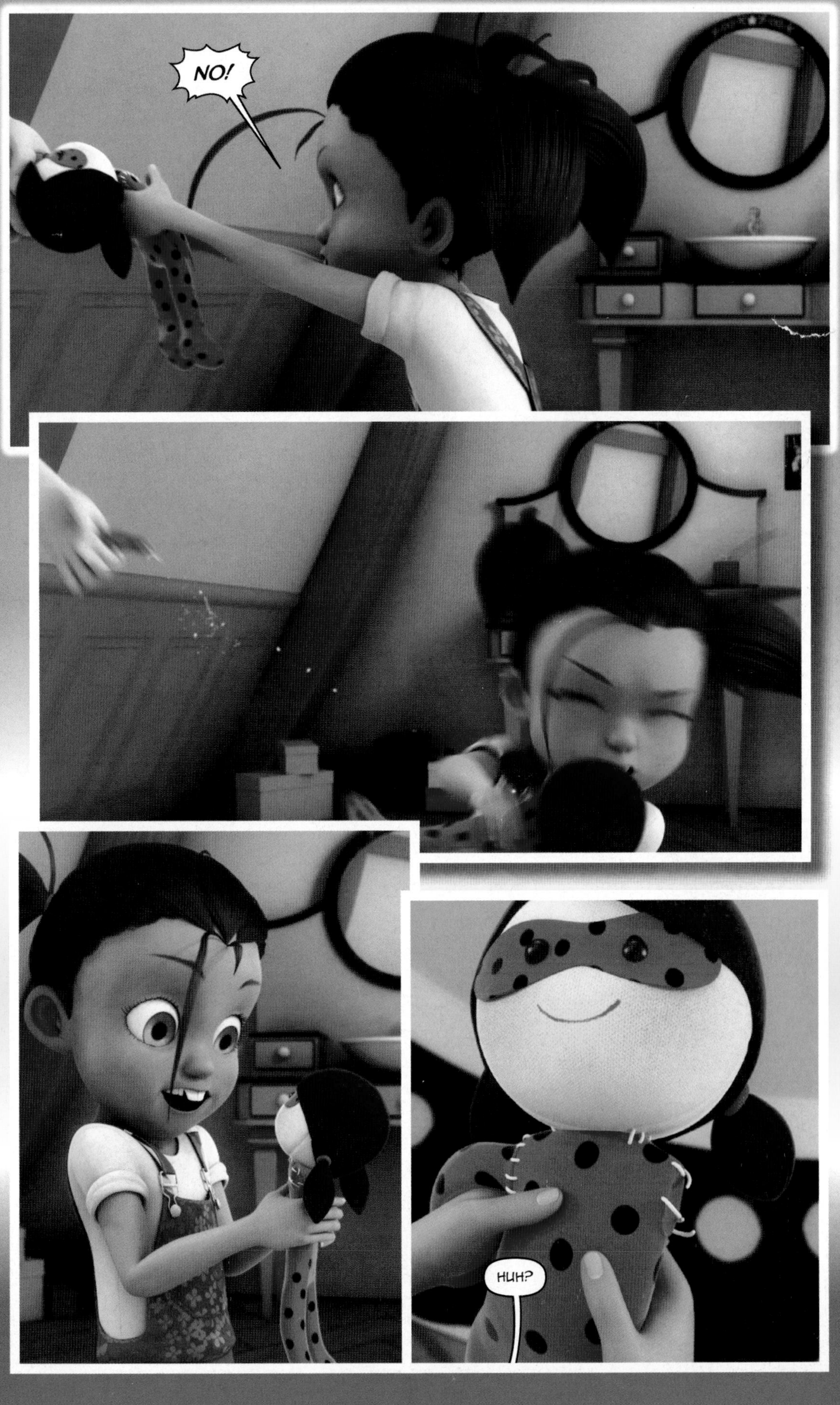
NO!
HUH?

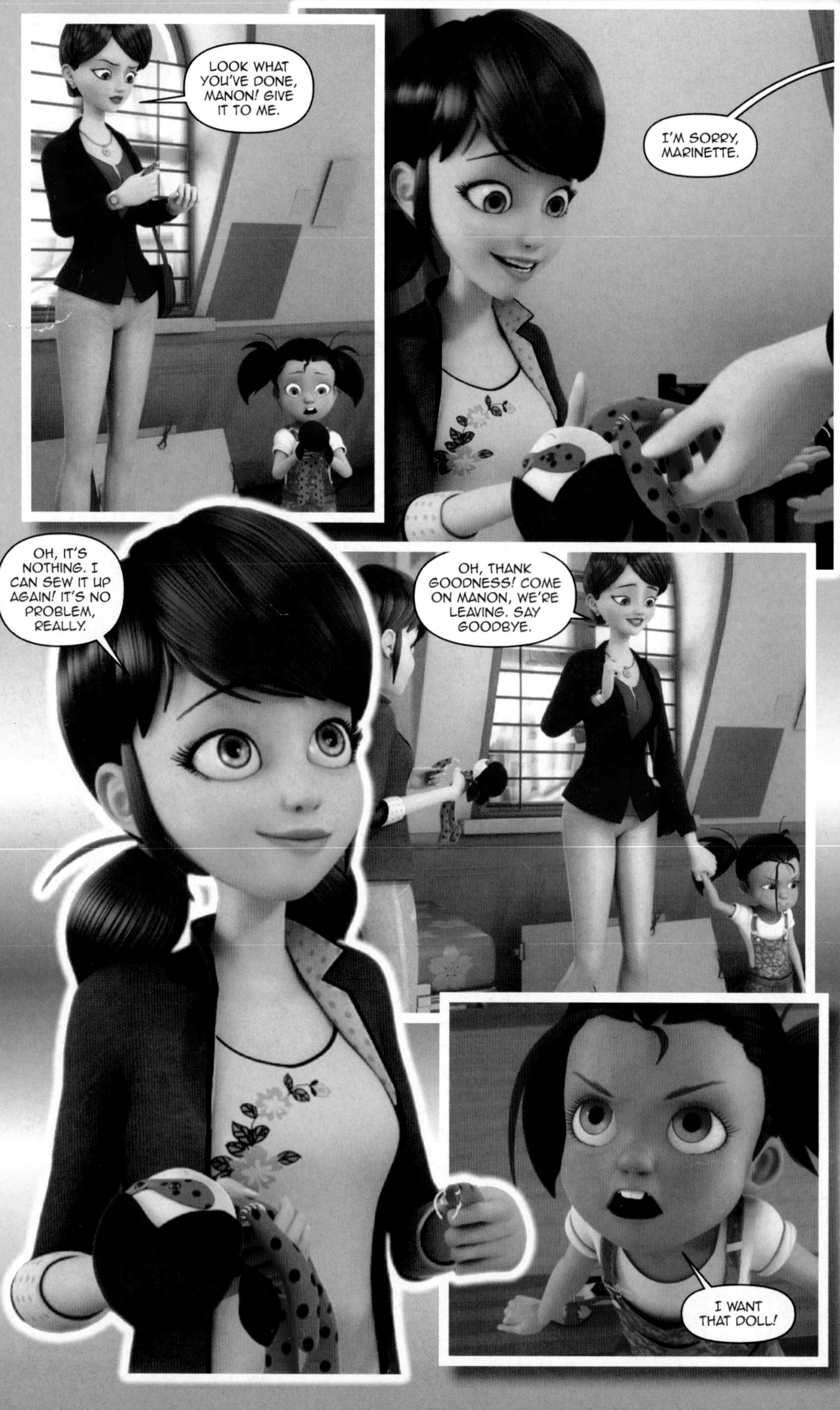
LOOK WHAT YOU'VE DONE, MANON! GIVE IT TO ME.
I'M SORRY, MARINETTE.
OH, IT'S NOTHING. I CAN SEW IT UP AGAIN! IT'S NO PROBLEM, REALLY.
OH, THANK GOODNESS! COME ON MANON, WE'RE LEAVING. SAY GOODBYE.
I WANT THAT DOLL!

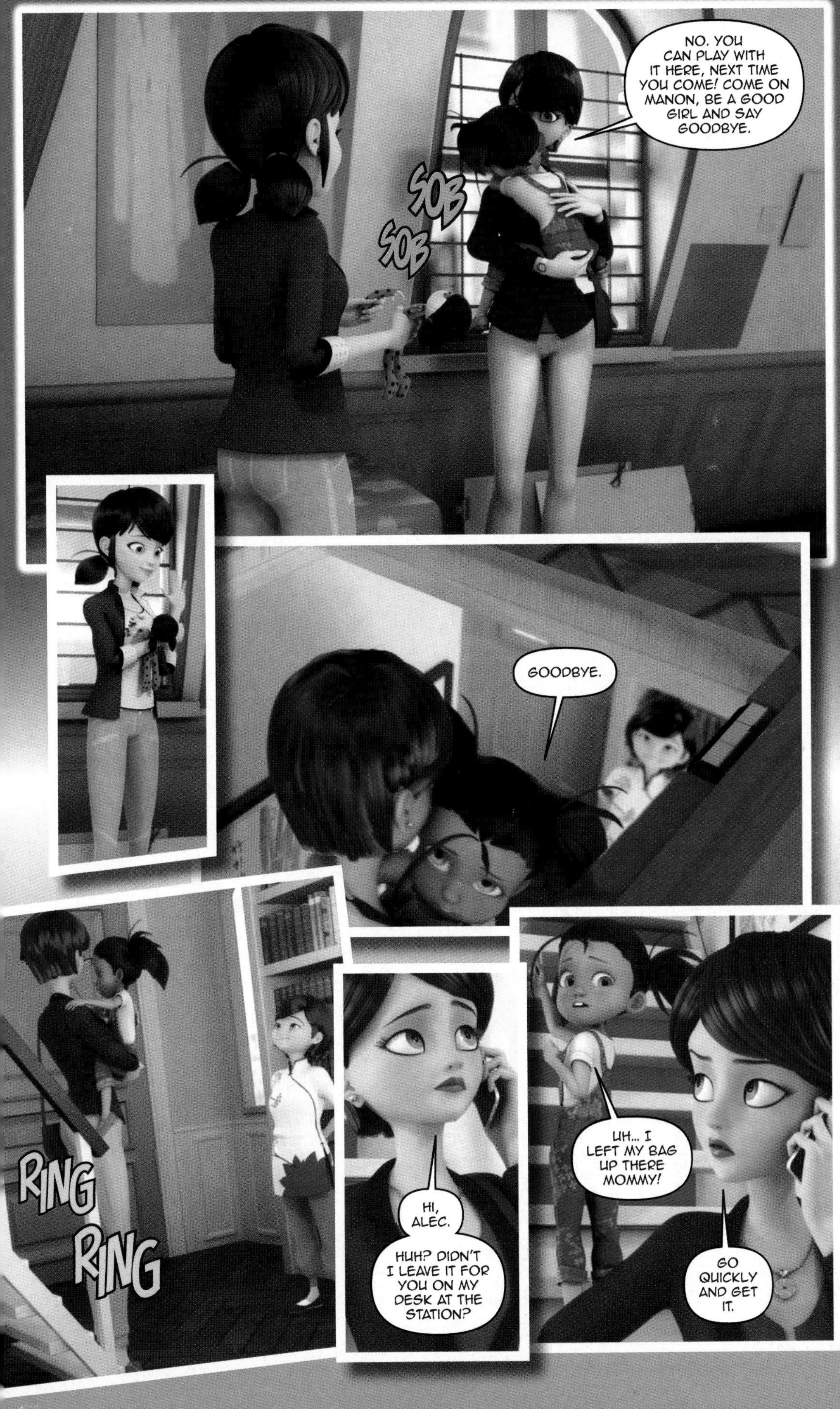
NO. YOU CAN PLAY WITH IT HERE, NEXT TIME YOU COME! COME ON MANON, BE A GOOD GIRL AND SAY GOODBYE.
SOB
SOB
GOODBYE.
RING
RING
HI, ALEC.
HUH? DIDN'T I LEAVE IT FOR YOU ON MY DESK AT THE STATION?
UH... I LEFT MY BAG UP THERE MOMMY!
GO QUICKLY AND GET IT.

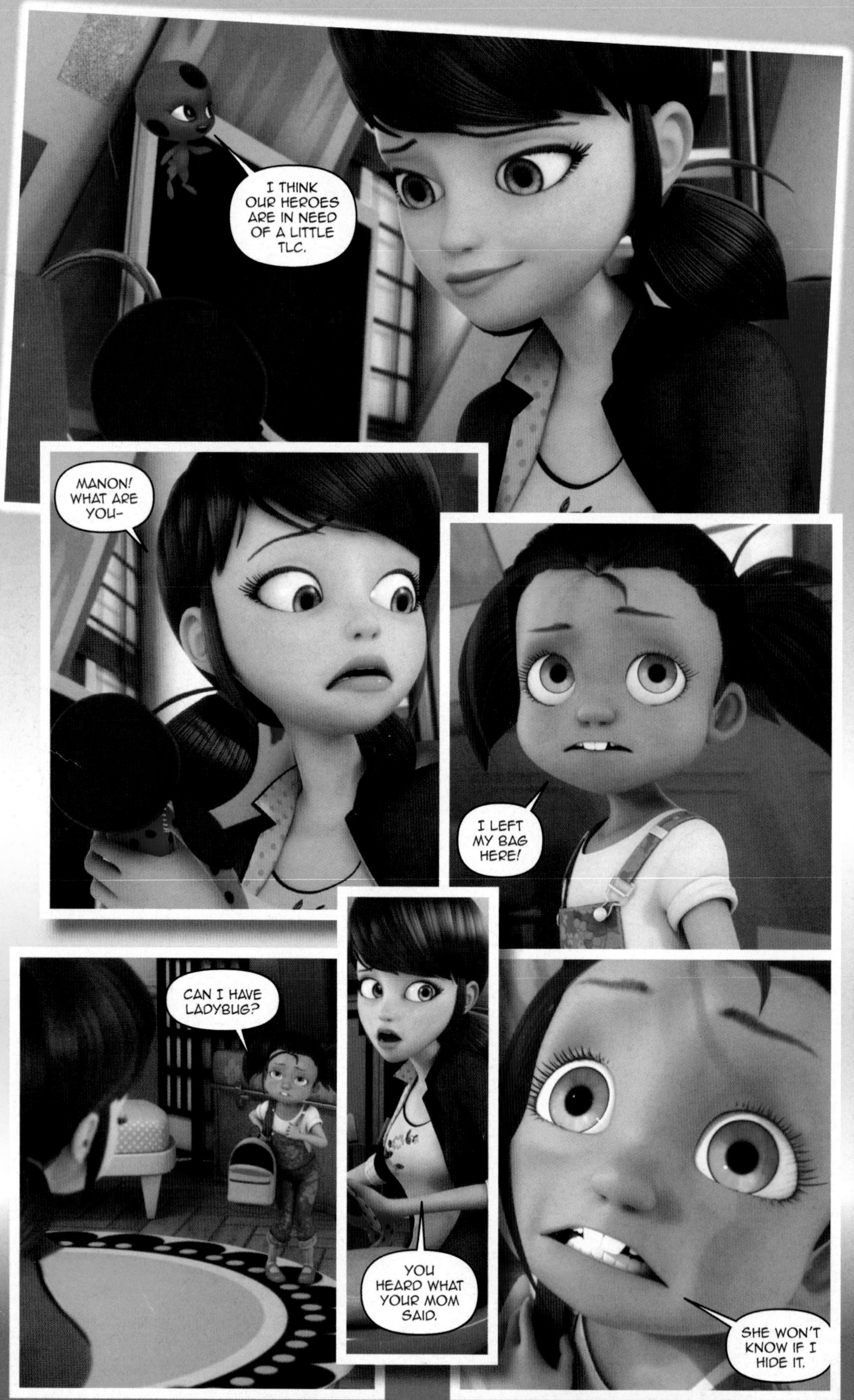
I THINK OUR HEROES ARE IN NEED OF A LITTLE TLC.
MANON! WHAT ARE YOU-
I LEFT MY BAG HERE!
CAN I HAVE LADYBUG?
YOU HEARD WHAT YOUR MOM SAID.
SHE WON'T KNOW IF I HIDE IT.

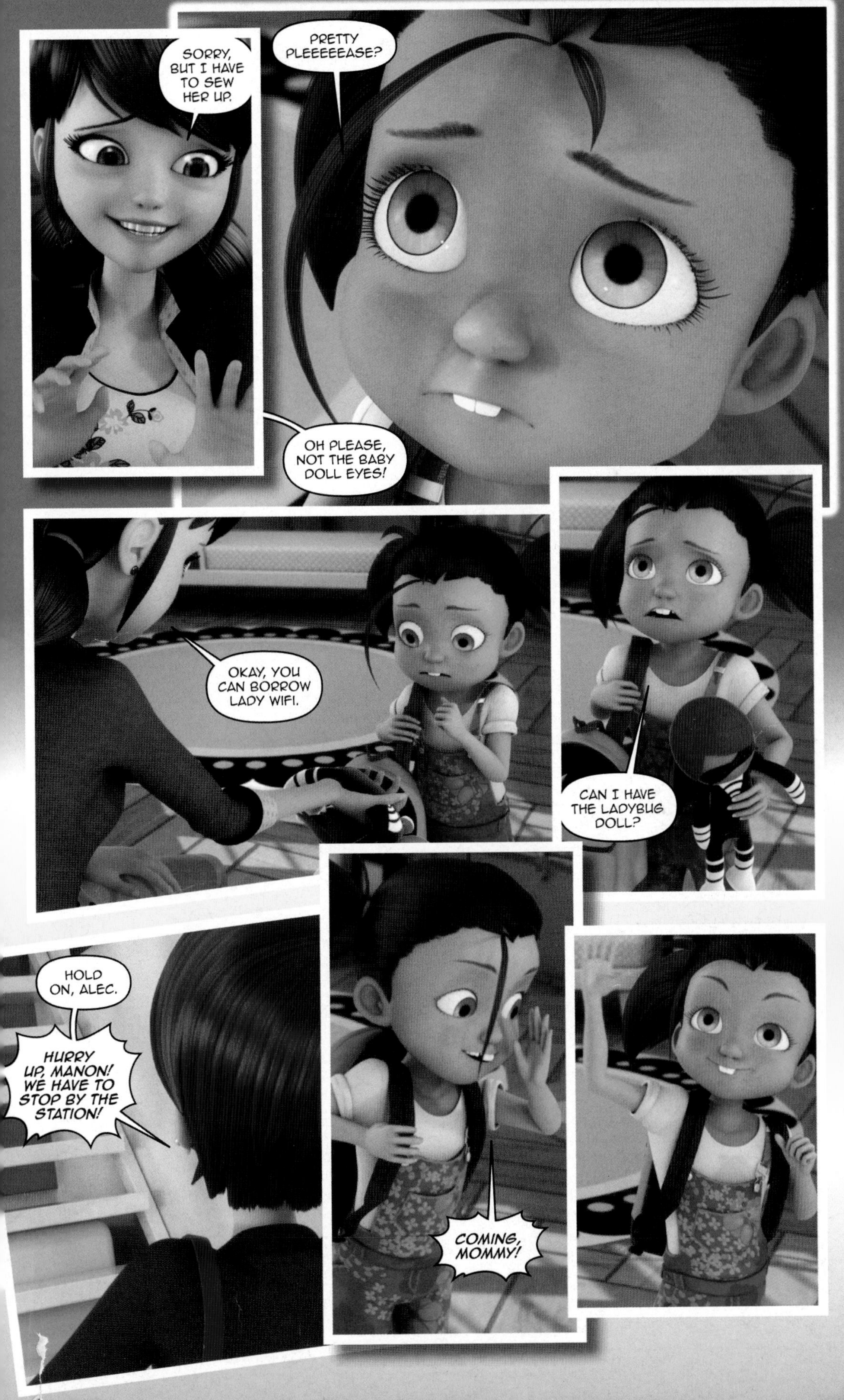
SORRY, BUT I HAVE TO SEW HER UP.
PRETTY PLEEEEEASE?
OH PLEASE, NOT THE BABY DOLL EYES!
OKAY, YOU CAN BORROW LADY WIFI.
CAN I HAVE THE LADYBUG DOLL?
HOLD ON, ALEC.
HURRY UP, MANON! WE HAVE TO STOP BY THE STATION!
COMING, MOMMY!

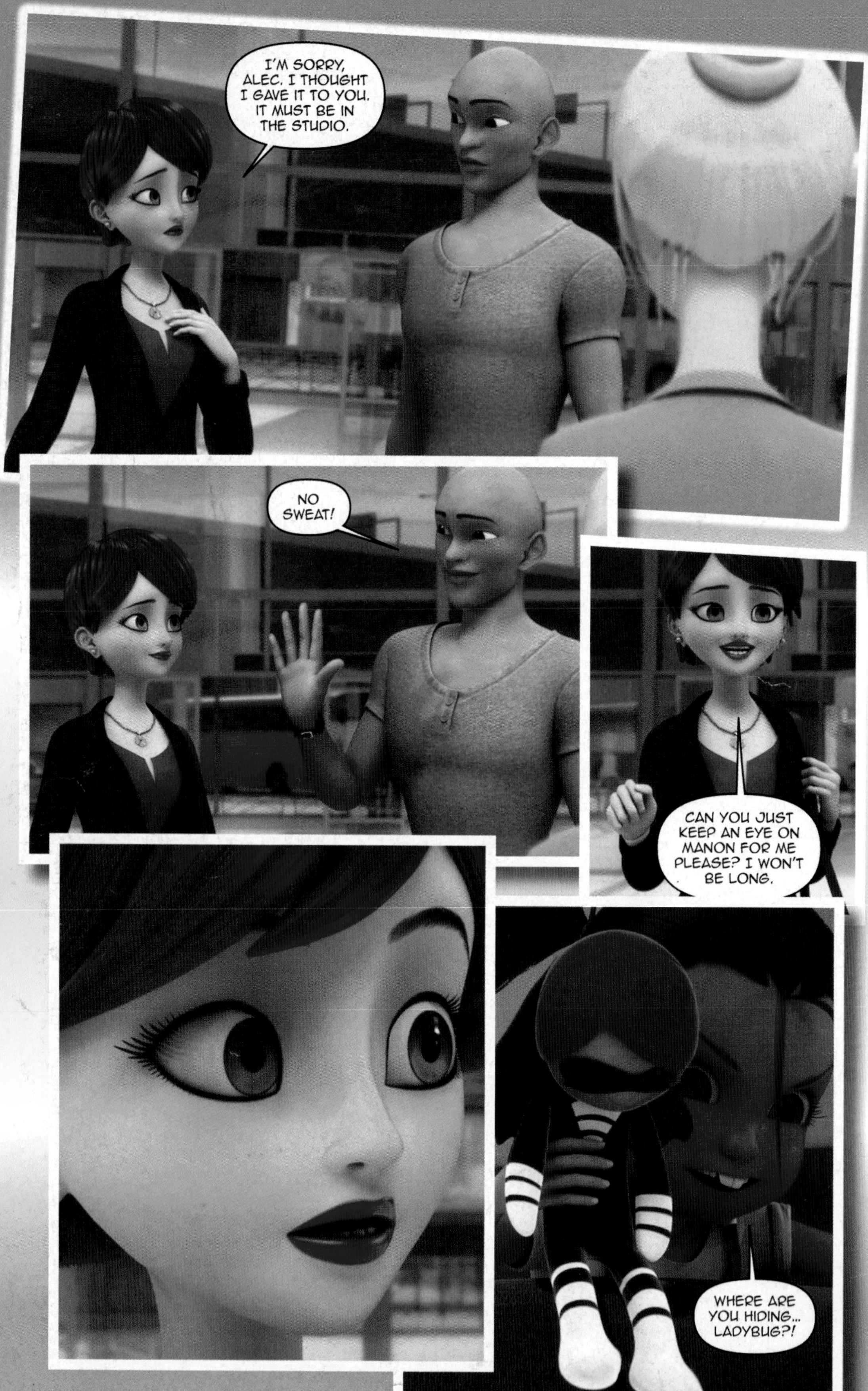
I'M SORRY, ALEC. I THOUGHT I GAVE IT TO YOU. IT MUST BE IN THE STUDIO.
NO SWEAT!
CAN YOU JUST KEEP AN EYE ON MANON FOR ME PLEASE? I WON'T BE LONG.
WHERE ARE YOU HIDING... LADYBUG?!

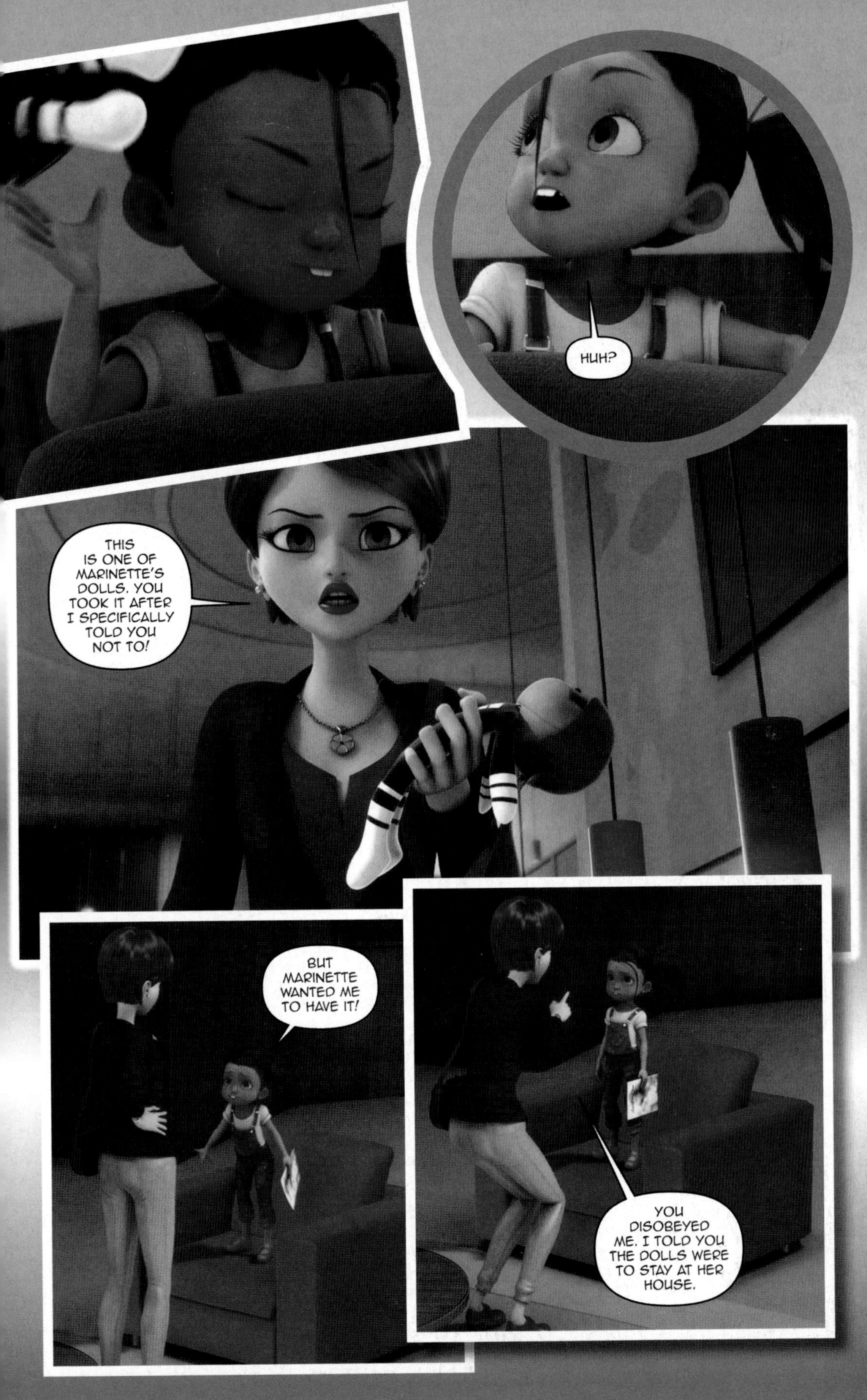
HUH?
THIS IS ONE OF MARINETTE'S DOLLS. YOU TOOK IT AFTER I SPECIFICALLY TOLD YOU NOT TO!
BUT MARINETTE WANTED ME TO HAVE IT!
YOU DISOBEYED ME. I TOLD YOU THE DOLLS WERE TO STAY AT HER HOUSE.

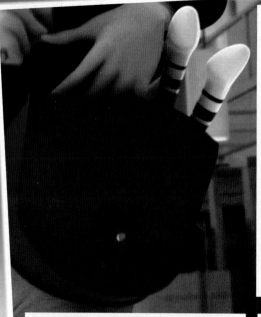

=GASP=

YOU WON'T BE NEEDING THIS ANYMORE.

NO!

MOMMY, PLEASE DON'T!

I'M NOT HAPPY ABOUT THIS. WAIT FOR ME HERE.

I DIDN'T STEAL THAT DOLL.

I WANT THAT DOLL!

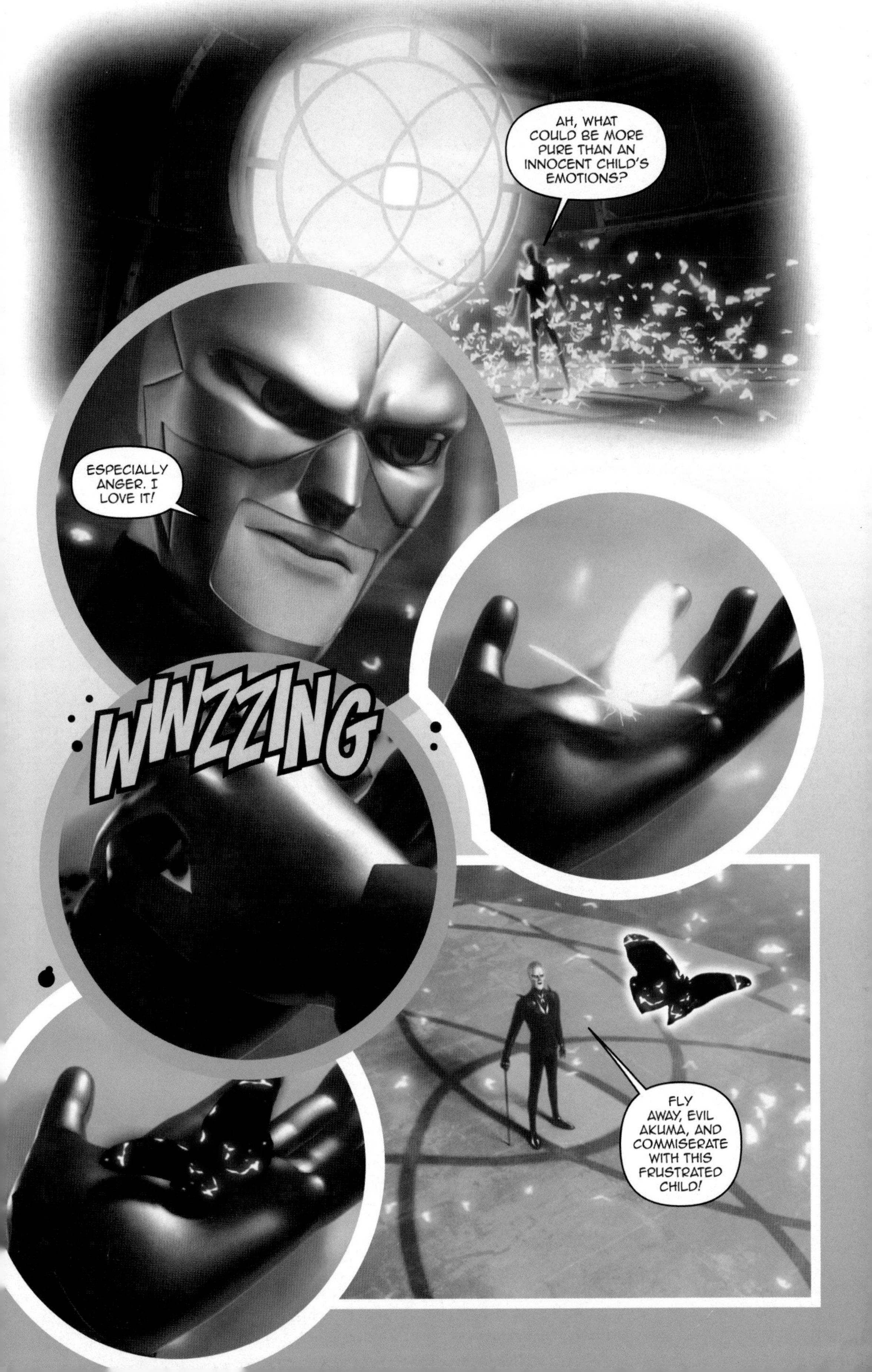
AH, WHAT COULD BE MORE PURE THAN AN INNOCENT CHILD'S EMOTIONS?
ESPECIALLY ANGER. I LOVE IT!
WWZZING
FLY AWAY, EVIL AKUMA, AND COMMISERATE WITH THIS FRUSTRATED CHILD!

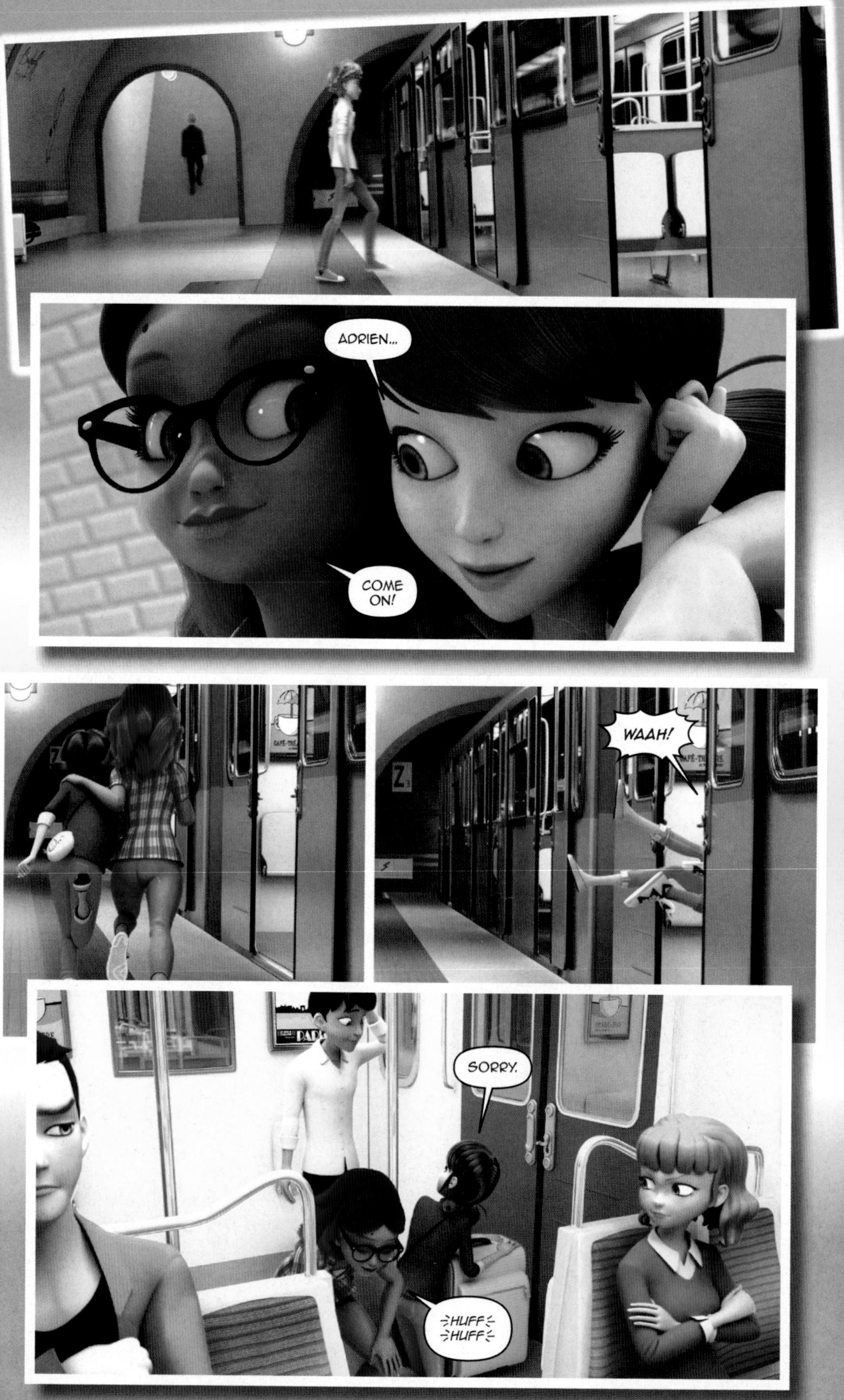
ADRIEN...
COME ON!
WAAH!
SORRY.
HUFF HUFF

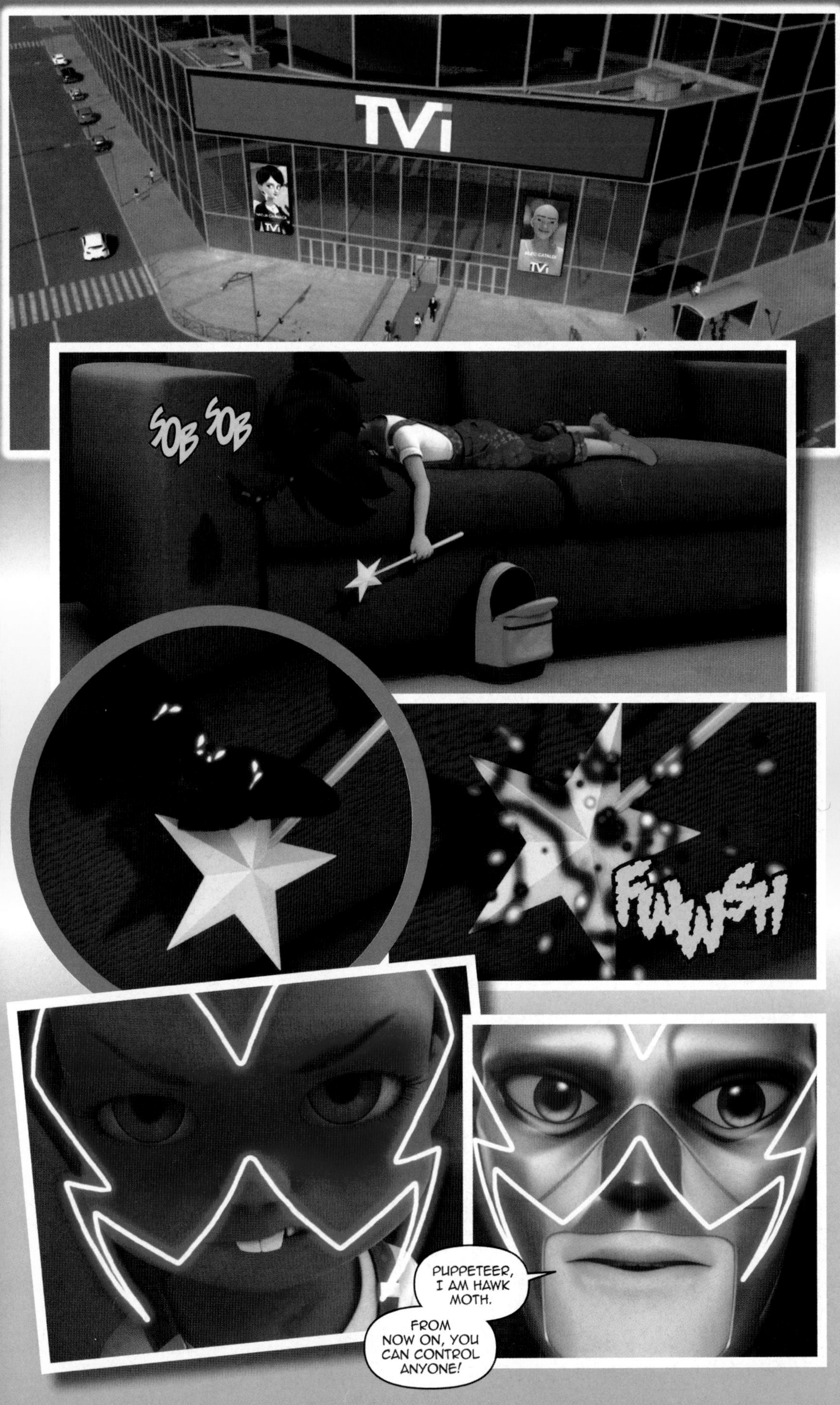
TVi
SOB SOB
FWWSH
PUPPETEER, I AM HAWK MOTH.
FROM NOW ON, YOU CAN CONTROL ANYONE!

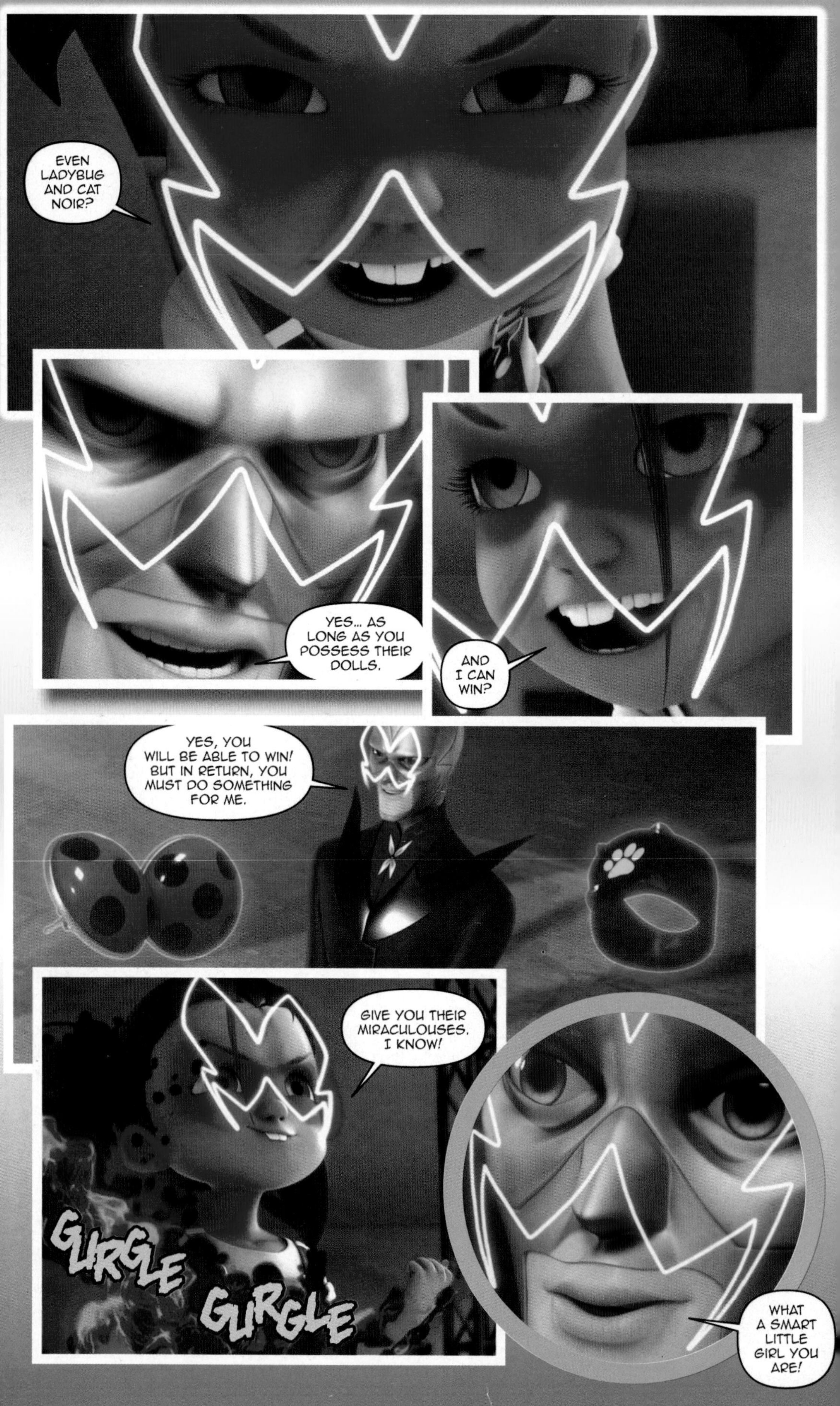
EVEN LADYBUG AND CAT NOIR?
YES... AS LONG AS YOU POSSESS THEIR DOLLS.
AND I CAN WIN?
YES, YOU WILL BE ABLE TO WIN! BUT IN RETURN, YOU MUST DO SOMETHING FOR ME.
GIVE YOU THEIR MIRACULOUSES. I KNOW!
GURGLE
GURGLE
WHAT A SMART LITTLE GIRL YOU ARE!

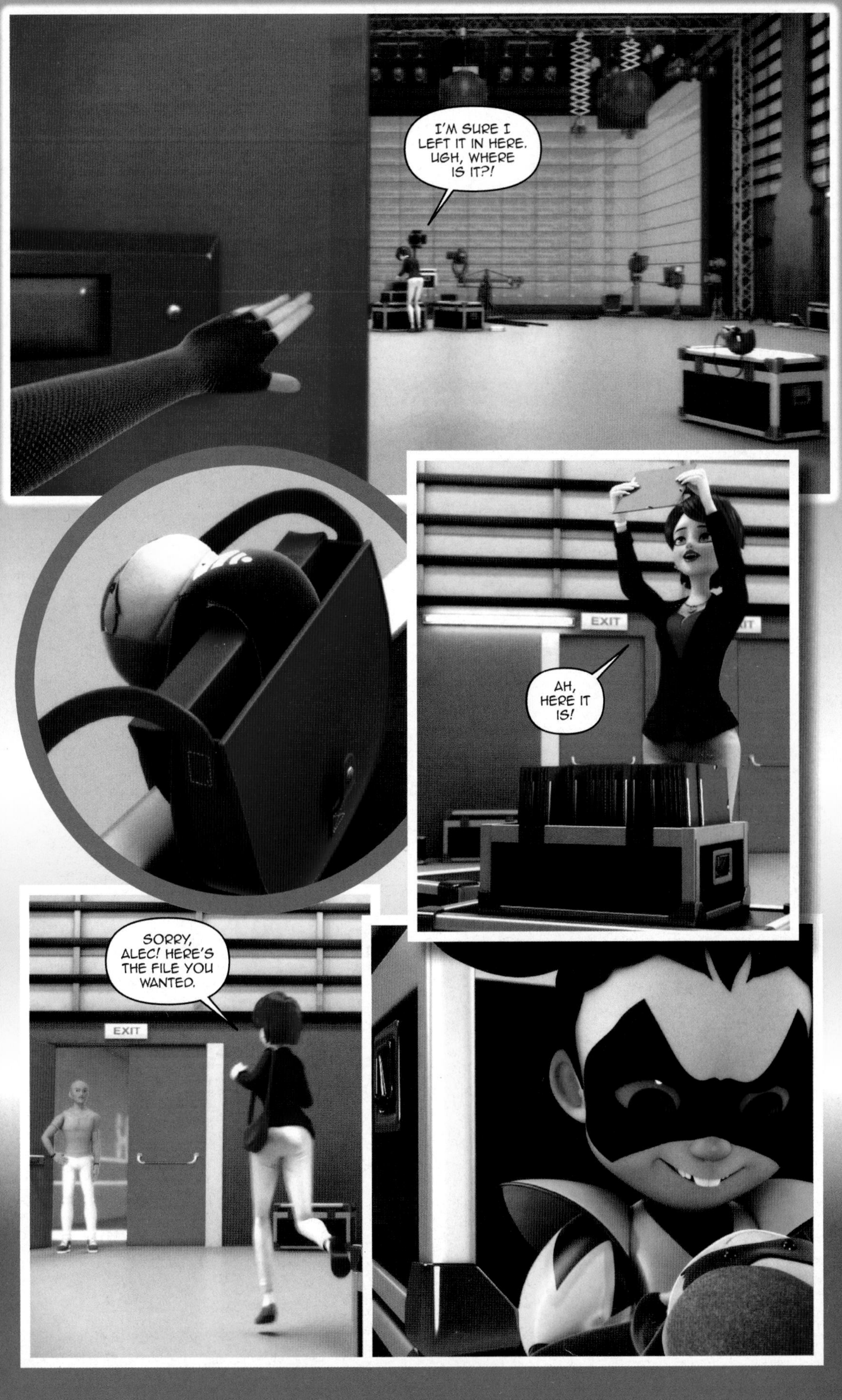
I'M SURE I LEFT IT IN HERE. UGH, WHERE IS IT?!
AH, HERE IT IS!
EXIT
SORRY, ALEC! HERE'S THE FILE YOU WANTED.
EXIT

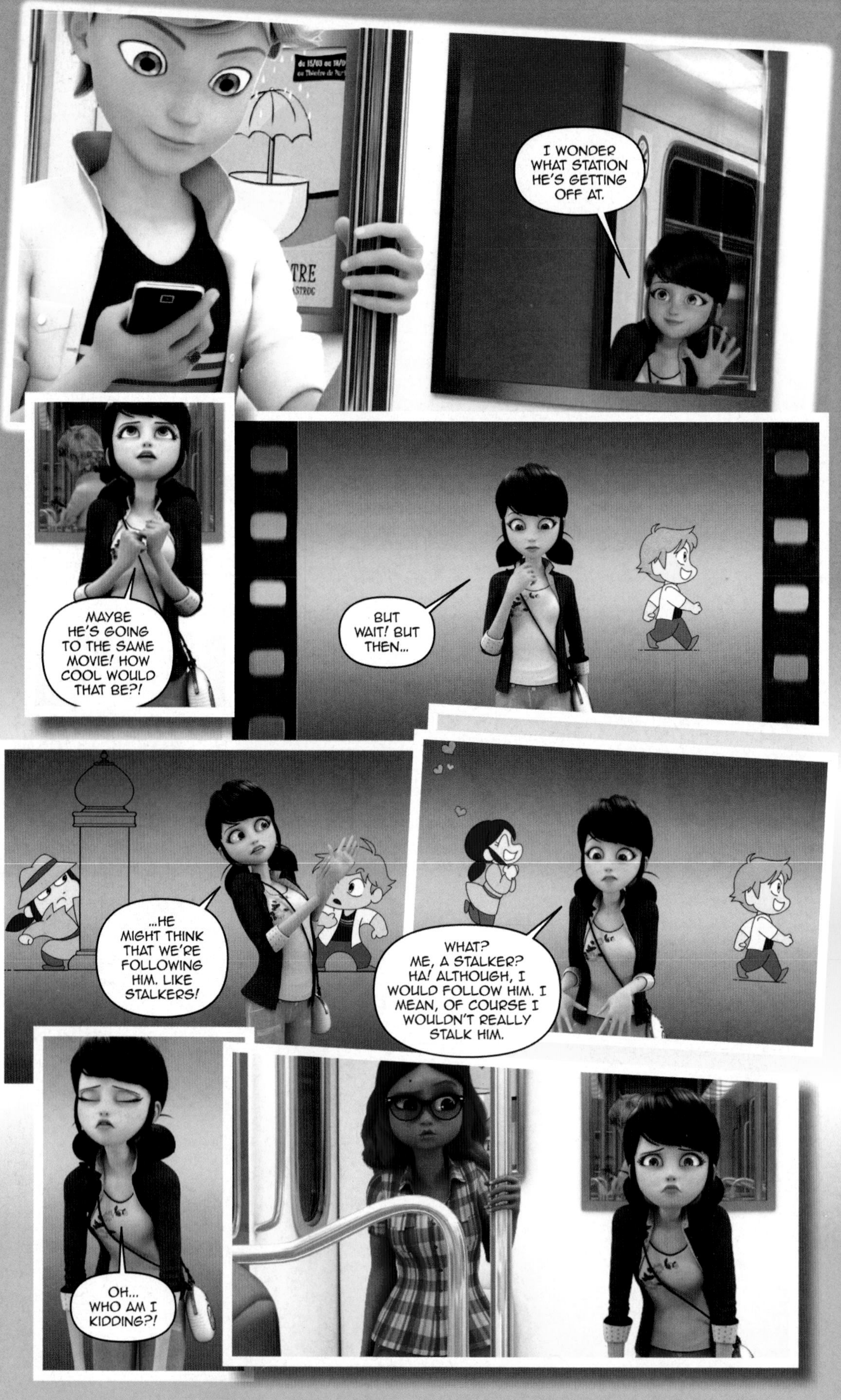
I WONDER WHAT STATION HE'S GETTING OFF AT.
MAYBE HE'S GOING TO THE SAME MOVIE! HOW COOL WOULD THAT BE?!
BUT WAIT! BUT THEN...
...HE MIGHT THINK THAT WE'RE FOLLOWING HIM. LIKE STALKERS!
WHAT? ME, A STALKER? HA! ALTHOUGH, I WOULD FOLLOW HIM. I MEAN, OF COURSE I WOULDN'T REALLY STALK HIM.
OH... WHO AM I KIDDING?!

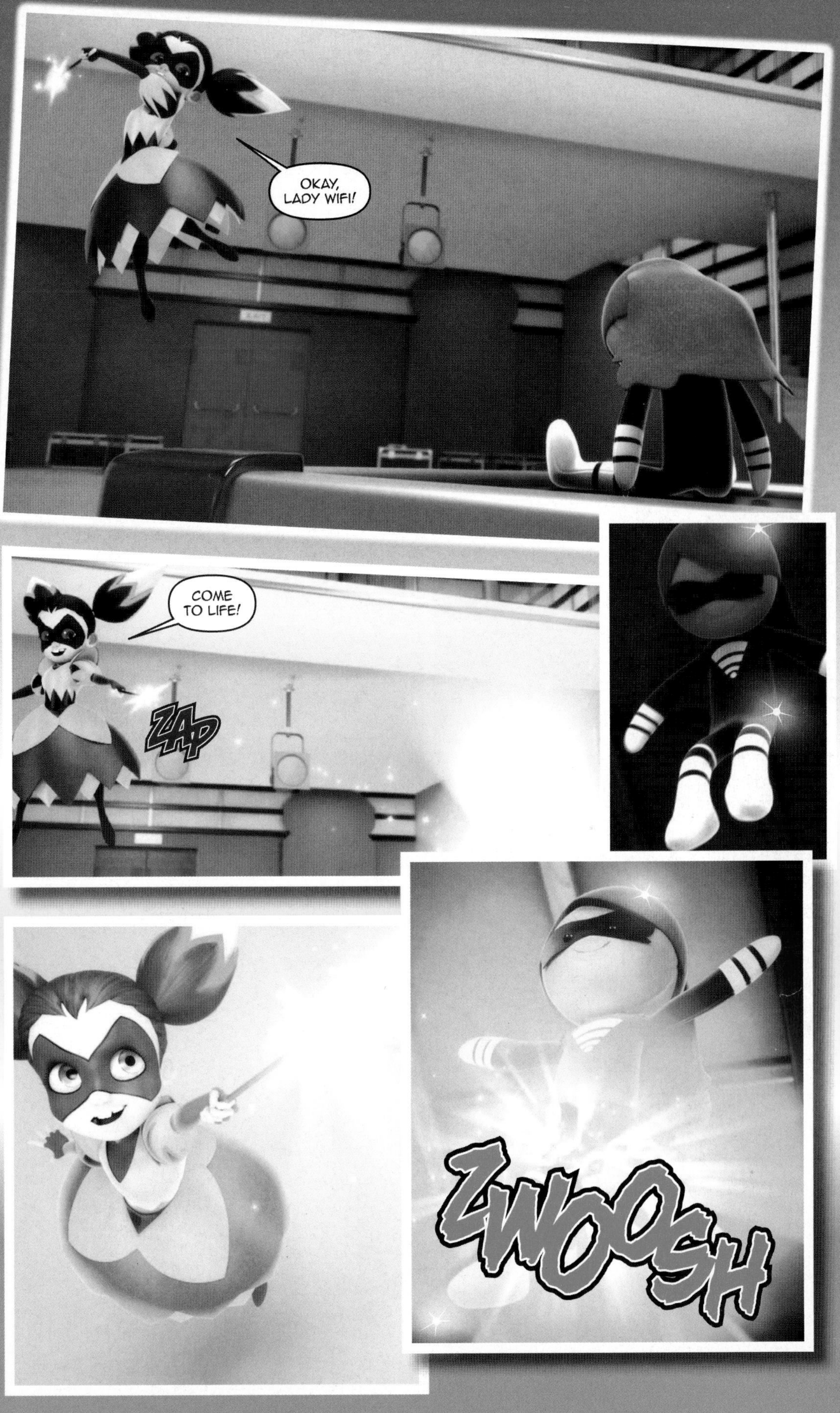
OKAY, LADY WIFI!
COME TO LIFE!
ZAP
ZWOOSH

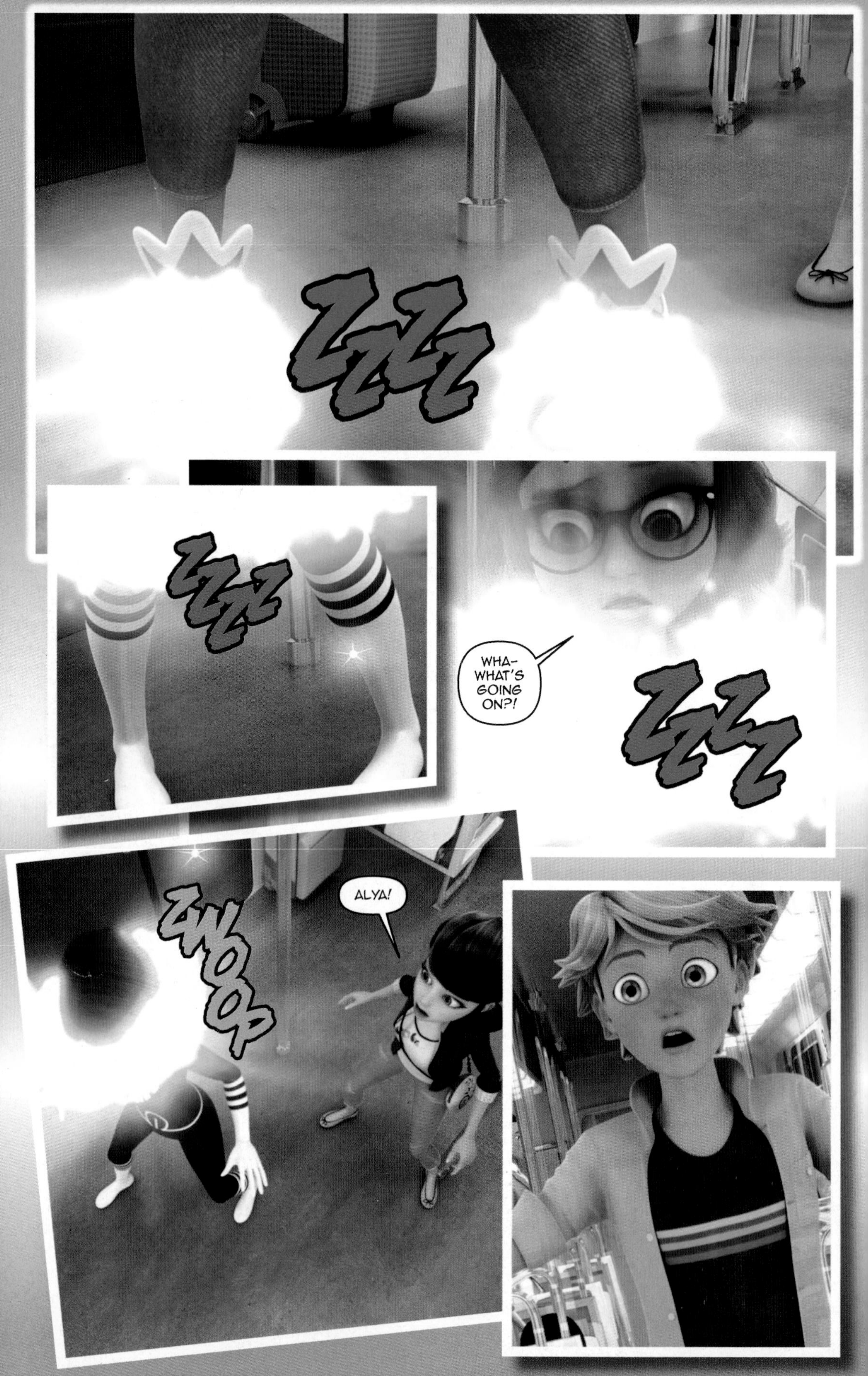
ZZZZ
ZZZZ
WHA-WHAT'S GOING ON?!
ZZZZ
ZWOOP
ALYA!

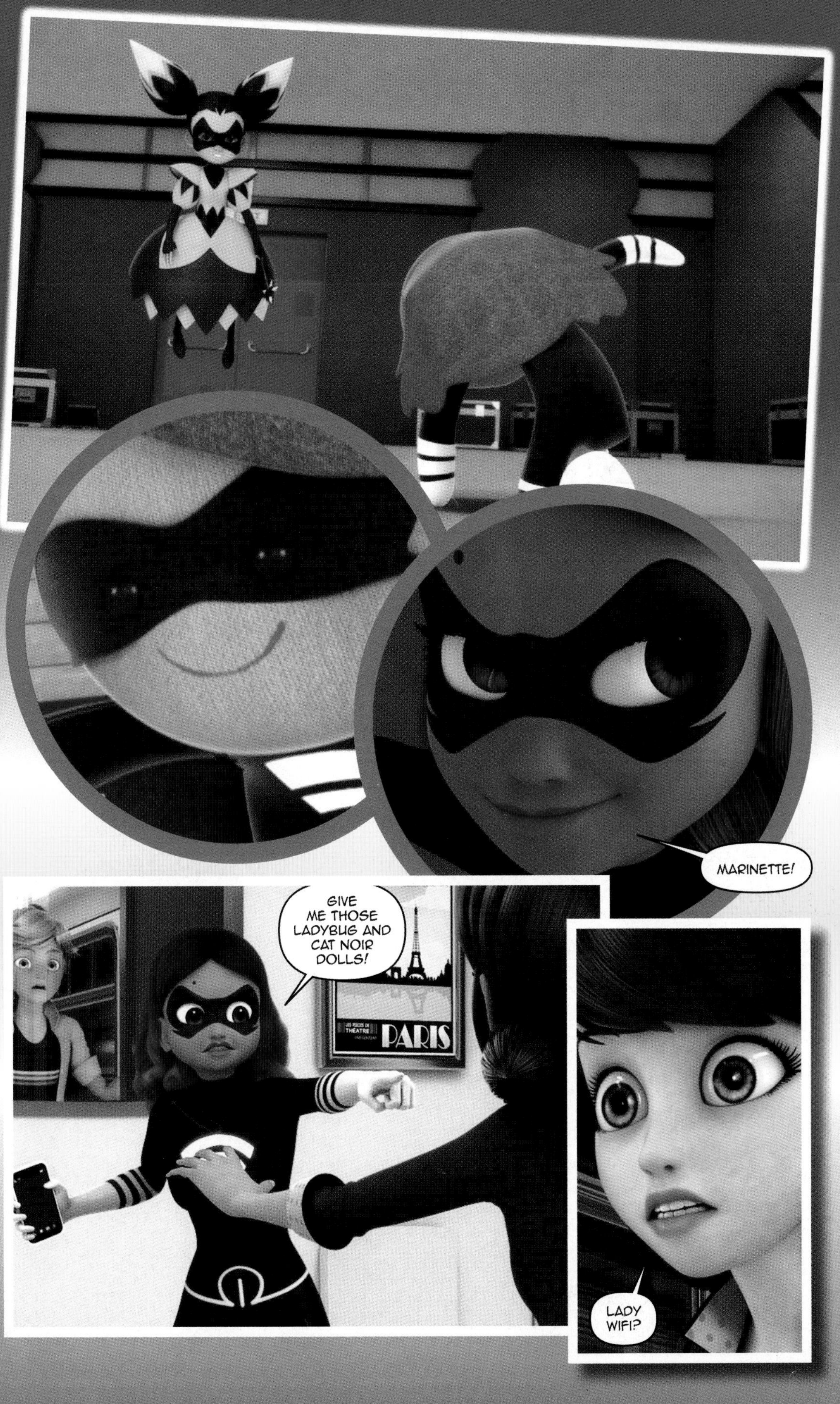
MARINETTE!
GIVE ME THOSE LADYBUG AND CAT NOIR DOLLS!
LADY WIFI?

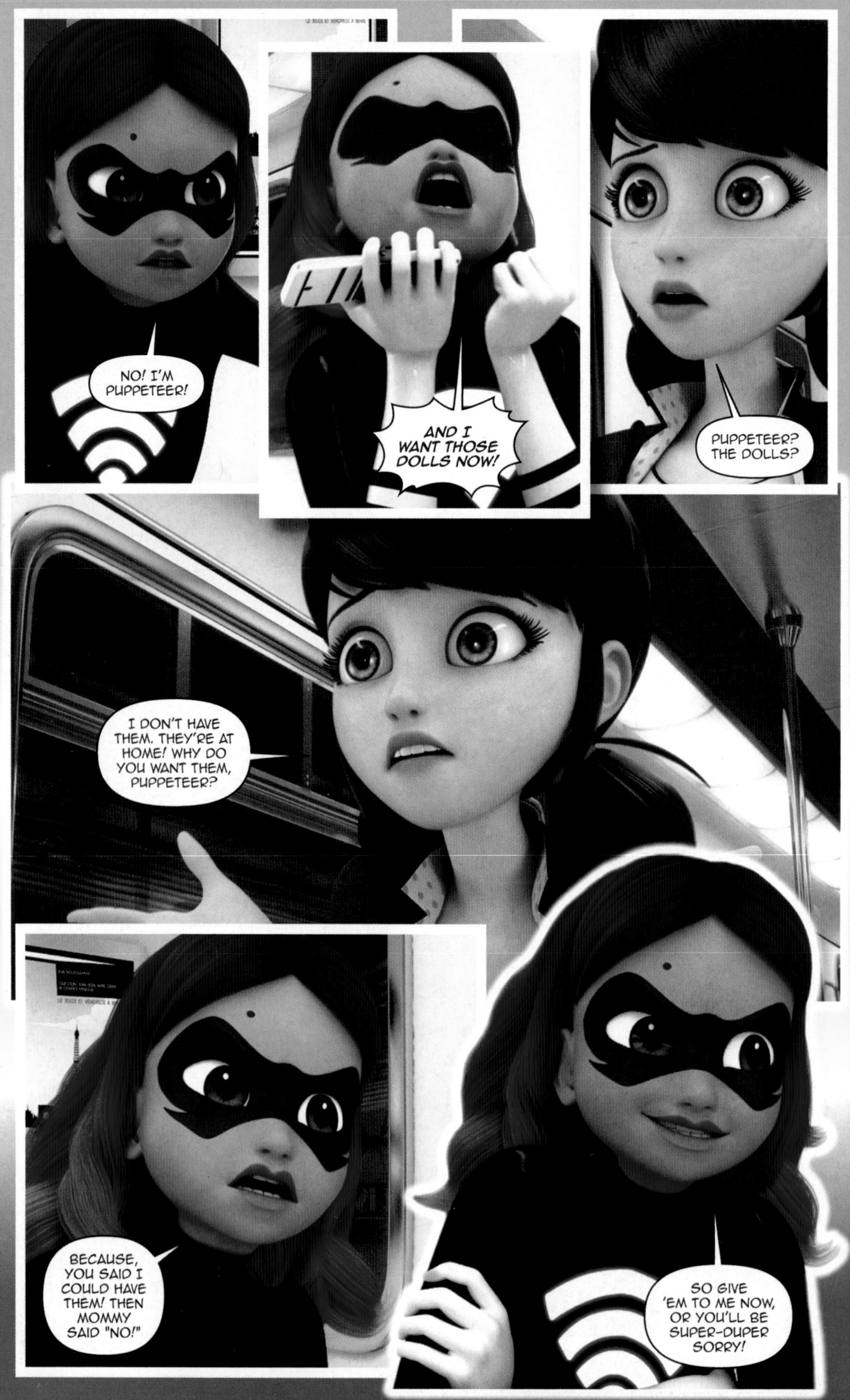
NO! I'M PUPPETEER!
AND I WANT THOSE DOLLS NOW!
PUPPETEER? THE DOLLS?
I DON'T HAVE THEM. THEY'RE AT HOME! WHY DO YOU WANT THEM, PUPPETEER?
BECAUSE, YOU SAID I COULD HAVE THEM! THEN MOMMY SAID "NO!"
SO GIVE 'EM TO ME NOW, OR YOU'LL BE SUPER-DUPER SORRY!

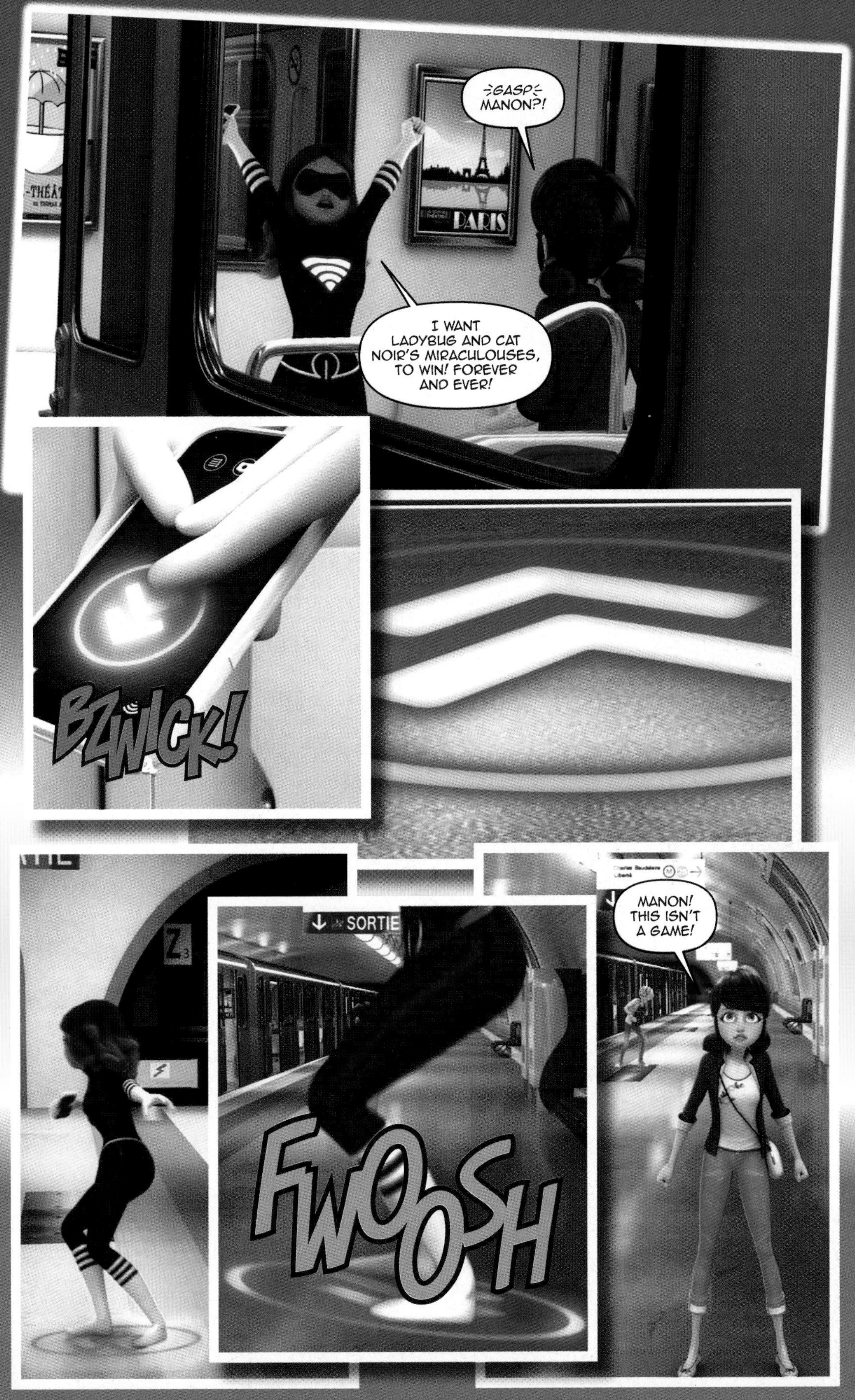
PARIS
GASP
MANON?!
I WANT LADYBUG AND CAT NOIR'S MIRACULOUSES, TO WIN! FOREVER AND EVER!
BZWICK!
SORTIE
FWOOSH
MANON! THIS ISN'T A GAME!

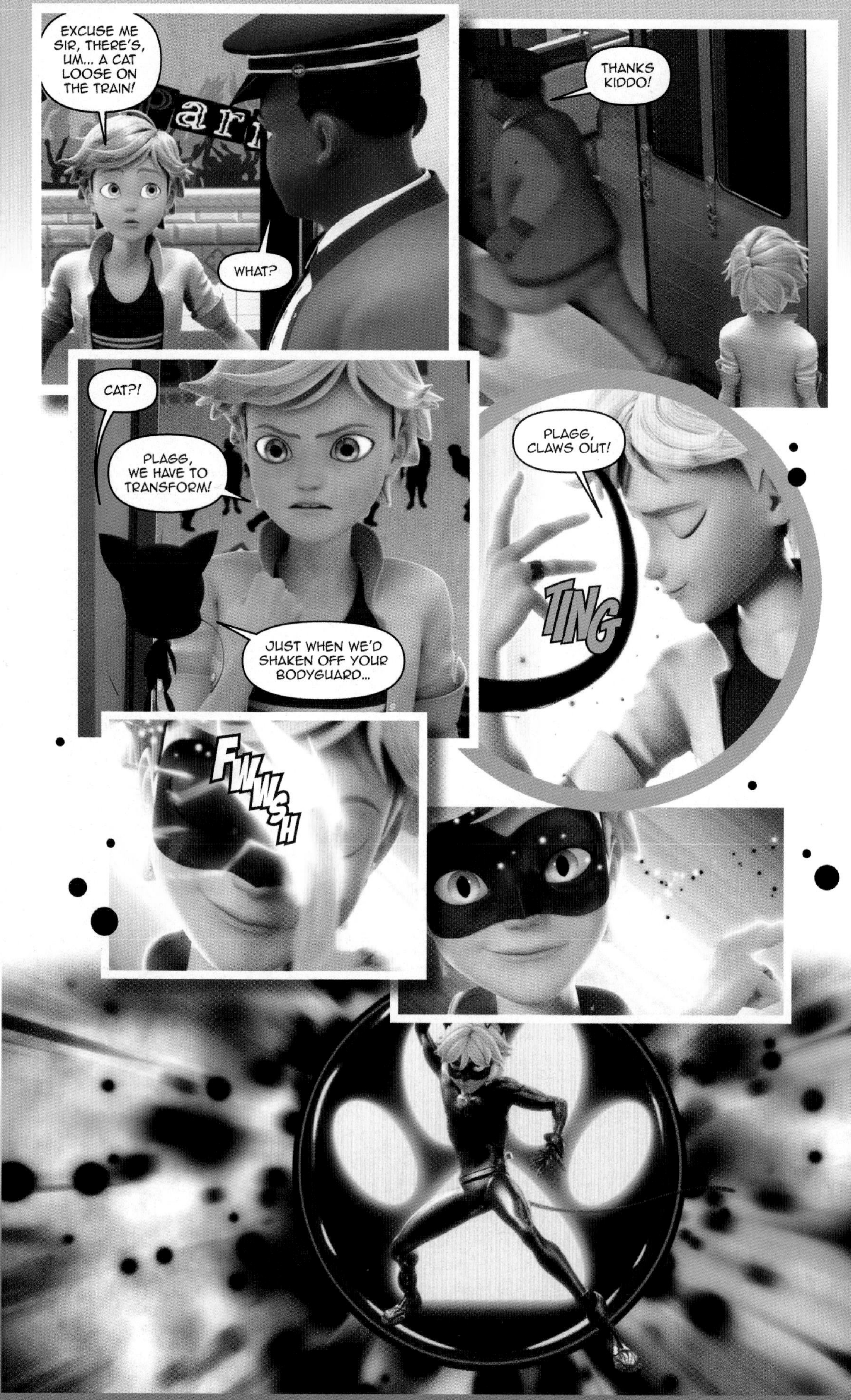

EXCUSE ME SIR, THERE'S, UM... A CAT LOOSE ON THE TRAIN!
WHAT?
THANKS KIDDO!
CAT?!
PLAGG, WE HAVE TO TRANSFORM!
JUST WHEN WE'D SHAKEN OFF YOUR BODYGUARD...
PLAGG, CLAWS OUT!
TING
FWWSH

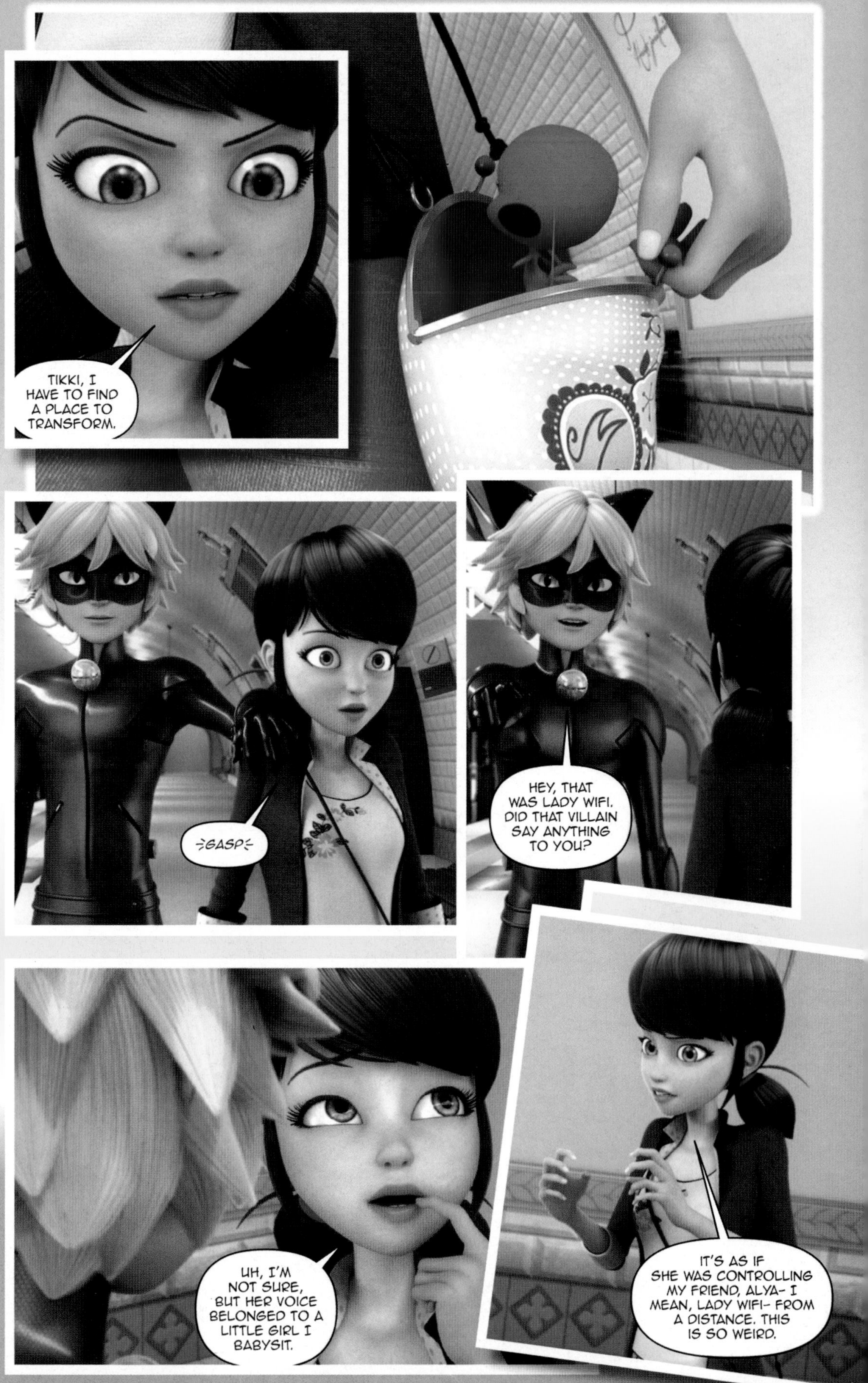
TIKKI, I HAVE TO FIND A PLACE TO TRANSFORM.
GASP
HEY, THAT WAS LADY WIFI. DID THAT VILLAIN SAY ANYTHING TO YOU?
UH, I'M NOT SURE, BUT HER VOICE BELONGED TO A LITTLE GIRL I BABYSIT.
IT'S AS IF SHE WAS CONTROLLING MY FRIEND, ALYA- I MEAN, LADY WIFI- FROM A DISTANCE. THIS IS SO WEIRD.

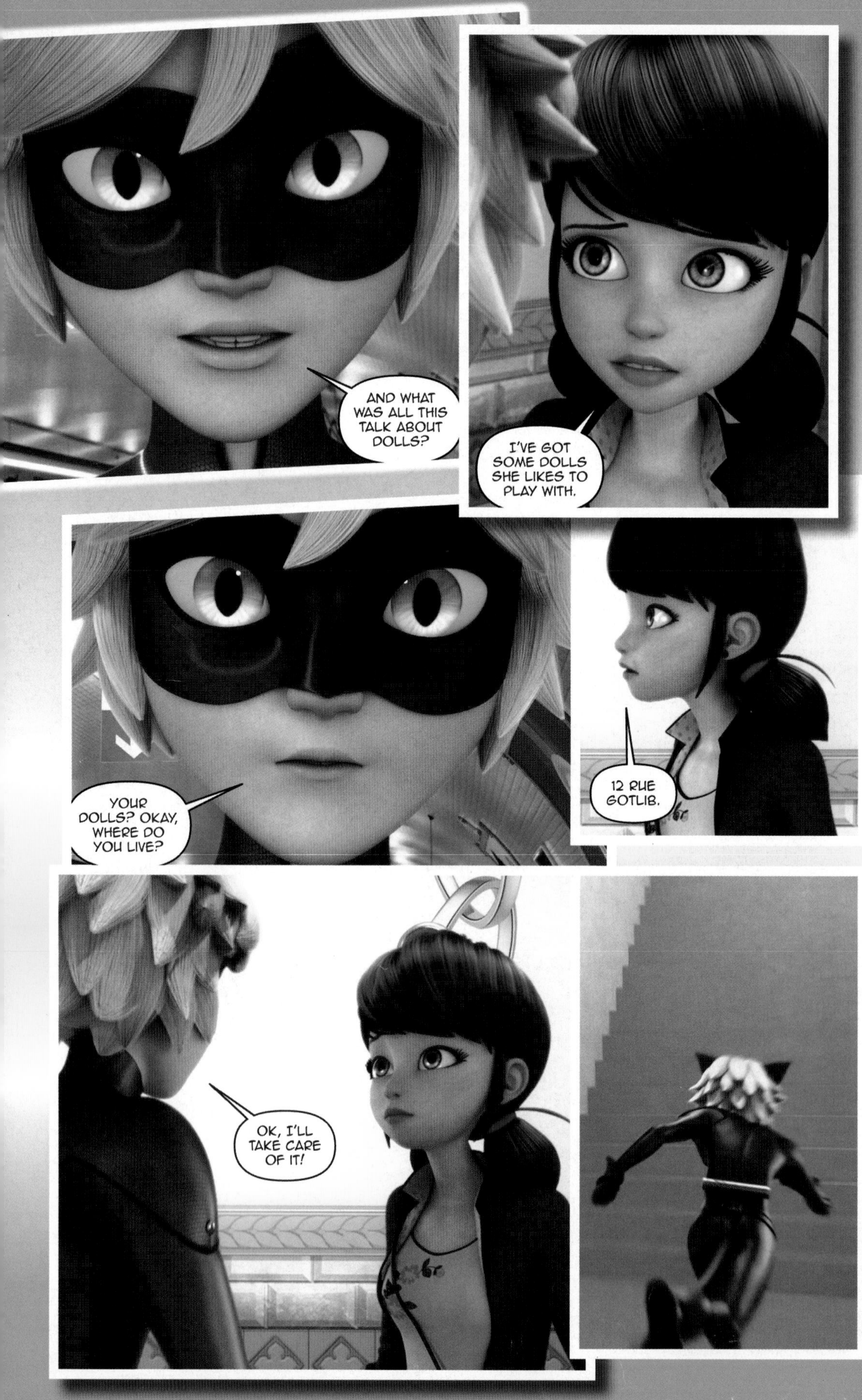
AND WHAT WAS ALL THIS TALK ABOUT DOLLS?
I'VE GOT SOME DOLLS SHE LIKES TO PLAY WITH.
YOUR DOLLS? OKAY, WHERE DO YOU LIVE?
12 RUE GOTLIB.
OK, I'LL TAKE CARE OF IT!

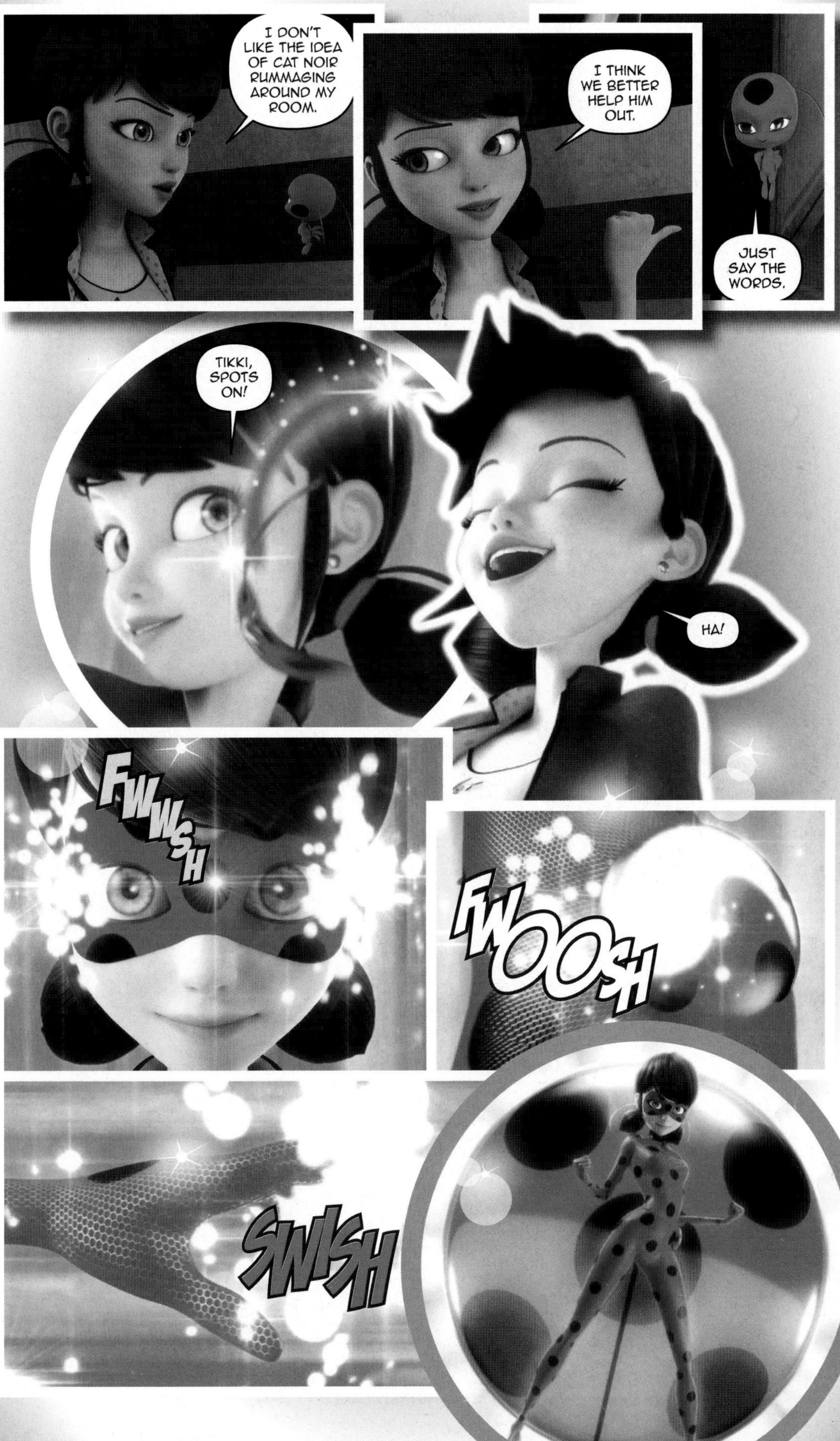
I DON'T LIKE THE IDEA OF CAT NOIR RUMMAGING AROUND MY ROOM.
I THINK WE BETTER HELP HIM OUT.
JUST SAY THE WORDS.
TIKKI, SPOTS ON!
HA!
FWWSH
FWOOSH
SWISH

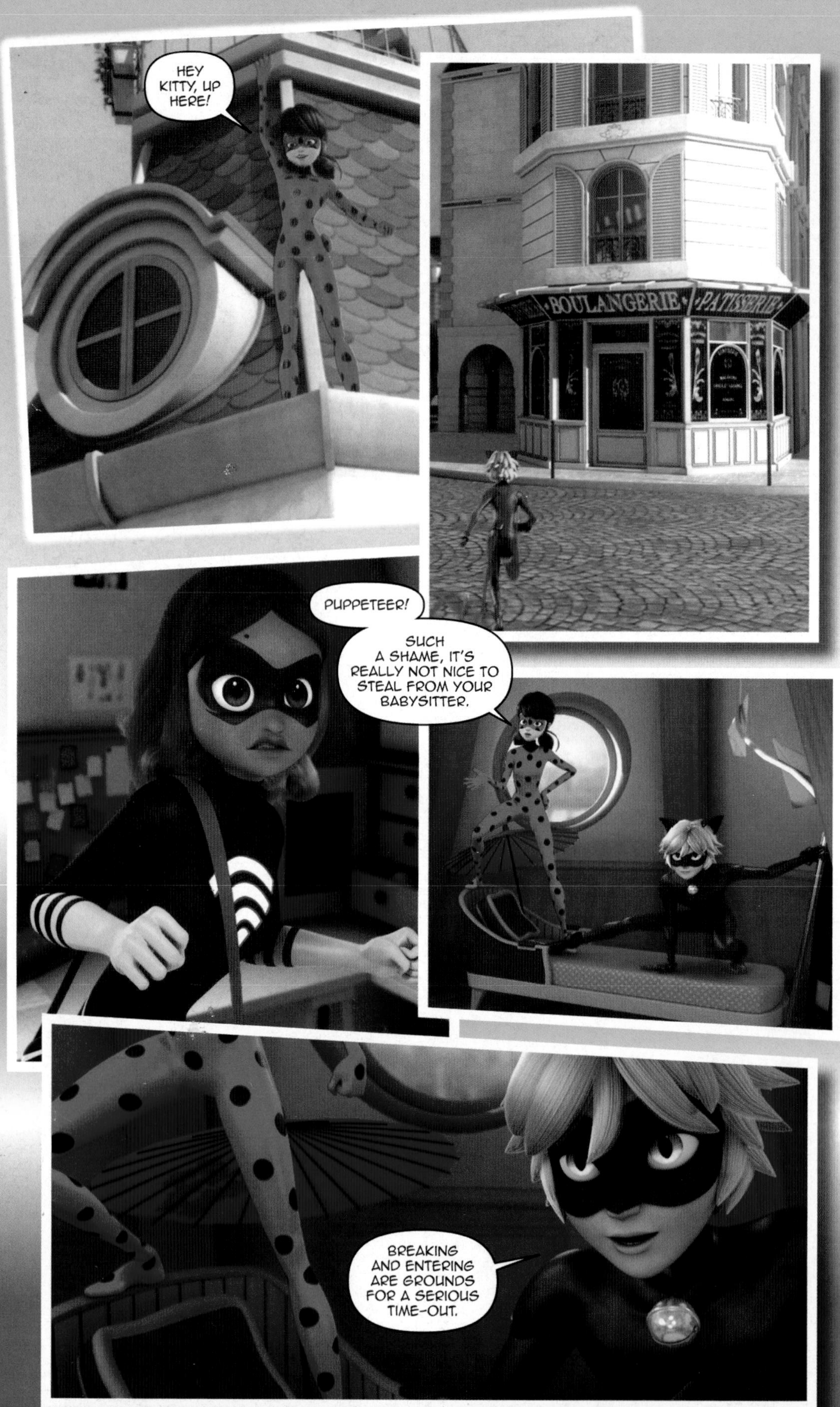
HEY KITTY, UP HERE!
BOULANGERIE · PATISSERIE
PUPPETEER!
SUCH A SHAME, IT'S REALLY NOT NICE TO STEAL FROM YOUR BABYSITTER.
BREAKING AND ENTERING ARE GROUNDS FOR A SERIOUS TIME-OUT.

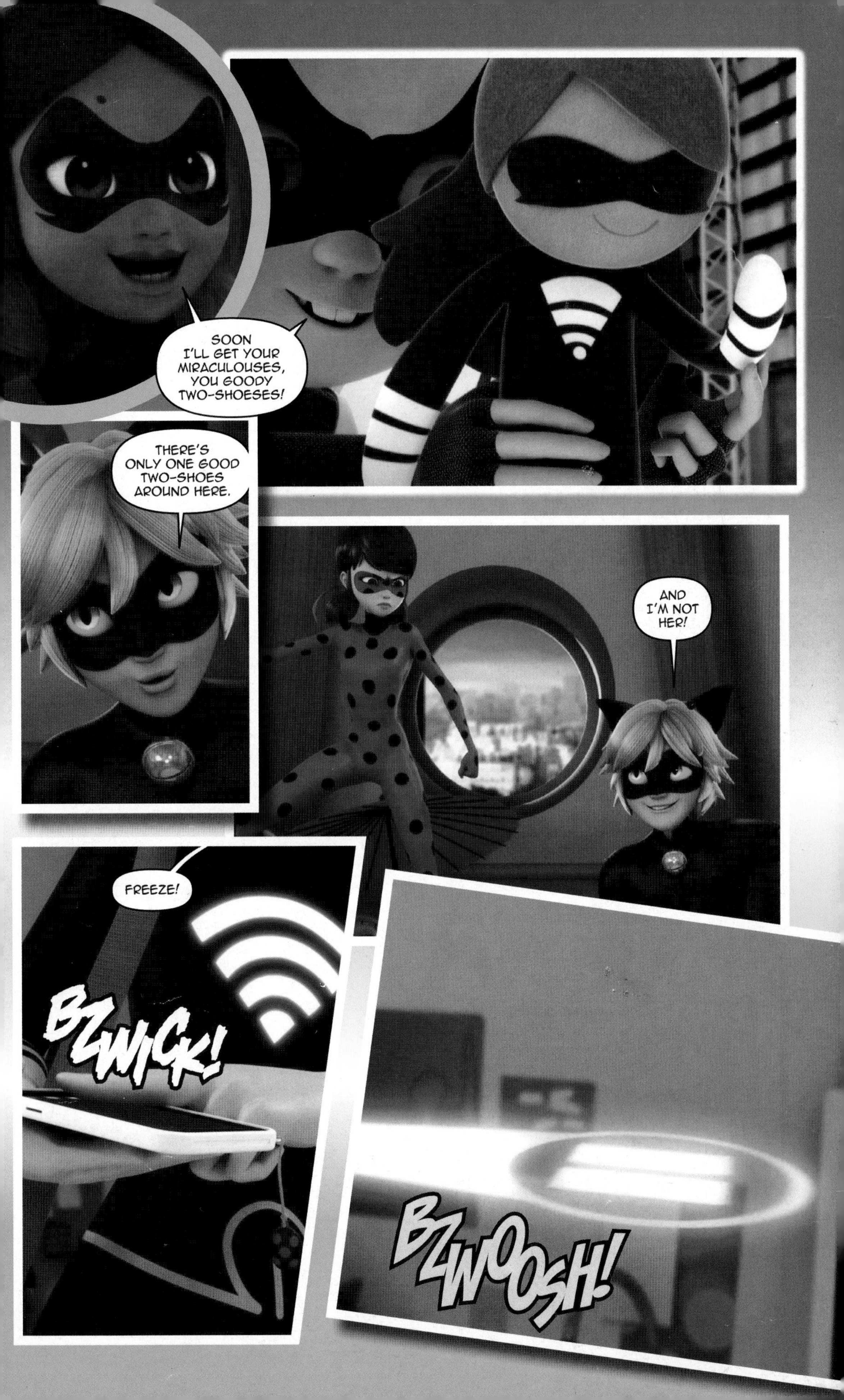
SOON I'LL GET YOUR MIRACULOUSES, YOU GOODY TWO-SHOESES!
THERE'S ONLY ONE GOOD TWO-SHOES AROUND HERE.
AND I'M NOT HER!
FREEZE!
BZWICK!
BZWOOSH!

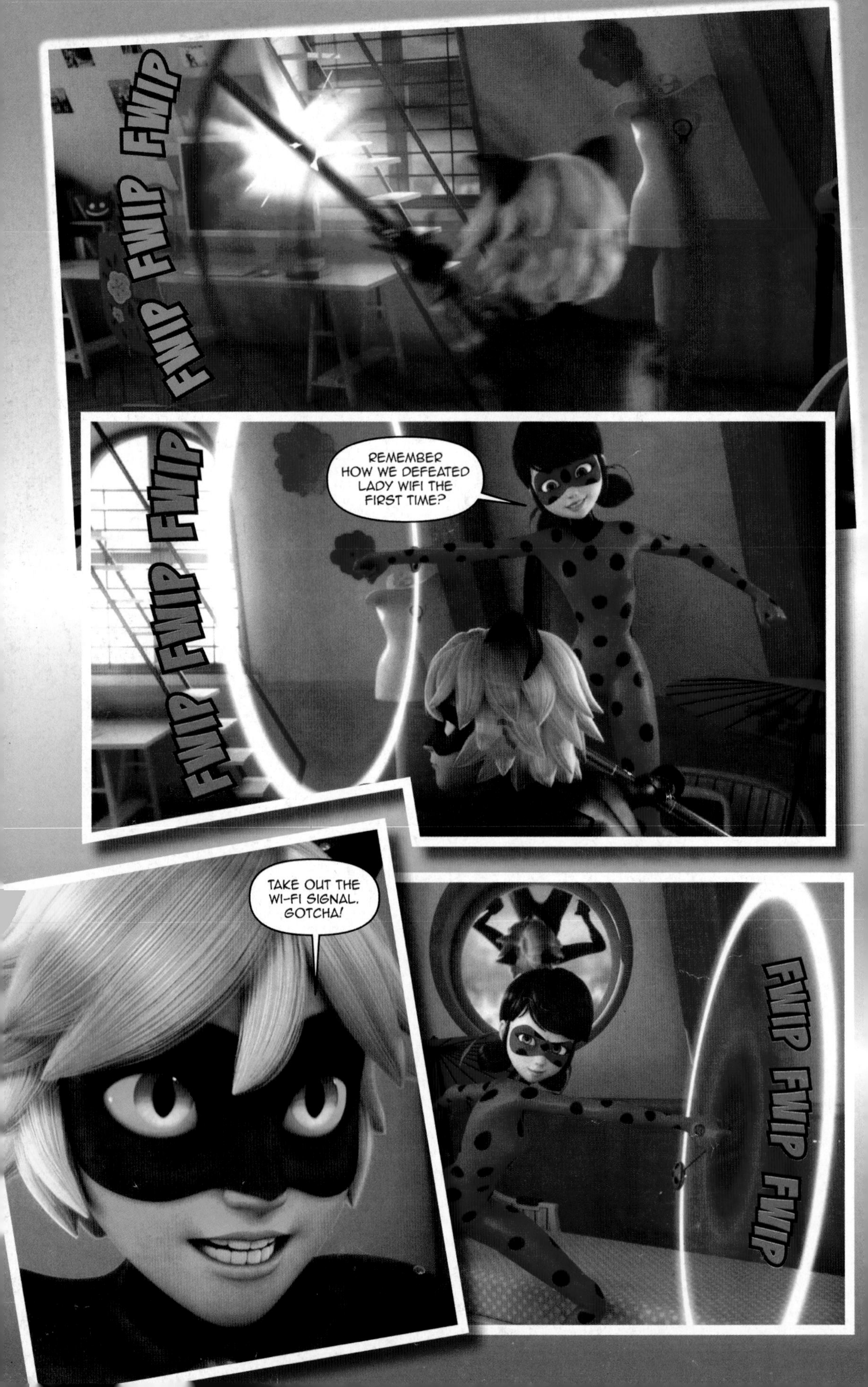
FWIP FWIP FWIP
FWIP FWIP FWIP
REMEMBER HOW WE DEFEATED LADY WIFI THE FIRST TIME?
TAKE OUT THE WI-FI SIGNAL. GOTCHA!
FWIP FWIP FWIP

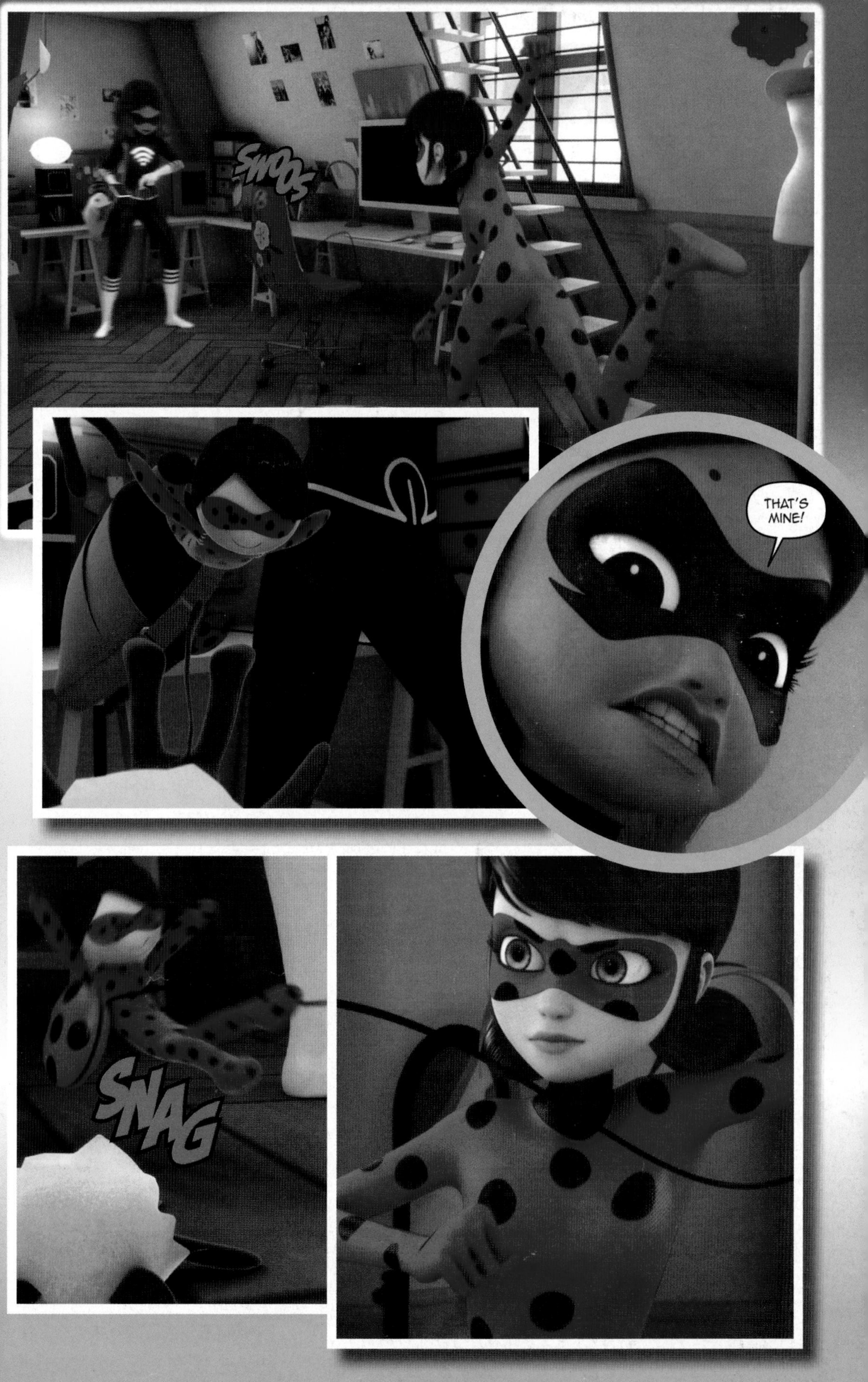
SWOOS
THAT'S MINE!
SNAG

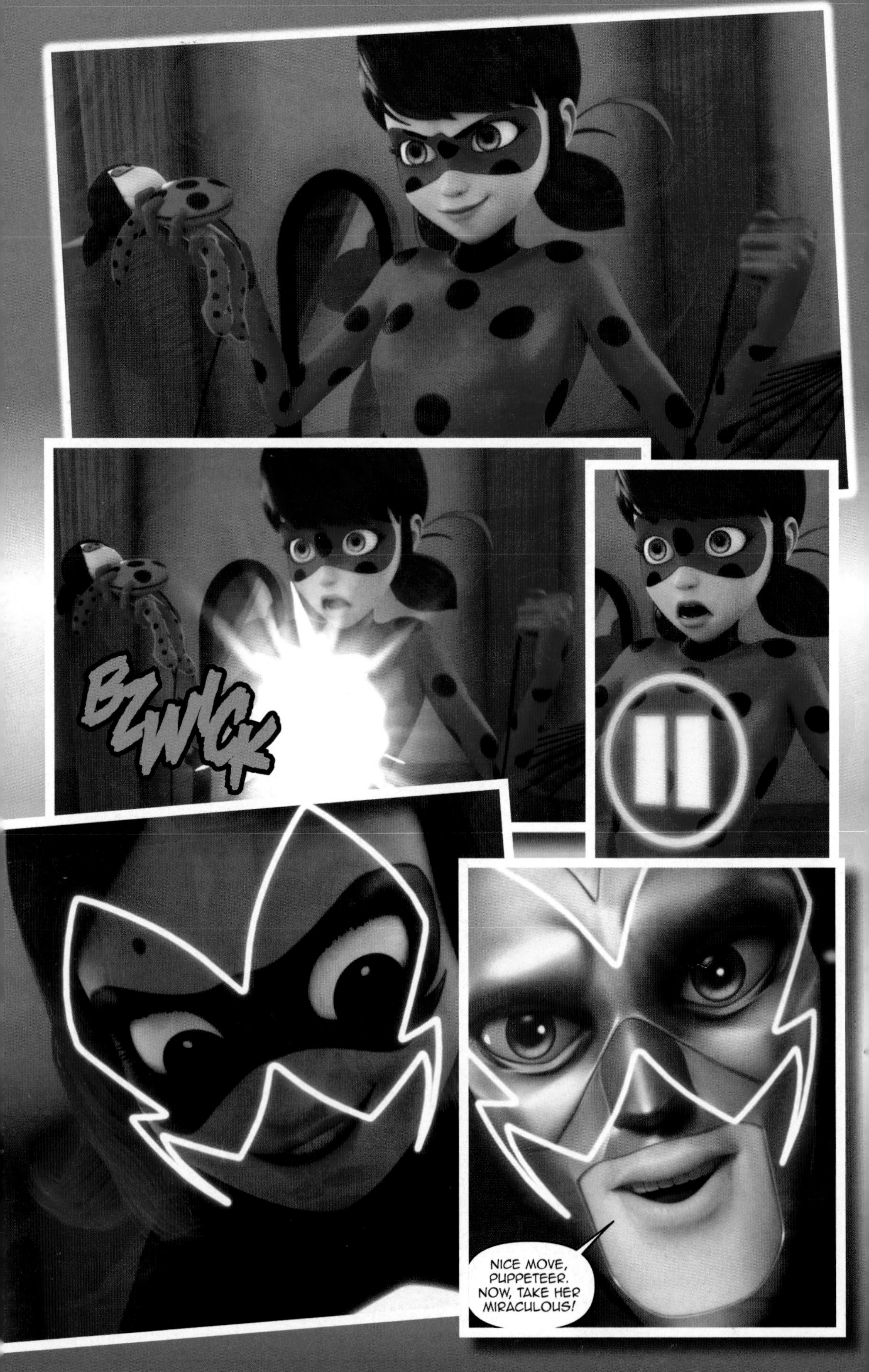
BZWICK
NICE MOVE, PUPPETEER. NOW, TAKE HER MIRACULOUS!

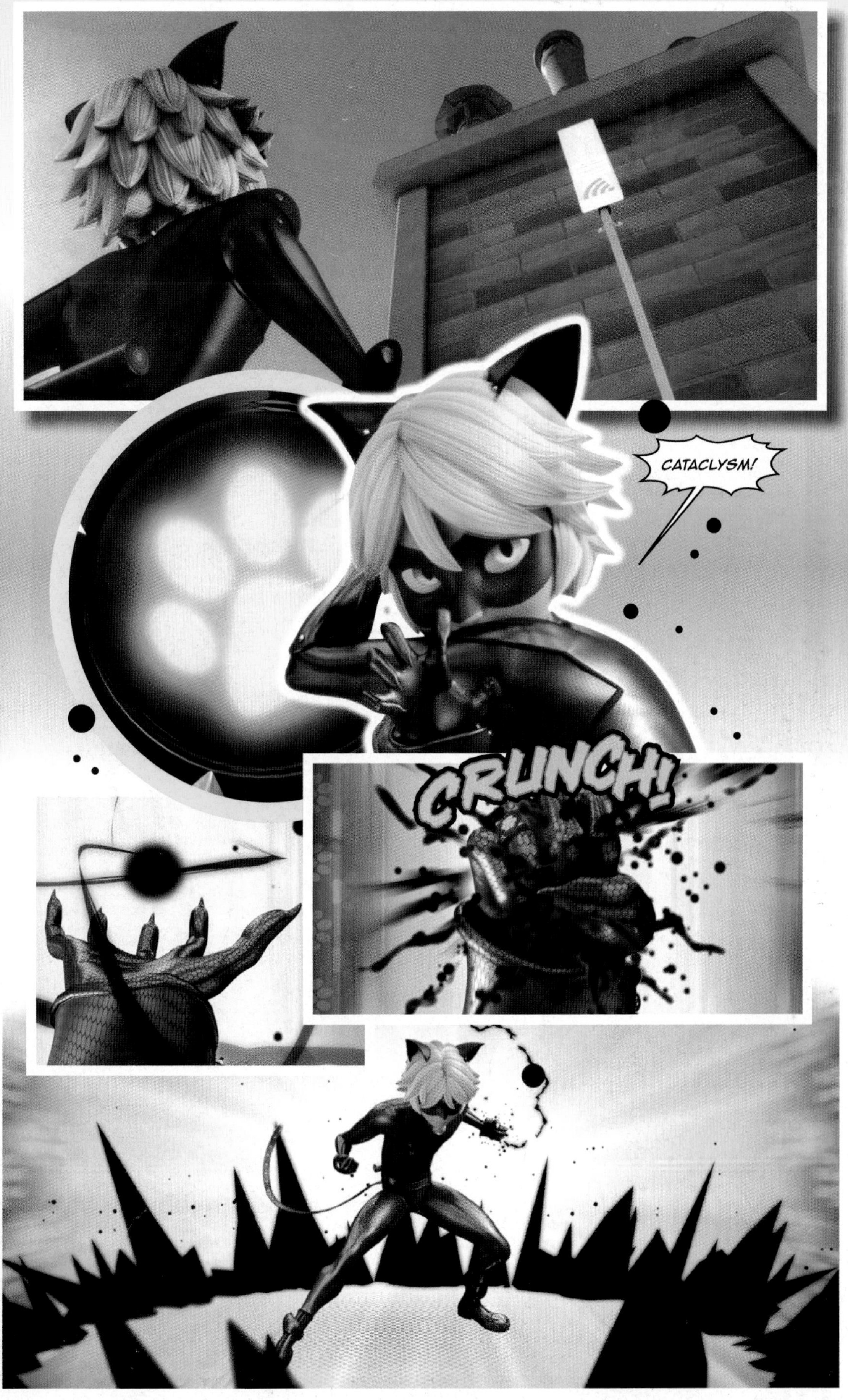
CATACLYSM!
CRUNCH!

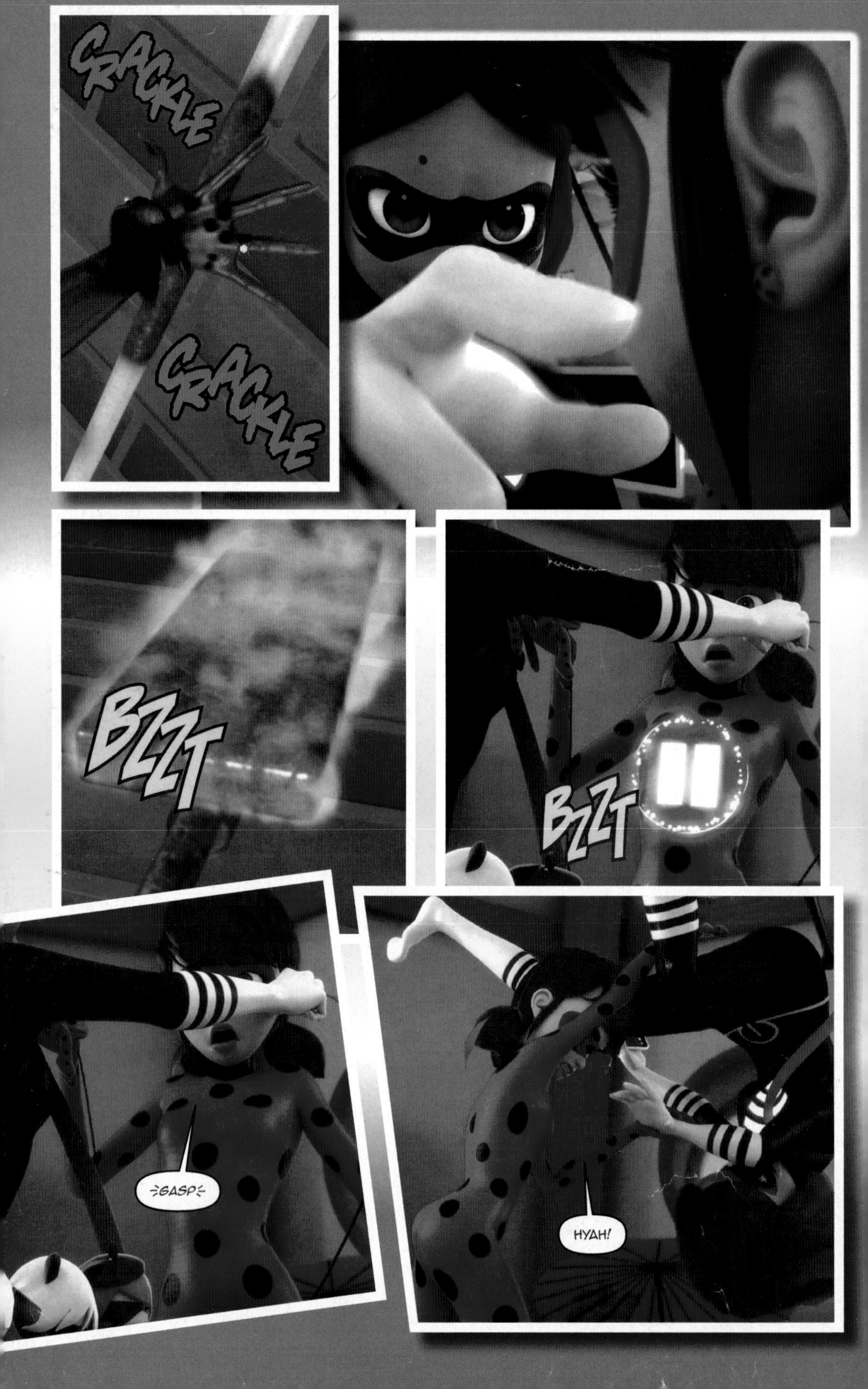
CRACKLE
CRACKLE
BZZT
BZZT
GASP
HYAH!

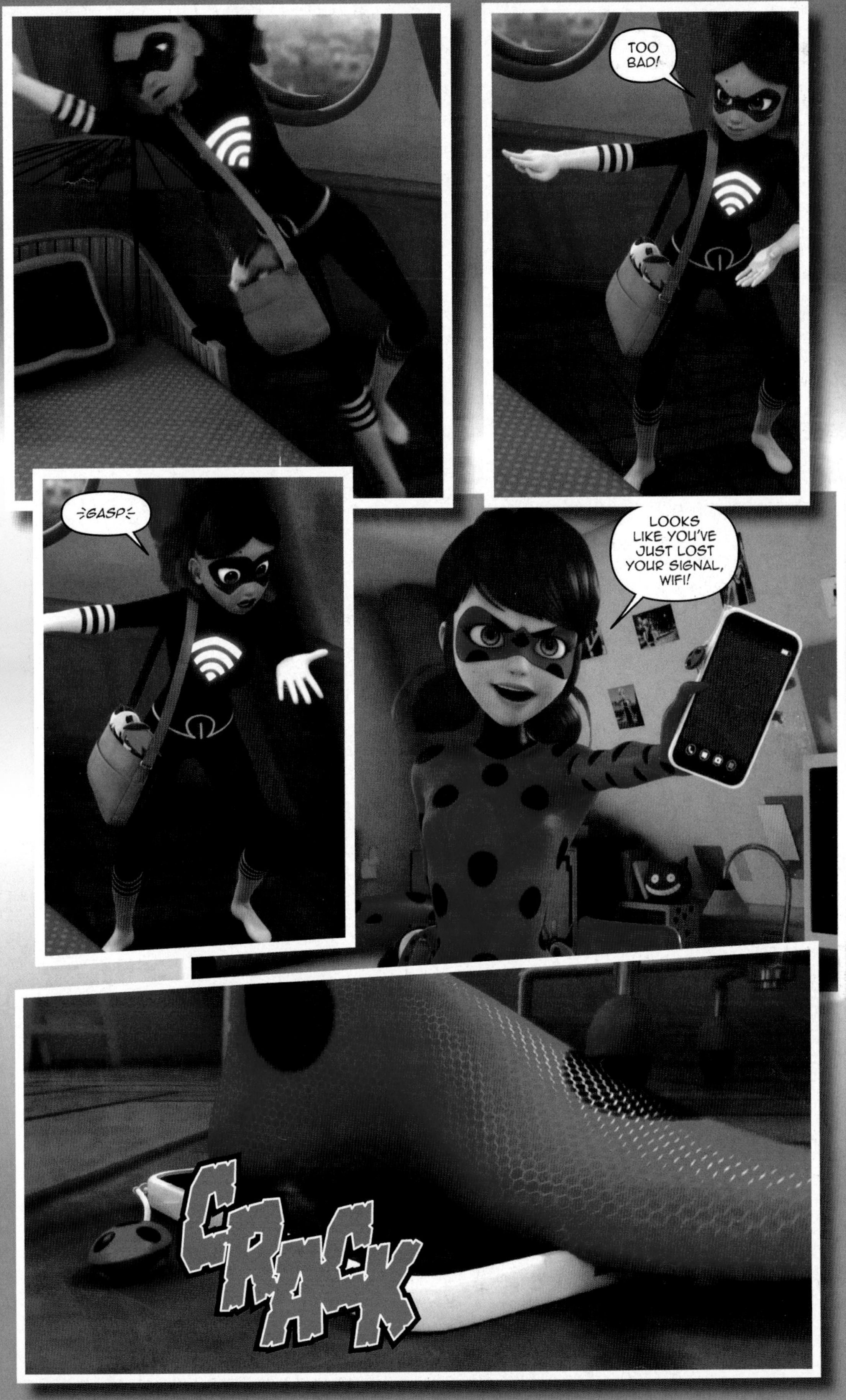
TOO BAD!
GASP
LOOKS LIKE YOU'VE JUST LOST YOUR SIGNAL, WIFI!
CRACK

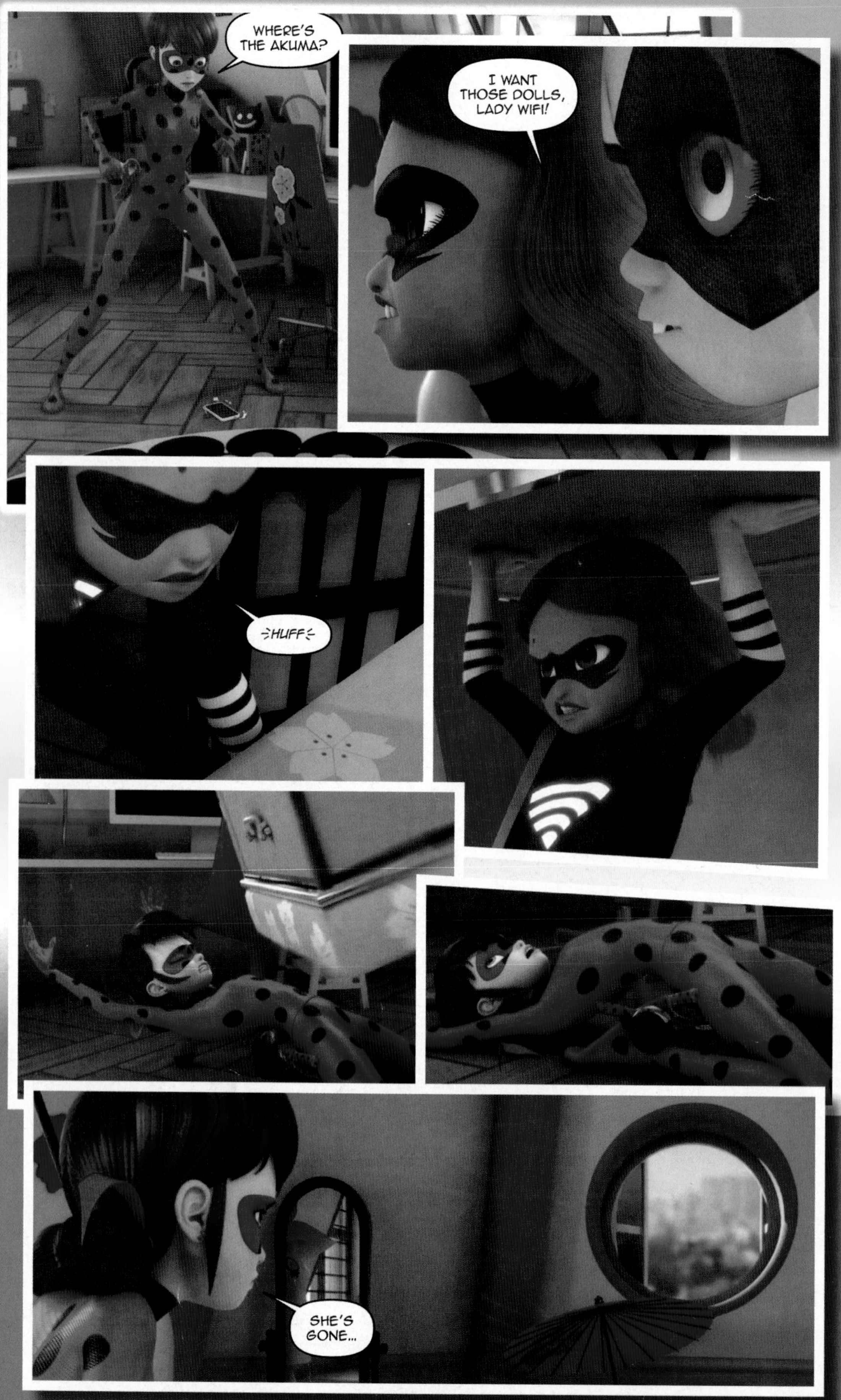
WHERE'S THE AKUMA?
I WANT THOSE DOLLS, LADY WIFI!
HUFF
SHE'S GONE...

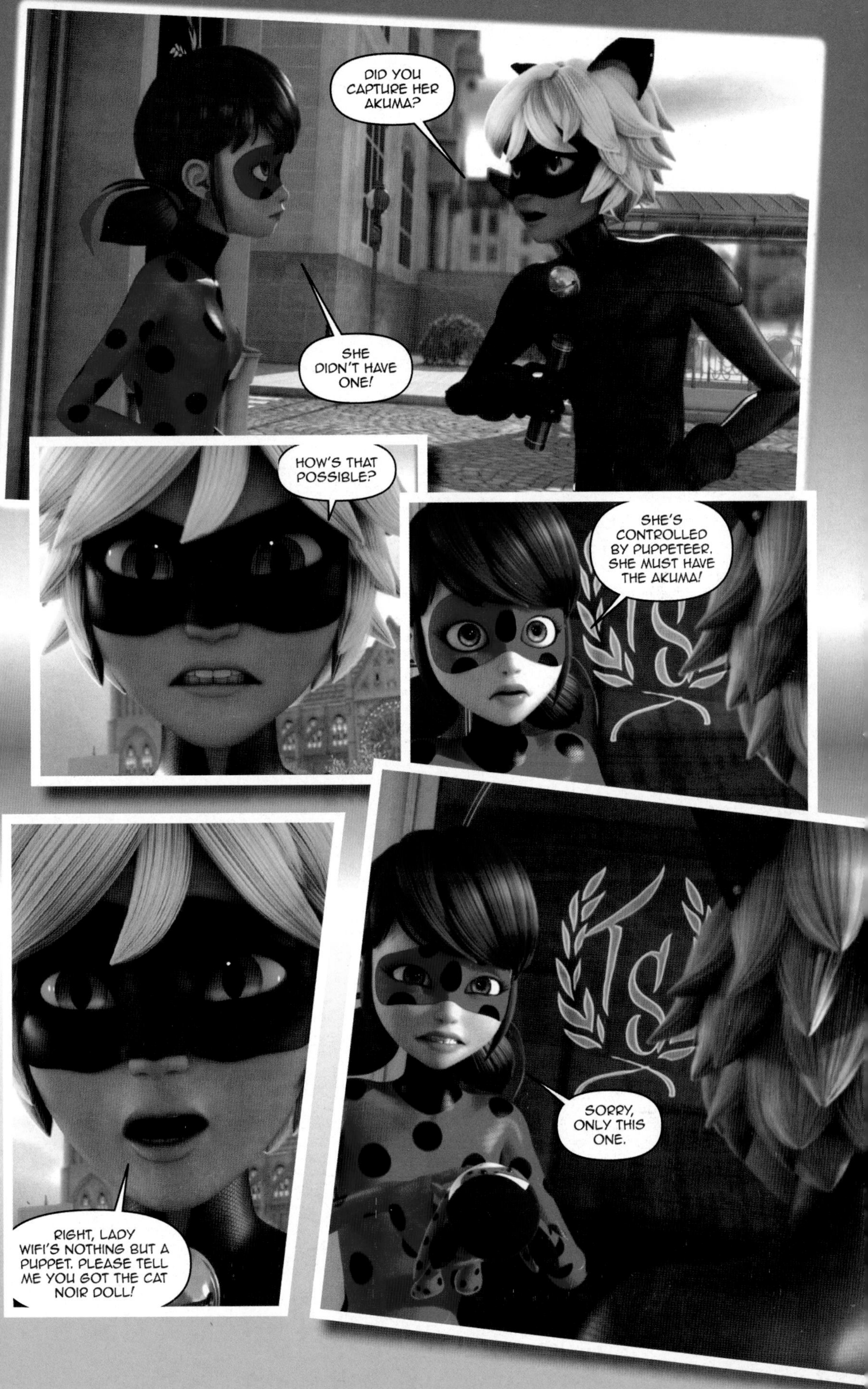
DID YOU CAPTURE HER AKUMA?
SHE DIDN'T HAVE ONE!
HOW'S THAT POSSIBLE?
SHE'S CONTROLLED BY PUPPETEER. SHE MUST HAVE THE AKUMA!
RIGHT, LADY WIFI'S NOTHING BUT A PUPPET. PLEASE TELL ME YOU GOT THE CAT NOIR DOLL!
SORRY, ONLY THIS ONE.

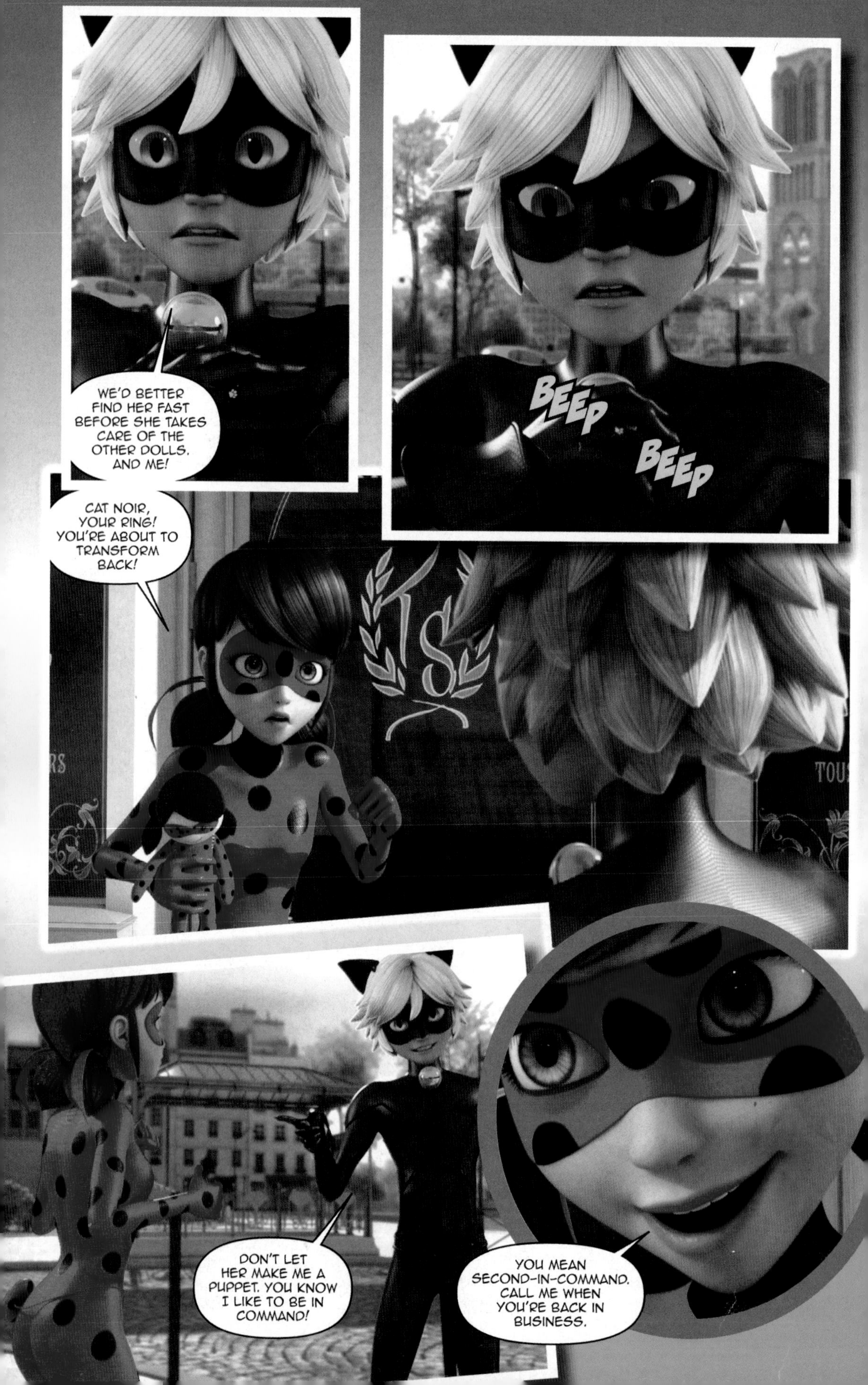
WE'D BETTER FIND HER FAST BEFORE SHE TAKES CARE OF THE OTHER DOLLS. AND ME!
BEEP
BEEP
CAT NOIR, YOUR RING! YOU'RE ABOUT TO TRANSFORM BACK!
DON'T LET HER MAKE ME A PUPPET. YOU KNOW I LIKE TO BE IN COMMAND!
YOU MEAN SECOND-IN-COMMAND. CALL ME WHEN YOU'RE BACK IN BUSINESS.

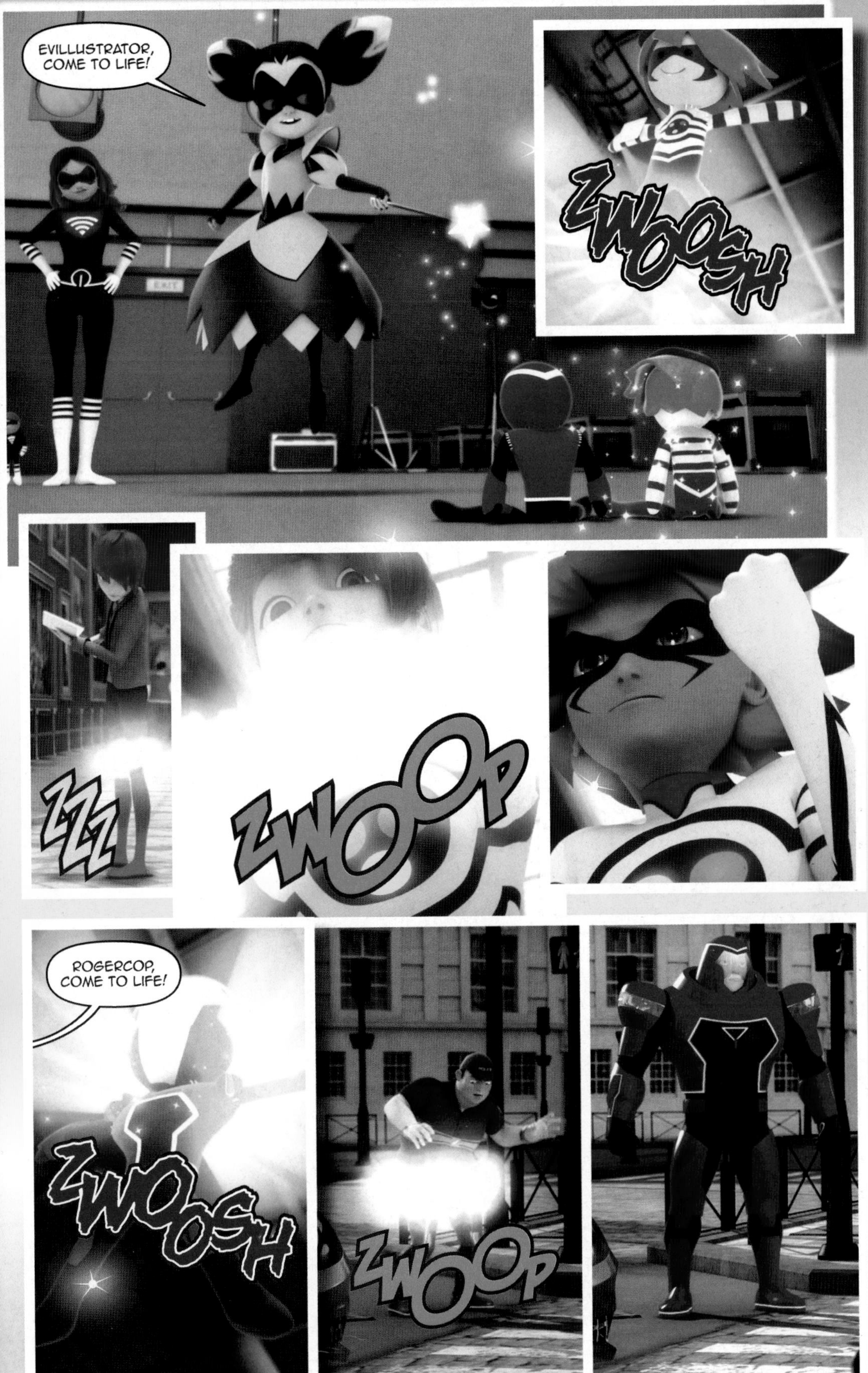
EVILLUSTRATOR, COME TO LIFE!
ZWOOSH
ZZZ
ZWOOP
ROGERCOP, COME TO LIFE!
ZWOOSH
ZWOOP

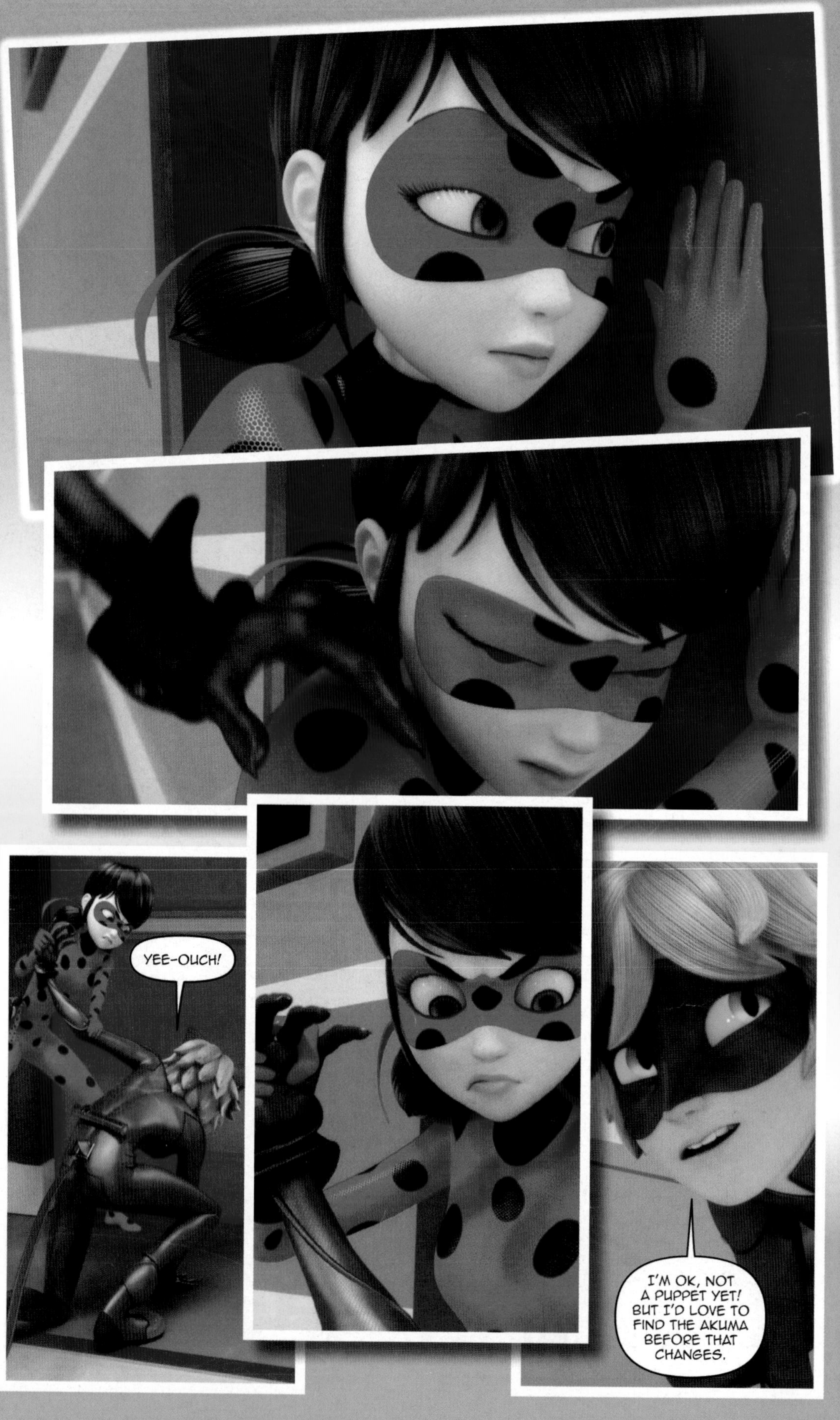
YEE-OUCH!
I'M OK, NOT A PUPPET YET! BUT I'D LOVE TO FIND THE AKUMA BEFORE THAT CHANGES.

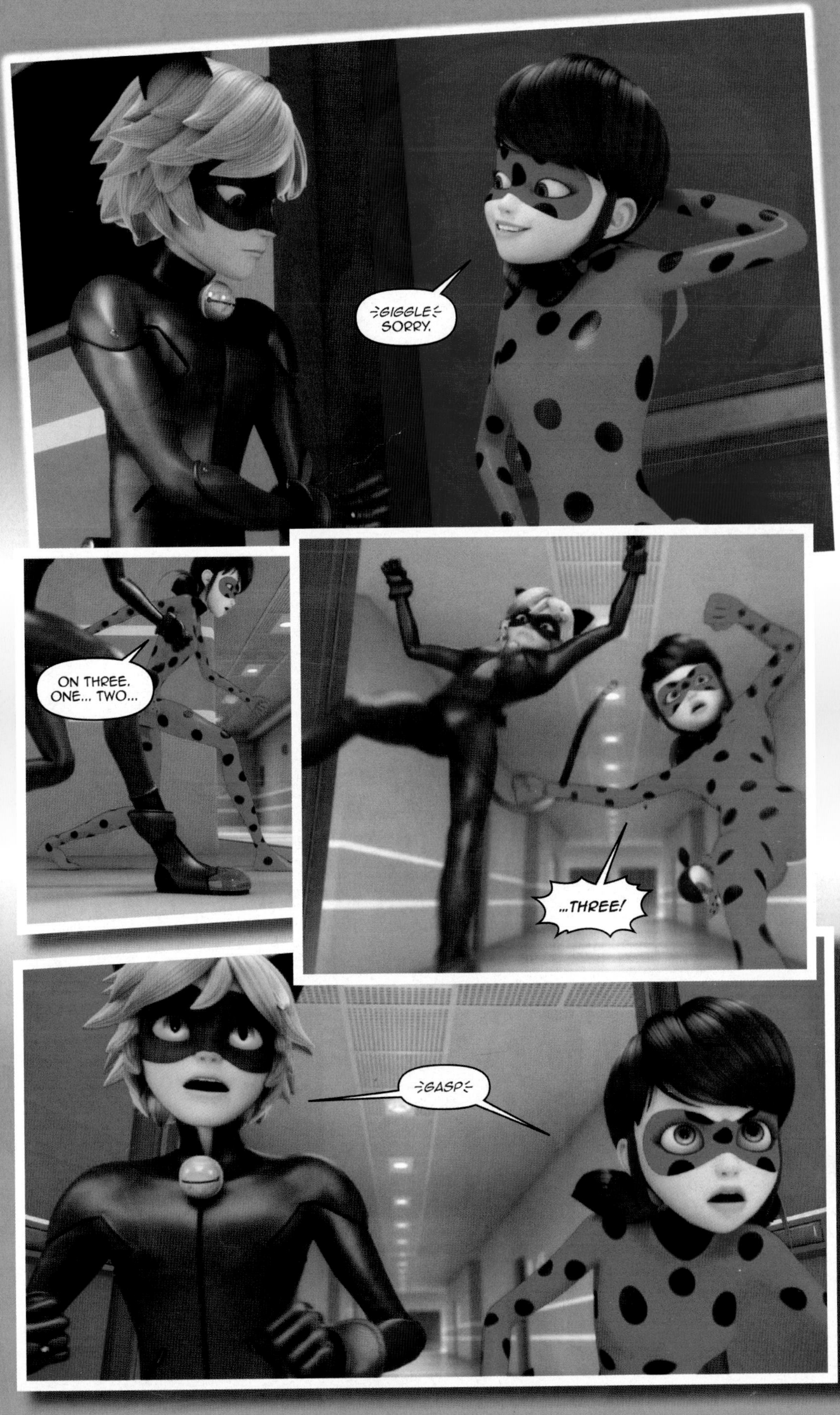

~GIGGLE~ SORRY.
ON THREE. ONE... TWO...
...THREE!
~GASP~

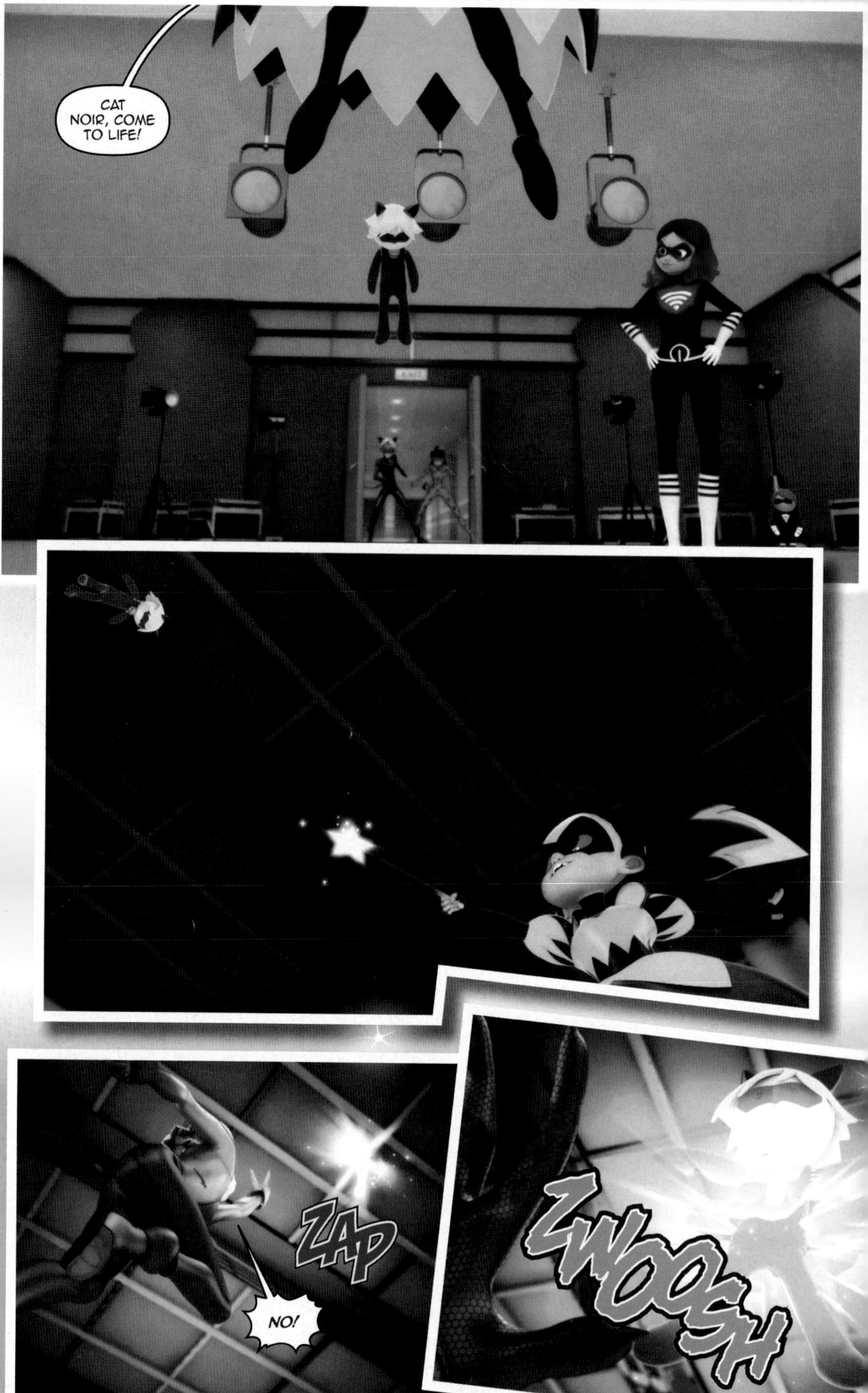
CAT NOIR, COME TO LIFE!
ZAP
NO!
ZWOOSH

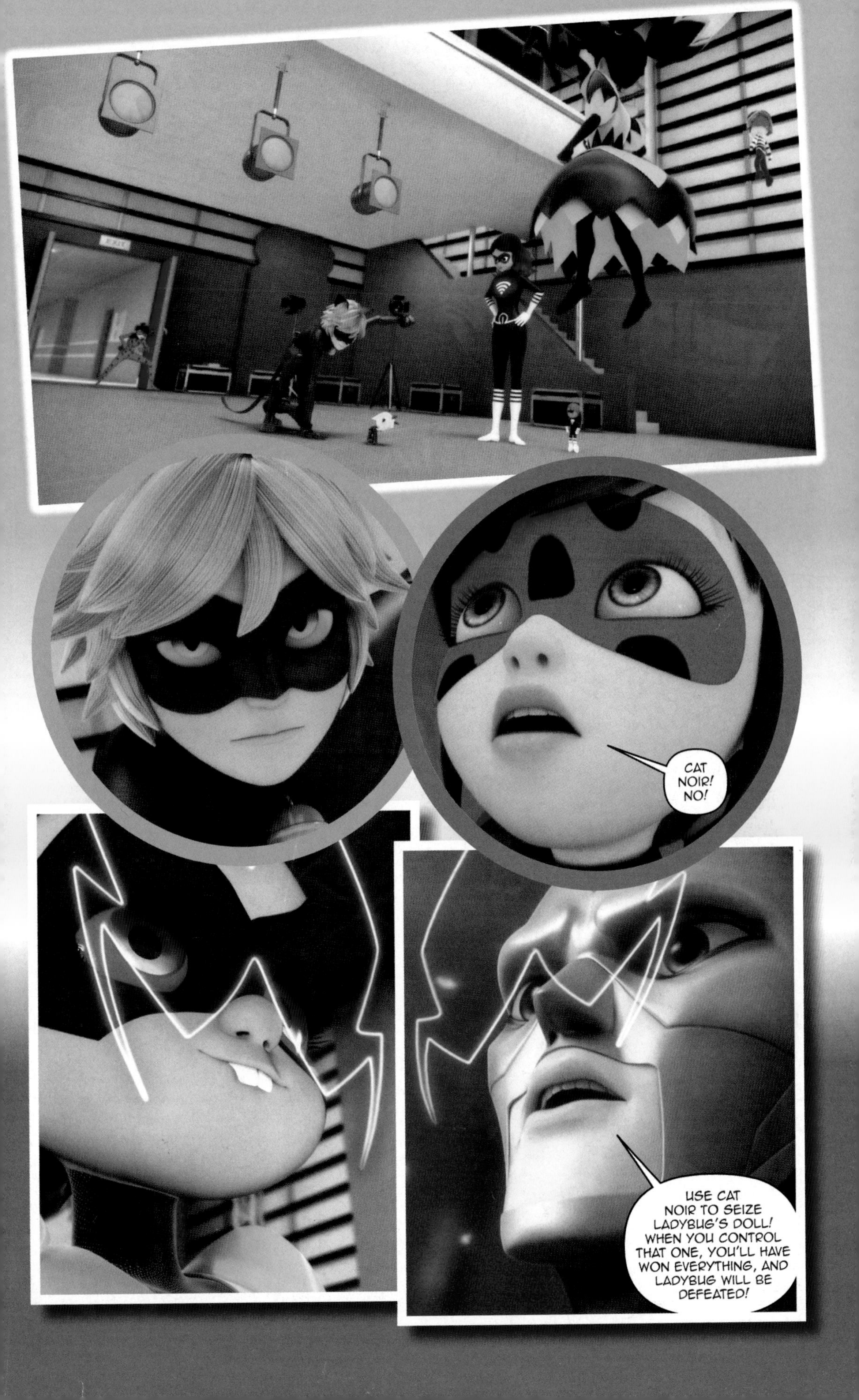
CAT NOIR! NO!
USE CAT NOIR TO SEIZE LADYBUG'S DOLL! WHEN YOU CONTROL THAT ONE, YOU'LL HAVE WON EVERYTHING, AND LADYBUG WILL BE DEFEATED!

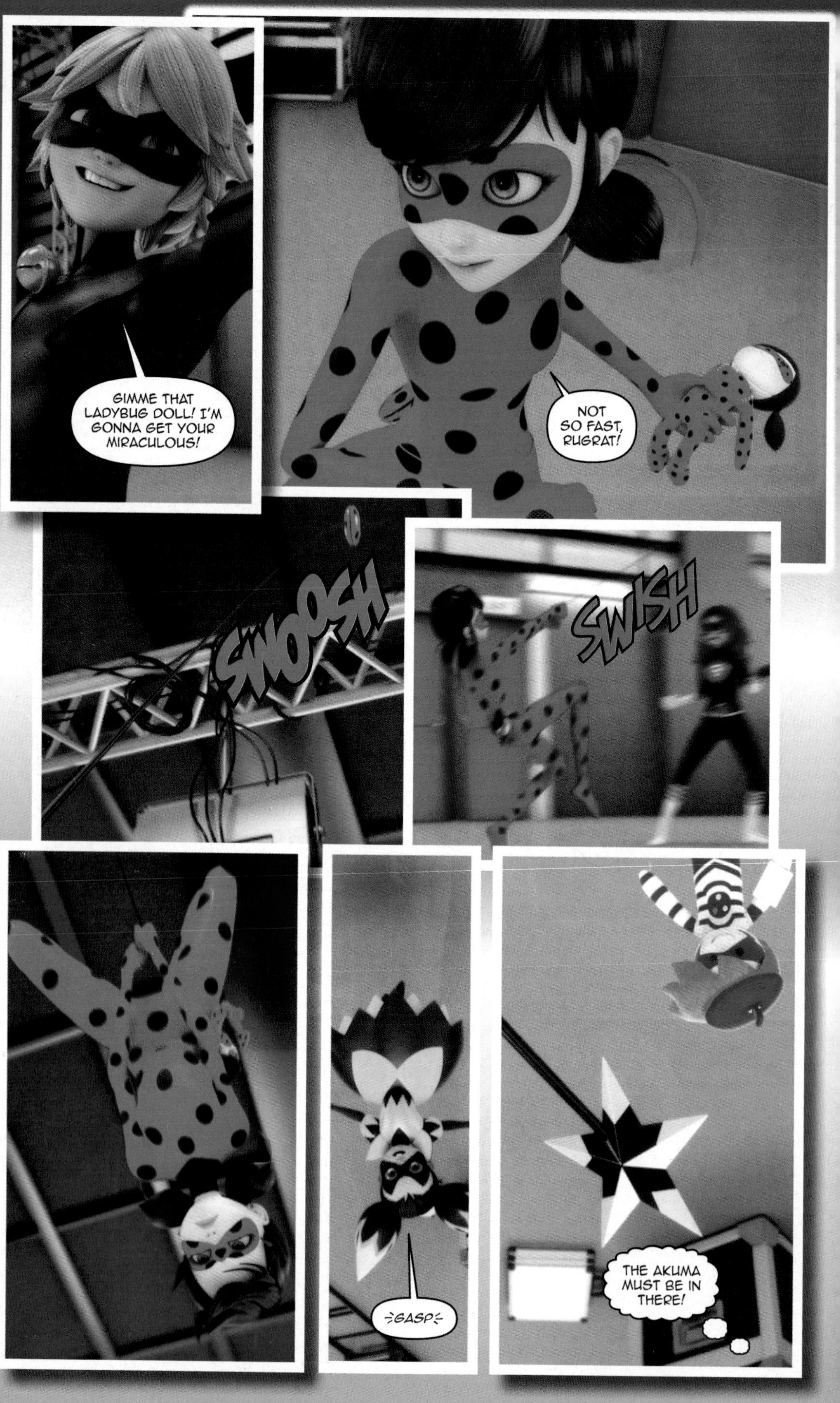
GIMME THAT LADYBUG DOLL! I'M GONNA GET YOUR MIRACULOUS!
NOT SO FAST, RUGRAT!
SWOOSH
SWISH
GASP
THE AKUMA MUST BE IN THERE!

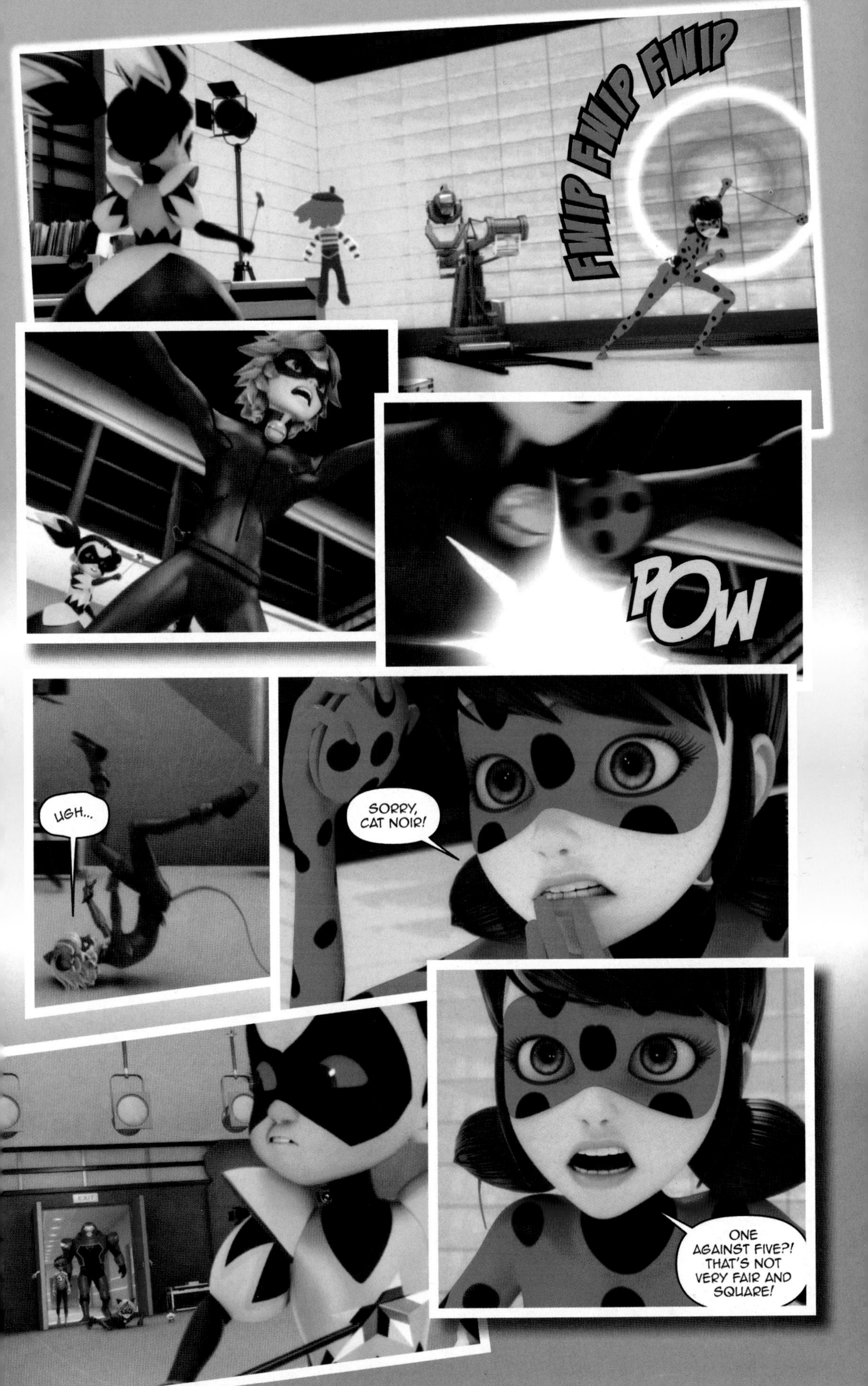
FWIP FWIP FWIP
POW
UGH...
SORRY, CAT NOIR!
ONE AGAINST FIVE?! THAT'S NOT VERY FAIR AND SQUARE!

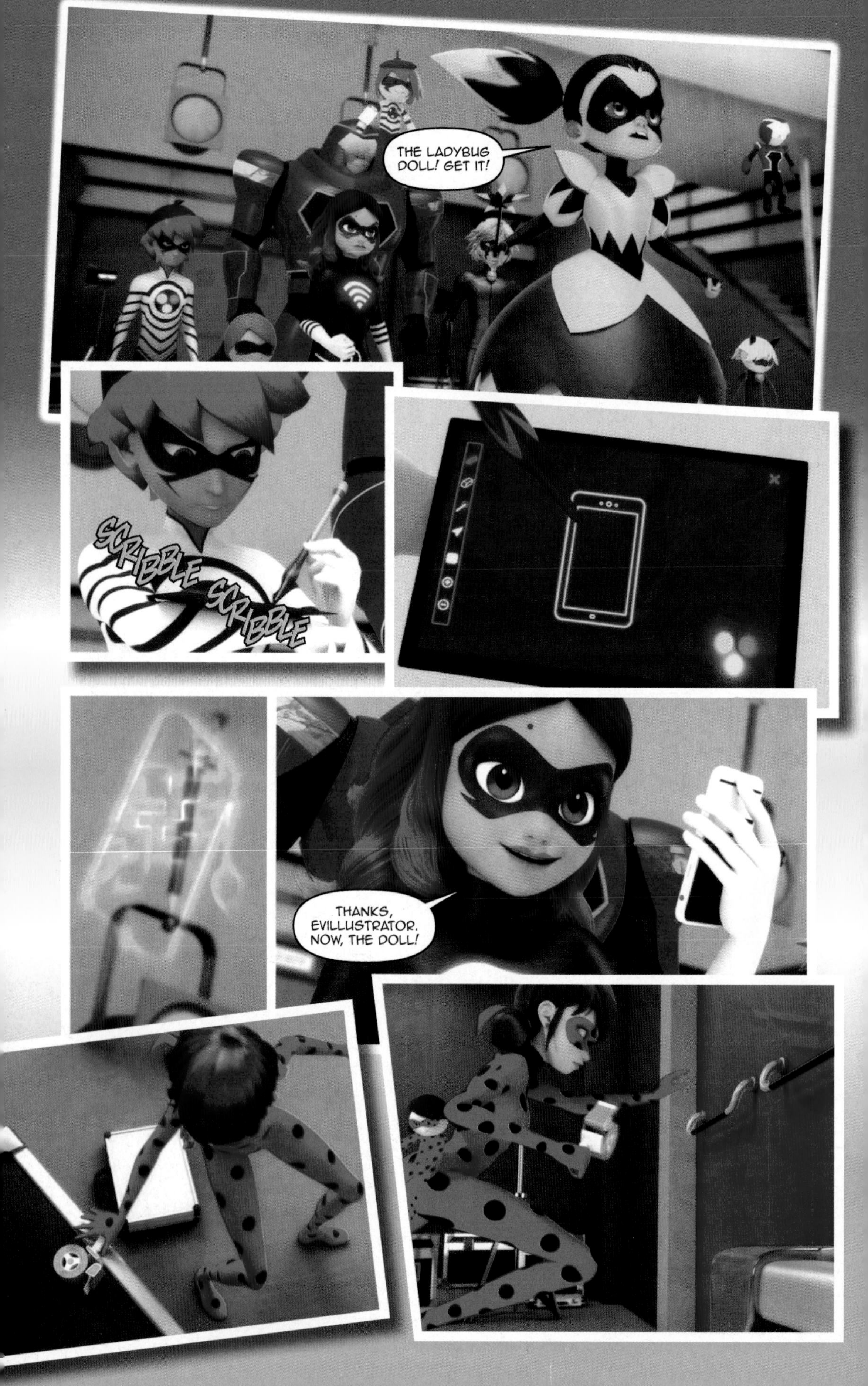
THE LADYBUG DOLL! GET IT!
SCRIBBLE SCRIBBLE
THANKS, EVILLUSTRATOR. NOW, THE DOLL!

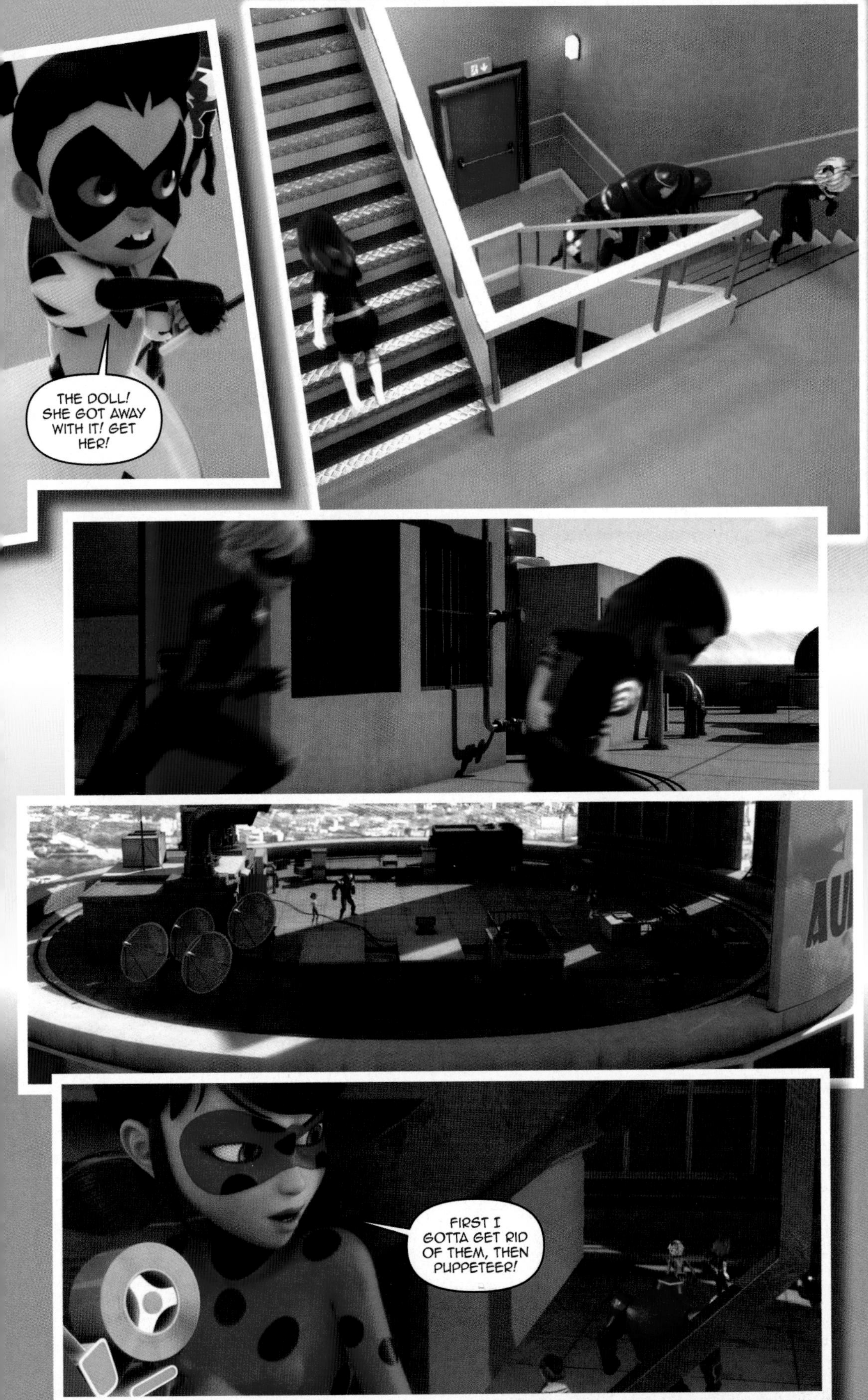
THE DOLL! SHE GOT AWAY WITH IT! GET HER!
FIRST I GOTTA GET RID OF THEM, THEN PUPPETEER!

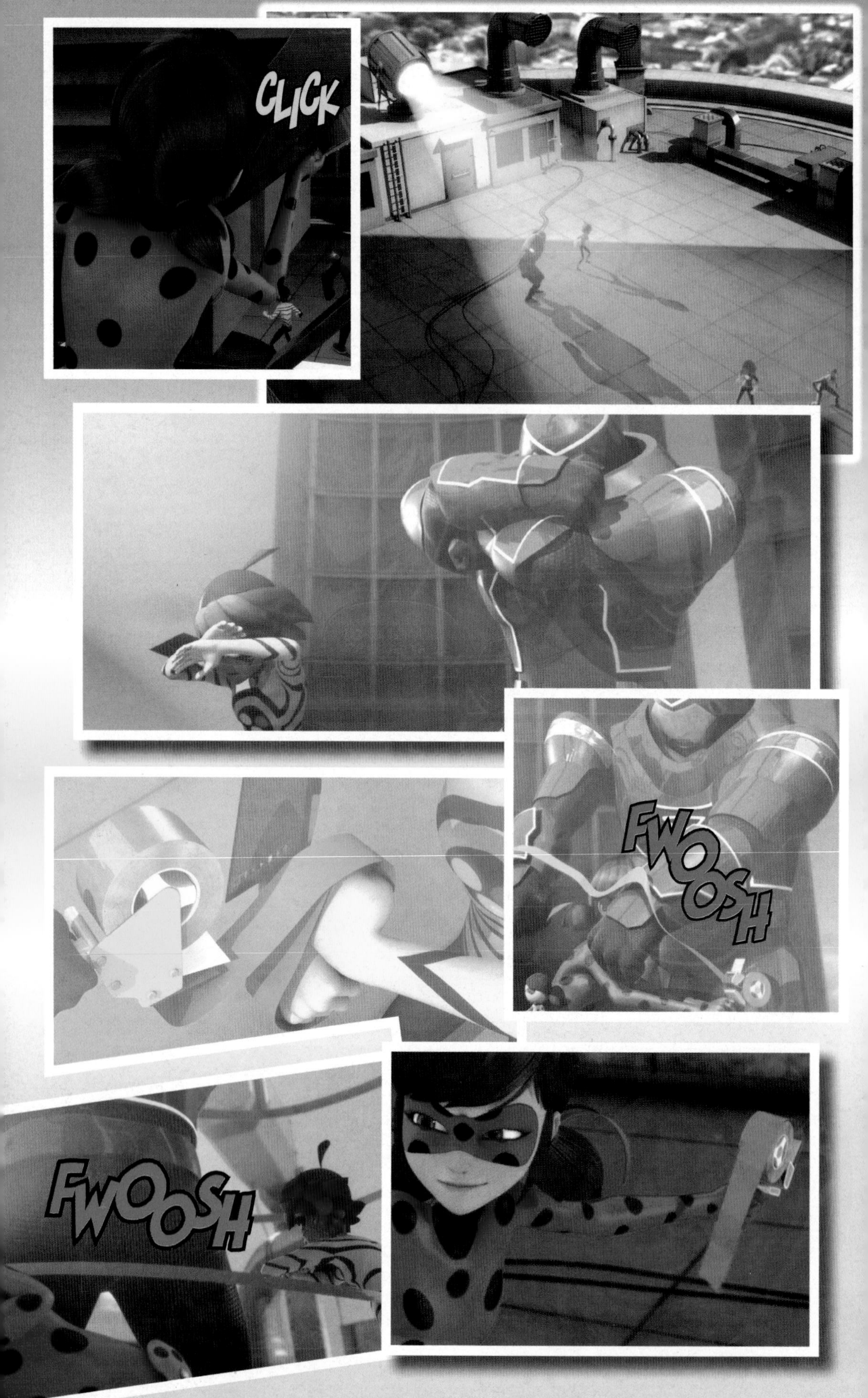
CLICK
FWOOSH
FWOOSH

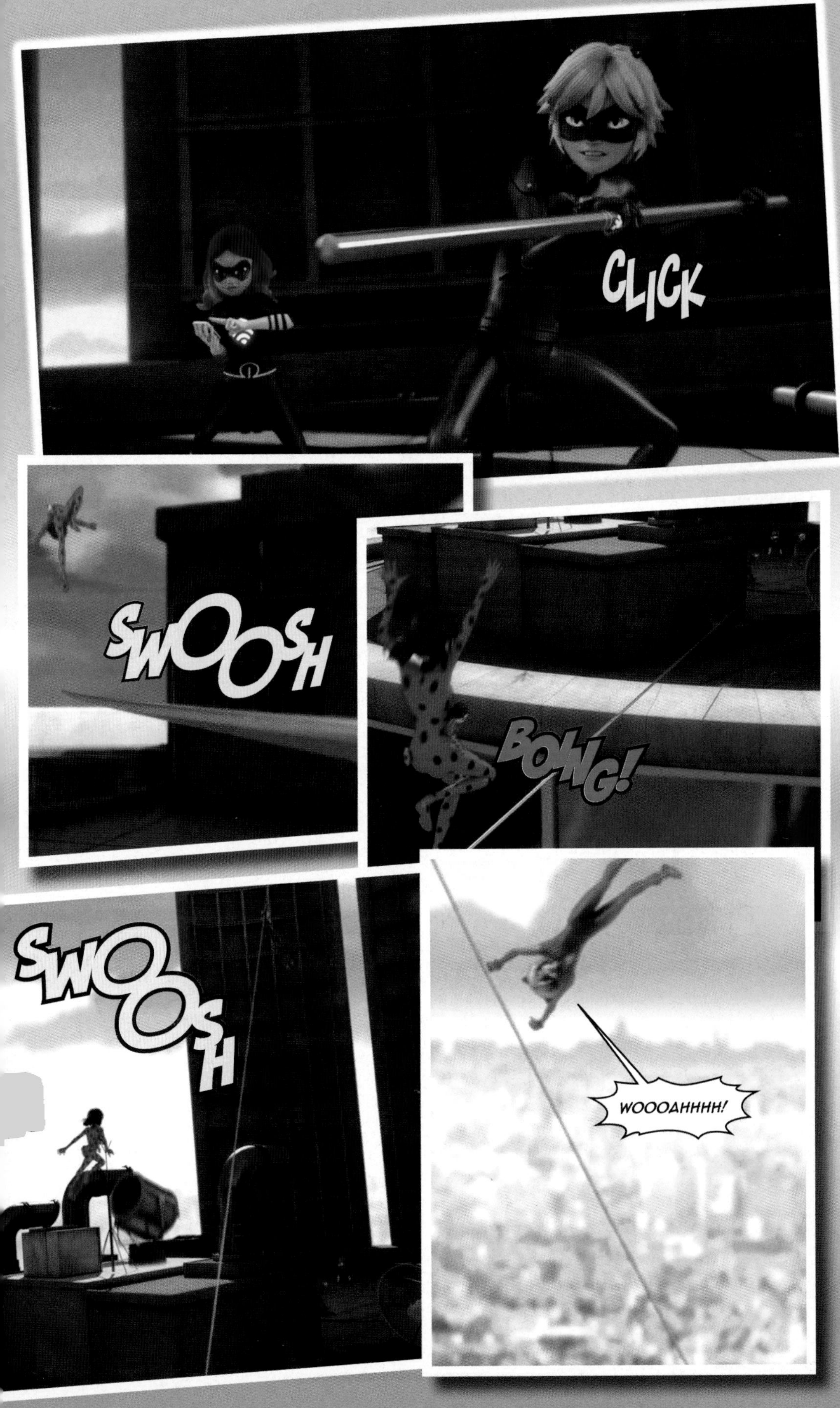
CLICK
SWOOSH
BOING!
SWOOSH
WOOOAHHHH!

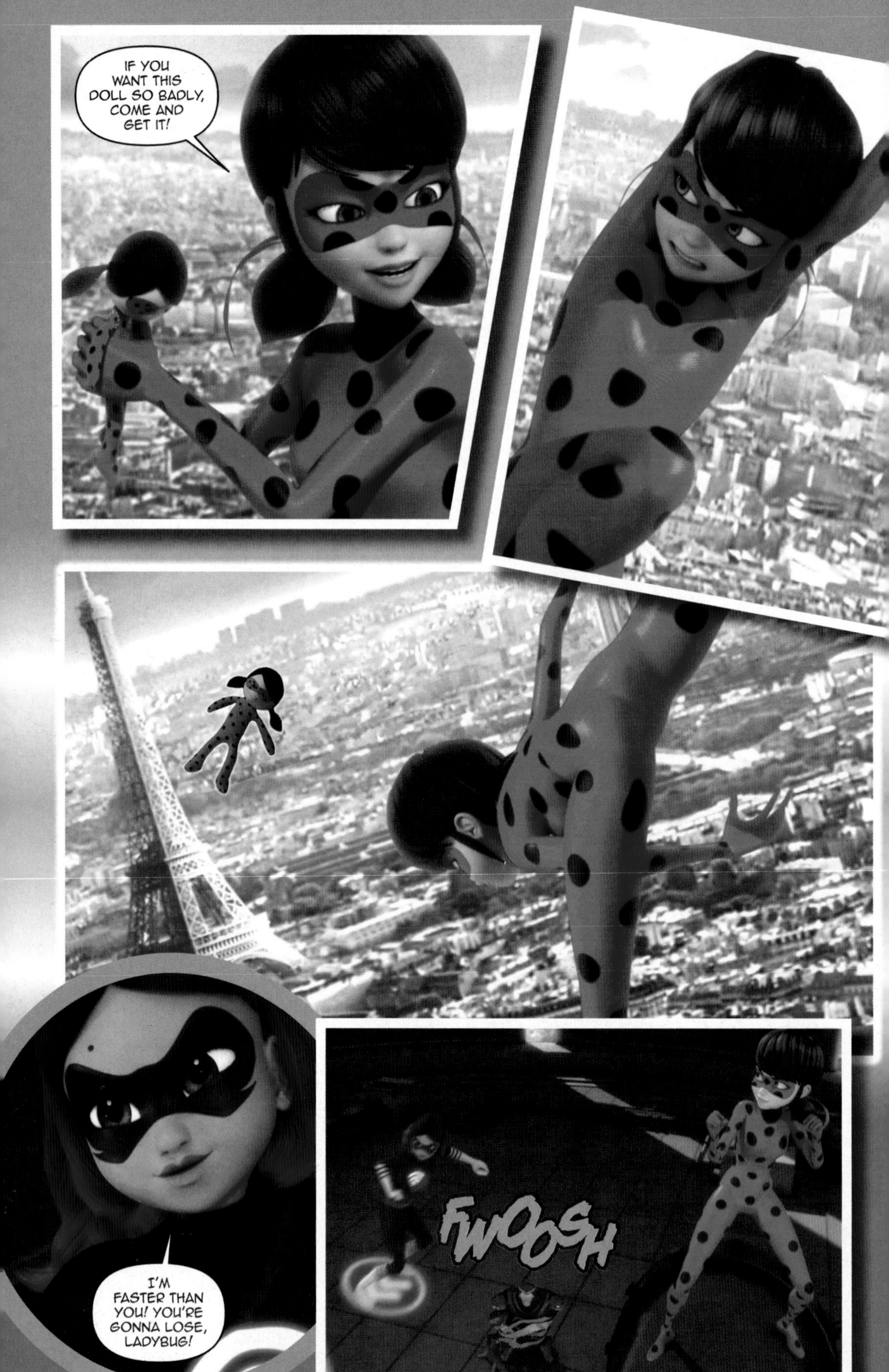
IF YOU WANT THIS DOLL SO BADLY, COME AND GET IT!
I'M FASTER THAN YOU! YOU'RE GONNA LOSE, LADYBUG!
FWOOSH

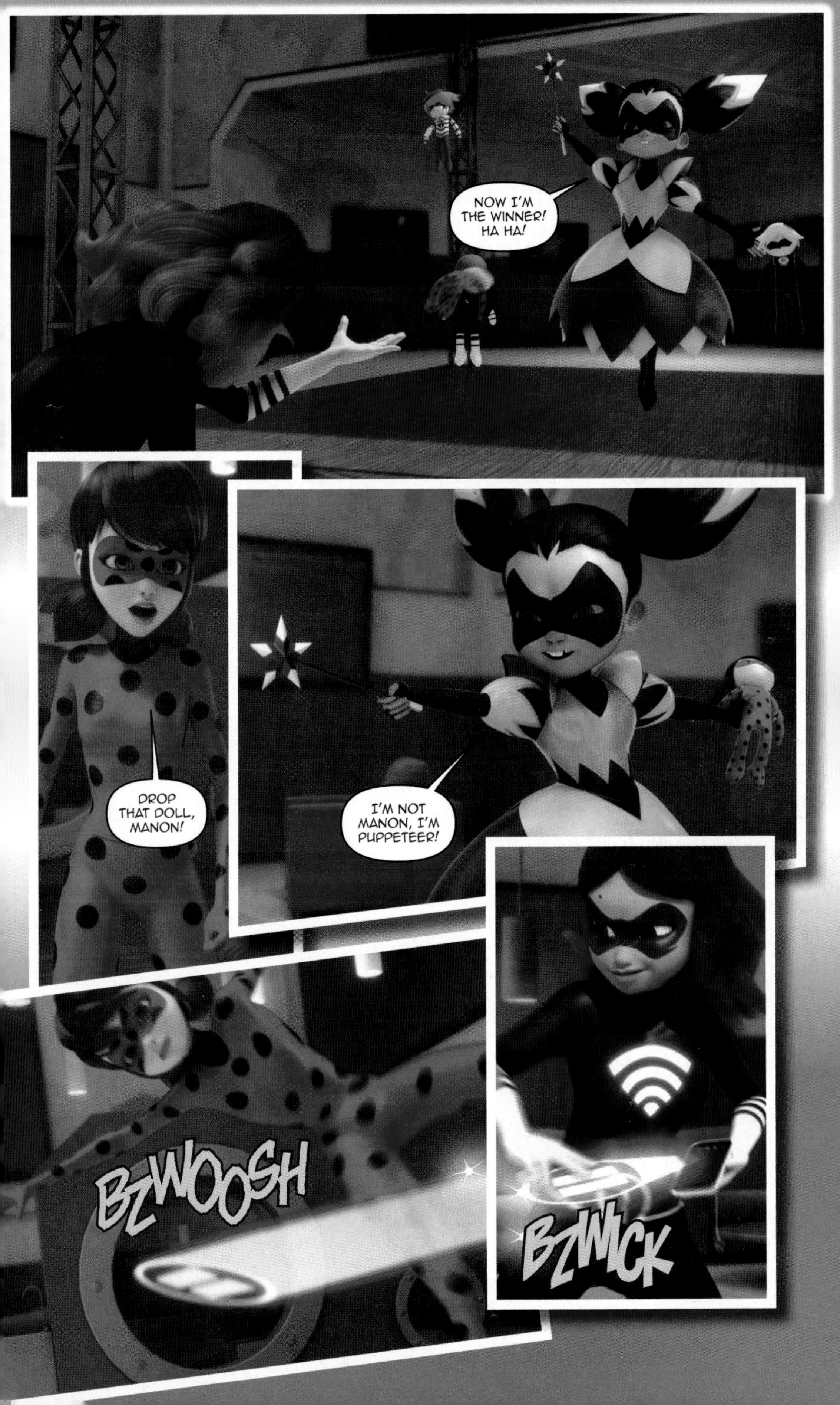

NOW I'M THE WINNER! HA HA!
DROP THAT DOLL, MANON!
I'M NOT MANON, I'M PUPPETEER!
BZWOOSH
BZWICK

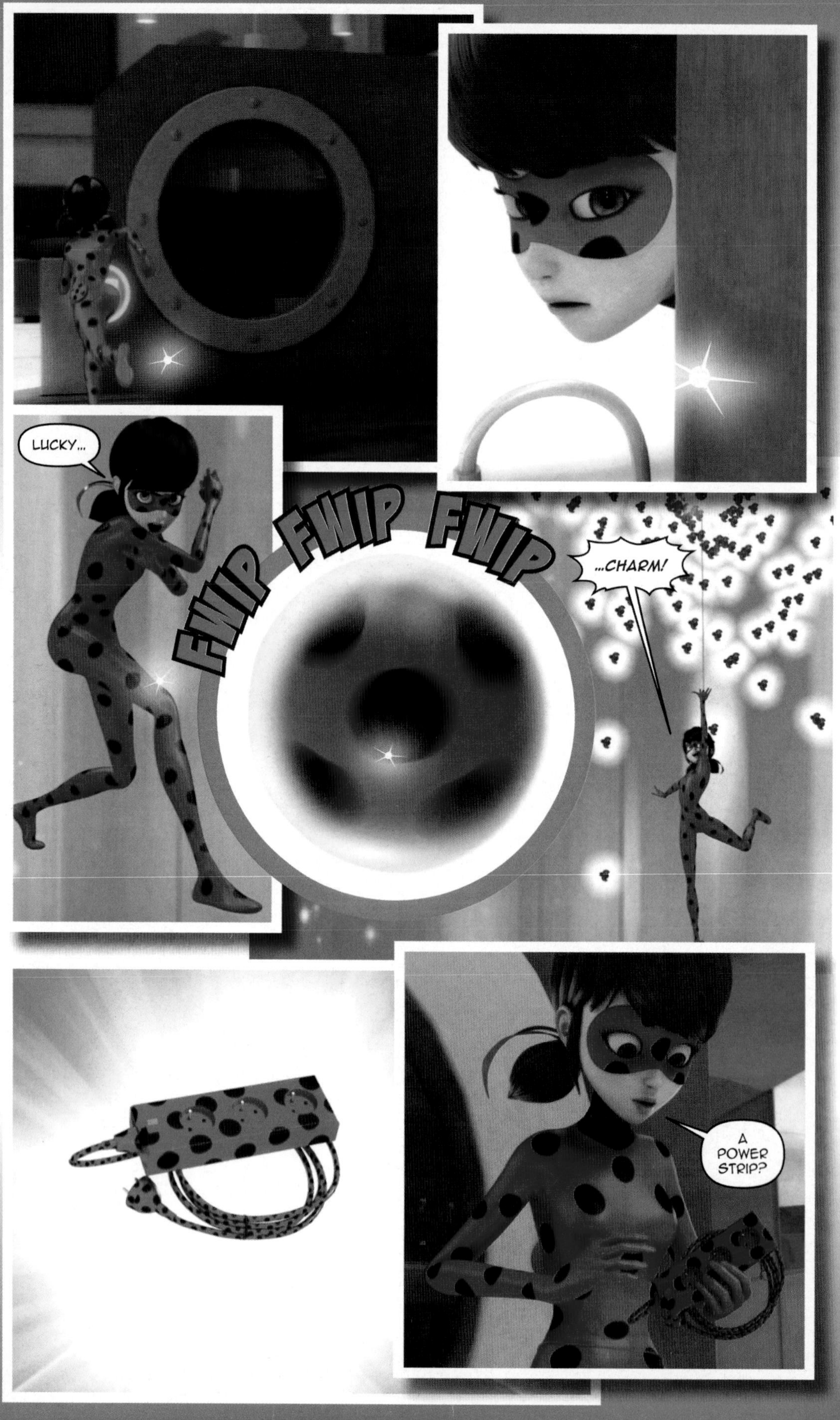
LUCKY...
FWIP FWIP FWIP
...CHARM!
A POWER STRIP?

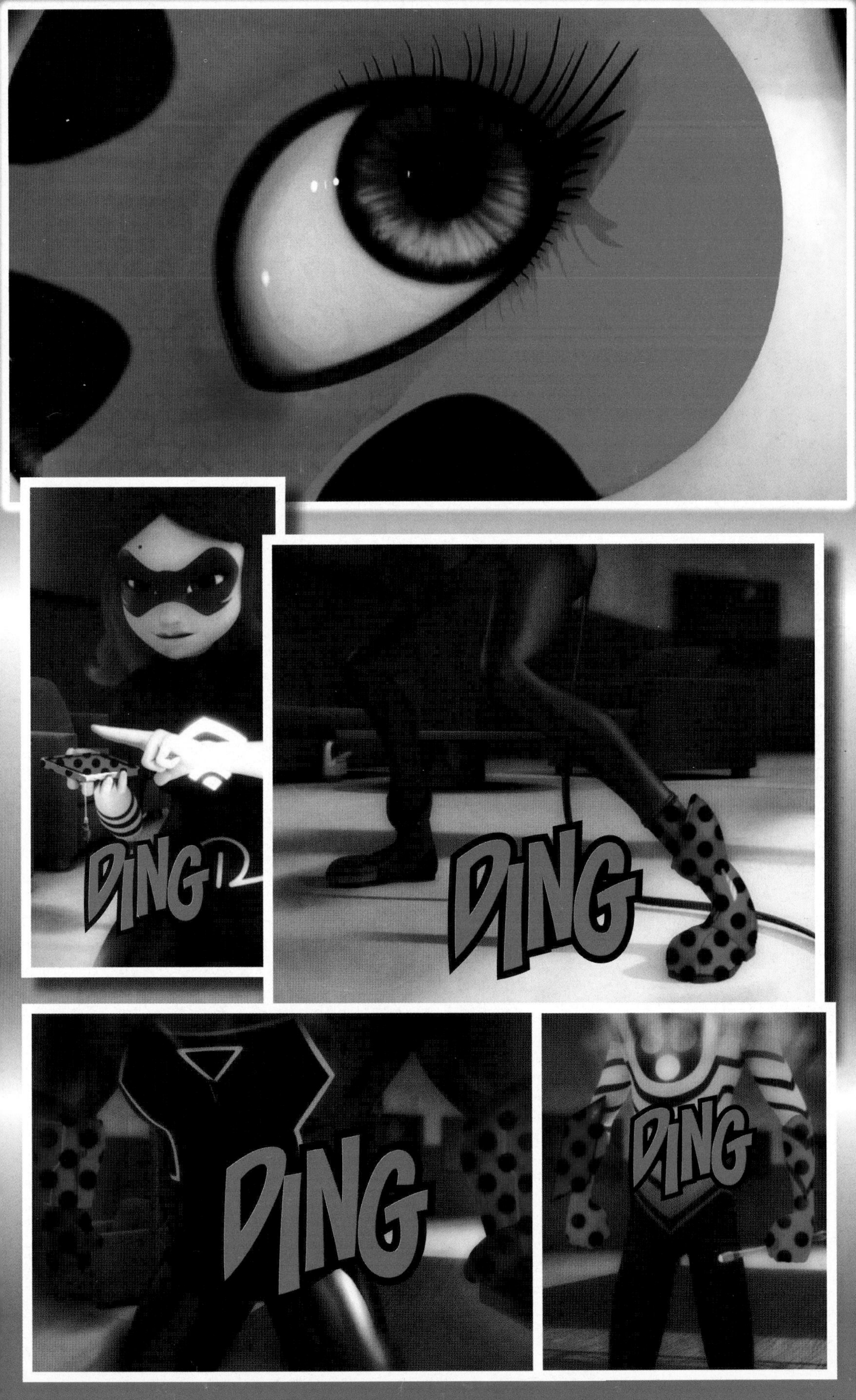
DING
DING
DING
DING

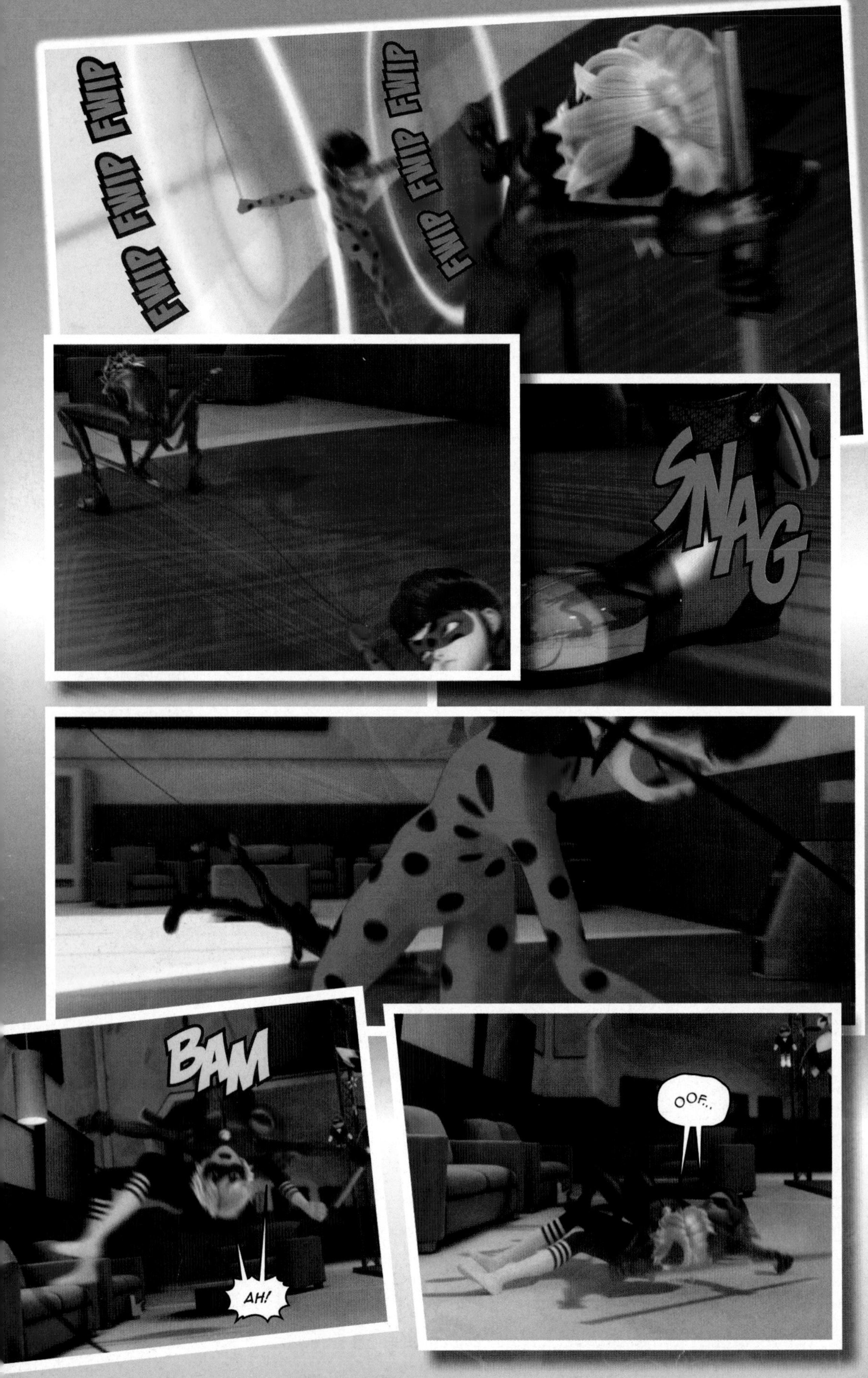
FWIP FWIP FWIP
FWIP FWIP FWIP
SNAG
BAM
AH!
OOF...

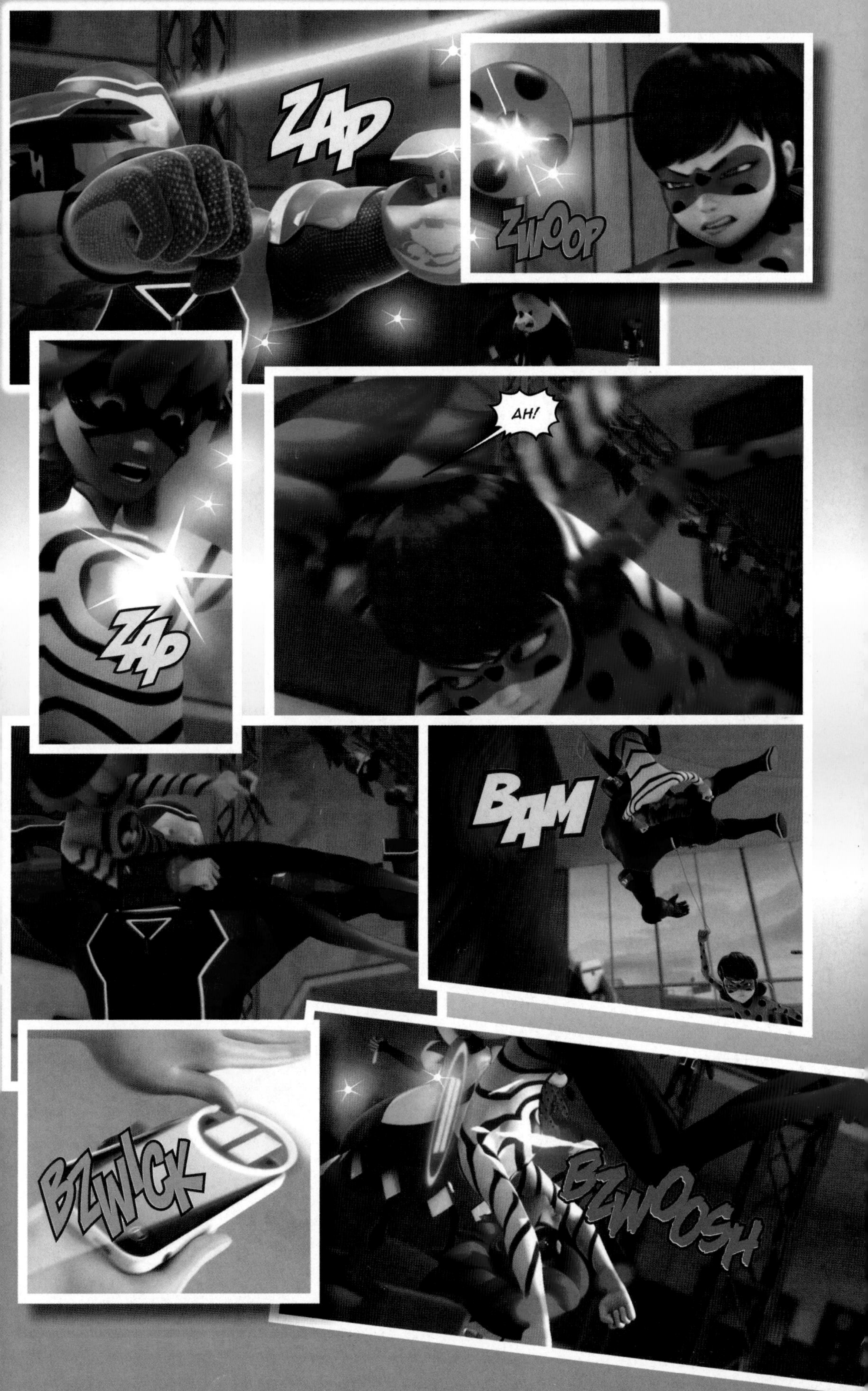
ZAP
ZWOOP
ZAP
AH!
BAM
BZWICK
BZWOOSH

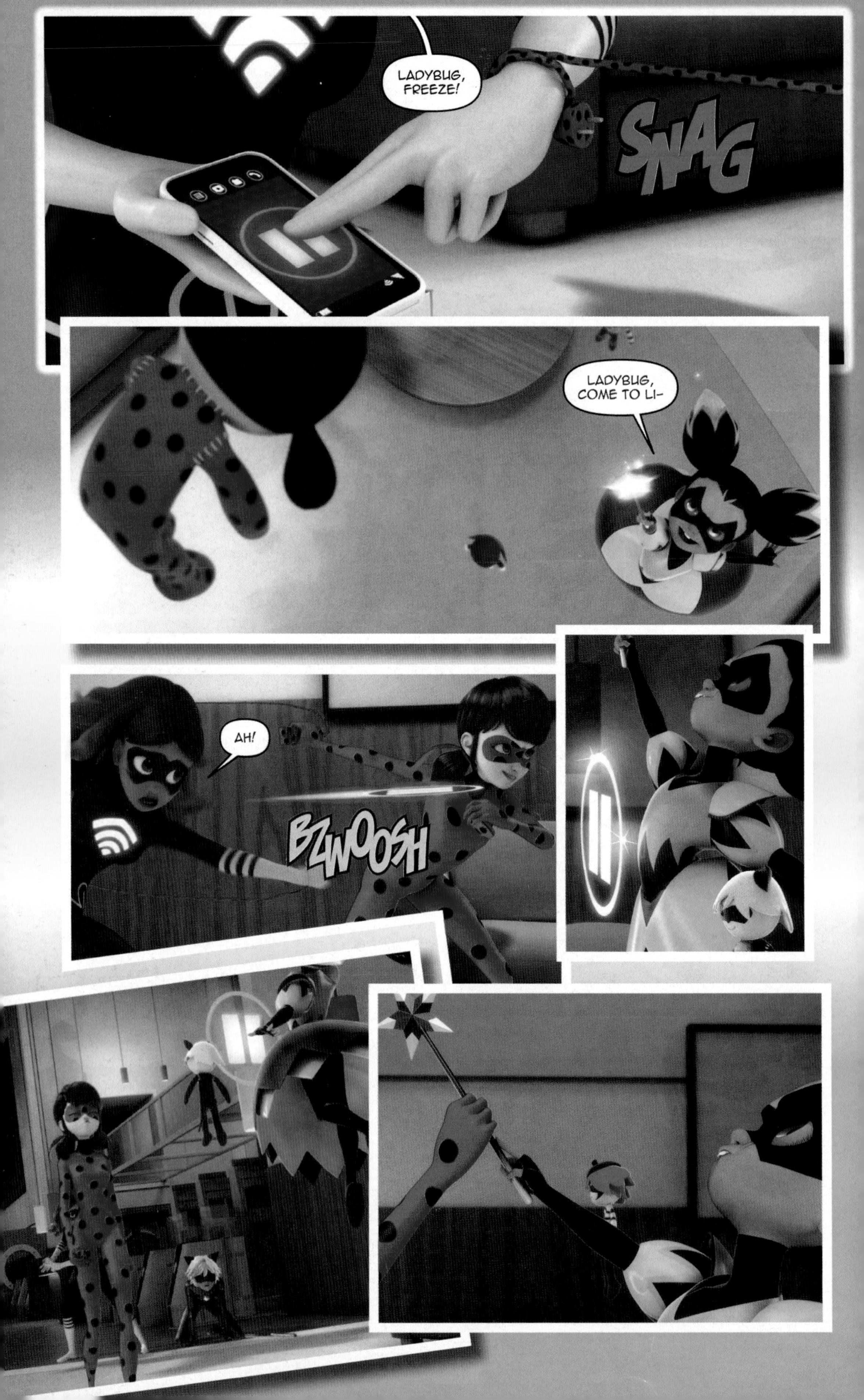
LADYBUG, FREEZE!
SNAG
LADYBUG, COME TO LI-
AH!
BZWOOSH

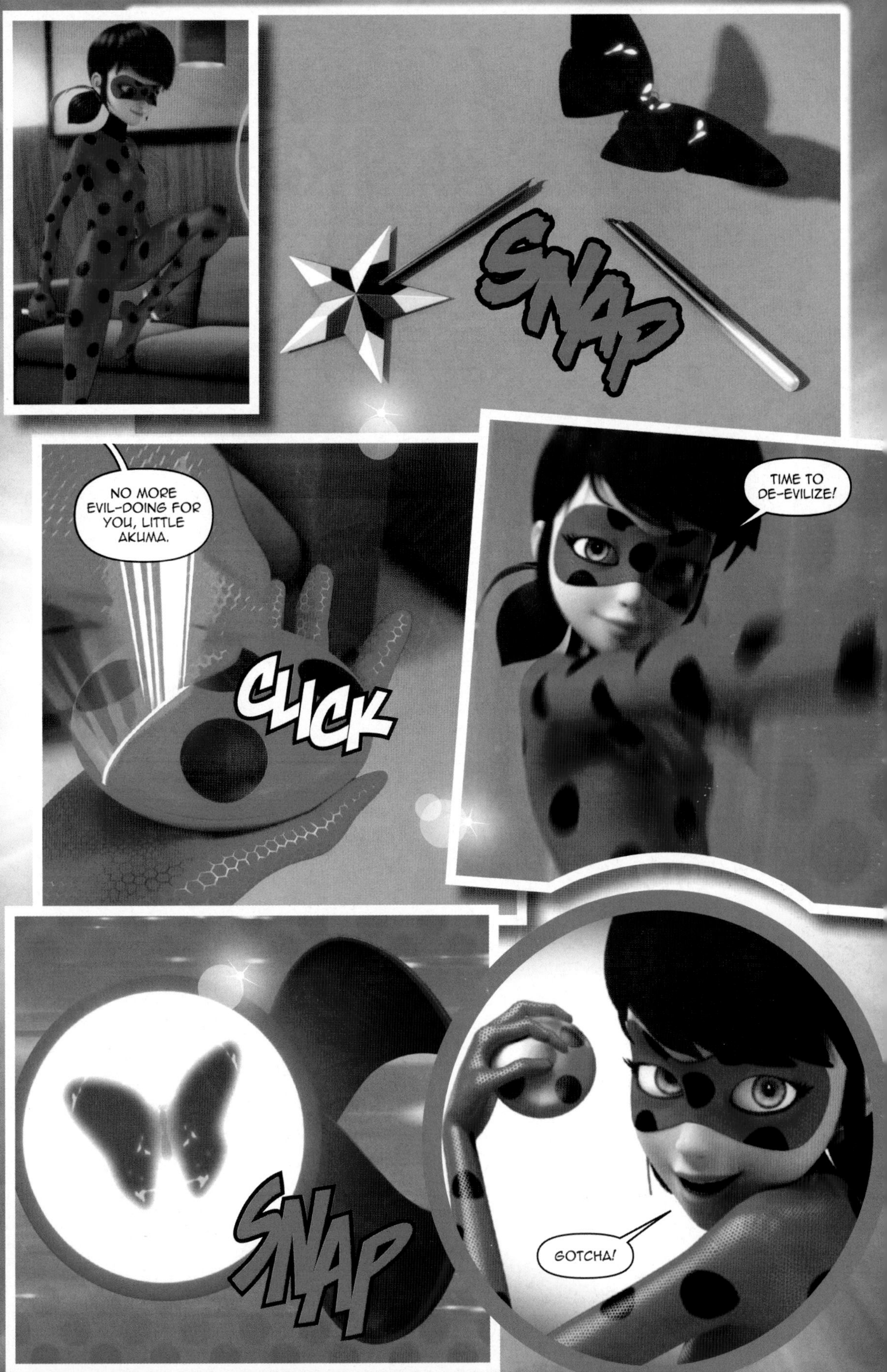
SNAP
NO MORE EVIL-DOING FOR YOU, LITTLE AKUMA.
CLICK
TIME TO DE-EVILIZE!
SNAP
GOTCHA!

BYE BYE, LITTLE BUTTERFLY!

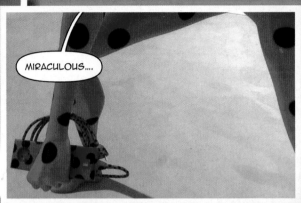

MIRACULOUS....

...LADYBUG!

FWWSH

FWOOSH

HUH?

GURGLE GURGLE

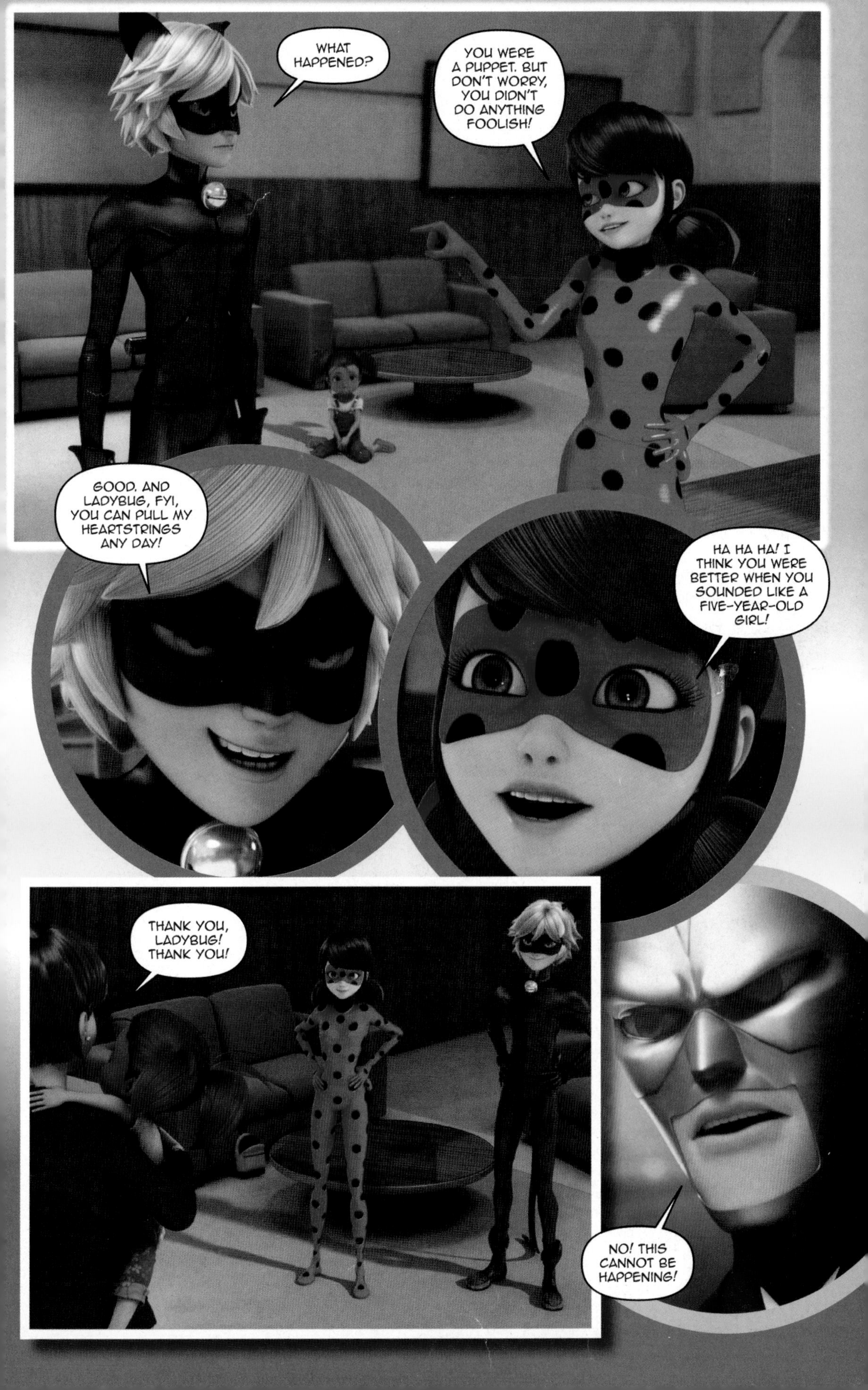
WHAT HAPPENED?
YOU WERE A PUPPET. BUT DON'T WORRY, YOU DIDN'T DO ANYTHING FOOLISH!
GOOD. AND LADYBUG, FYI, YOU CAN PULL MY HEARTSTRINGS ANY DAY!
HA HA HA! I THINK YOU WERE BETTER WHEN YOU SOUNDED LIKE A FIVE-YEAR-OLD GIRL!
THANK YOU, LADYBUG! THANK YOU!
NO! THIS CANNOT BE HAPPENING!

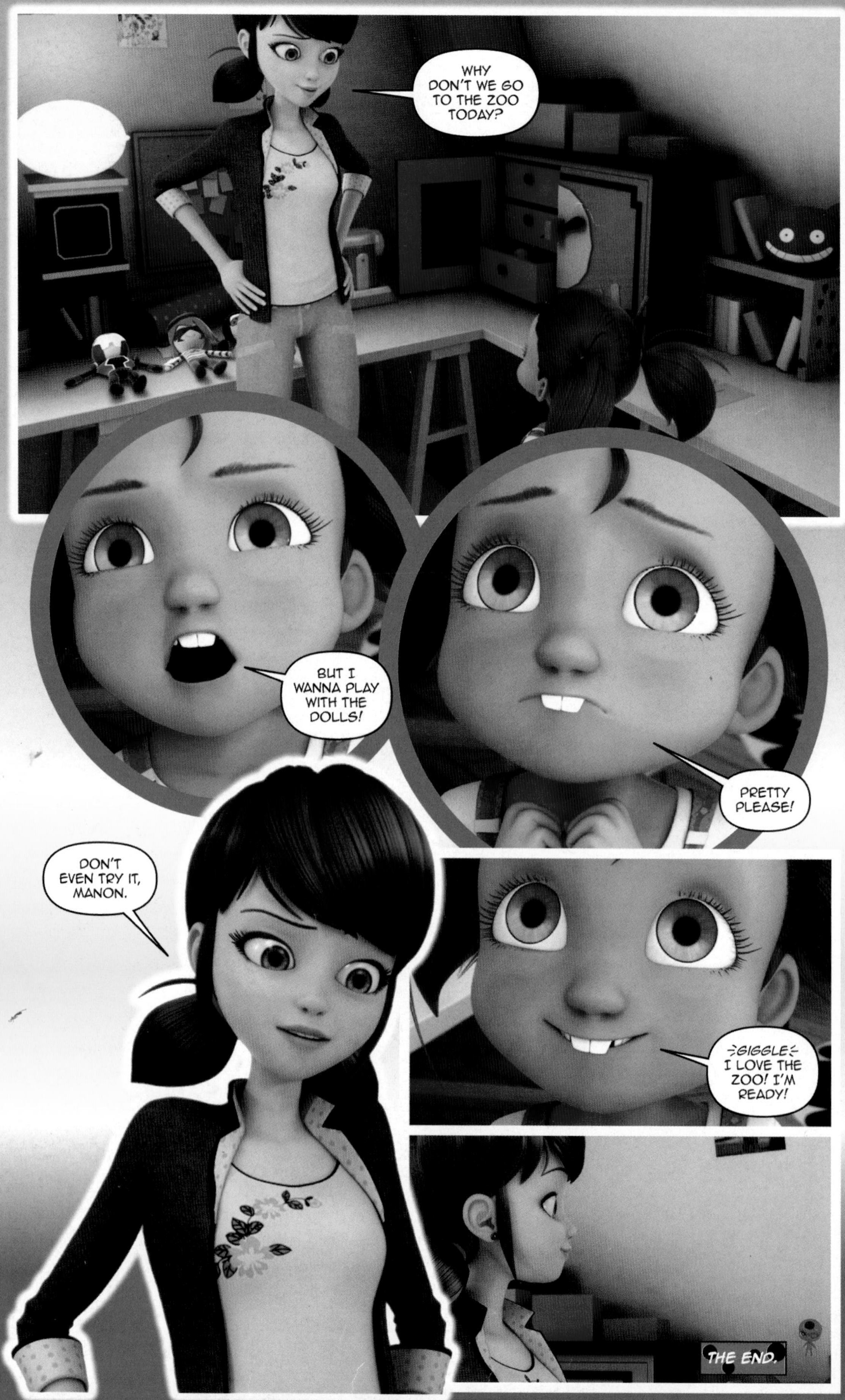
WHY DON'T WE GO TO THE ZOO TODAY?
BUT I WANNA PLAY WITH THE DOLLS!
PRETTY PLEASE!
DON'T EVEN TRY IT, MANON.
⇒GIGGLE⇐ I LOVE THE ZOO! I'M READY!
THE END.

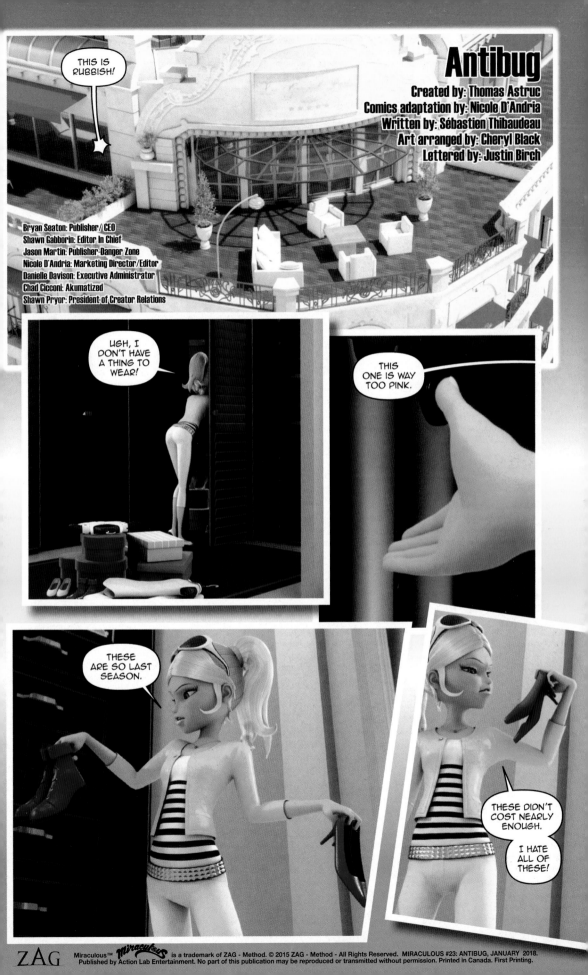

THIS IS RUBBISH!

Antibug

Created by: Thomas Astruc
Comics adaptation by: Nicole D'Andria
Written by: Sébastien Thibaudeau
Art arranged by: Cheryl Black
Lettered by: Justin Birch

Bryan Seaton: Publisher/CEO
Shawn Gabborin: Editor In Chief
Jason Martin: Publisher-Danger Zone
Nicole D'Andria: Marketing Director/Editor
Danielle Davison: Executive Administrator
Chad Cicconi: Akumatized
Shawn Pryor: President of Creator Relations

UGH, I DON'T HAVE A THING TO WEAR!

THIS ONE IS WAY TOO PINK.

THESE ARE SO LAST SEASON.

THESE DIDN'T COST NEARLY ENOUGH.

I HATE ALL OF THESE!

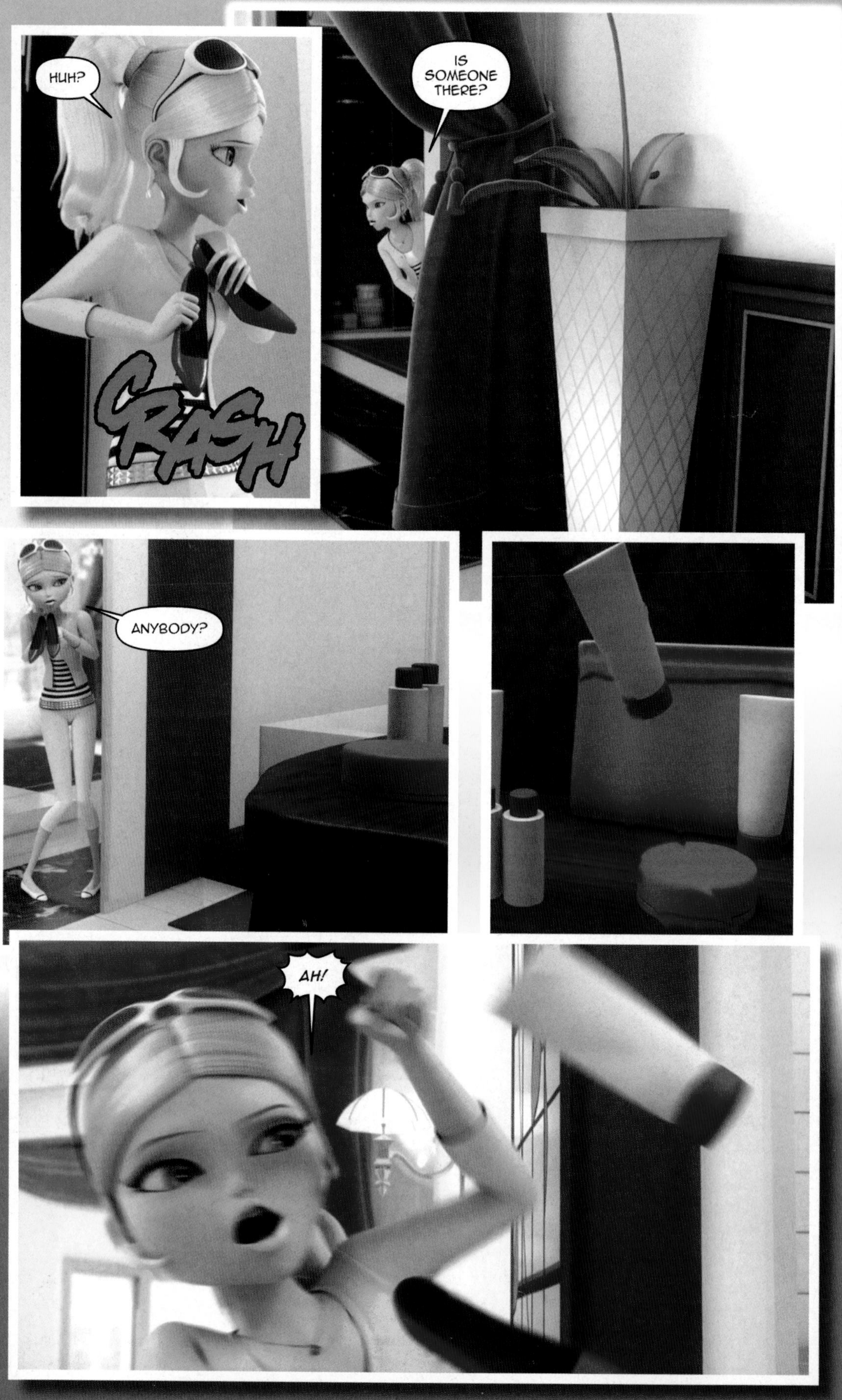
HUH?
IS SOMEONE THERE?
CRASH
ANYBODY?
AH!

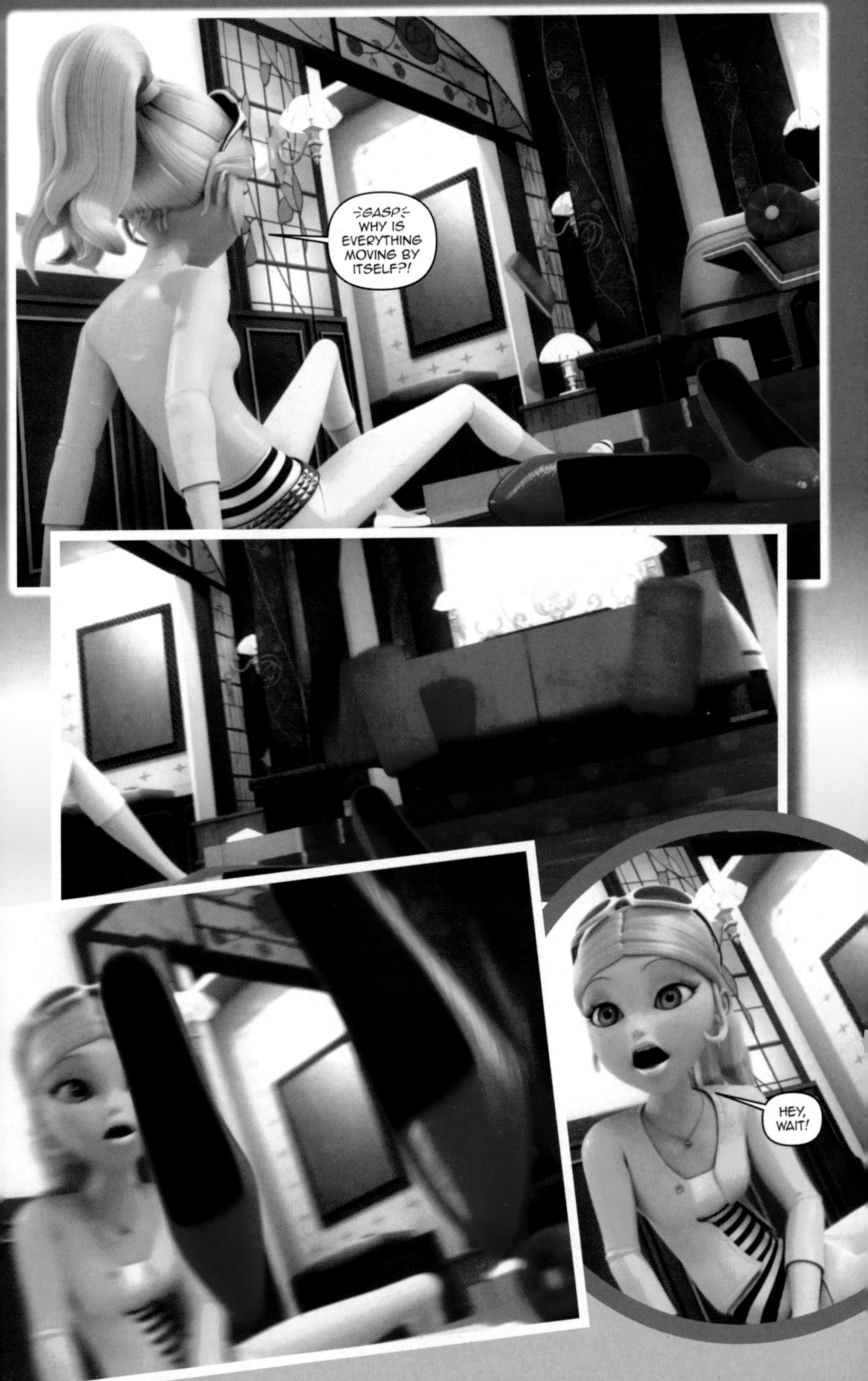

-GASP- WHY IS EVERYTHING MOVING BY ITSELF?!
HEY, WAIT!

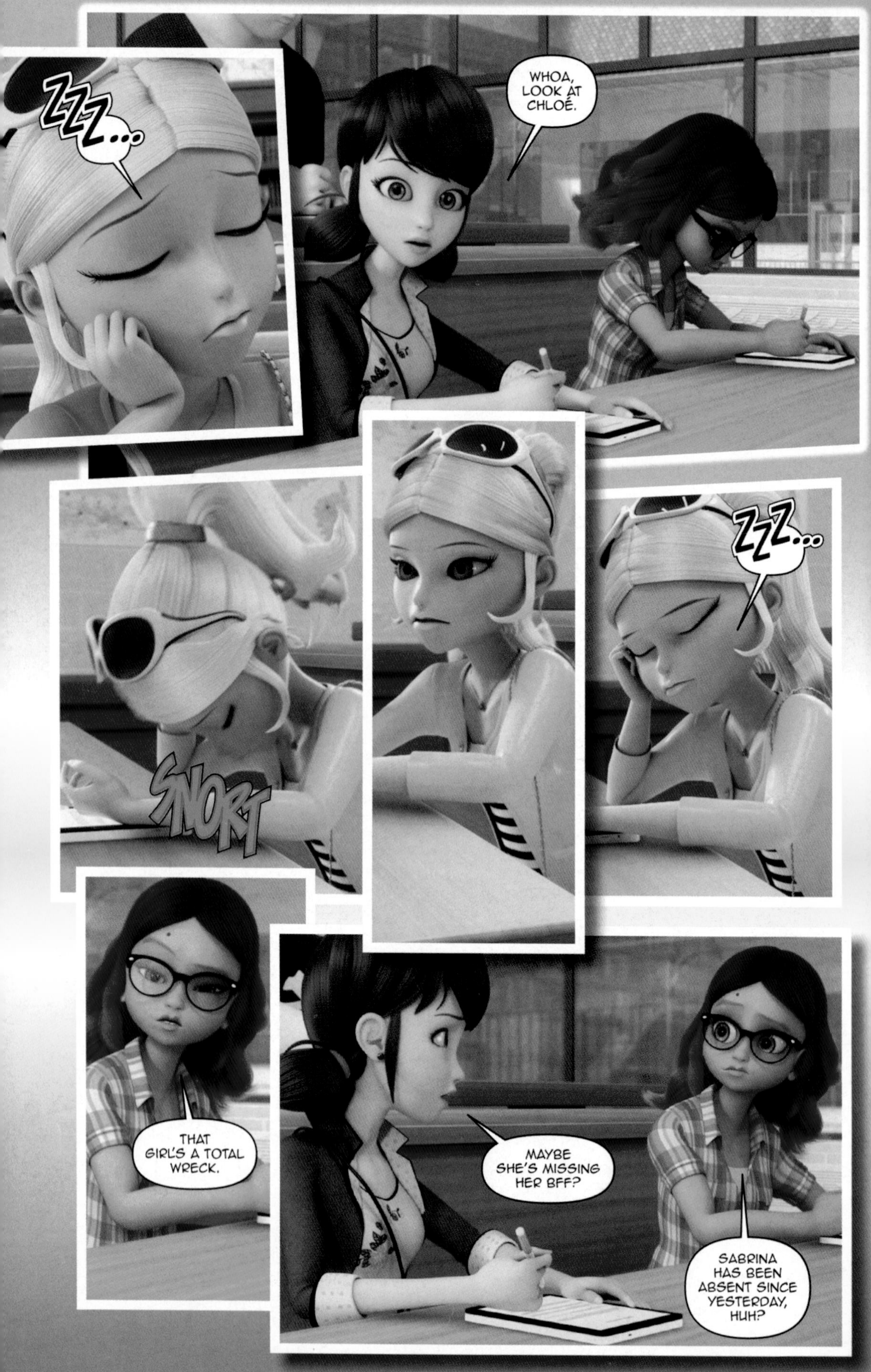
ZZZ...
WHOA, LOOK AT CHLOÉ.
SNORT
ZZZ...
THAT GIRL'S A TOTAL WRECK.
MAYBE SHE'S MISSING HER BFF?
SABRINA HAS BEEN ABSENT SINCE YESTERDAY, HUH?

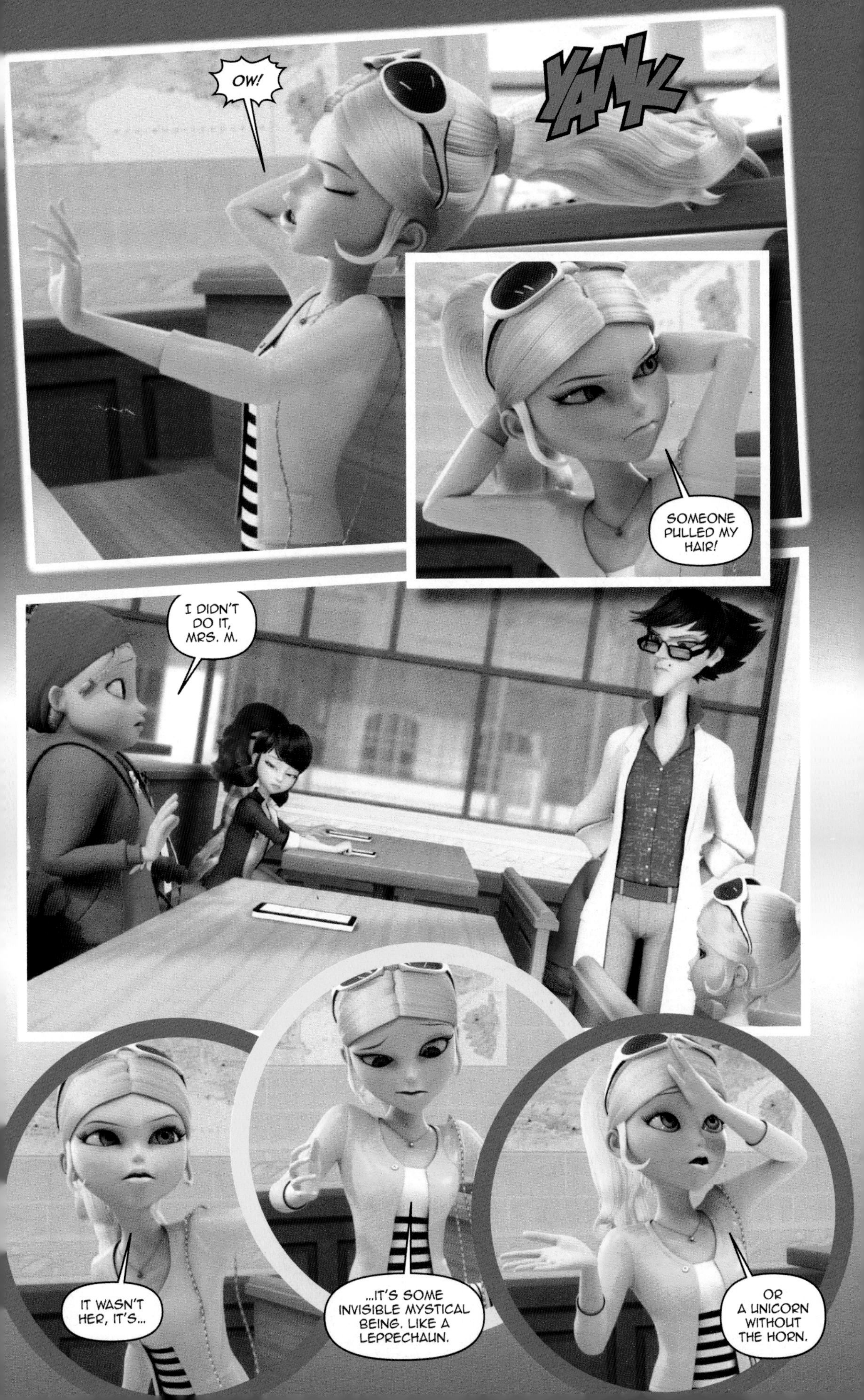
OW!
YANK
SOMEONE PULLED MY HAIR!
I DIDN'T DO IT, MRS. M.
IT WASN'T HER, IT'S...
...IT'S SOME INVISIBLE MYSTICAL BEING. LIKE A LEPRECHAUN.
OR A UNICORN WITHOUT THE HORN.

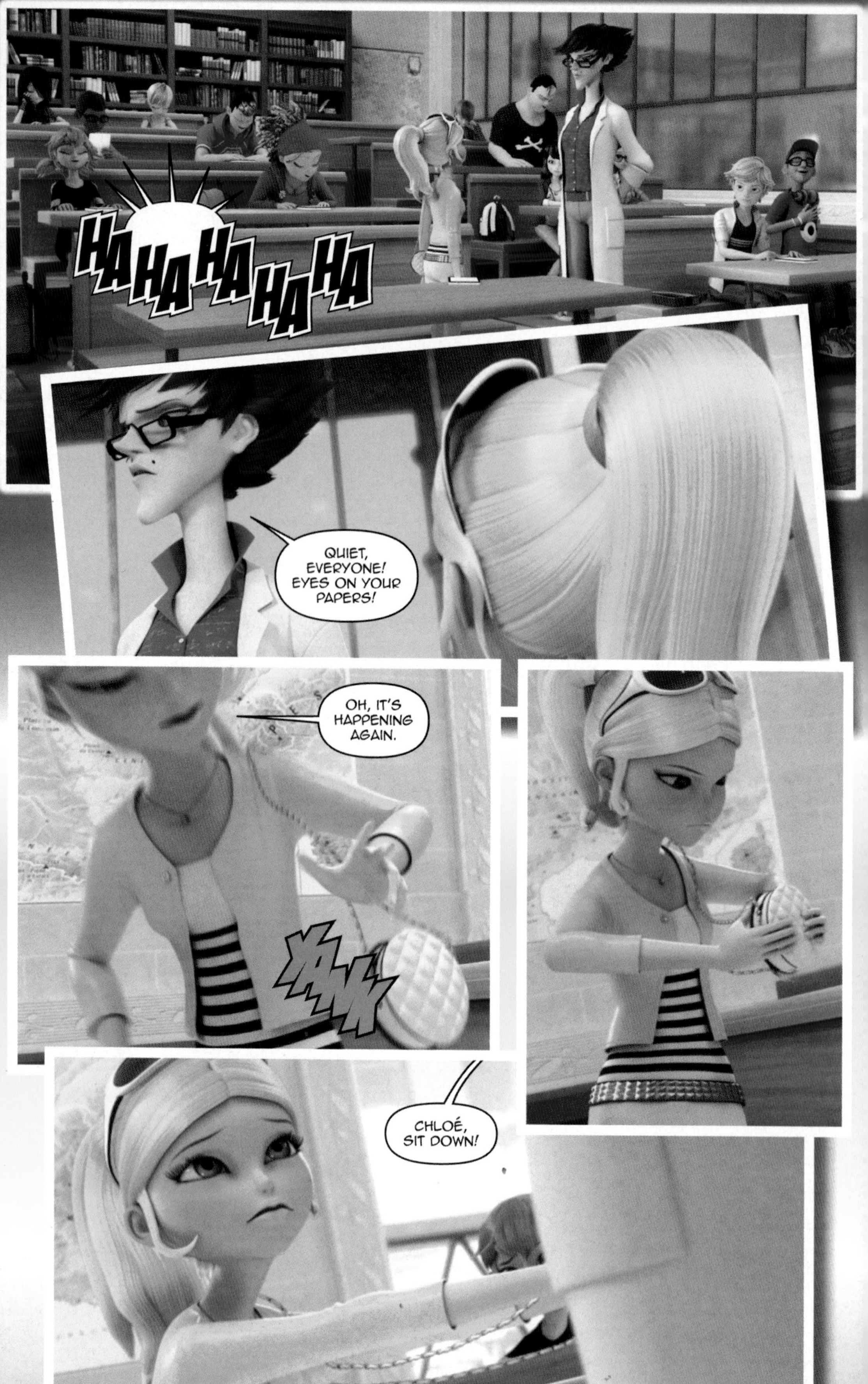
HAHAHAHAHAHA
QUIET, EVERYONE! EYES ON YOUR PAPERS!
OH, IT'S HAPPENING AGAIN.
YANK
CHLOÉ, SIT DOWN!

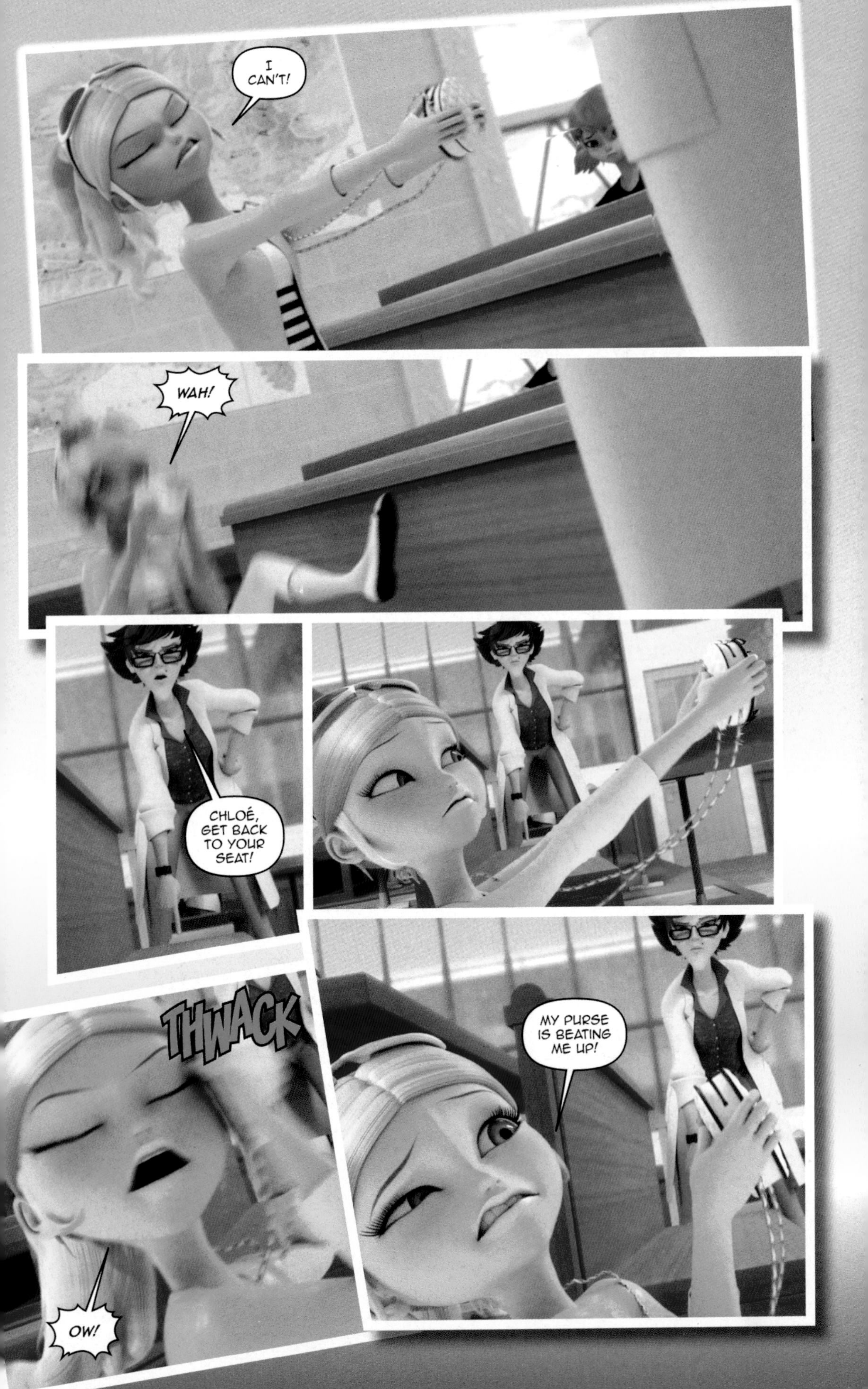
I CAN'T!
WAH!
CHLOÉ, GET BACK TO YOUR SEAT!
THWACK
OW!
MY PURSE IS BEATING ME UP!

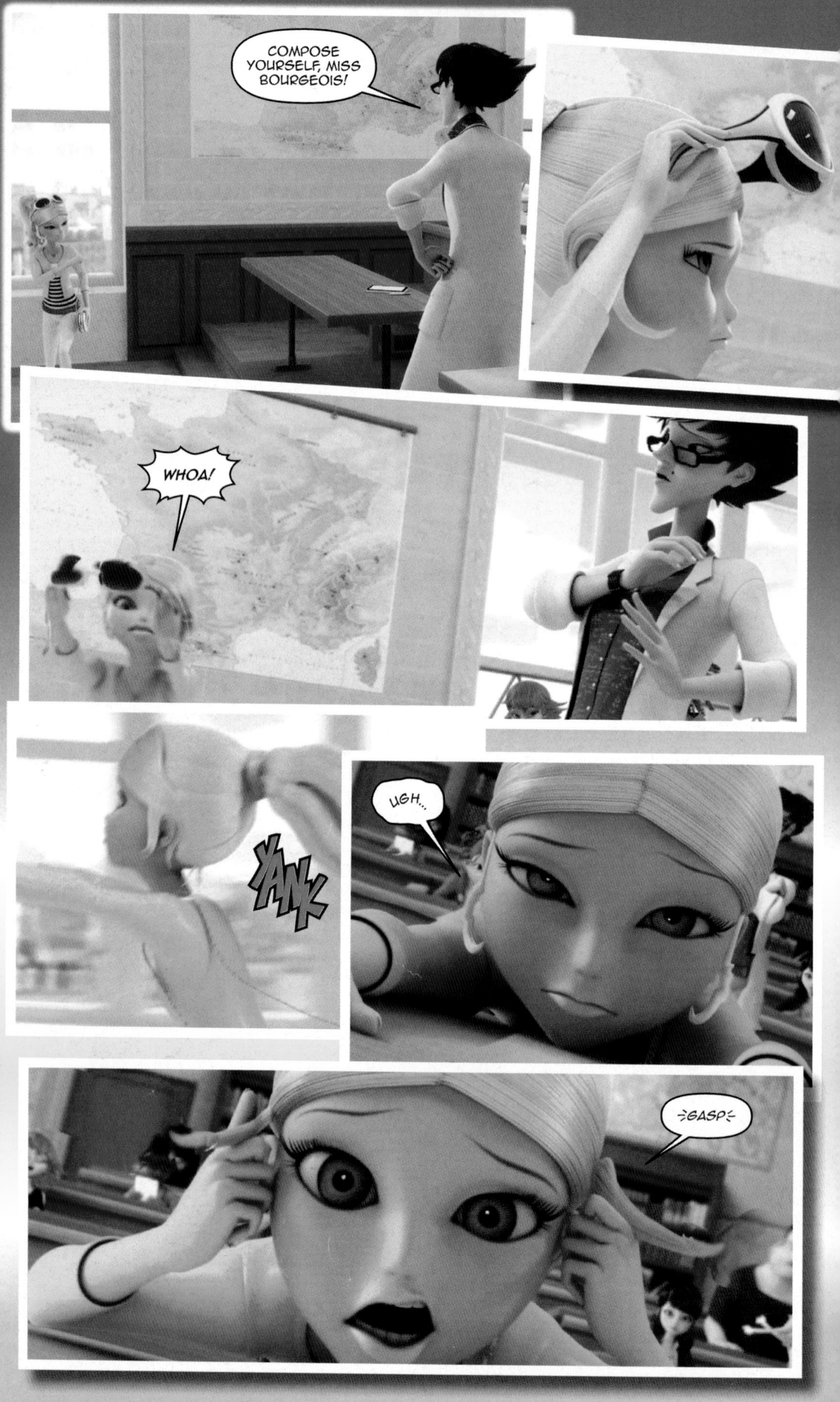
COMPOSE YOURSELF, MISS BOURGEOIS!
WHOA!
YANK
UGH...
GASP

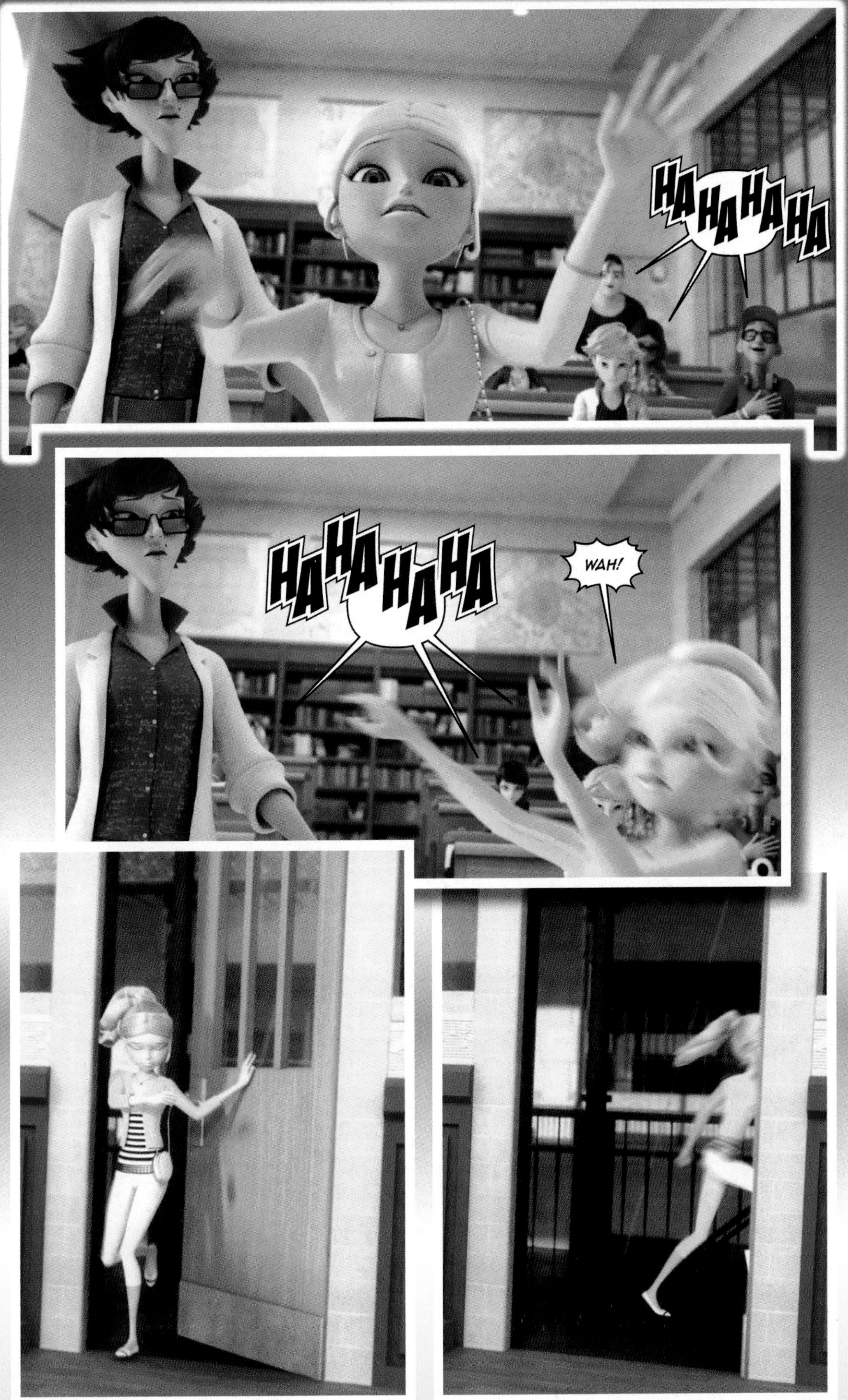
HAHAHAHAHA
HAHAHAHAHA
WAH!

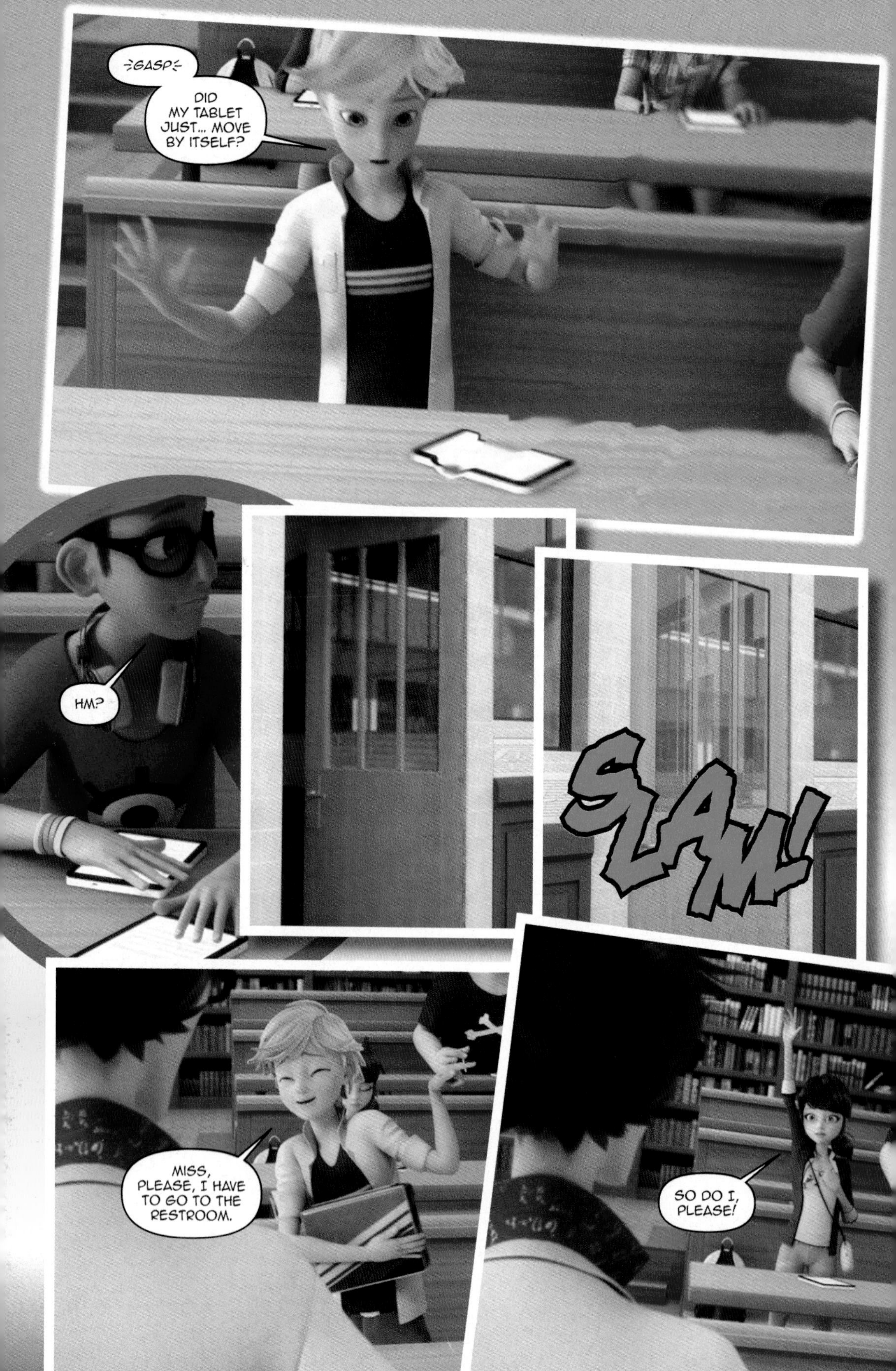

-GASP-
DID MY TABLET JUST... MOVE BY ITSELF?
HM?
SLAM!
MISS, PLEASE, I HAVE TO GO TO THE RESTROOM.
SO DO I, PLEASE!

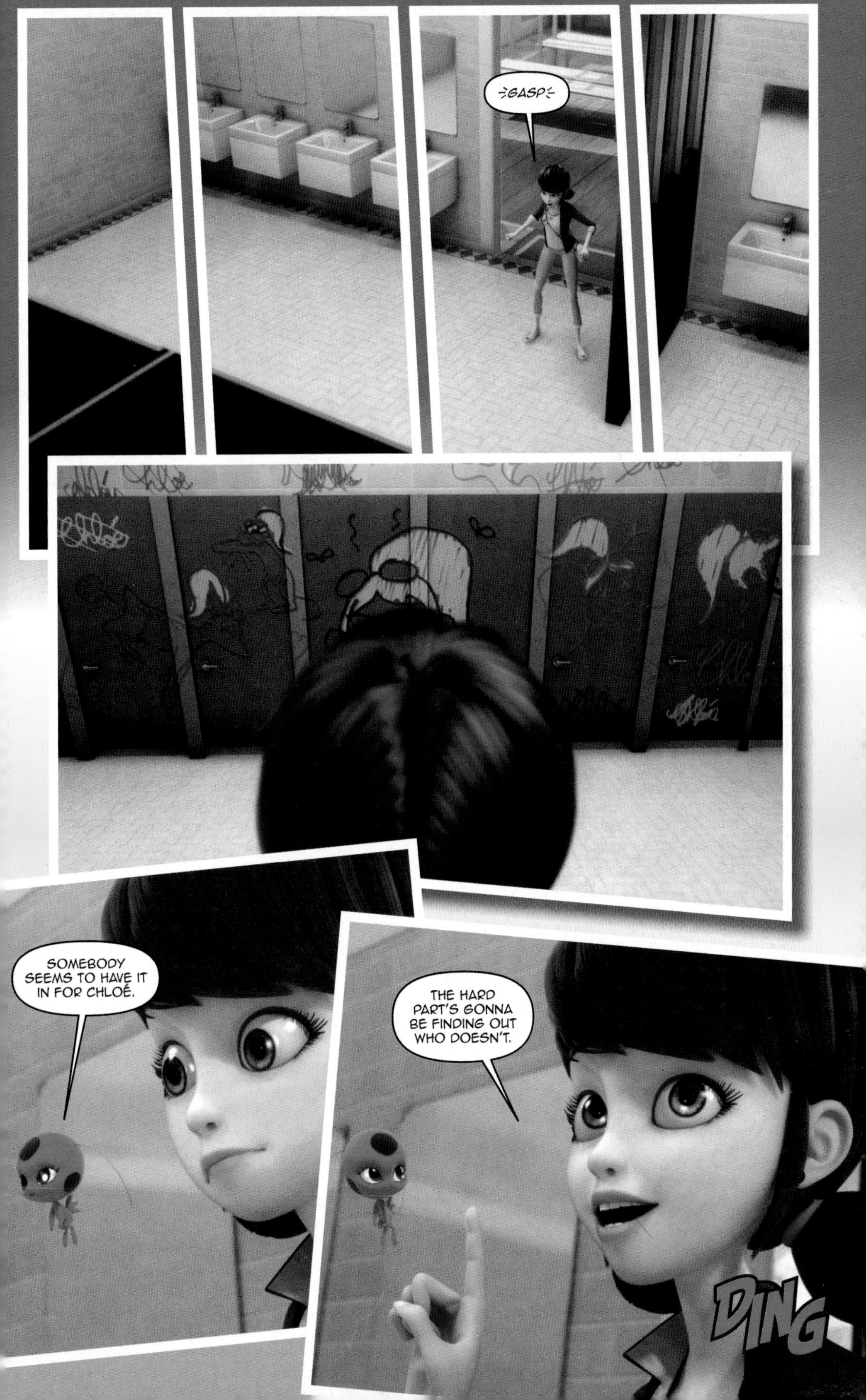

GASP
SOMEBODY SEEMS TO HAVE IT IN FOR CHLOÉ.
THE HARD PART'S GONNA BE FINDING OUT WHO DOESN'T.
DING

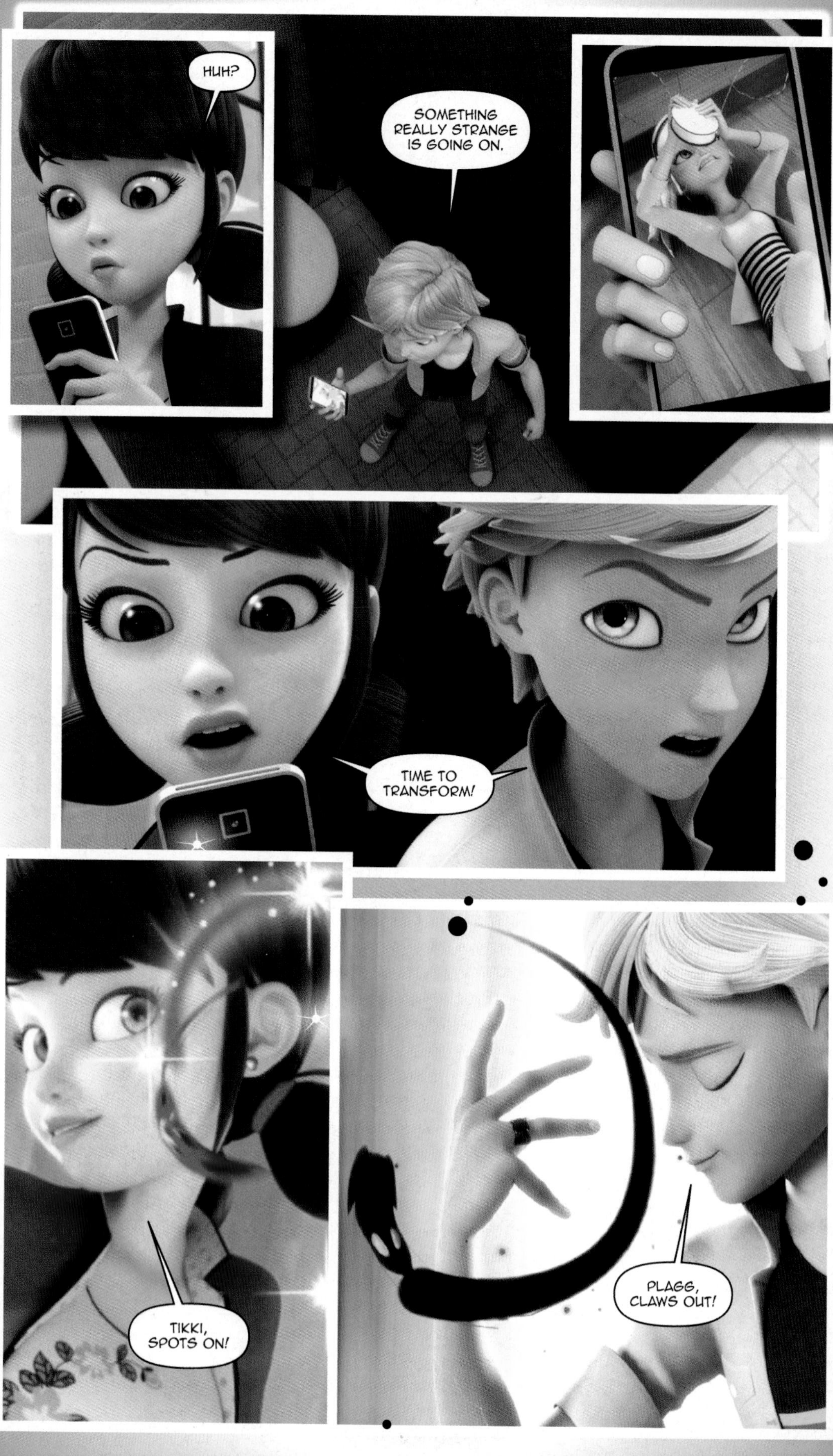
HUH?
SOMETHING REALLY STRANGE IS GOING ON.
TIME TO TRANSFORM!
TIKKI, SPOTS ON!
PLAGG, CLAWS OUT!

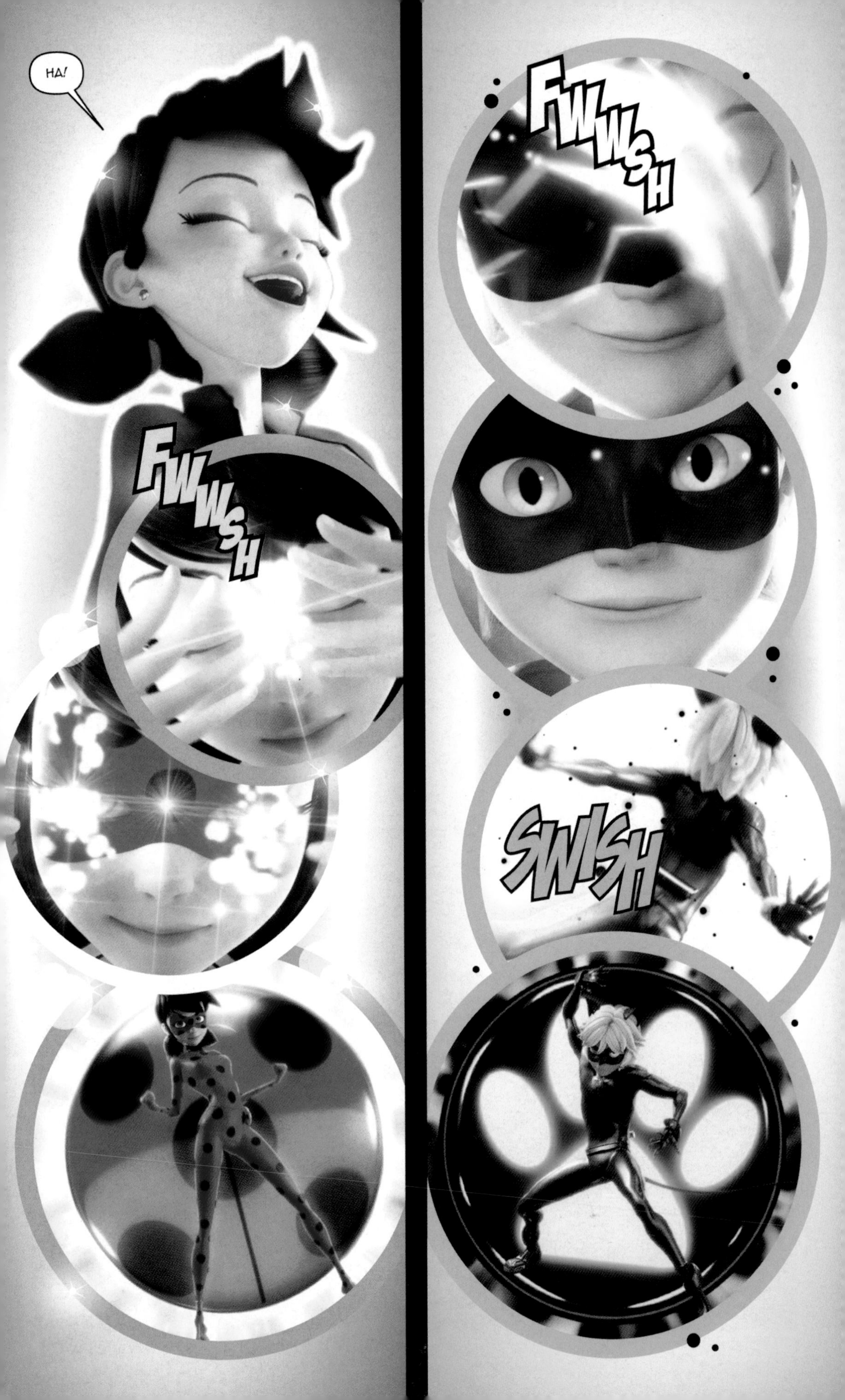
HA!
FWWSH
FWWSH
SWISH

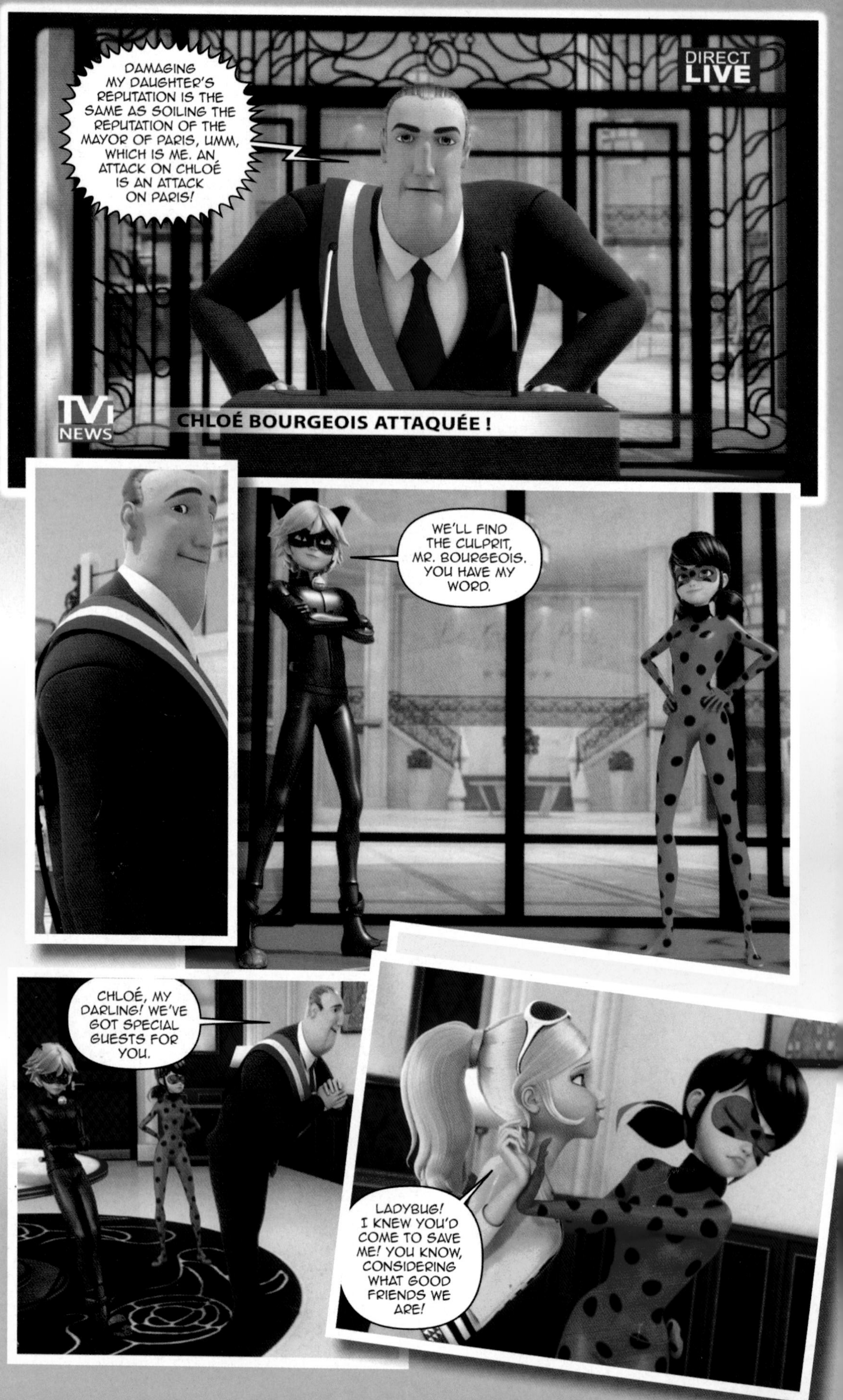
DAMAGING MY DAUGHTER'S REPUTATION IS THE SAME AS SOILING THE REPUTATION OF THE MAYOR OF PARIS, UMM, WHICH IS ME. AN ATTACK ON CHLOÉ IS AN ATTACK ON PARIS!
DIRECT LIVE
TVi NEWS
CHLOÉ BOURGEOIS ATTAQUÉE !
WE'LL FIND THE CULPRIT, MR. BOURGEOIS. YOU HAVE MY WORD.
CHLOÉ, MY DARLING! WE'VE GOT SPECIAL GUESTS FOR YOU.
LADYBUG! I KNEW YOU'D COME TO SAVE ME! YOU KNOW, CONSIDERING WHAT GOOD FRIENDS WE ARE!

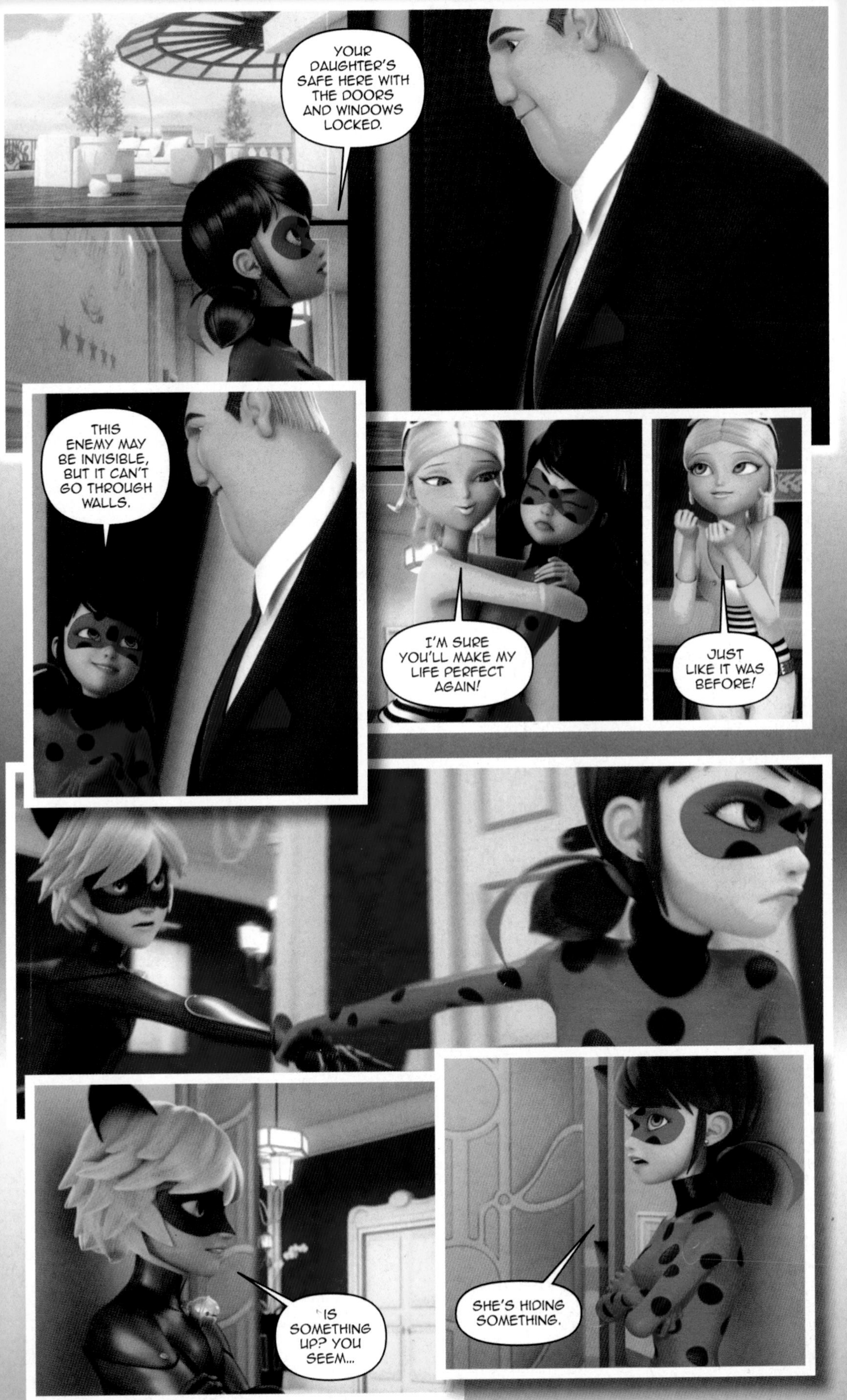
YOUR DAUGHTER'S SAFE HERE WITH THE DOORS AND WINDOWS LOCKED.
THIS ENEMY MAY BE INVISIBLE, BUT IT CAN'T GO THROUGH WALLS.
I'M SURE YOU'LL MAKE MY LIFE PERFECT AGAIN!
JUST LIKE IT WAS BEFORE!
IS SOMETHING UP? YOU SEEM...
SHE'S HIDING SOMETHING.

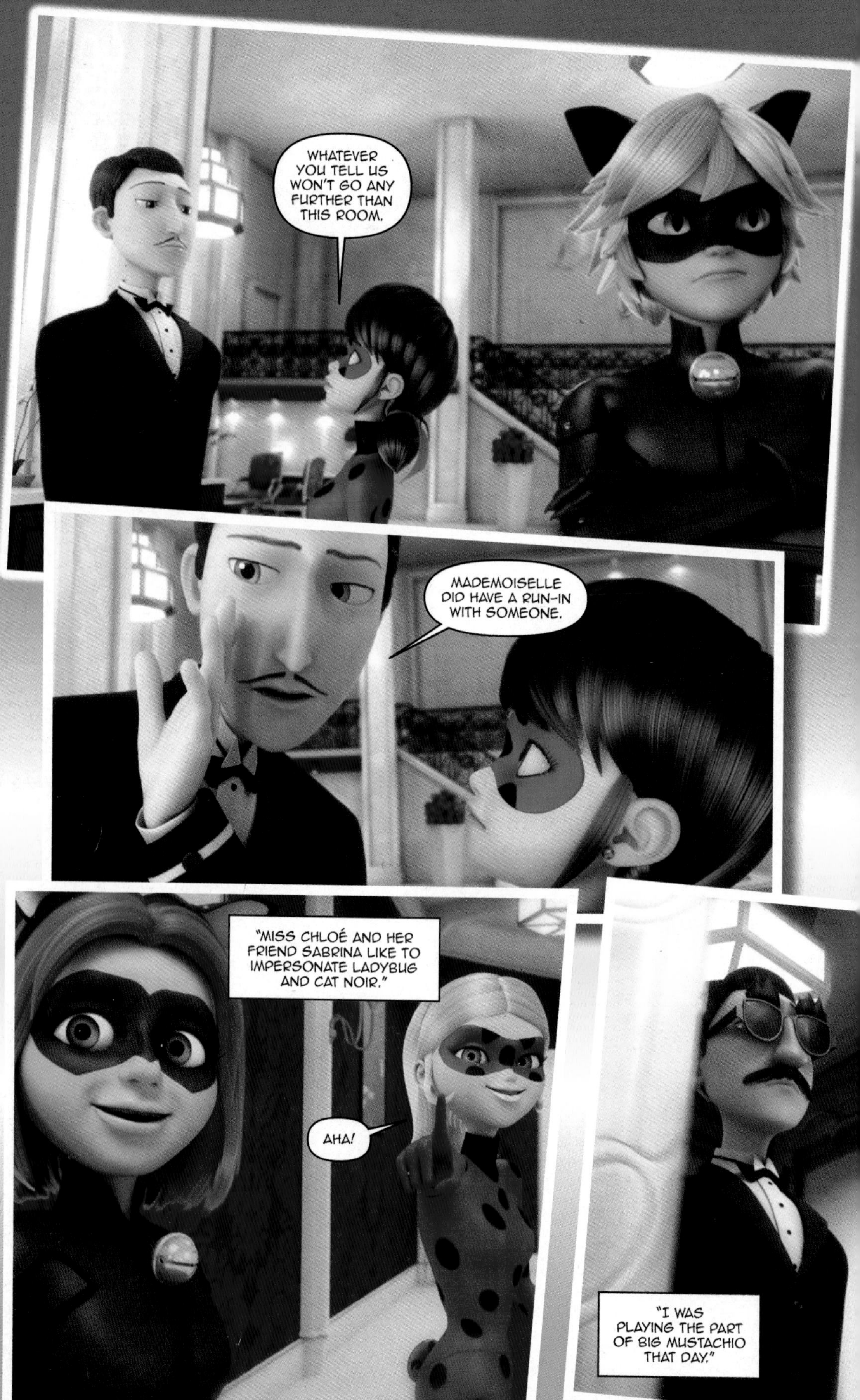
WHATEVER YOU TELL US WON'T GO ANY FURTHER THAN THIS ROOM.
MADEMOISELLE DID HAVE A RUN-IN WITH SOMEONE.
"MISS CHLOÉ AND HER FRIEND SABRINA LIKE TO IMPERSONATE LADYBUG AND CAT NOIR."
AHA!
"I WAS PLAYING THE PART OF BIG MUSTACHIO THAT DAY."

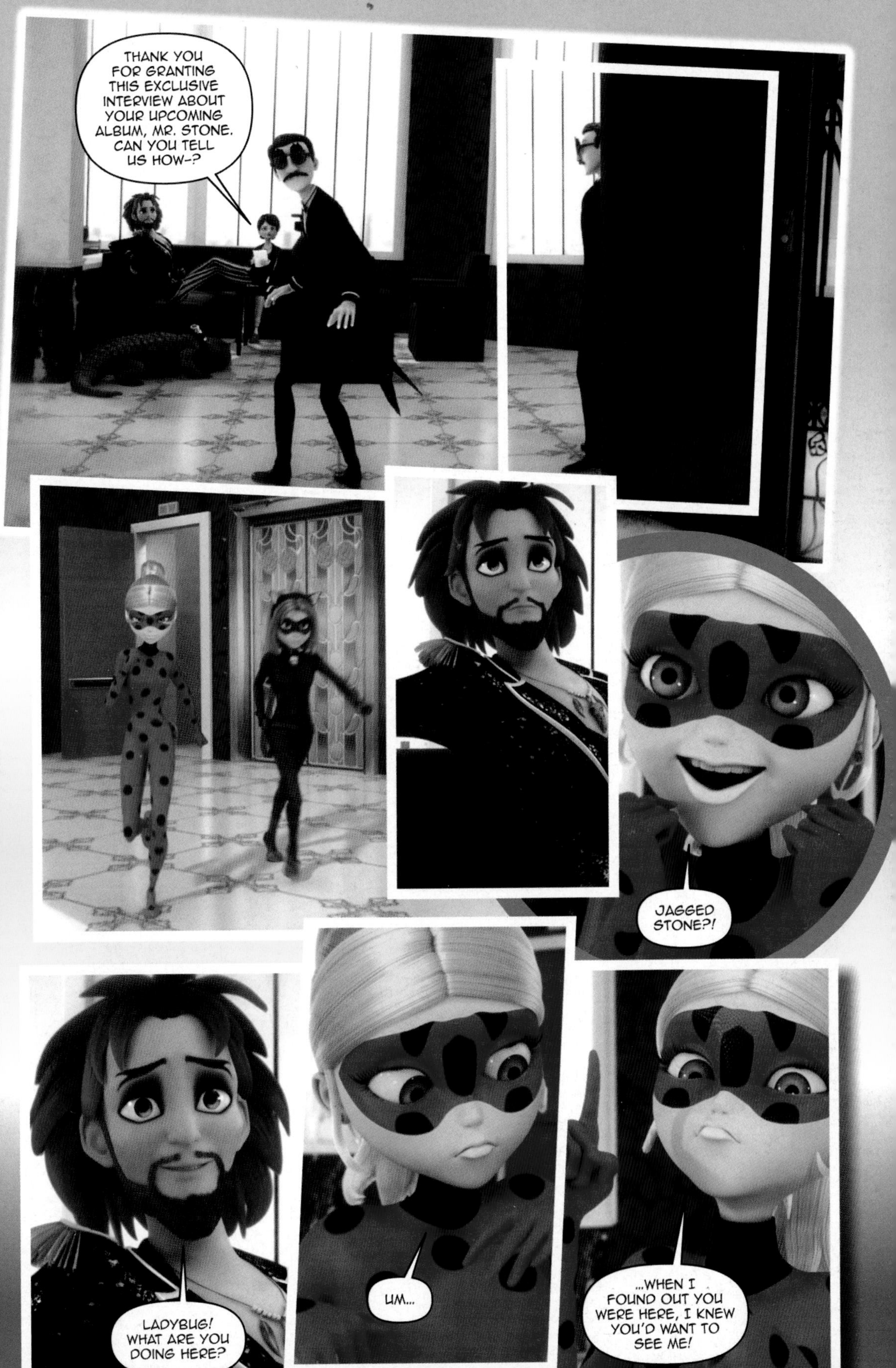
THANK YOU FOR GRANTING THIS EXCLUSIVE INTERVIEW ABOUT YOUR UPCOMING ALBUM, MR. STONE. CAN YOU TELL US HOW-?
JAGGED STONE?!
LADYBUG! WHAT ARE YOU DOING HERE?
UM...
...WHEN I FOUND OUT YOU WERE HERE, I KNEW YOU'D WANT TO SEE ME!

I HAD TO COME SAY HELLO.
WELL, YOU DID THE RIGHT THING.
HEY, WHAT'S THE DEALIO WITH YOUR HAIR?
UH...
OH. I...

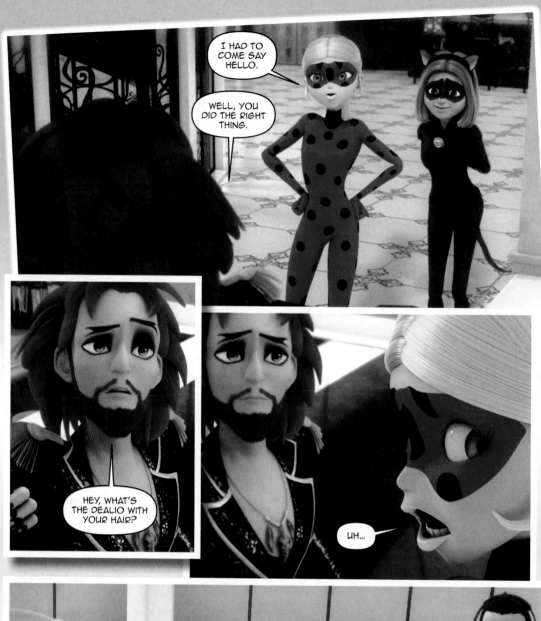

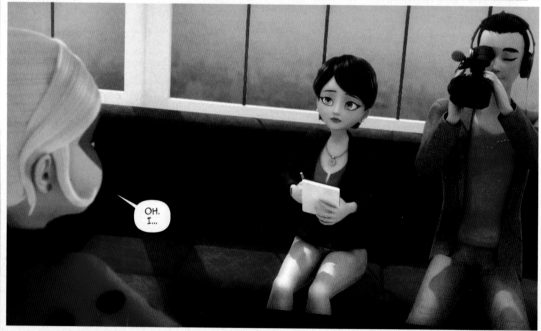

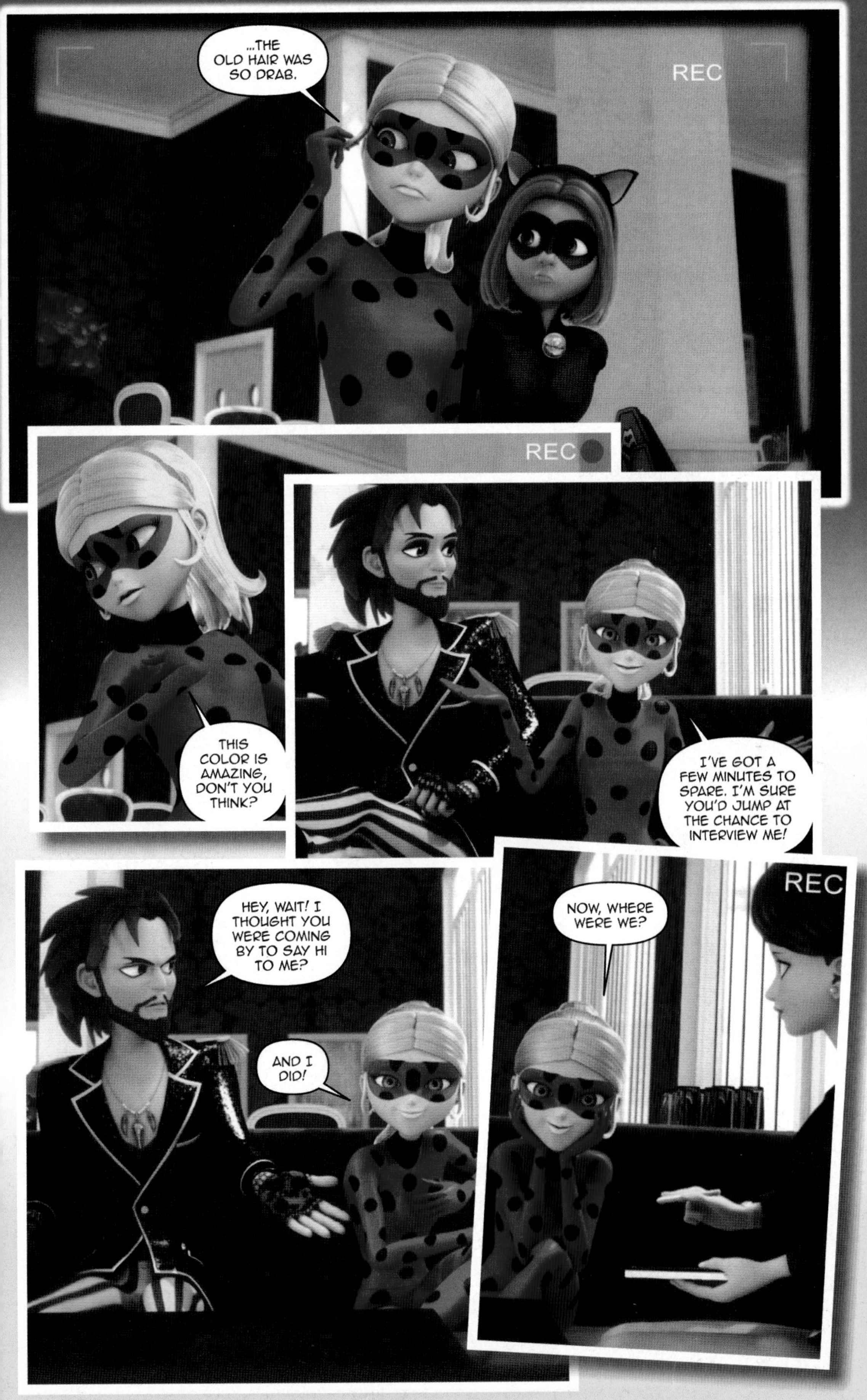
REC
...THE OLD HAIR WAS SO DRAB.
REC
THIS COLOR IS AMAZING, DON'T YOU THINK?
I'VE GOT A FEW MINUTES TO SPARE. I'M SURE YOU'D JUMP AT THE CHANCE TO INTERVIEW ME!
HEY, WAIT! I THOUGHT YOU WERE COMING BY TO SAY HI TO ME?
AND I DID!
REC
NOW, WHERE WERE WE?

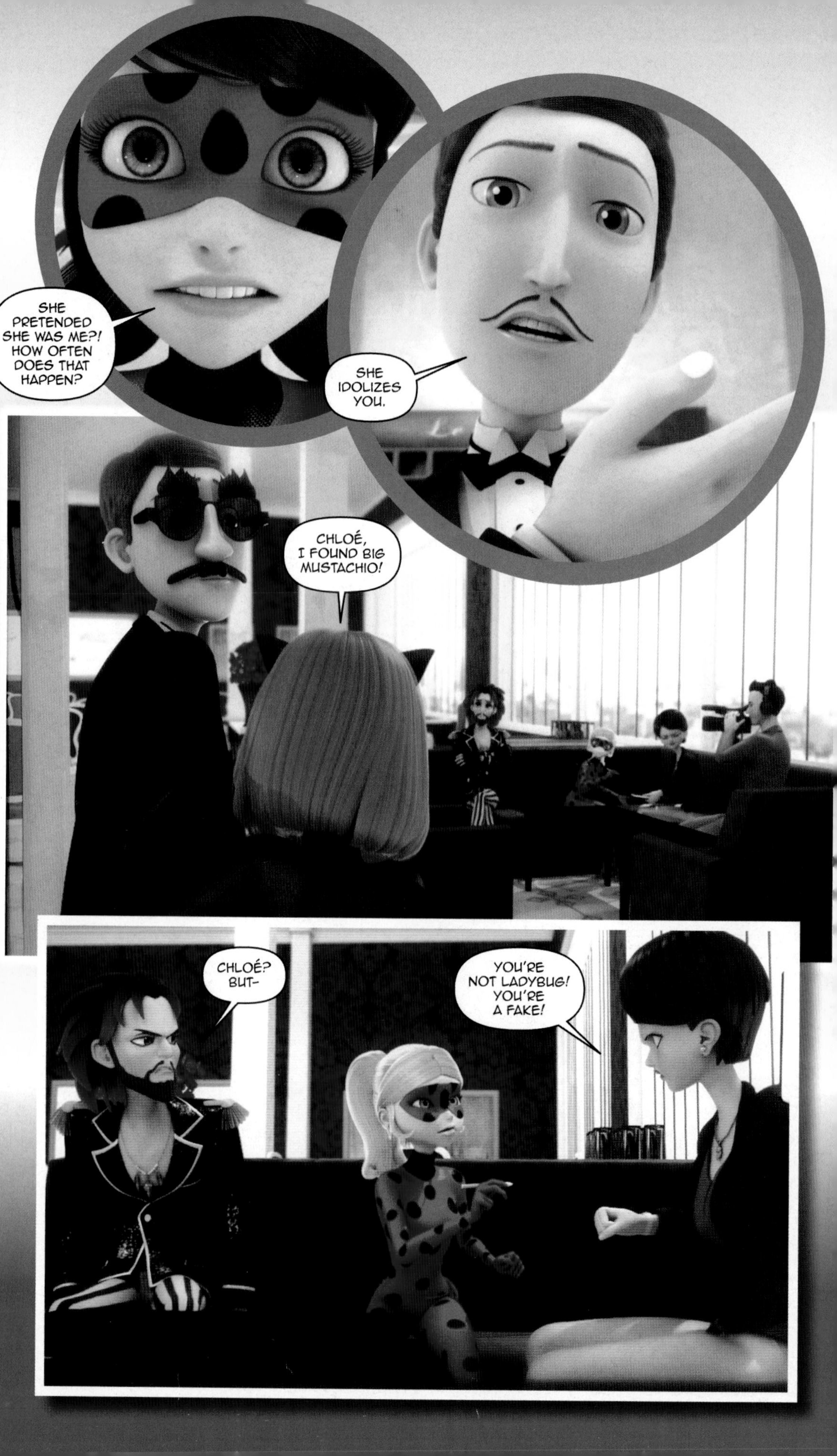

SHE PRETENDED SHE WAS ME?! HOW OFTEN DOES THAT HAPPEN?
SHE IDOLIZES YOU.
CHLOÉ, I FOUND BIG MUSTACHIO!
CHLOÉ? BUT-
YOU'RE NOT LADYBUG! YOU'RE A FAKE!

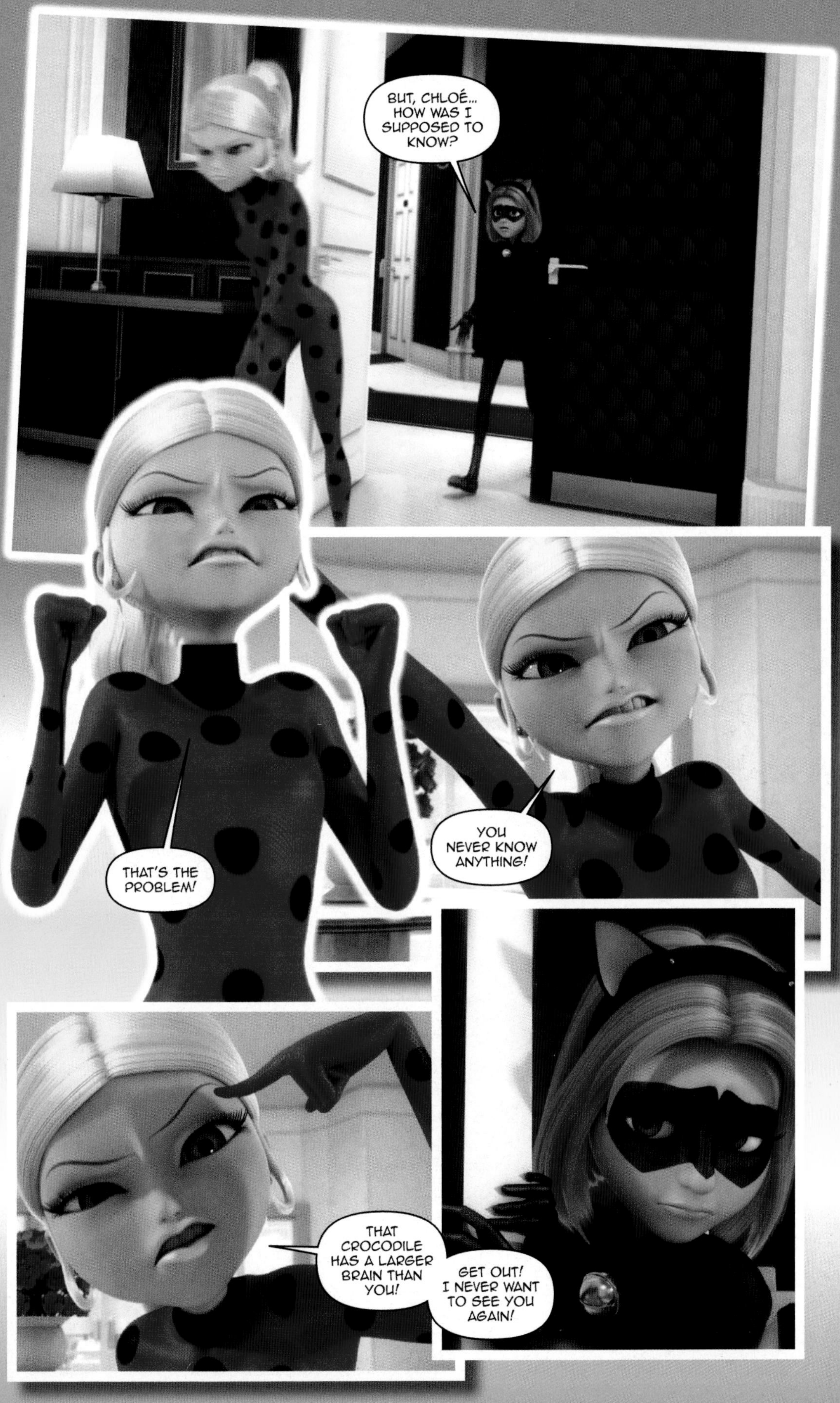
BUT, CHLOÉ... HOW WAS I SUPPOSED TO KNOW?
THAT'S THE PROBLEM!
YOU NEVER KNOW ANYTHING!
THAT CROCODILE HAS A LARGER BRAIN THAN YOU!
GET OUT! I NEVER WANT TO SEE YOU AGAIN!

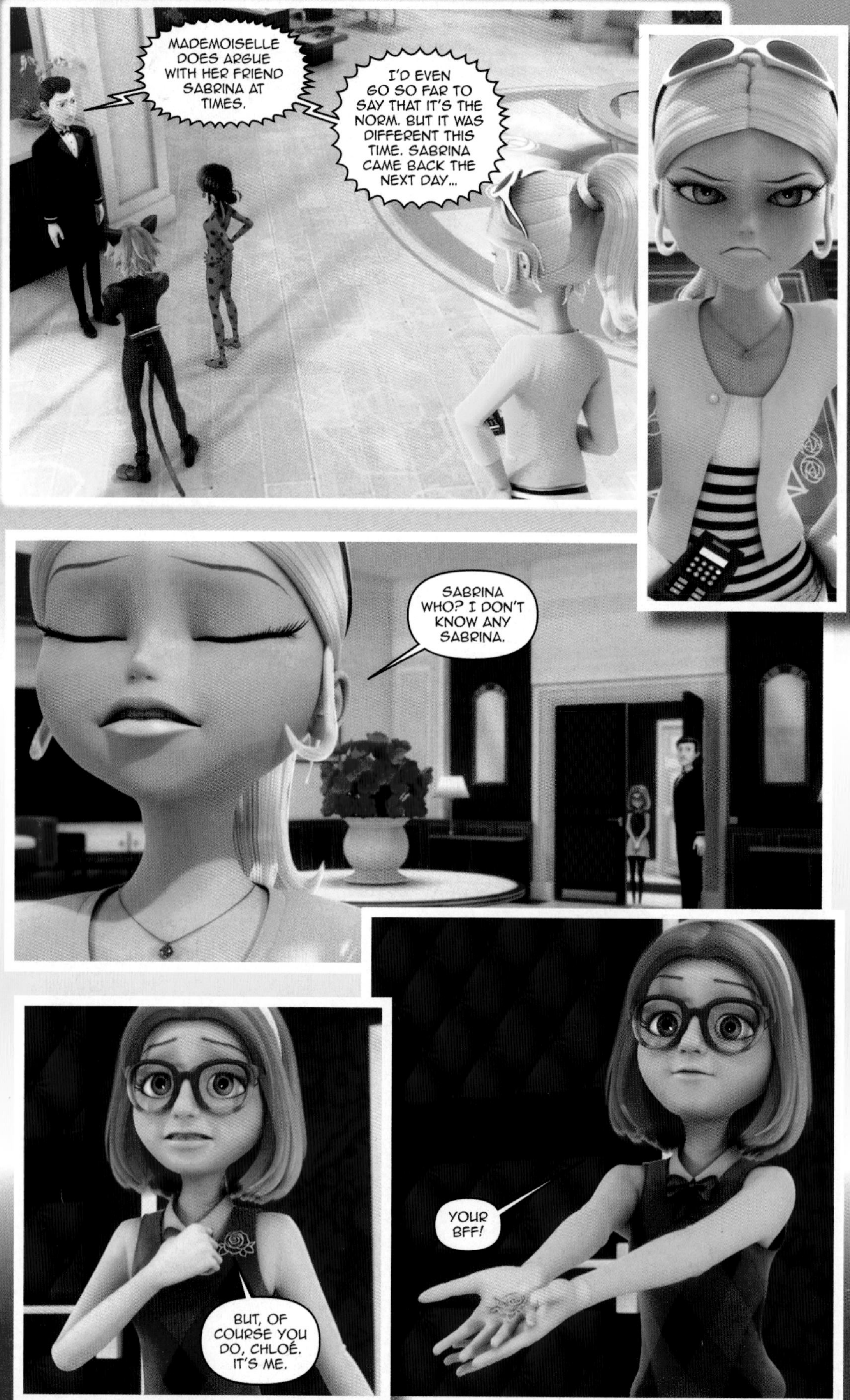
MADEMOISELLE DOES ARGUE WITH HER FRIEND SABRINA AT TIMES.
I'D EVEN GO SO FAR TO SAY THAT IT'S THE NORM. BUT IT WAS DIFFERENT THIS TIME. SABRINA CAME BACK THE NEXT DAY...
SABRINA WHO? I DON'T KNOW ANY SABRINA.
BUT, OF COURSE YOU DO, CHLOÉ. IT'S ME.
YOUR BFF!

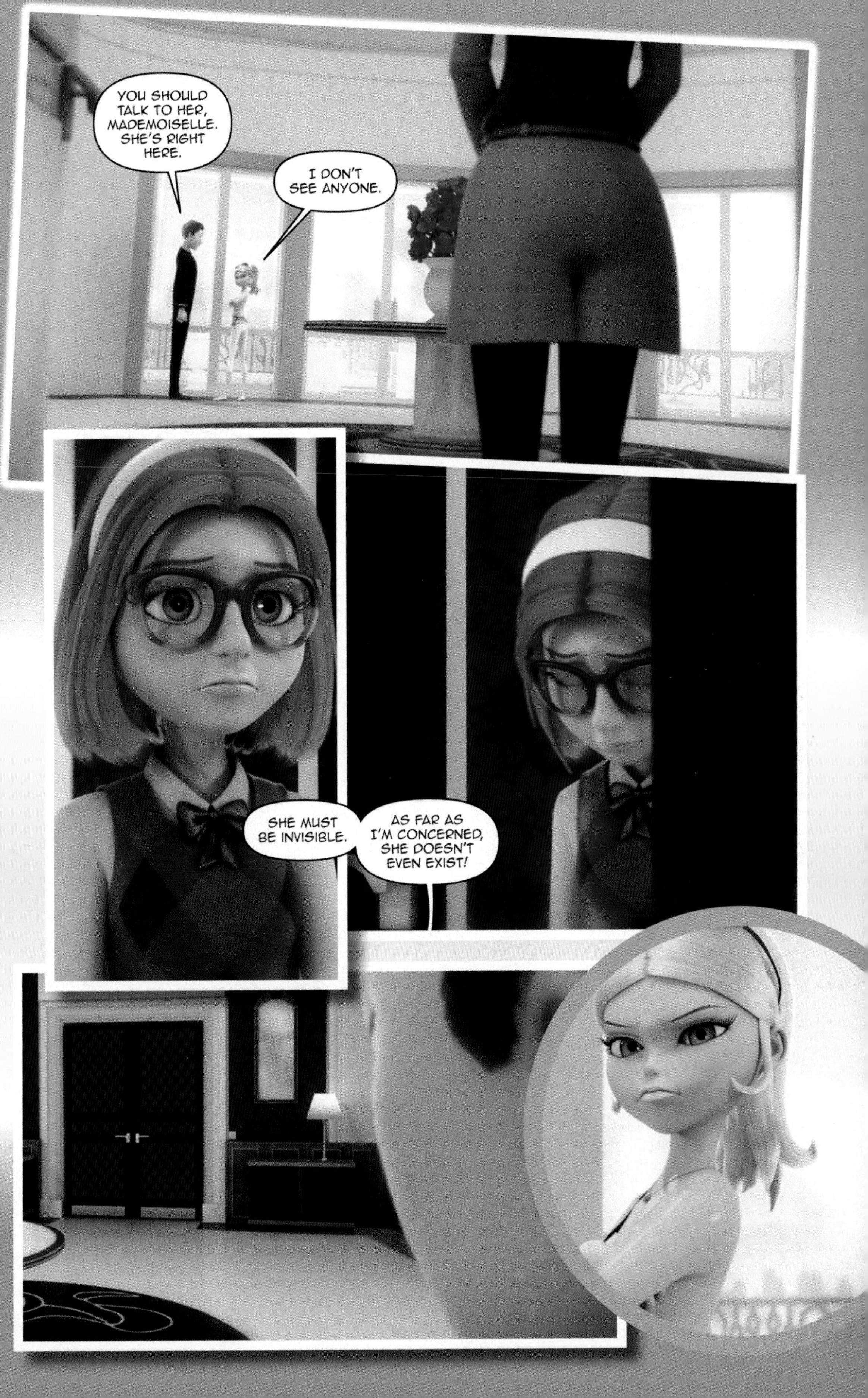
YOU SHOULD TALK TO HER, MADEMOISELLE. SHE'S RIGHT HERE.
I DON'T SEE ANYONE.
SHE MUST BE INVISIBLE.
AS FAR AS I'M CONCERNED, SHE DOESN'T EVEN EXIST!

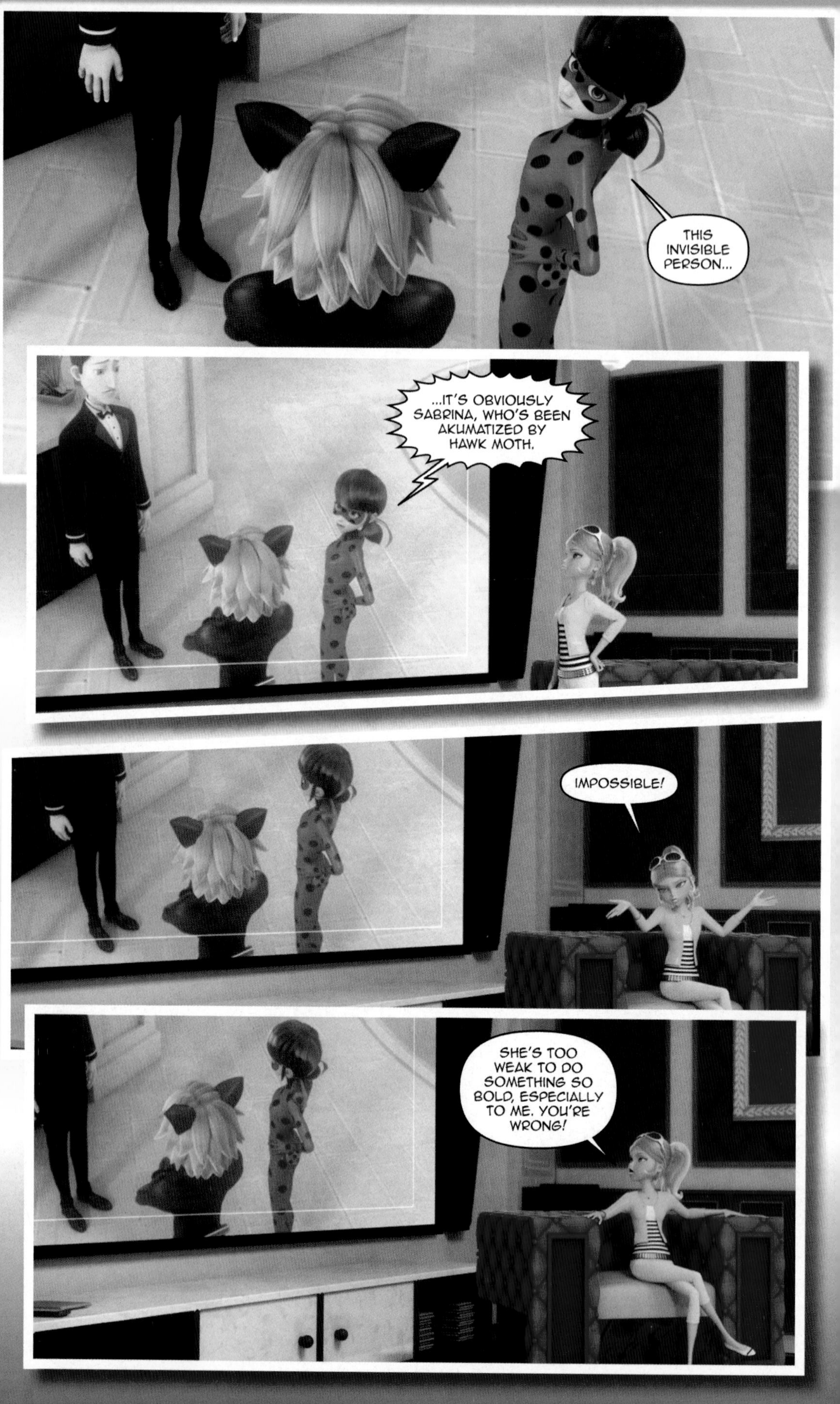
THIS INVISIBLE PERSON...
...IT'S OBVIOUSLY SABRINA, WHO'S BEEN AKUMATIZED BY HAWK MOTH.
IMPOSSIBLE!
SHE'S TOO WEAK TO DO SOMETHING SO BOLD, ESPECIALLY TO ME. YOU'RE WRONG!

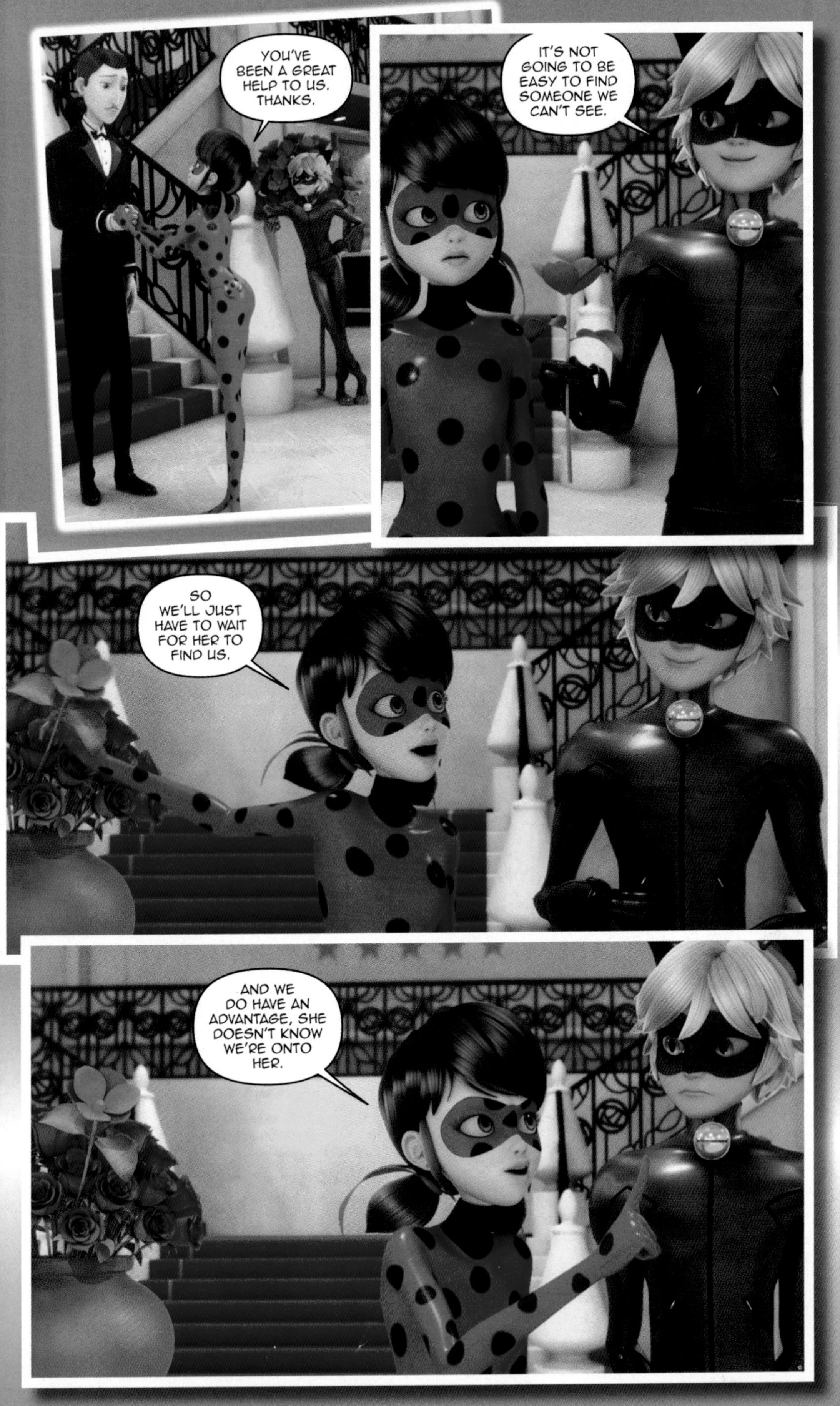
YOU'VE BEEN A GREAT HELP TO US. THANKS.
IT'S NOT GOING TO BE EASY TO FIND SOMEONE WE CAN'T SEE.
SO WE'LL JUST HAVE TO WAIT FOR HER TO FIND US.
AND WE DO HAVE AN ADVANTAGE, SHE DOESN'T KNOW WE'RE ONTO HER.

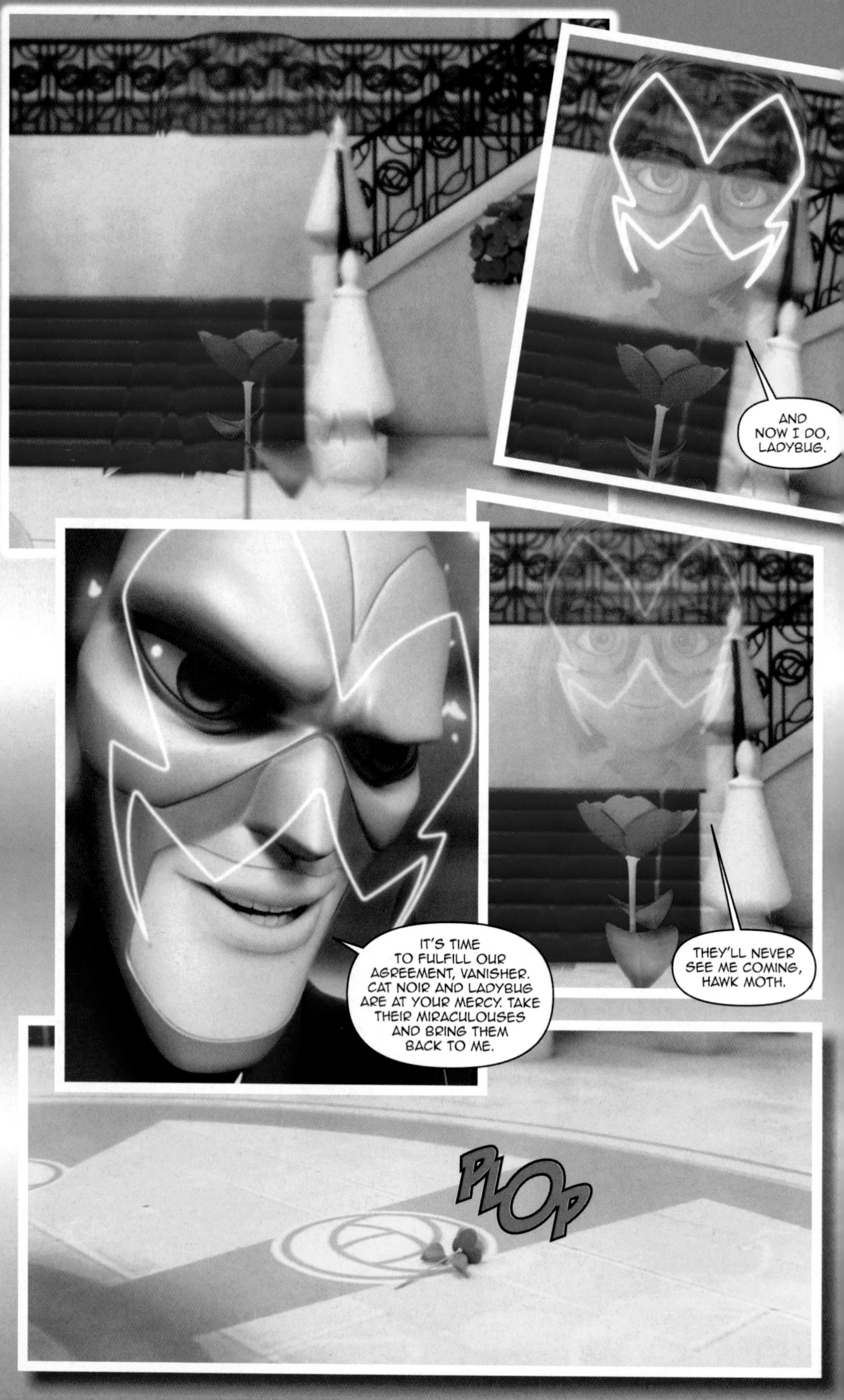
AND NOW I DO, LADYBUG.
IT'S TIME TO FULFILL OUR AGREEMENT, VANISHER. CAT NOIR AND LADYBUG ARE AT YOUR MERCY. TAKE THEIR MIRACULOUSES AND BRING THEM BACK TO ME.
THEY'LL NEVER SEE ME COMING, HAWK MOTH.
PLOP

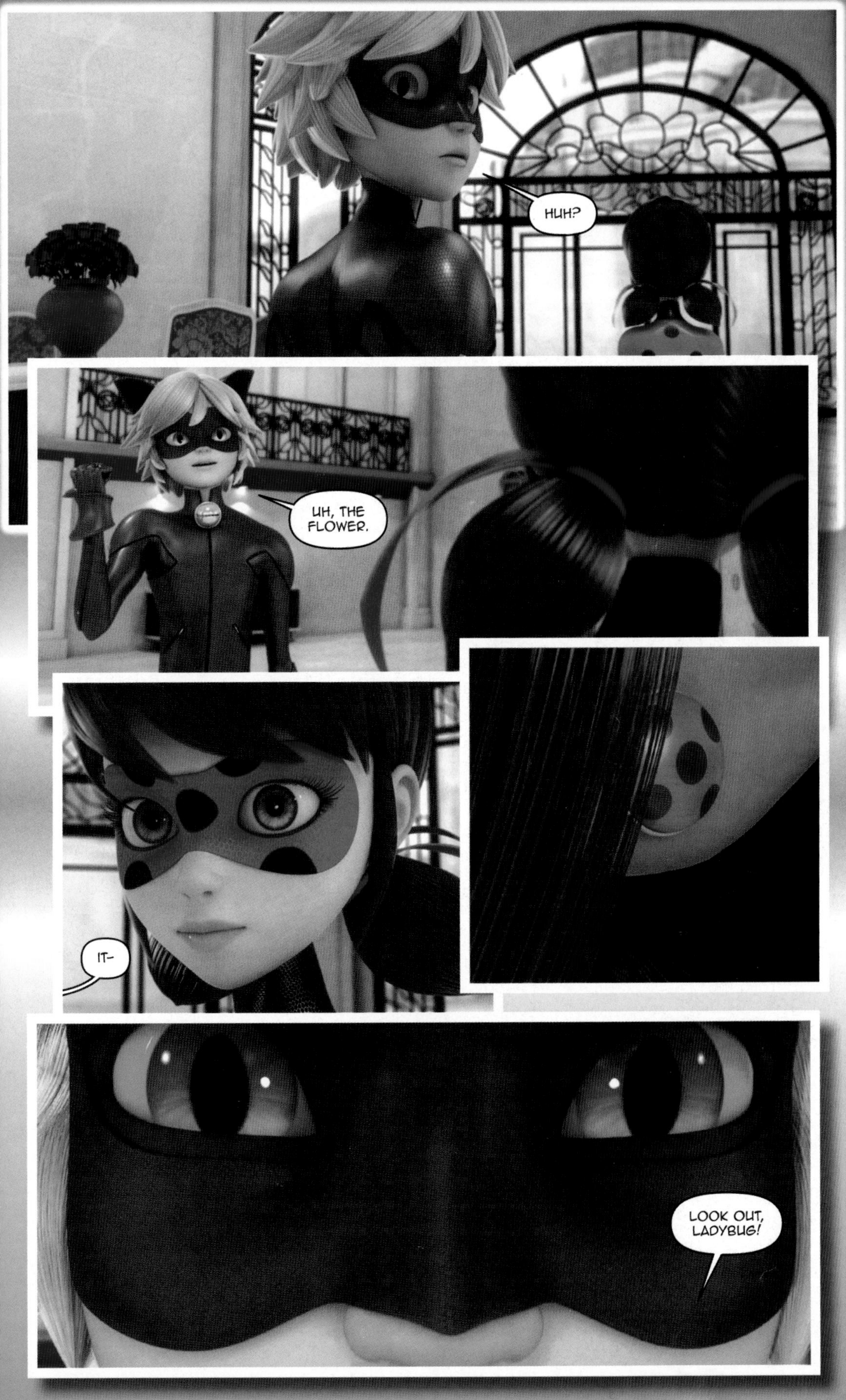
HUH?
UH, THE FLOWER.
IT-
LOOK OUT, LADYBUG!

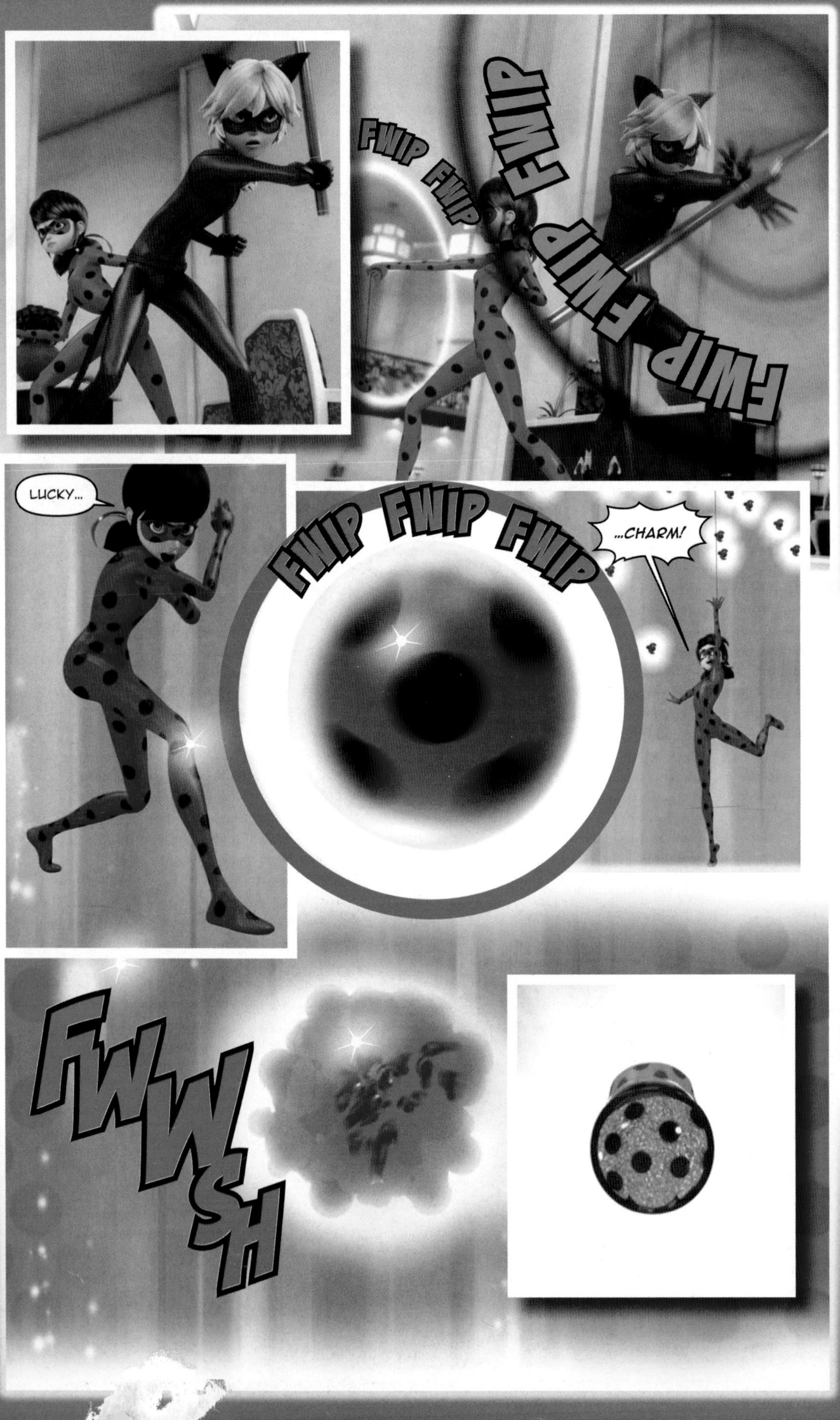
FWIP FWIP
FWIP FWIP FWIP
LUCKY...
FWIP FWIP FWIP
...CHARM!
FWWSH

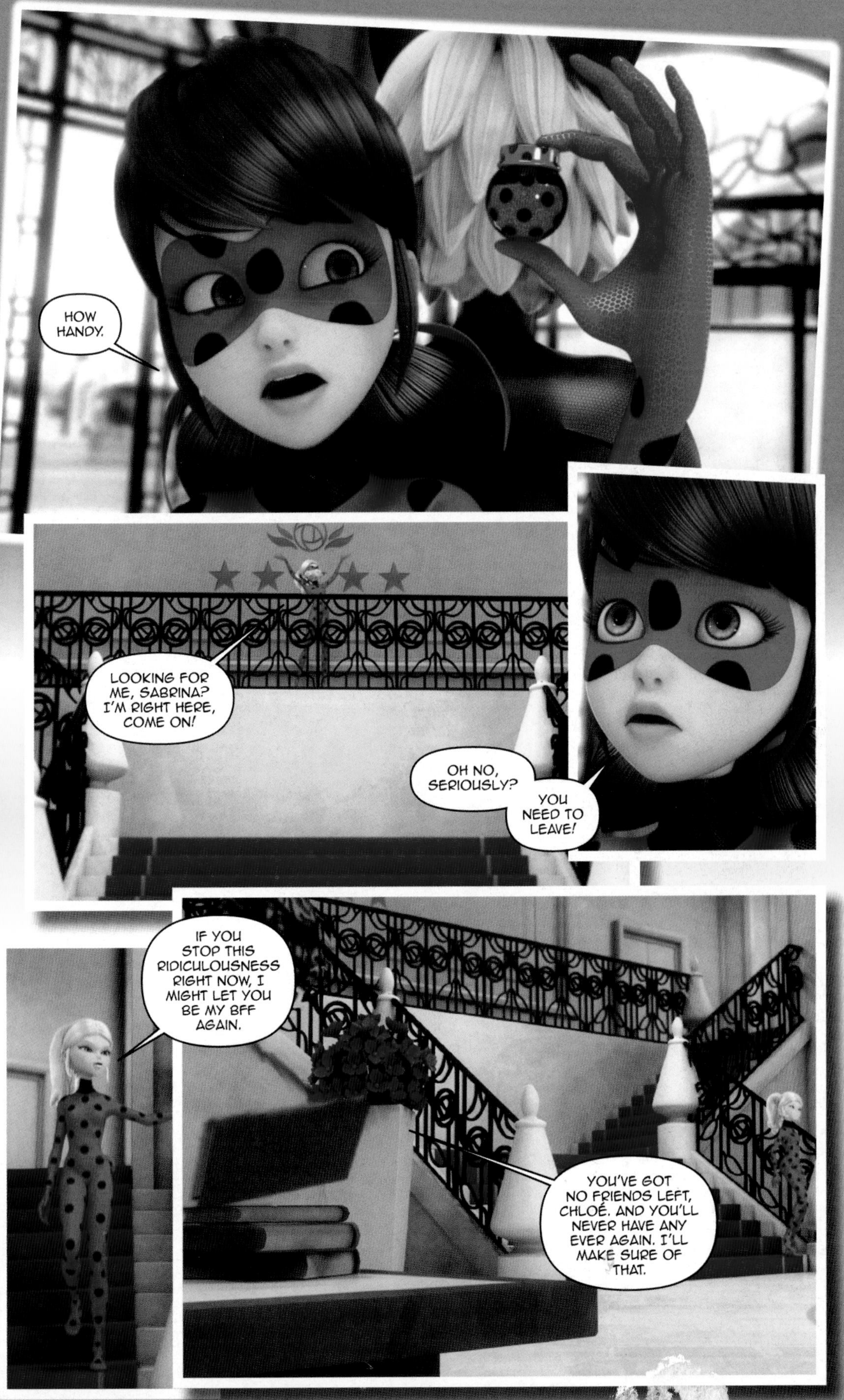
HOW HANDY.
LOOKING FOR ME, SABRINA? I'M RIGHT HERE, COME ON!
OH NO, SERIOUSLY?
YOU NEED TO LEAVE!
IF YOU STOP THIS RIDICULOUSNESS RIGHT NOW, I MIGHT LET YOU BE MY BFF AGAIN.
YOU'VE GOT NO FRIENDS LEFT, CHLOÉ. AND YOU'LL NEVER HAVE ANY EVER AGAIN. I'LL MAKE SURE OF THAT.

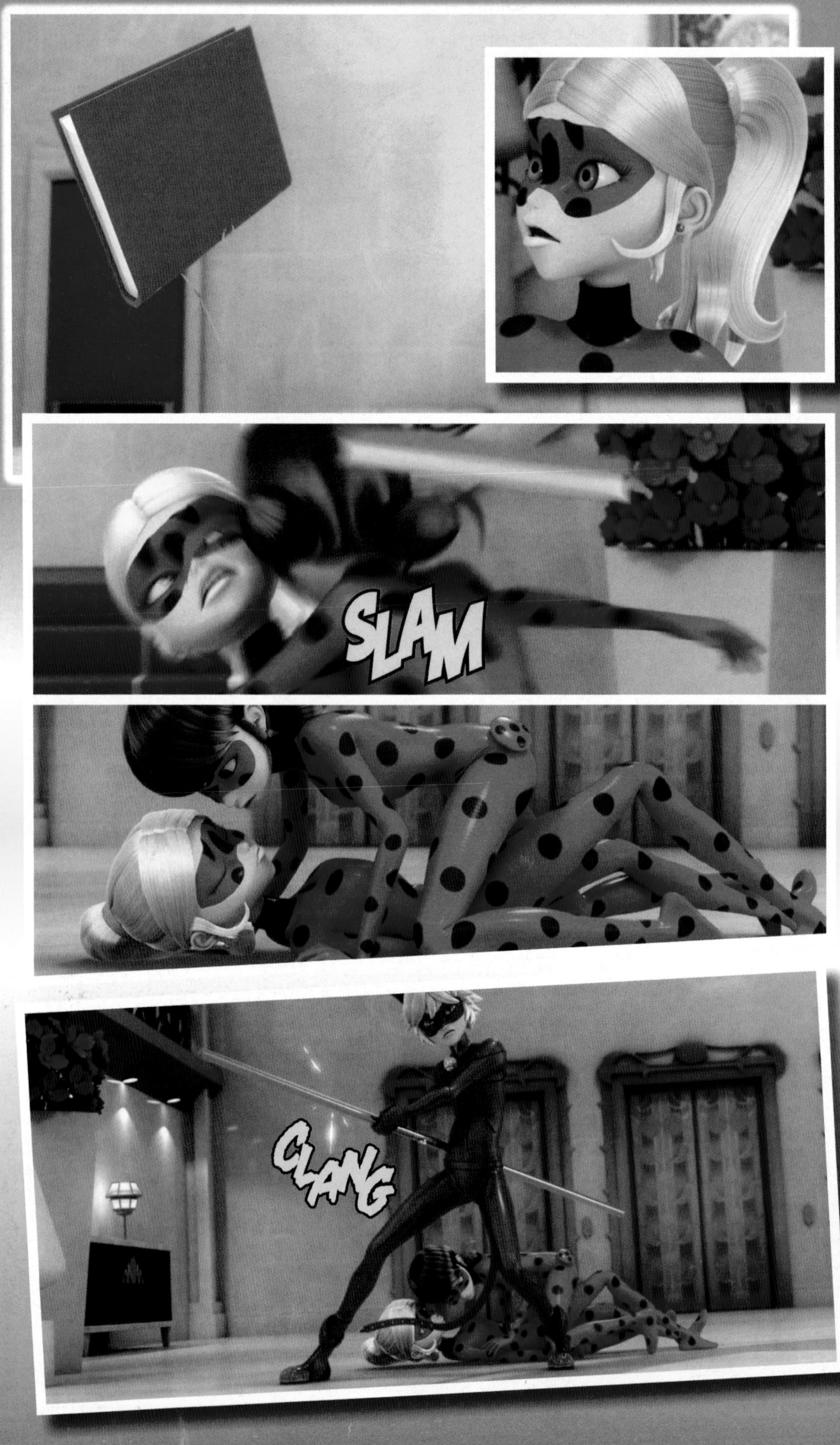
SLAM
CLANG

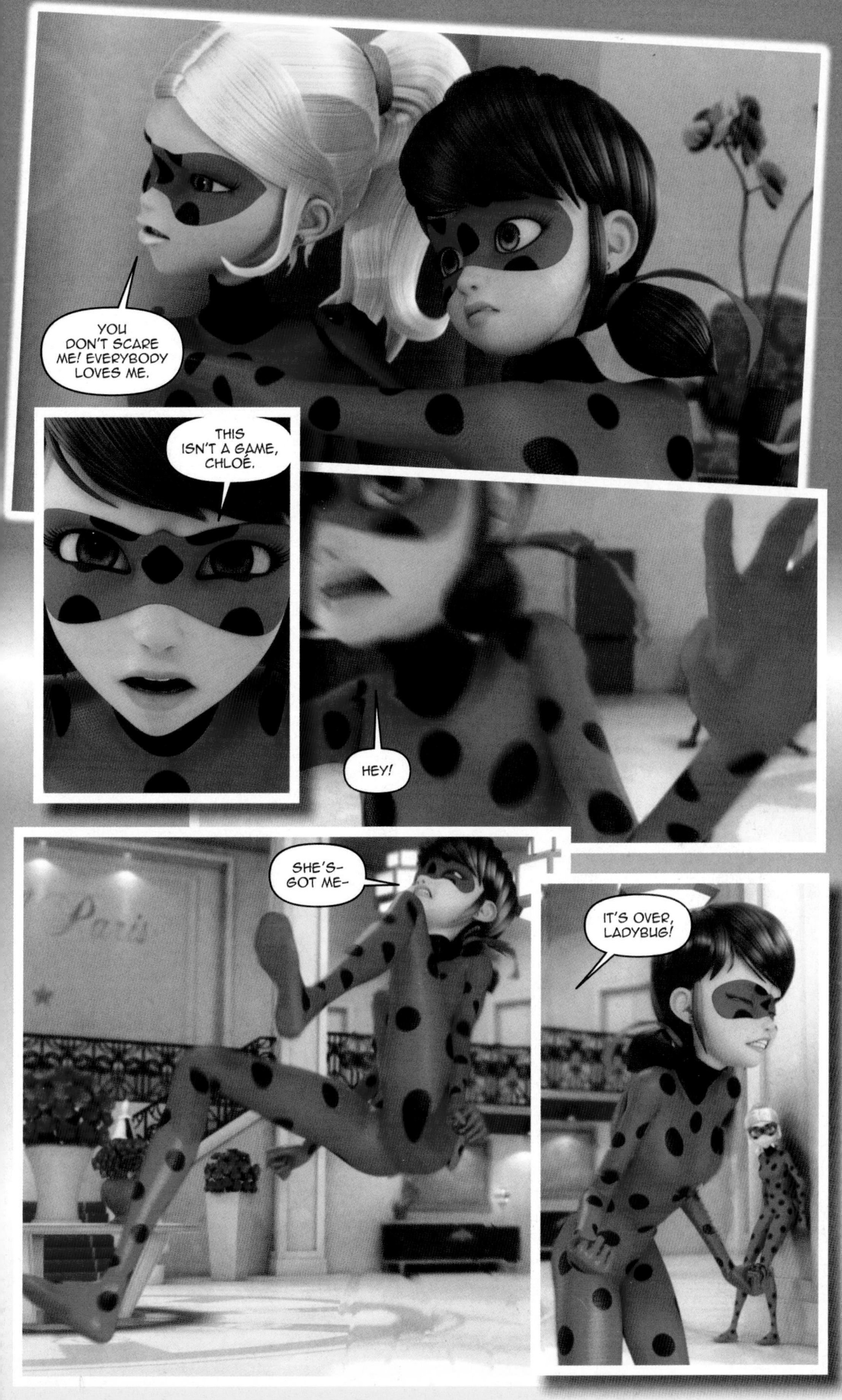
YOU DON'T SCARE ME! EVERYBODY LOVES ME.
THIS ISN'T A GAME, CHLOÉ.
HEY!
SHE'S- GOT ME-
IT'S OVER, LADYBUG!

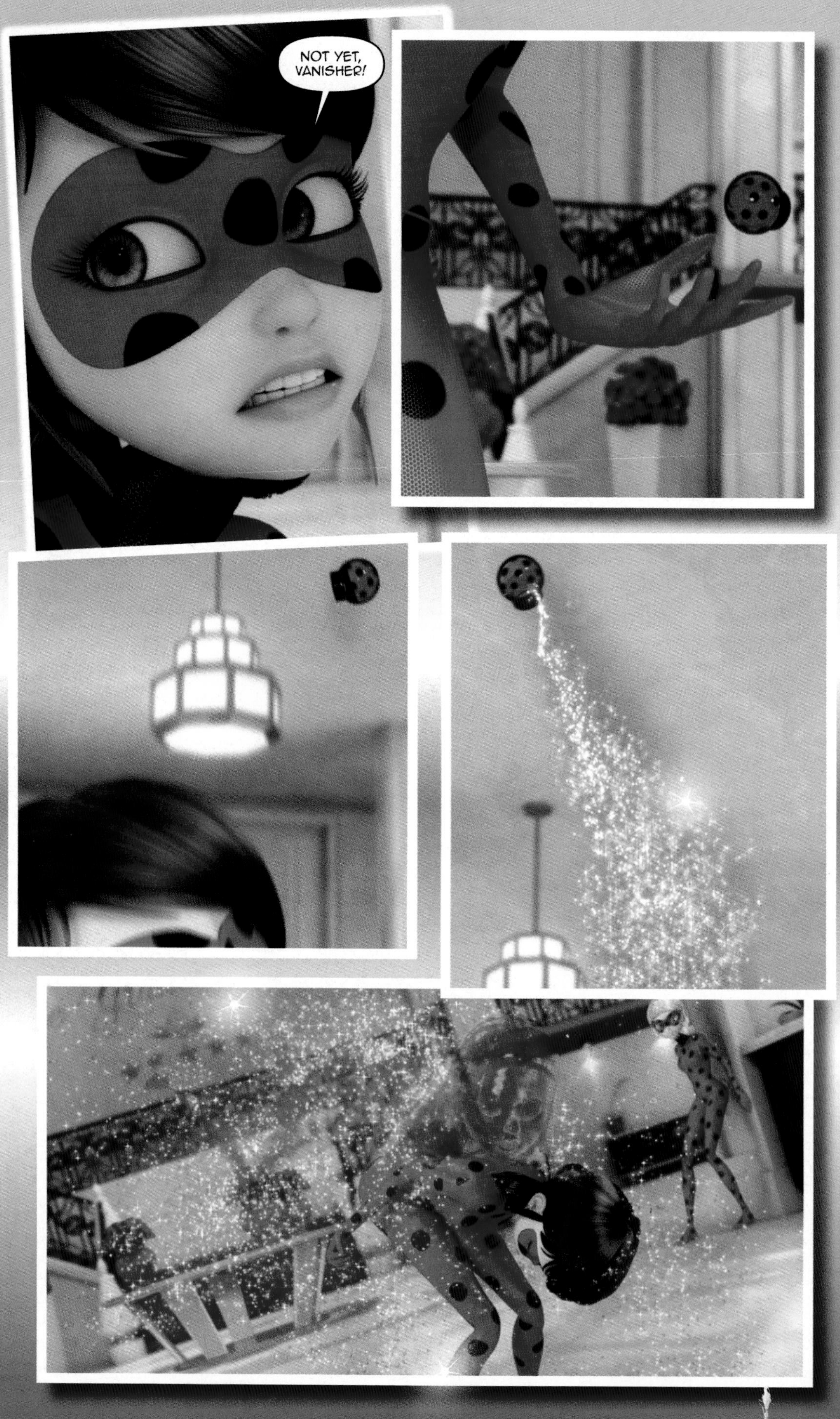
NOT YET, VANISHER!

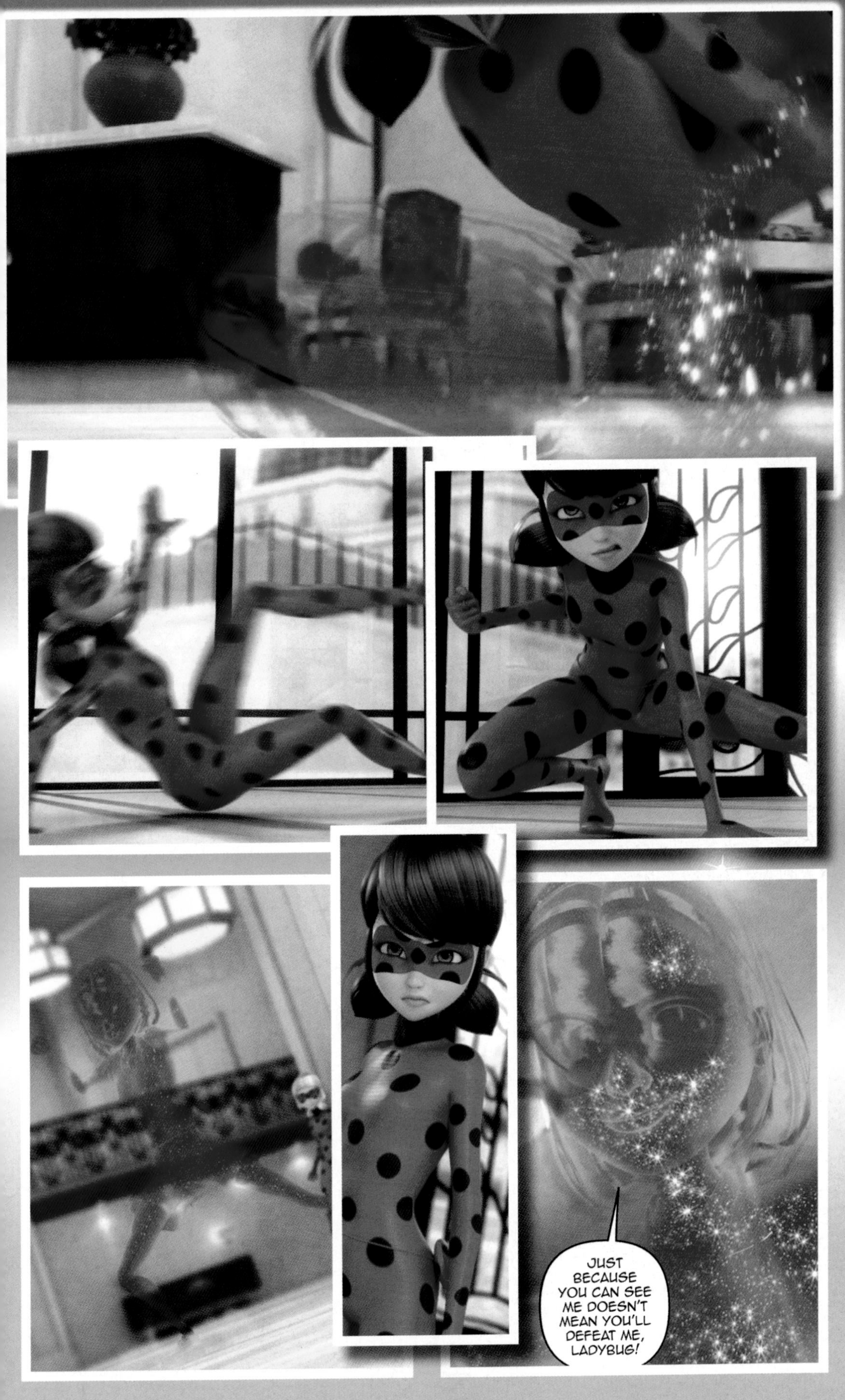
JUST BECAUSE YOU CAN SEE ME DOESN'T MEAN YOU'LL DEFEAT ME, LADYBUG!

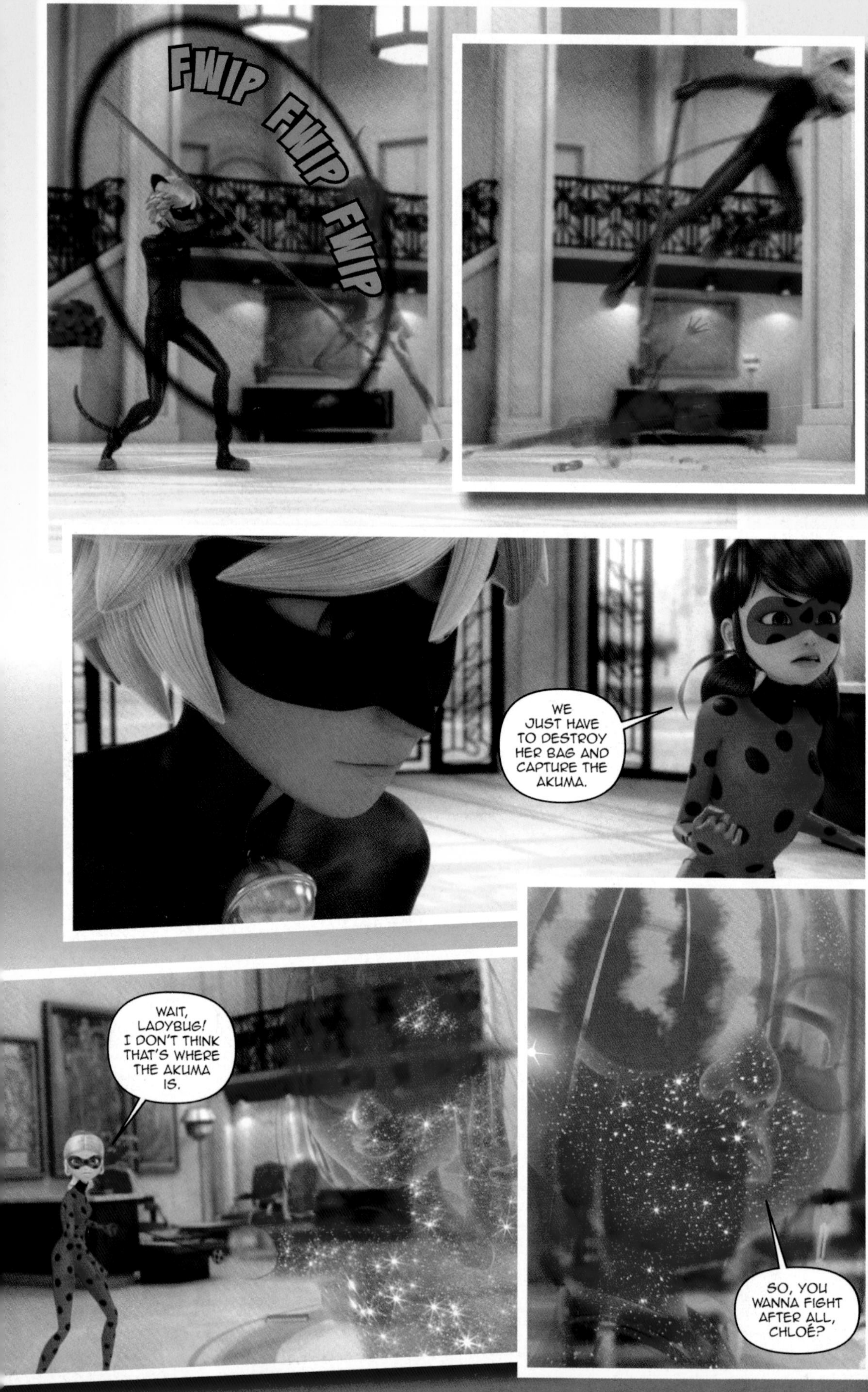
FWIP FWIP FWIP FWIP
WE JUST HAVE TO DESTROY HER BAG AND CAPTURE THE AKUMA.
WAIT, LADYBUG! I DON'T THINK THAT'S WHERE THE AKUMA IS.
SO, YOU WANNA FIGHT AFTER ALL, CHLOÉ?

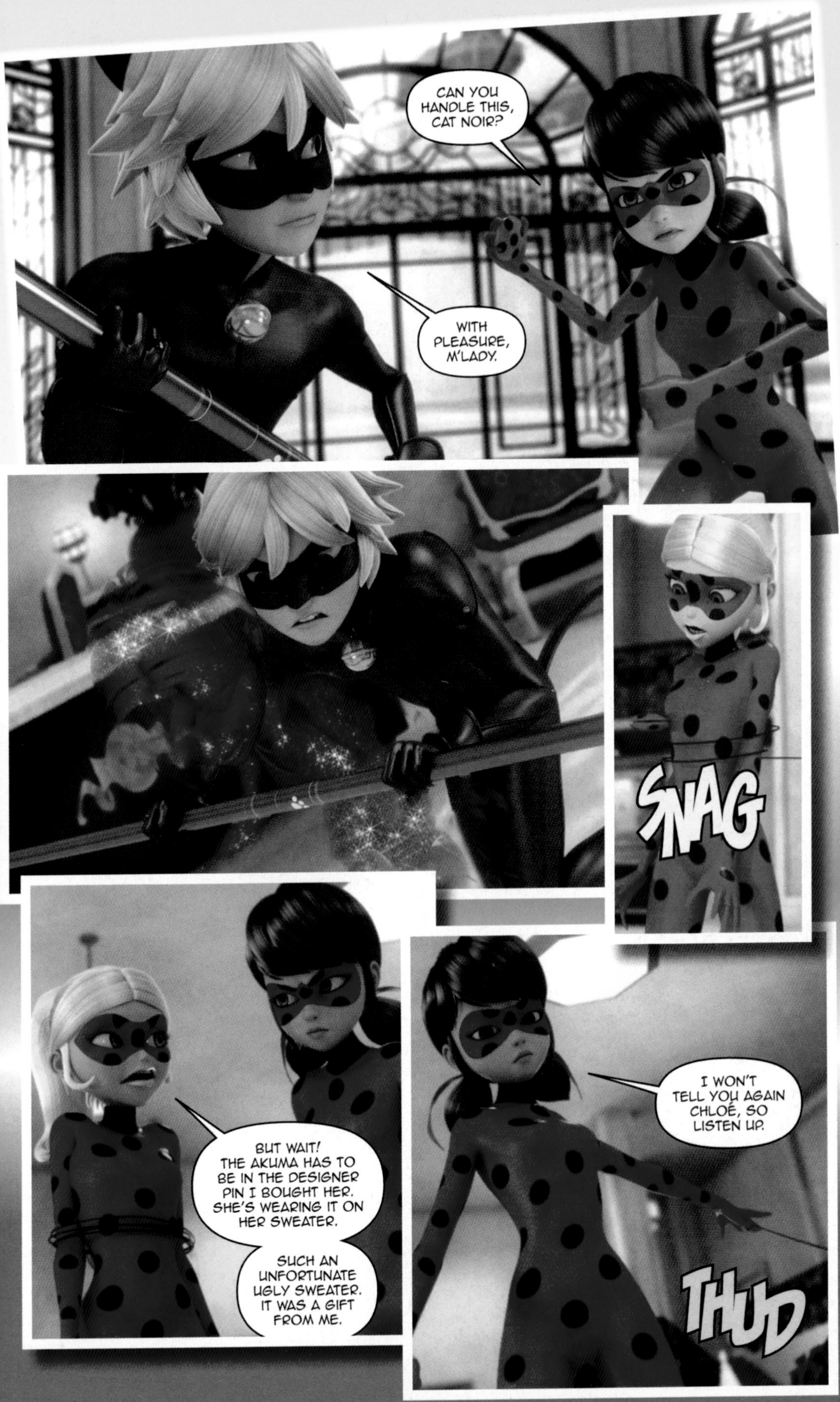
CAN YOU HANDLE THIS, CAT NOIR?
WITH PLEASURE, M'LADY.
SNAG
BUT WAIT! THE AKUMA HAS TO BE IN THE DESIGNER PIN I BOUGHT HER. SHE'S WEARING IT ON HER SWEATER.
SUCH AN UNFORTUNATE UGLY SWEATER. IT WAS A GIFT FROM ME.
I WON'T TELL YOU AGAIN CHLOÉ, SO LISTEN UP.
THUD

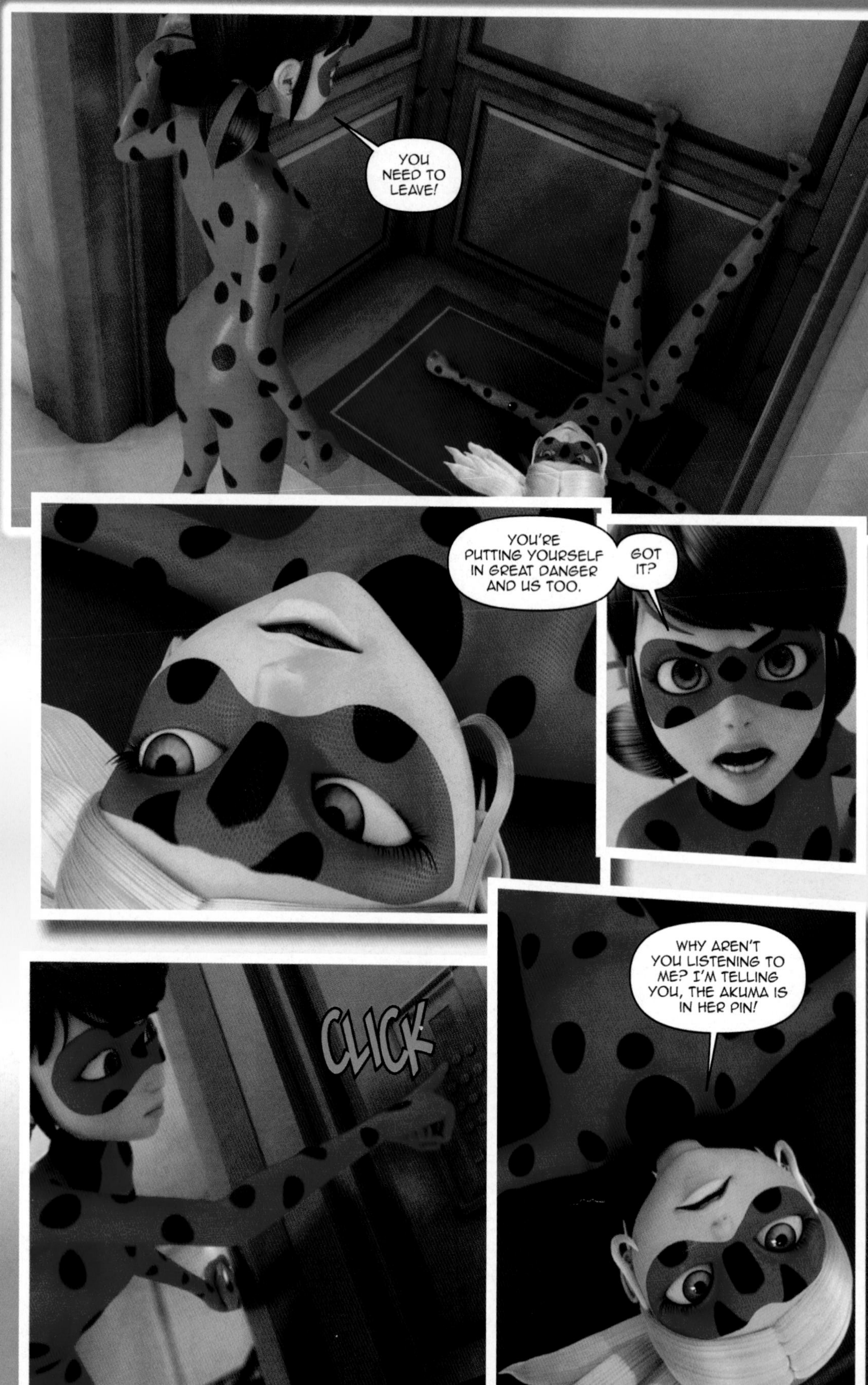
YOU NEED TO LEAVE!
YOU'RE PUTTING YOURSELF IN GREAT DANGER AND US TOO.
GOT IT?
CLICK
WHY AREN'T YOU LISTENING TO ME? I'M TELLING YOU, THE AKUMA IS IN HER PIN!

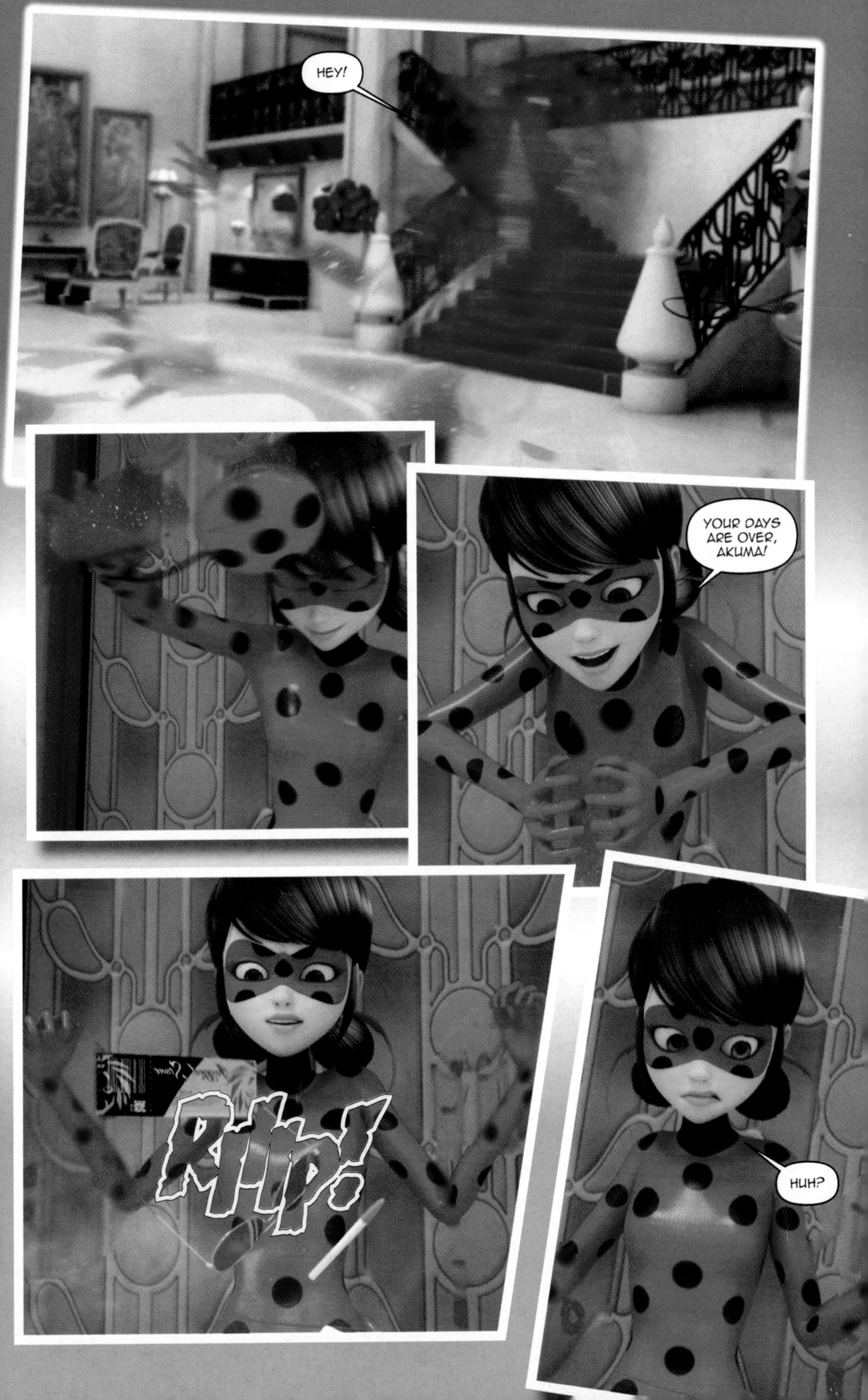
HEY!
YOUR DAYS ARE OVER, AKUMA!
HUH?

ARGH!

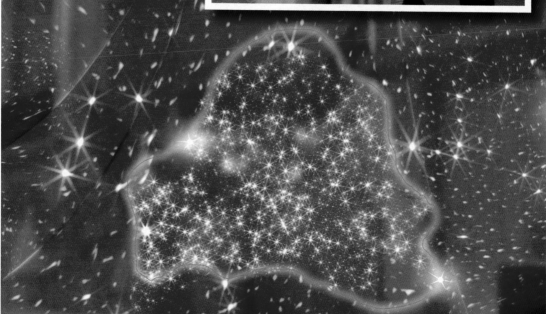

SLAM!

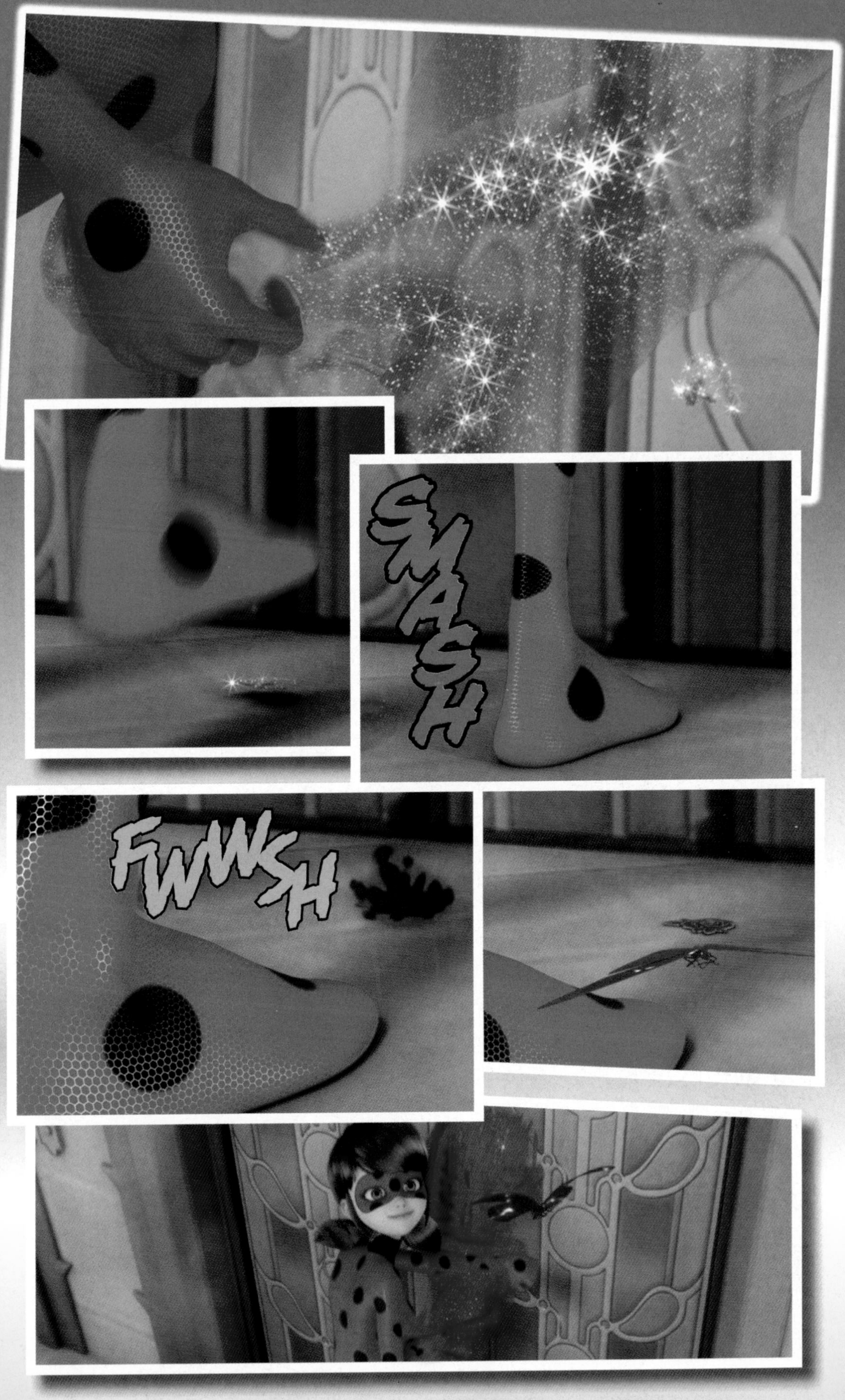
SMASH
FWWSH

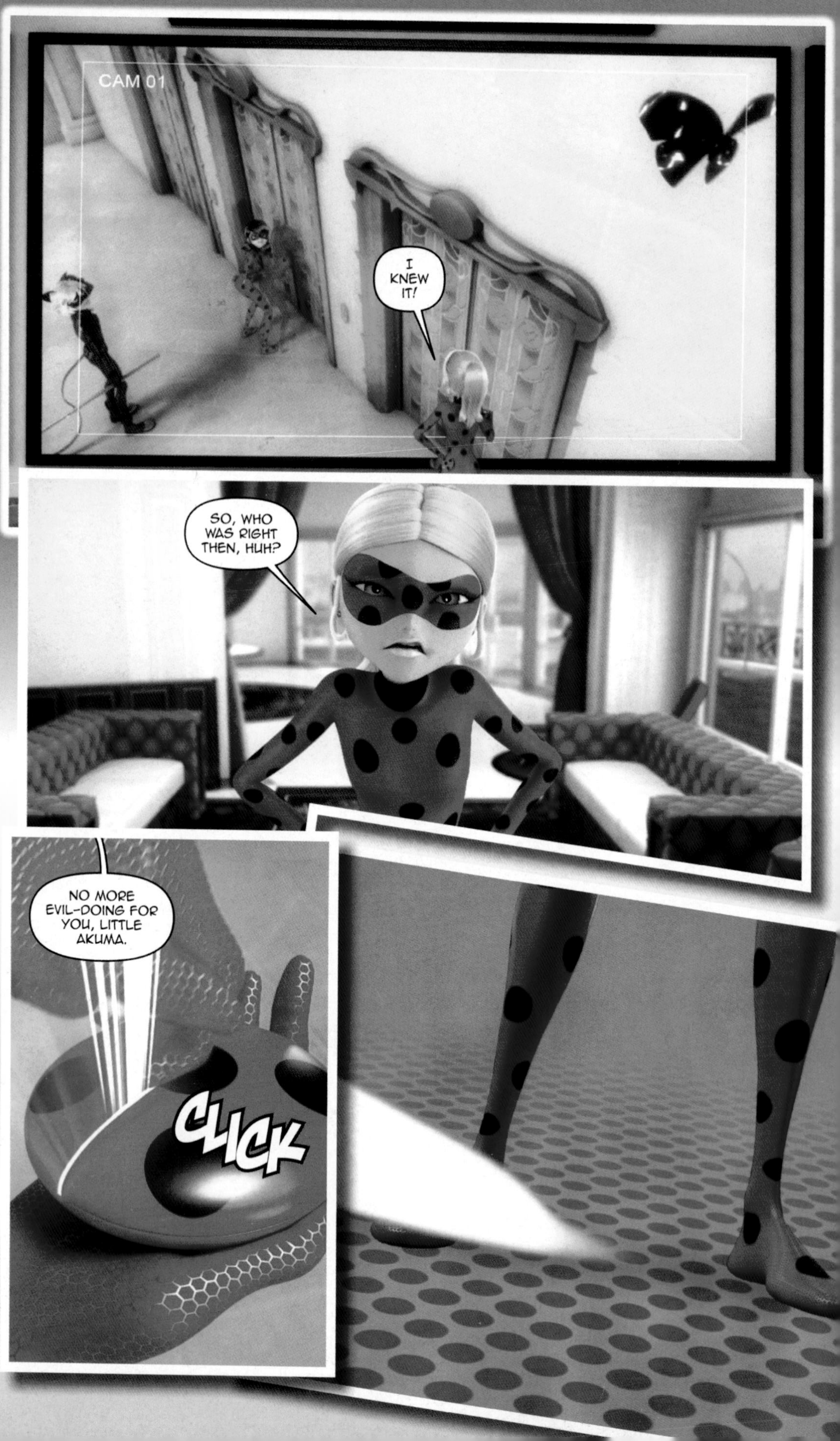
CAM 01
I KNEW IT!
SO, WHO WAS RIGHT THEN, HUH?
NO MORE EVIL-DOING FOR YOU, LITTLE AKUMA.
CLICK

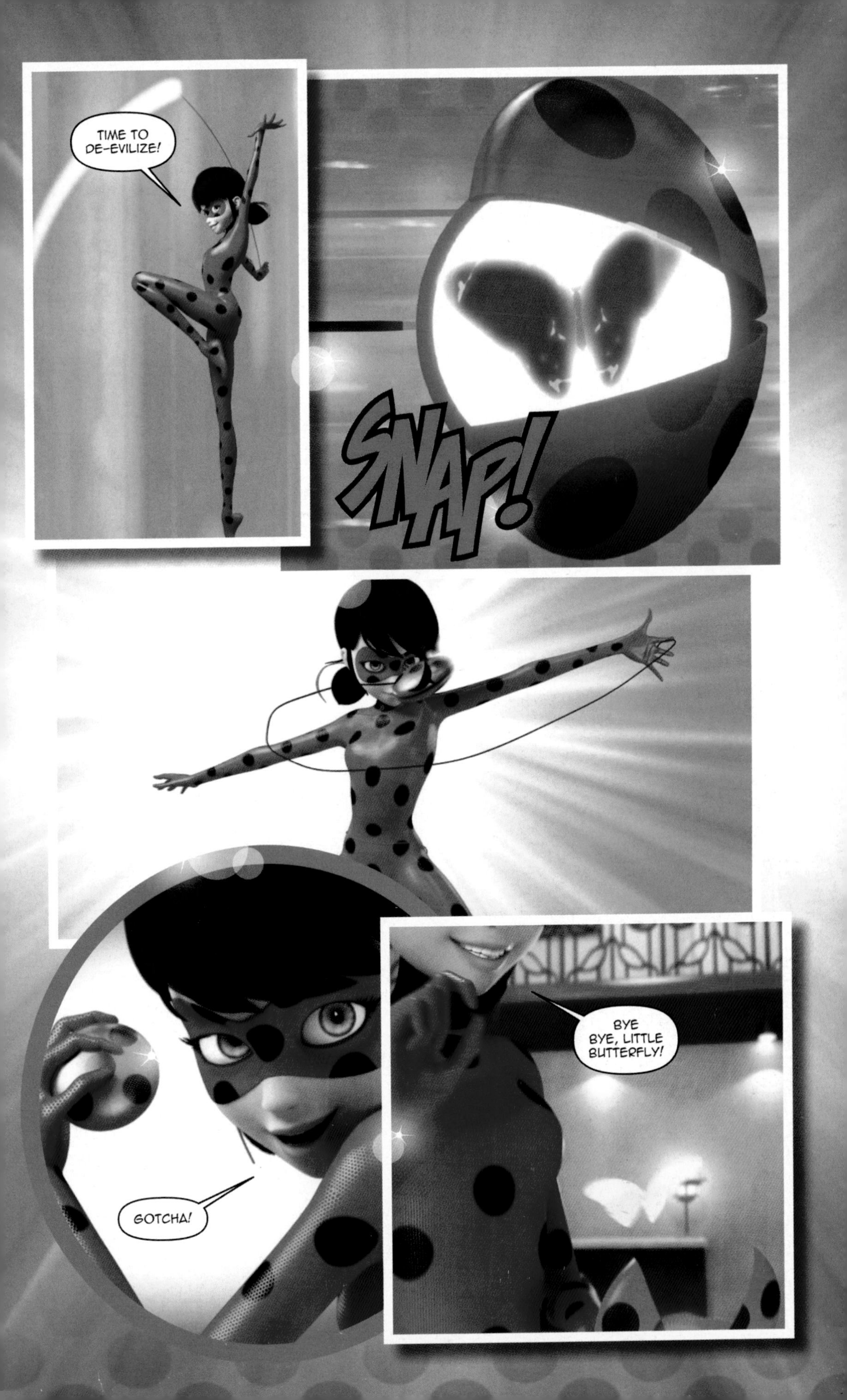
TIME TO DE-EVILIZE!
SNAP!
GOTCHA!
BYE BYE, LITTLE BUTTERFLY!

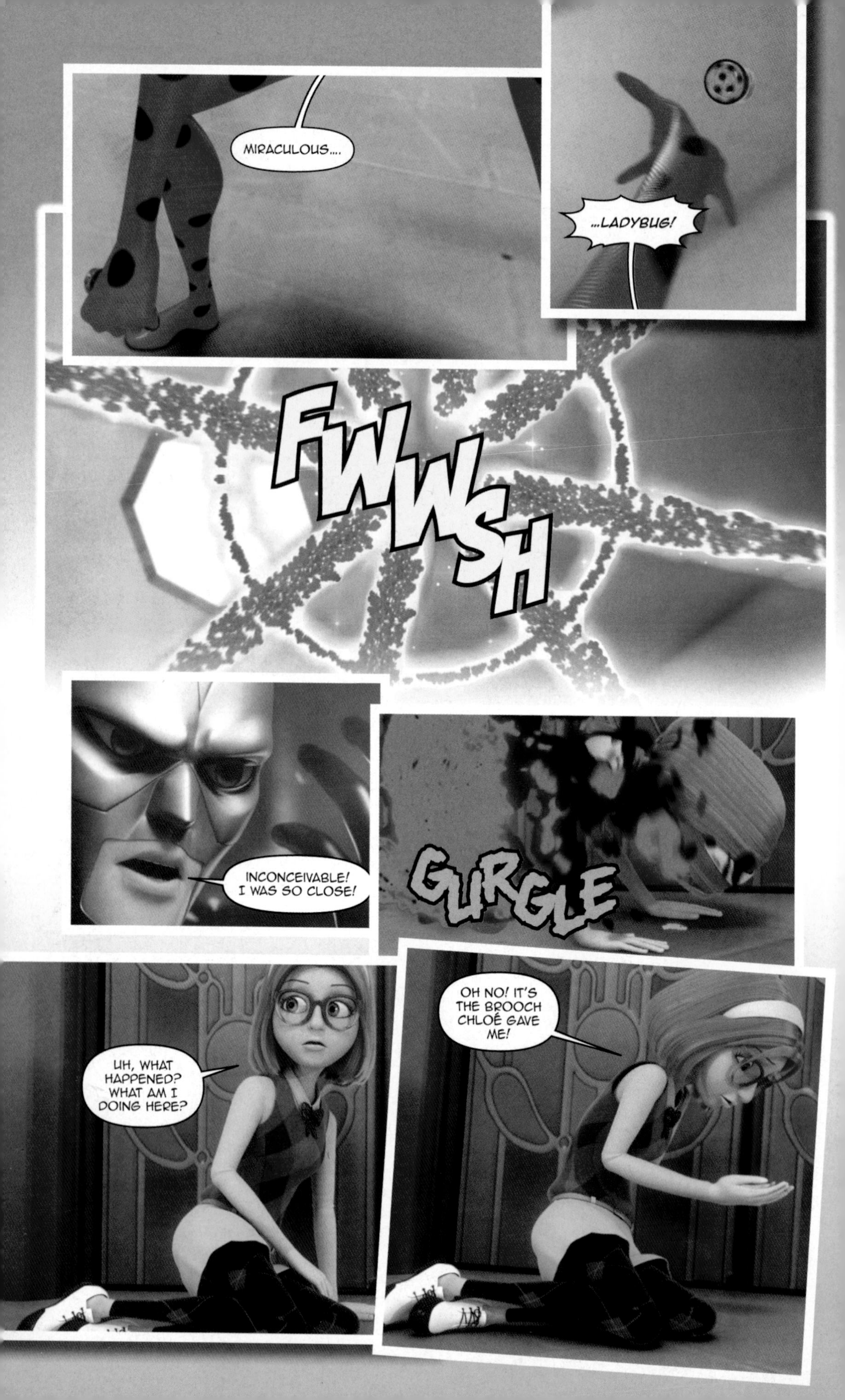

MIRACULOUS....
...LADYBUG!
FWWSH
INCONCEIVABLE! I WAS SO CLOSE!
GURGLE
UH, WHAT HAPPENED? WHAT AM I DOING HERE?
OH NO! IT'S THE BROOCH CHLOÉ GAVE ME!

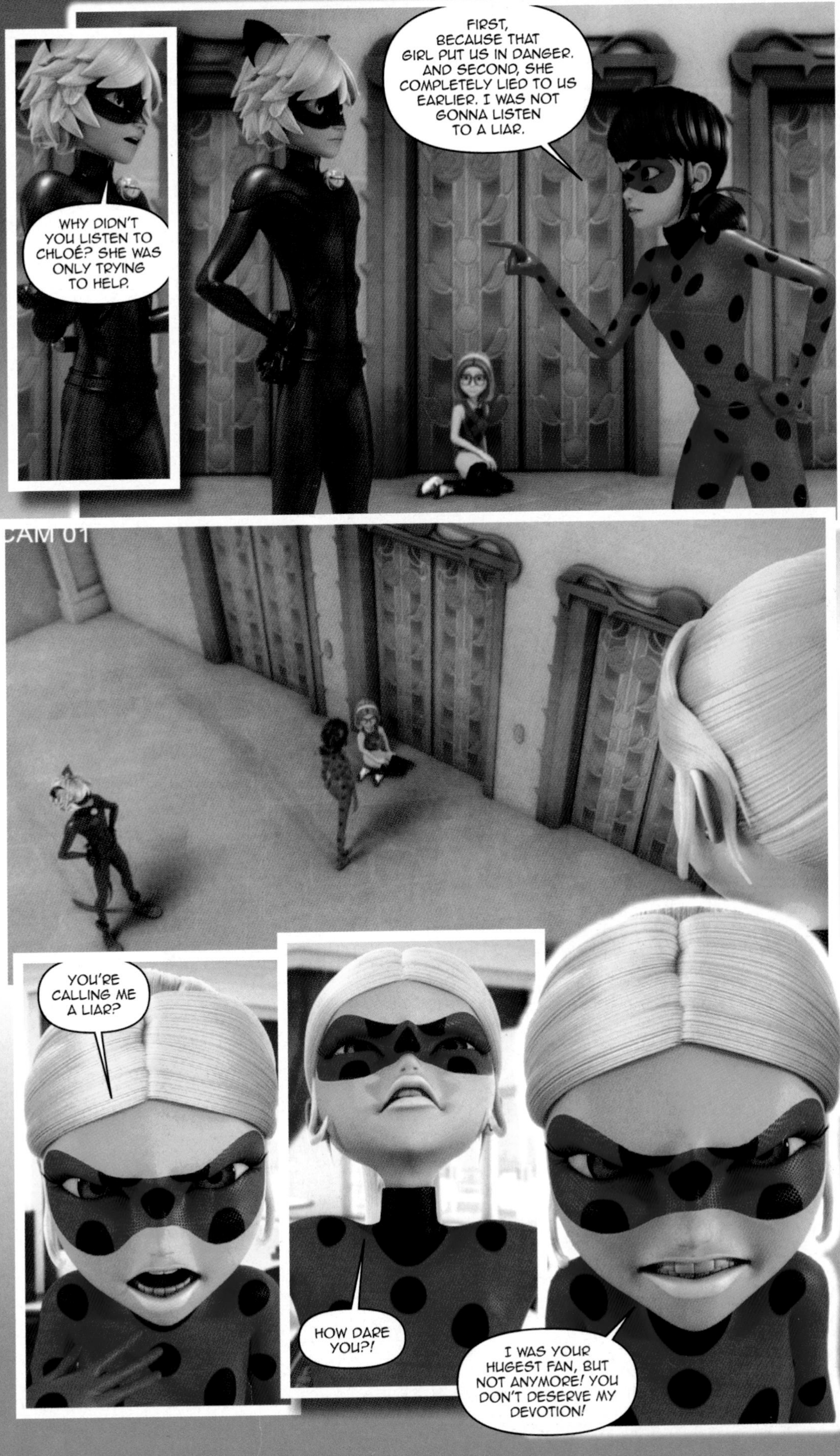
WHY DIDN'T YOU LISTEN TO CHLOÉ? SHE WAS ONLY TRYING TO HELP.
FIRST, BECAUSE THAT GIRL PUT US IN DANGER. AND SECOND, SHE COMPLETELY LIED TO US EARLIER. I WAS NOT GONNA LISTEN TO A LIAR.
CAM 01
YOU'RE CALLING ME A LIAR?
HOW DARE YOU?!
I WAS YOUR HUGEST FAN, BUT NOT ANYMORE! YOU DON'T DESERVE MY DEVOTION!

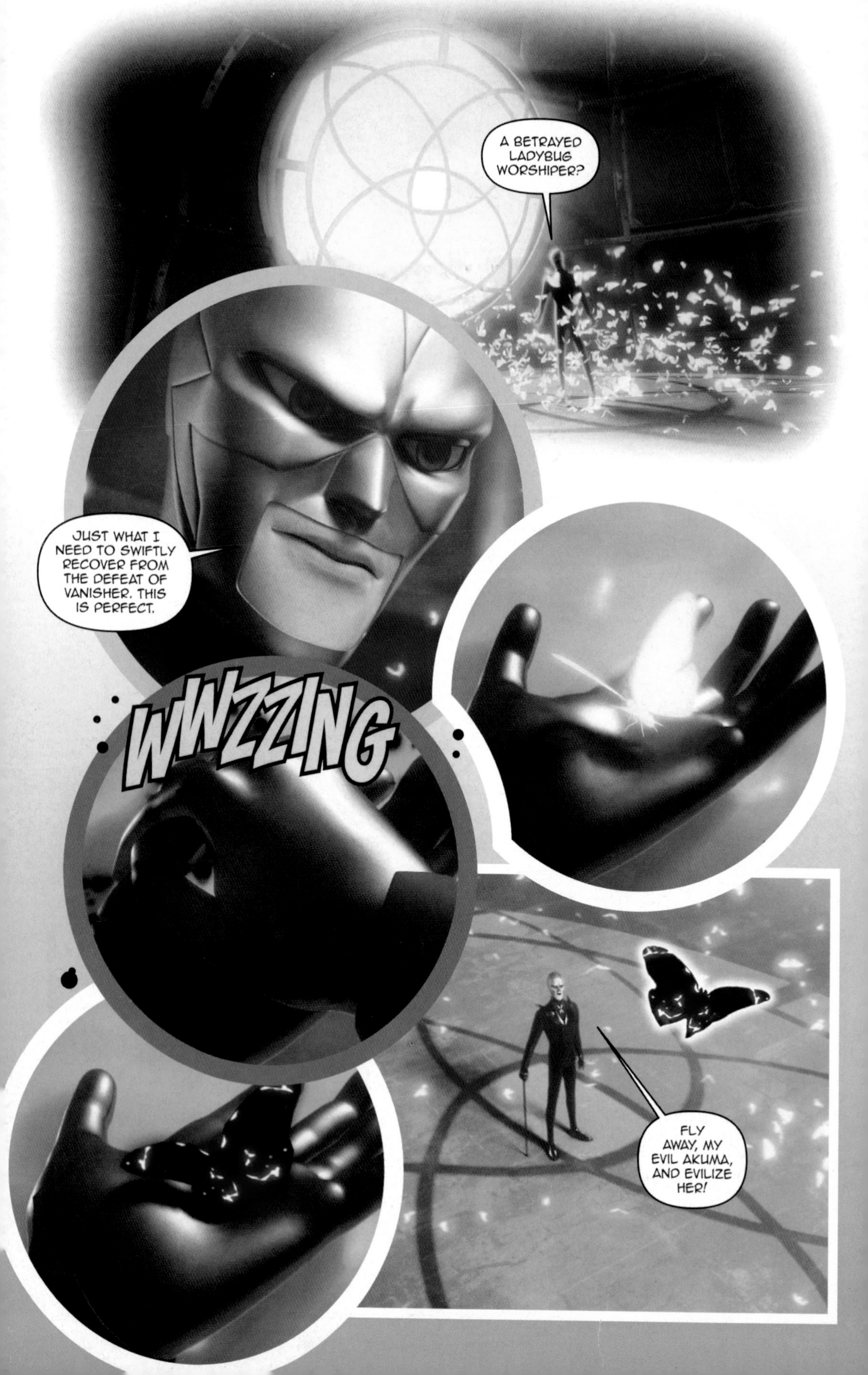
A BETRAYED LADYBUG WORSHIPER?
JUST WHAT I NEED TO SWIFTLY RECOVER FROM THE DEFEAT OF VANISHER. THIS IS PERFECT.
WWZZING
FLY AWAY, MY EVIL AKUMA, AND EVILIZE HER!

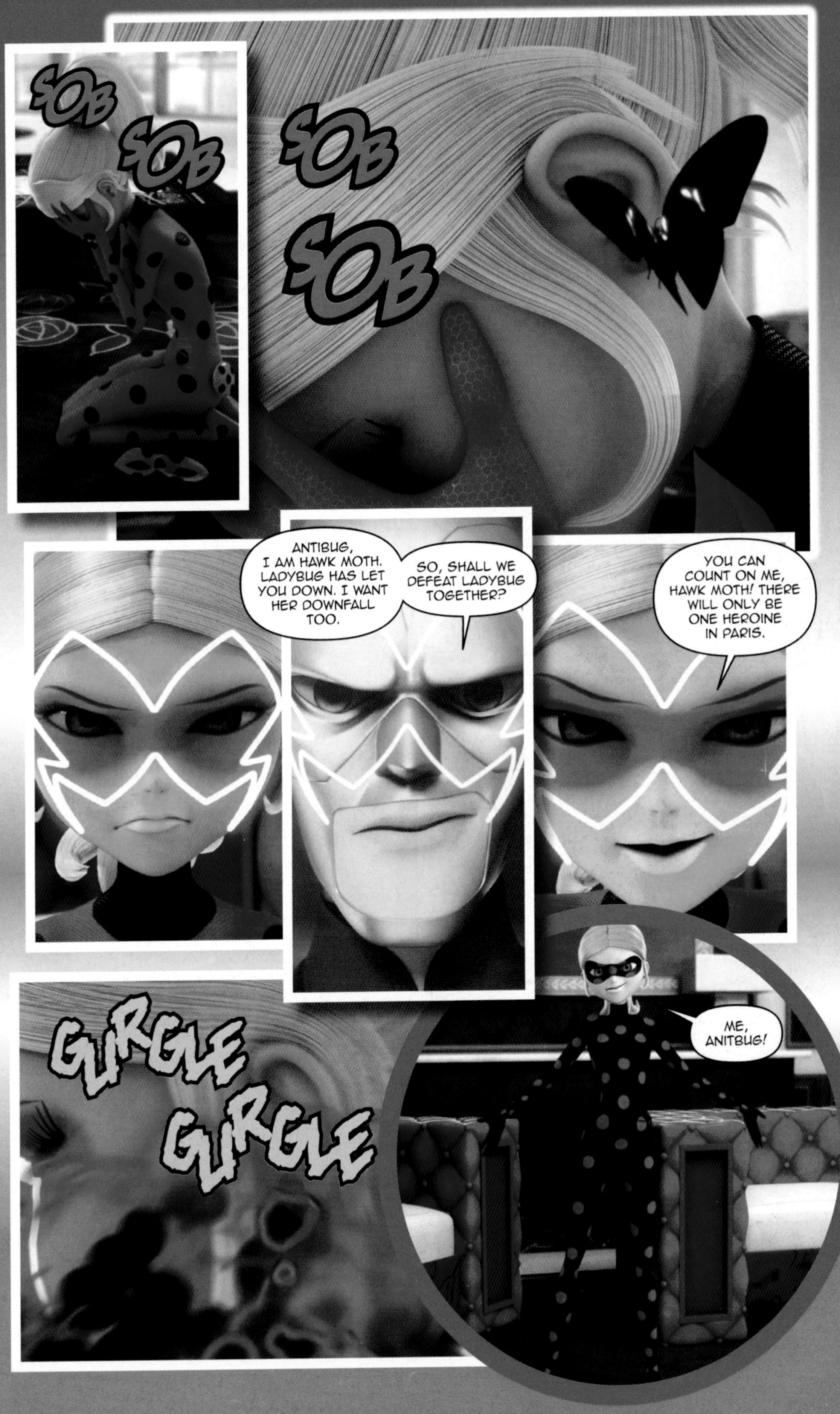
SOB
SOB
SOB
SOB
ANTIBUG, I AM HAWK MOTH. LADYBUG HAS LET YOU DOWN. I WANT HER DOWNFALL TOO.
SO, SHALL WE DEFEAT LADYBUG TOGETHER?
YOU CAN COUNT ON ME, HAWK MOTH! THERE WILL ONLY BE ONE HEROINE IN PARIS.
GURGLE
GURGLE
ME, ANITBUG!

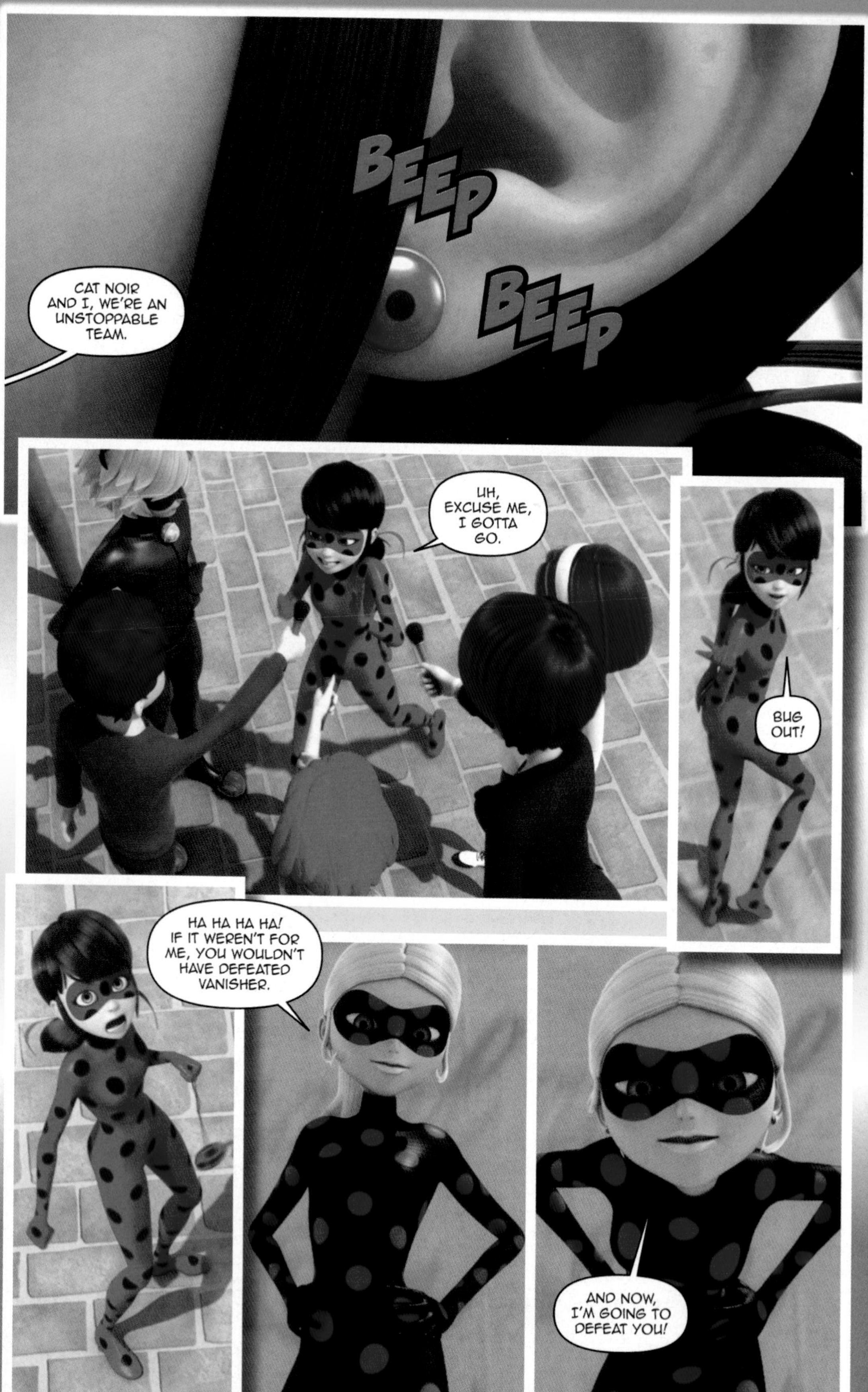
BEEP
BEEP
CAT NOIR AND I, WE'RE AN UNSTOPPABLE TEAM.
UH, EXCUSE ME, I GOTTA GO.
BUG OUT!
HA HA HA HA! IF IT WEREN'T FOR ME, YOU WOULDN'T HAVE DEFEATED VANISHER.
AND NOW, I'M GOING TO DEFEAT YOU!

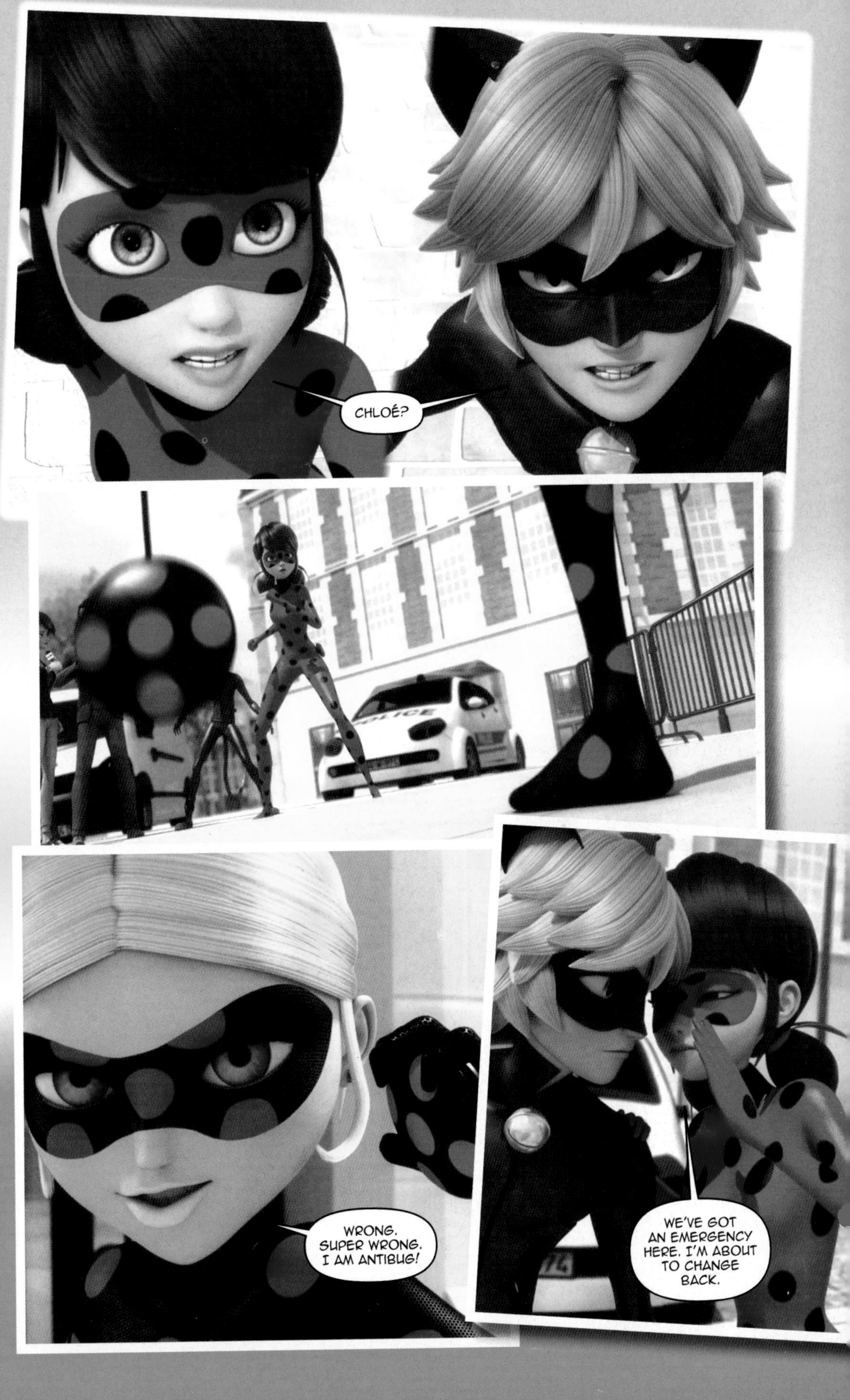
CHLOÉ?
WRONG. SUPER WRONG. I AM ANTIBUG!
WE'VE GOT AN EMERGENCY HERE. I'M ABOUT TO CHANGE BACK.

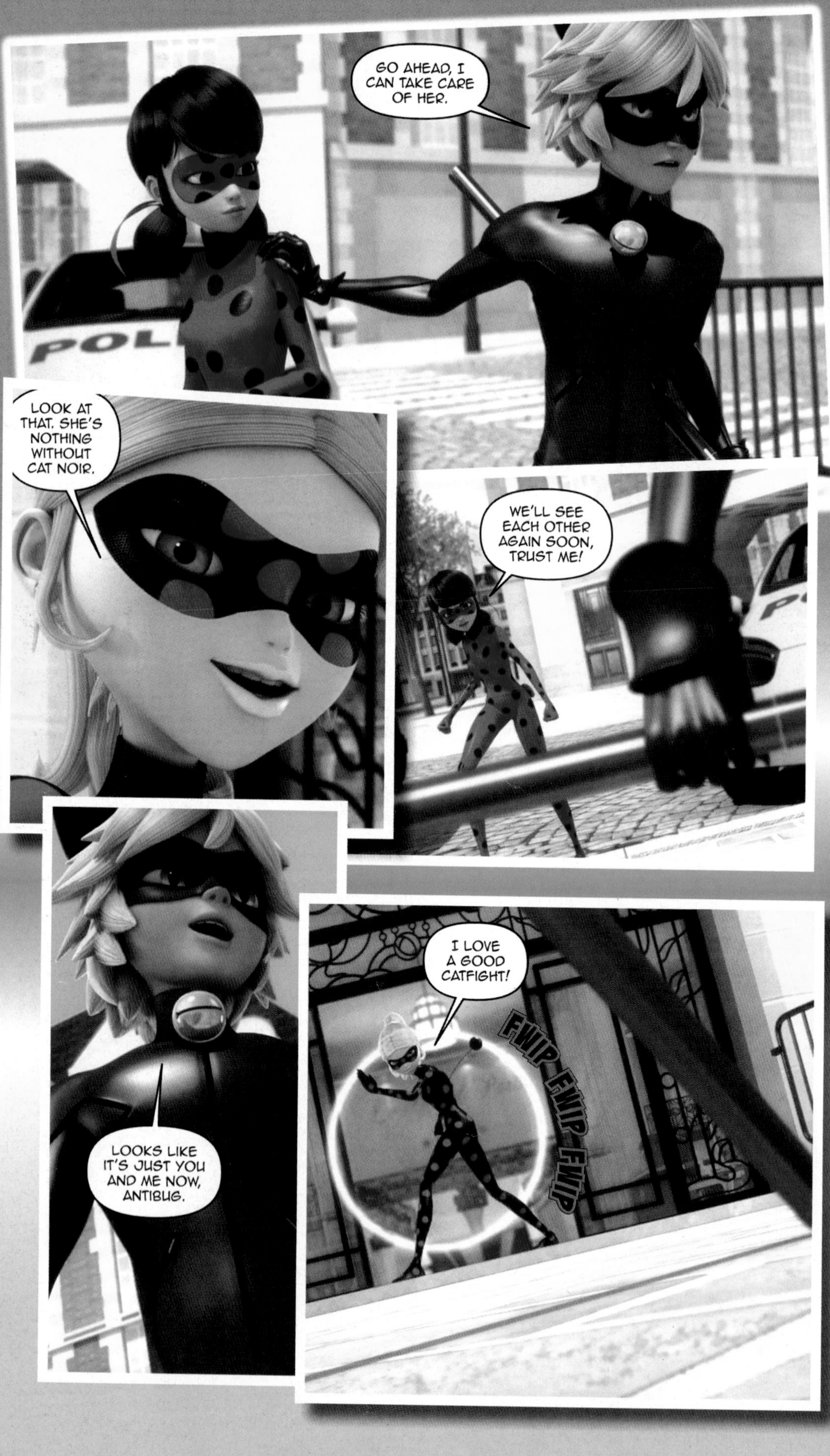

GO AHEAD, I CAN TAKE CARE OF HER.
LOOK AT THAT. SHE'S NOTHING WITHOUT CAT NOIR.
WE'LL SEE EACH OTHER AGAIN SOON, TRUST ME!
LOOKS LIKE IT'S JUST YOU AND ME NOW, ANTIBUG.
I LOVE A GOOD CATFIGHT!
FWIP FWIP FWIP FWIP

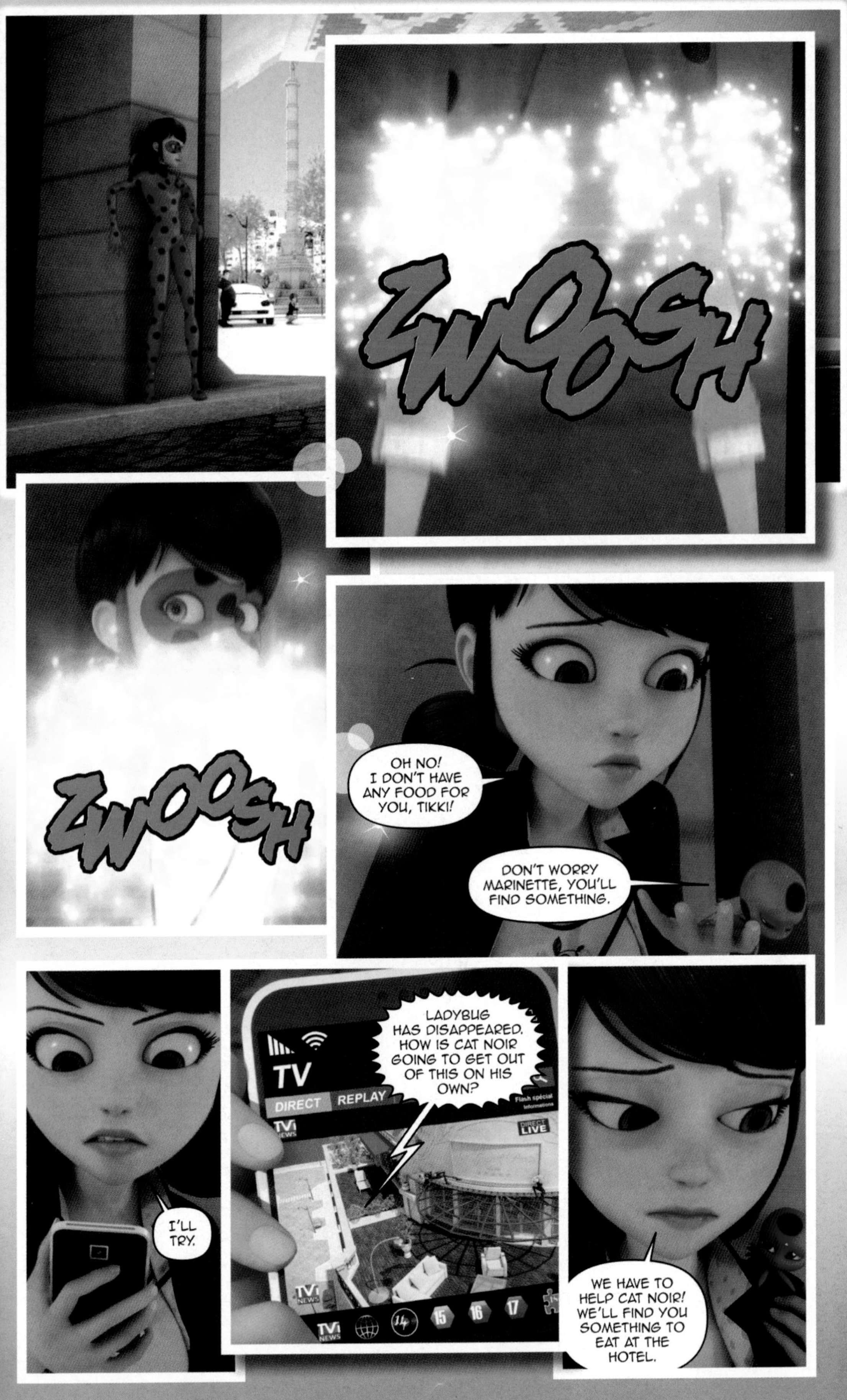
ZWOOSH
ZWOOSH
OH NO! I DON'T HAVE ANY FOOD FOR YOU, TIKKI!
DON'T WORRY MARINETTE, YOU'LL FIND SOMETHING.
I'LL TRY.
LADYBUG HAS DISAPPEARED. HOW IS CAT NOIR GOING TO GET OUT OF THIS ON HIS OWN?
TV
DIRECT
REPLAY
WE HAVE TO HELP CAT NOIR! WE'LL FIND YOU SOMETHING TO EAT AT THE HOTEL.

÷GIGGLE÷

CAT NOIR!

NIBBLE NIBBLE

HURRY UP, TIKKI!

I'M EATING AS FAST AS I CAN!

AREN'T YOU TIRED OF PLAYING SECOND FIDDLE TO LADYBUG?

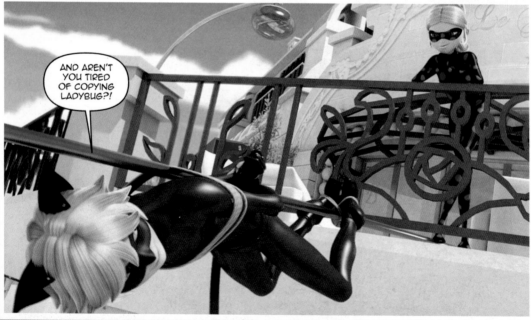

AND AREN'T YOU TIRED OF COPYING LADYBUG?!

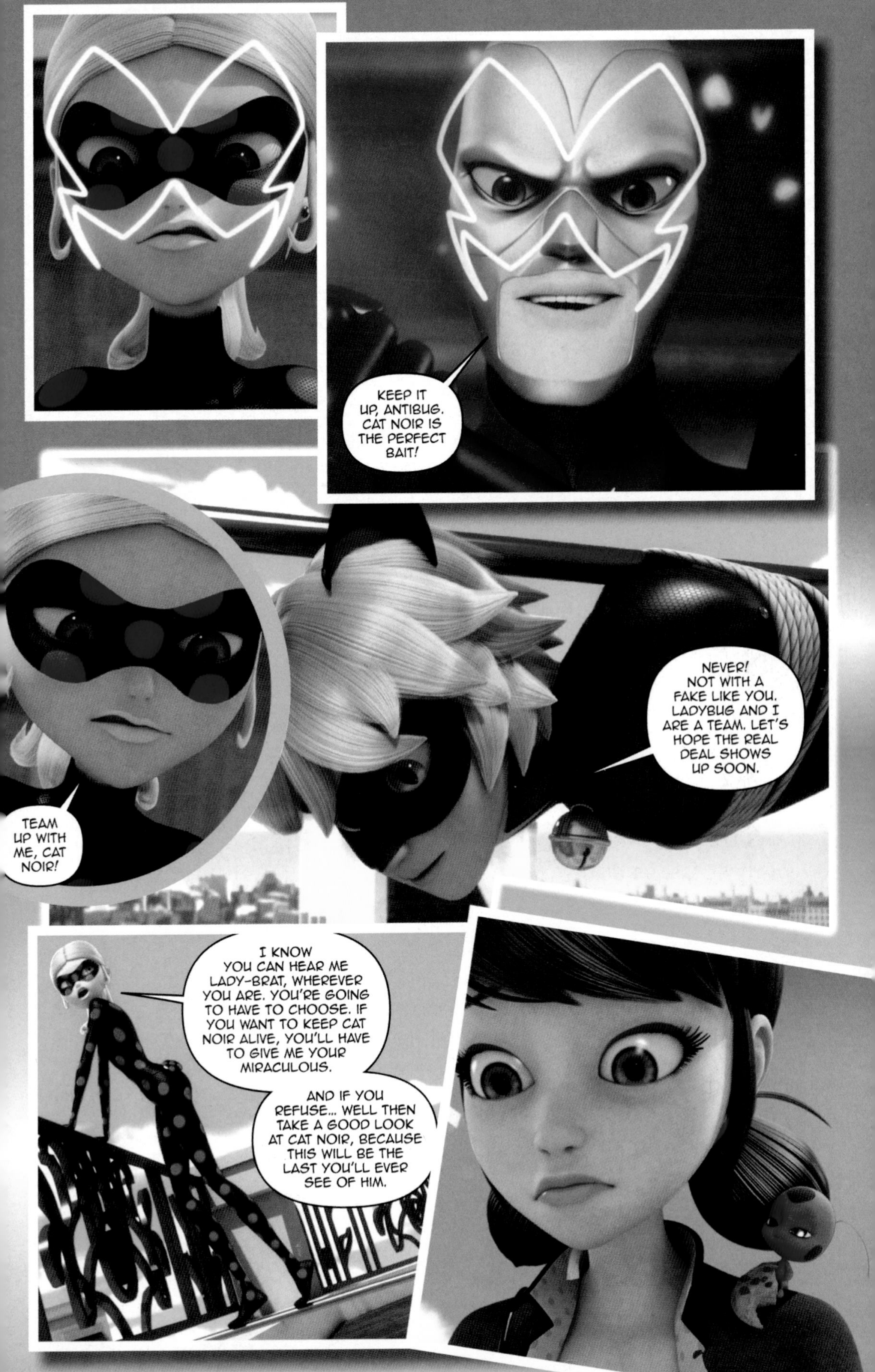
KEEP IT UP, ANTIBUG. CAT NOIR IS THE PERFECT BAIT!
TEAM UP WITH ME, CAT NOIR!
NEVER! NOT WITH A FAKE LIKE YOU. LADYBUG AND I ARE A TEAM. LET'S HOPE THE REAL DEAL SHOWS UP SOON.
I KNOW YOU CAN HEAR ME LADY-BRAT, WHEREVER YOU ARE. YOU'RE GOING TO HAVE TO CHOOSE. IF YOU WANT TO KEEP CAT NOIR ALIVE, YOU'LL HAVE TO GIVE ME YOUR MIRACULOUS.
AND IF YOU REFUSE... WELL THEN TAKE A GOOD LOOK AT CAT NOIR, BECAUSE THIS WILL BE THE LAST YOU'LL EVER SEE OF HIM.

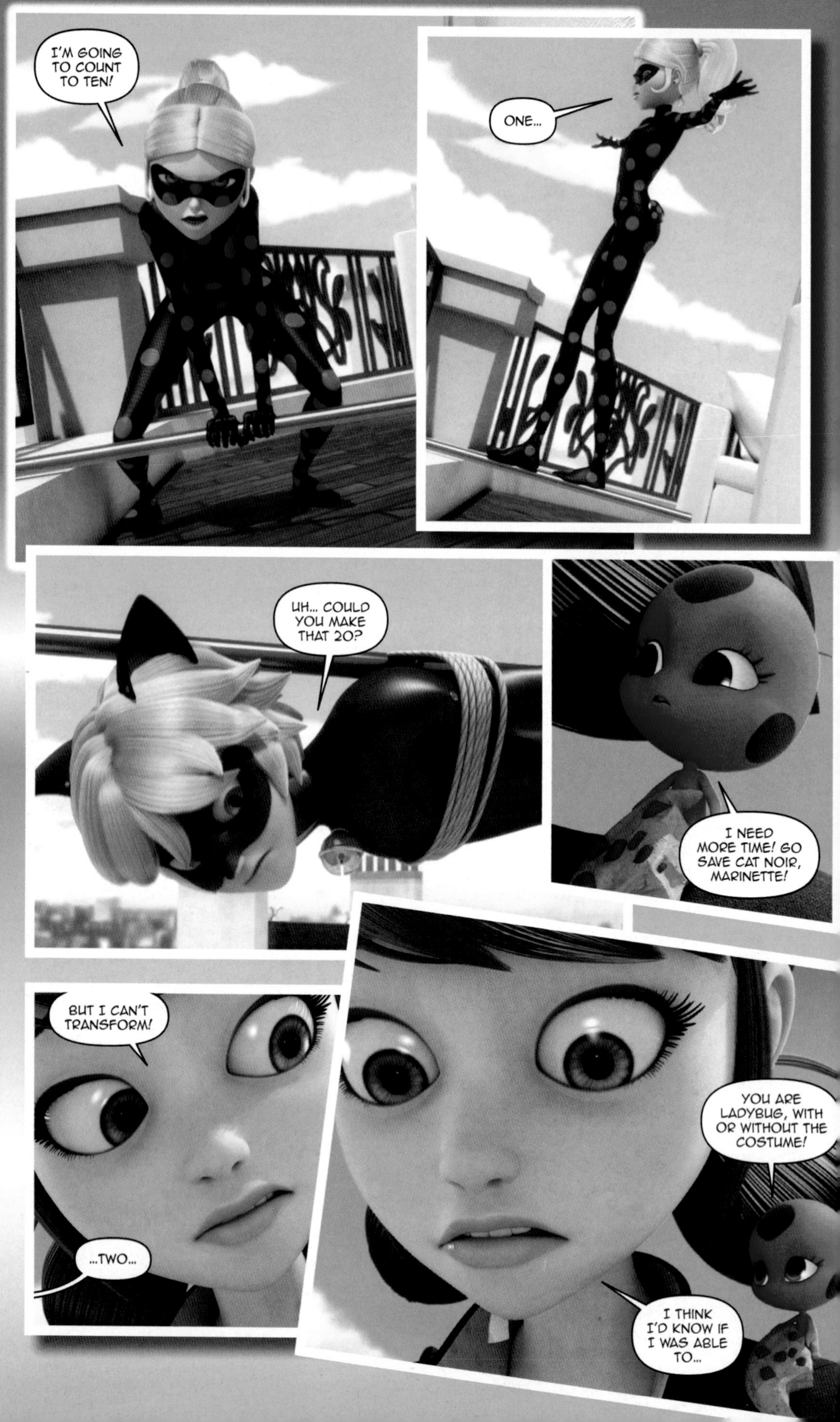
I'M GOING TO COUNT TO TEN!
ONE...
UH... COULD YOU MAKE THAT 20?
I NEED MORE TIME! GO SAVE CAT NOIR, MARINETTE!
BUT I CAN'T TRANSFORM!
...TWO...
YOU ARE LADYBUG, WITH OR WITHOUT THE COSTUME!
I THINK I'D KNOW IF I WAS ABLE TO...

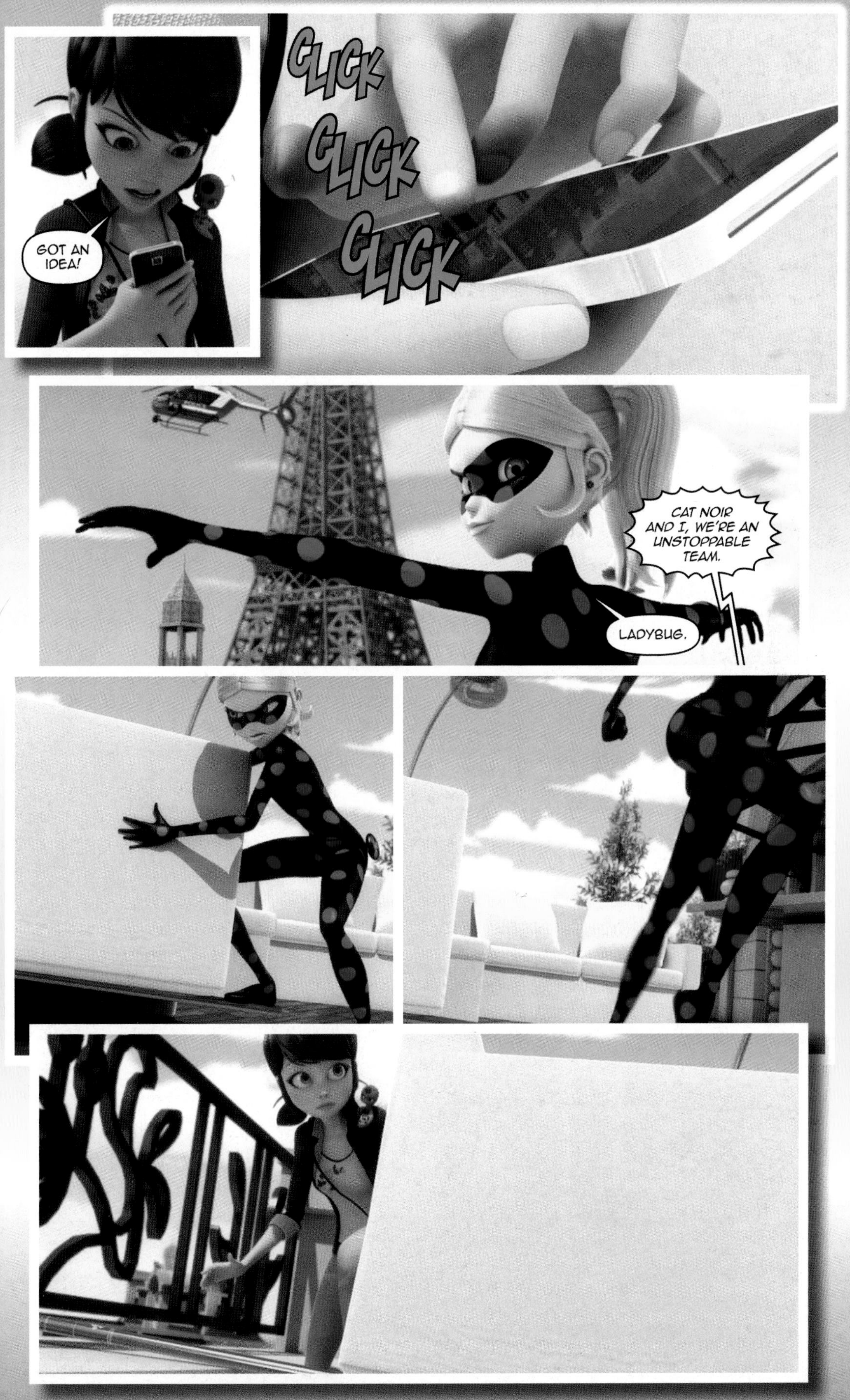

GOT AN IDEA!
CLICK
CLICK
CLICK
CAT NOIR AND I, WE'RE AN UNSTOPPABLE TEAM.
LADYBUG.

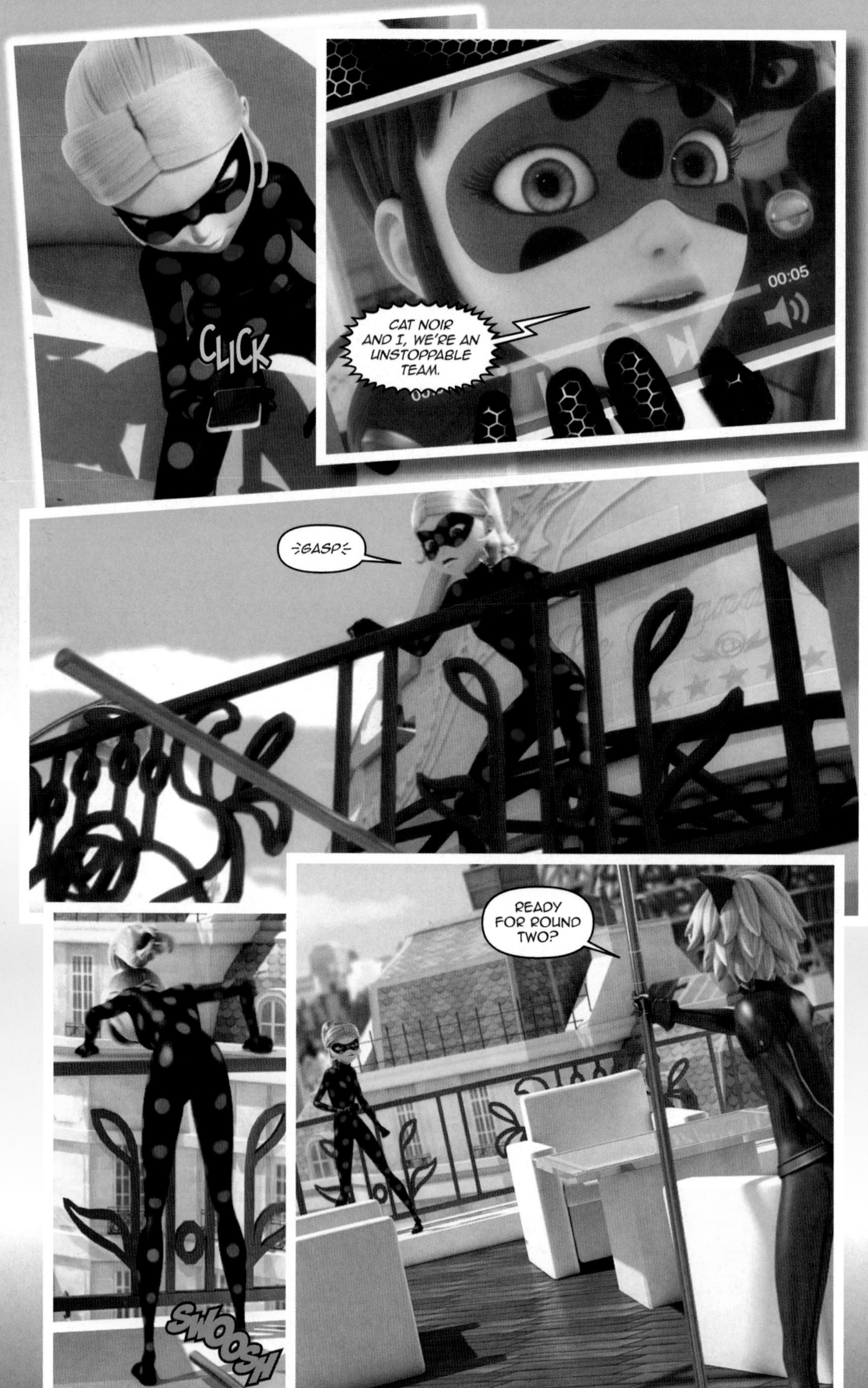
CLICK
00:05
CAT NOIR AND I, WE'RE AN UNSTOPPABLE TEAM.
GASP
SWOOSH
READY FOR ROUND TWO?

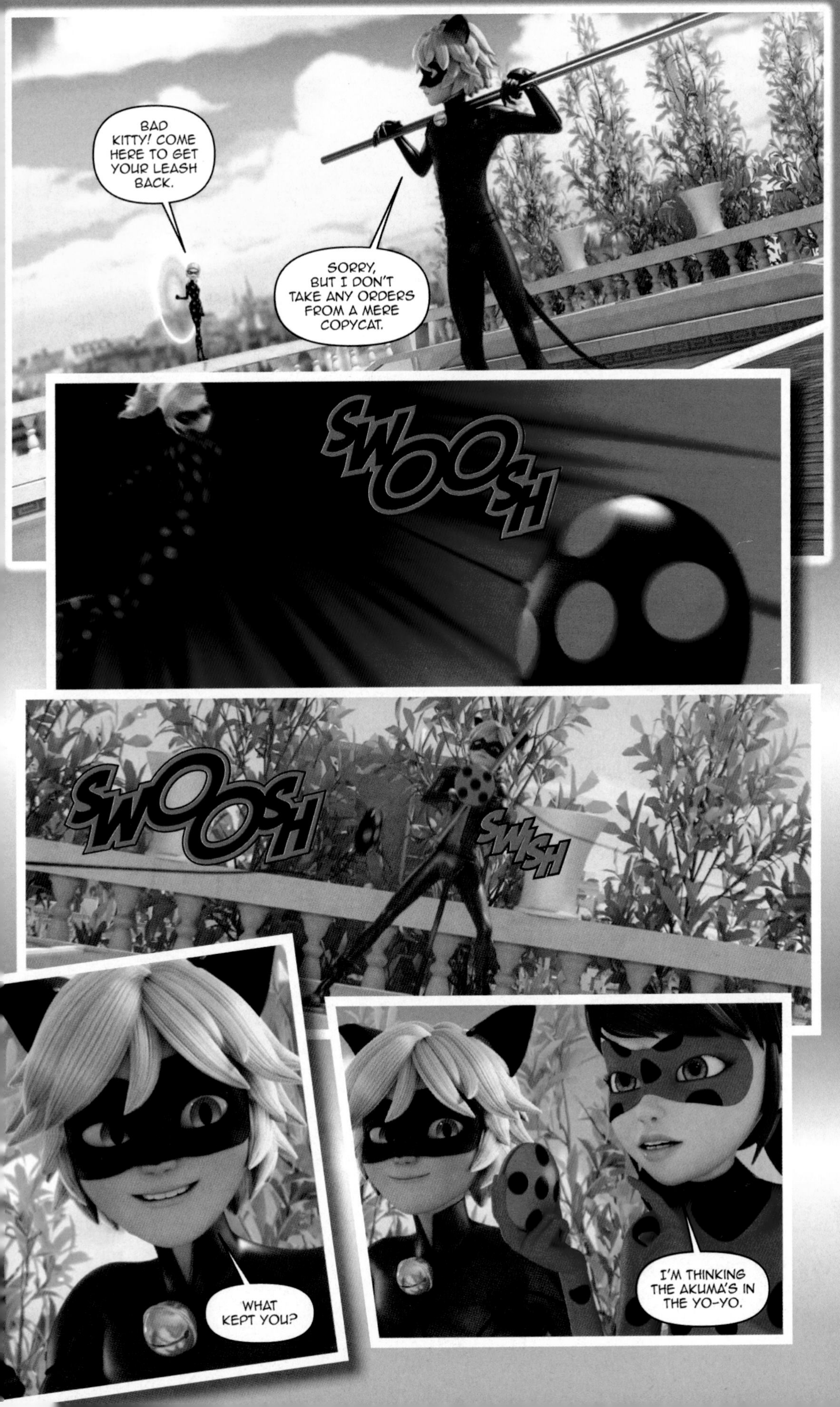
BAD KITTY! COME HERE TO GET YOUR LEASH BACK.
SORRY, BUT I DON'T TAKE ANY ORDERS FROM A MERE COPYCAT.
SWOOSH
SWOOSH
SWISH
WHAT KEPT YOU?
I'M THINKING THE AKUMA'S IN THE YO-YO.

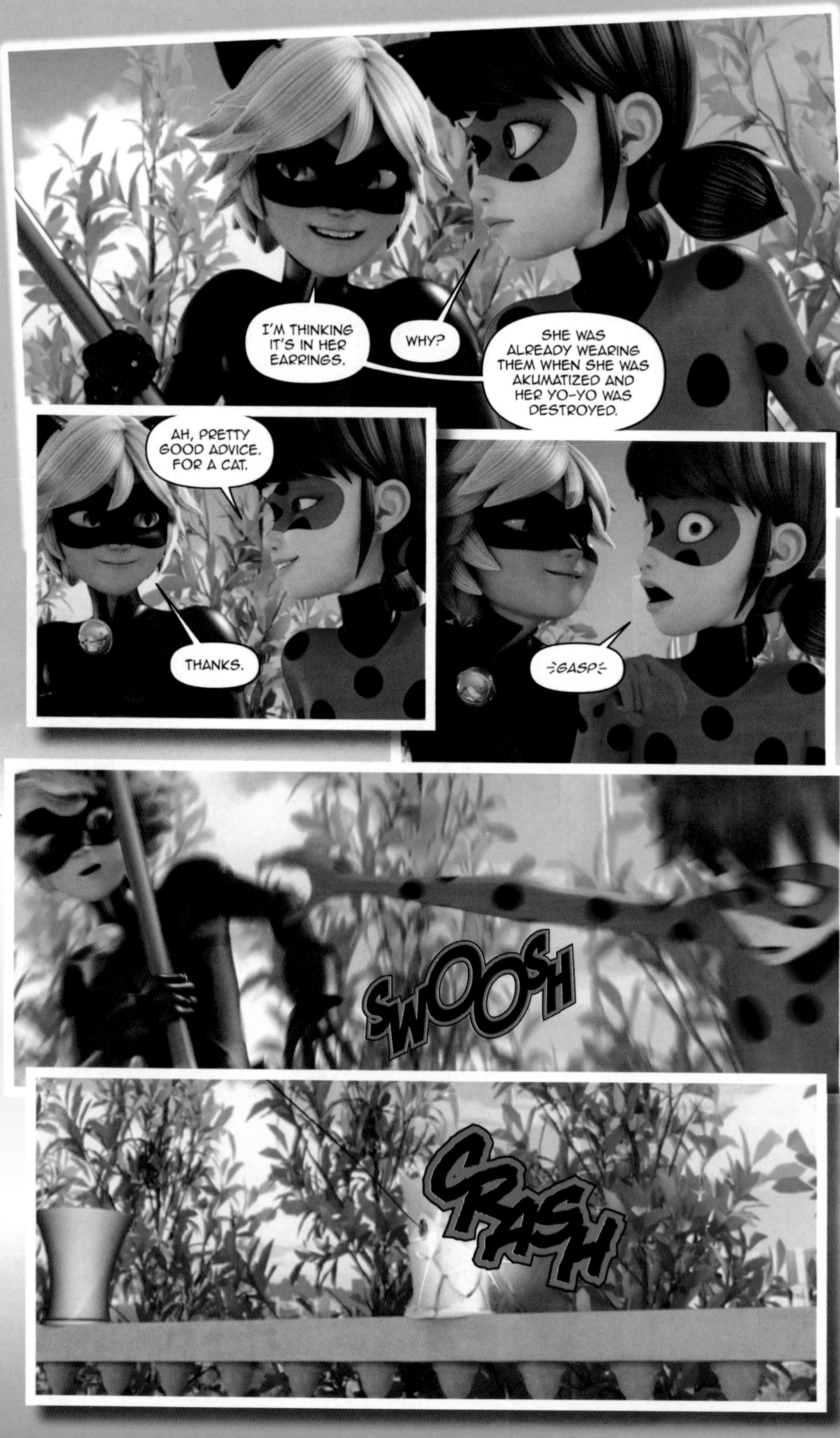
I'M THINKING IT'S IN HER EARRINGS.
WHY?
SHE WAS ALREADY WEARING THEM WHEN SHE WAS AKUMATIZED AND HER YO-YO WAS DESTROYED.
AH, PRETTY GOOD ADVICE. FOR A CAT.
THANKS.
GASP
SWOOSH
CRASH

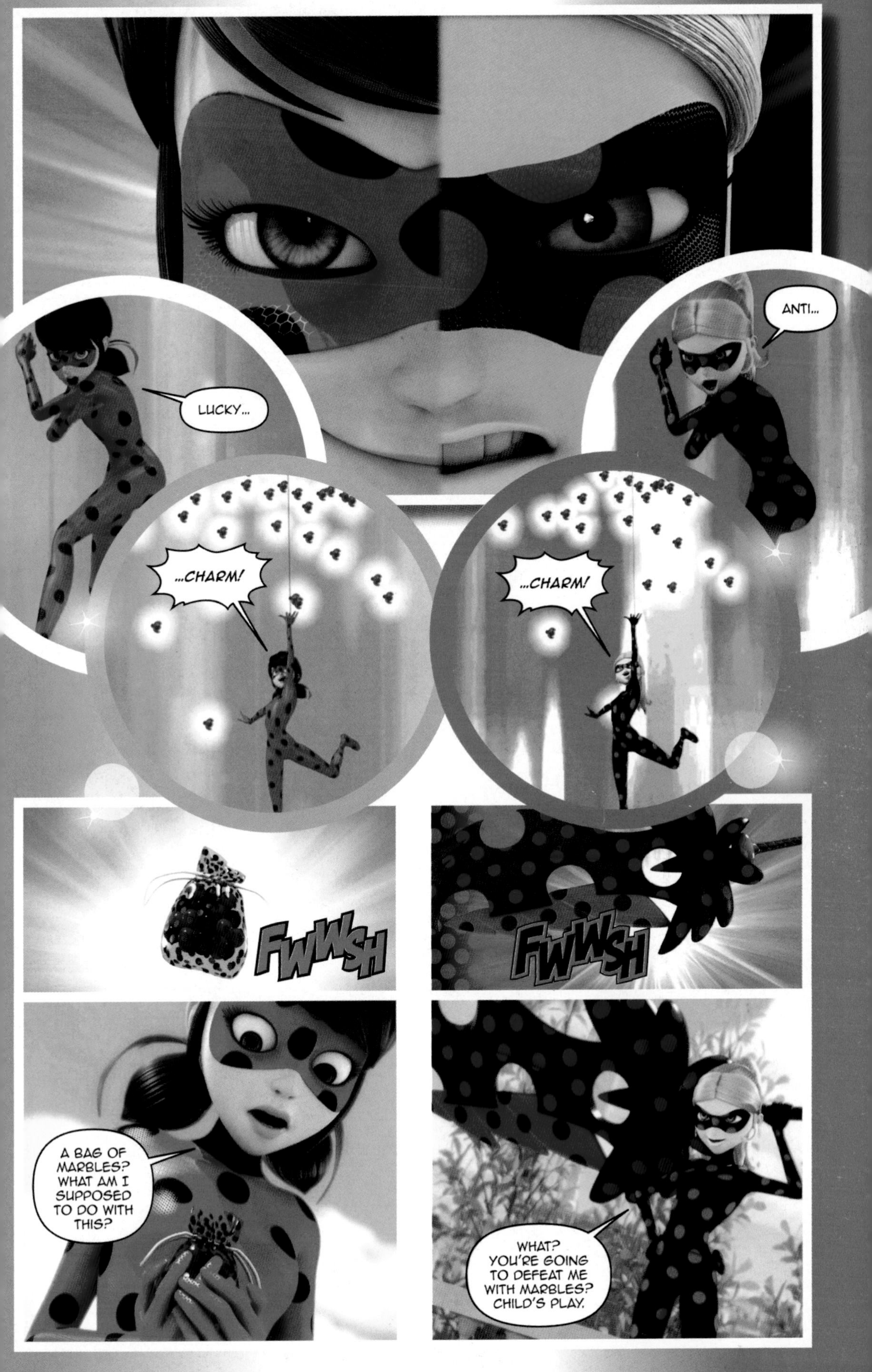
LUCKY...
ANTI...
...CHARM!
...CHARM!
FWWSH
FWWSH
A BAG OF MARBLES? WHAT AM I SUPPOSED TO DO WITH THIS?
WHAT? YOU'RE GOING TO DEFEAT ME WITH MARBLES? CHILD'S PLAY.

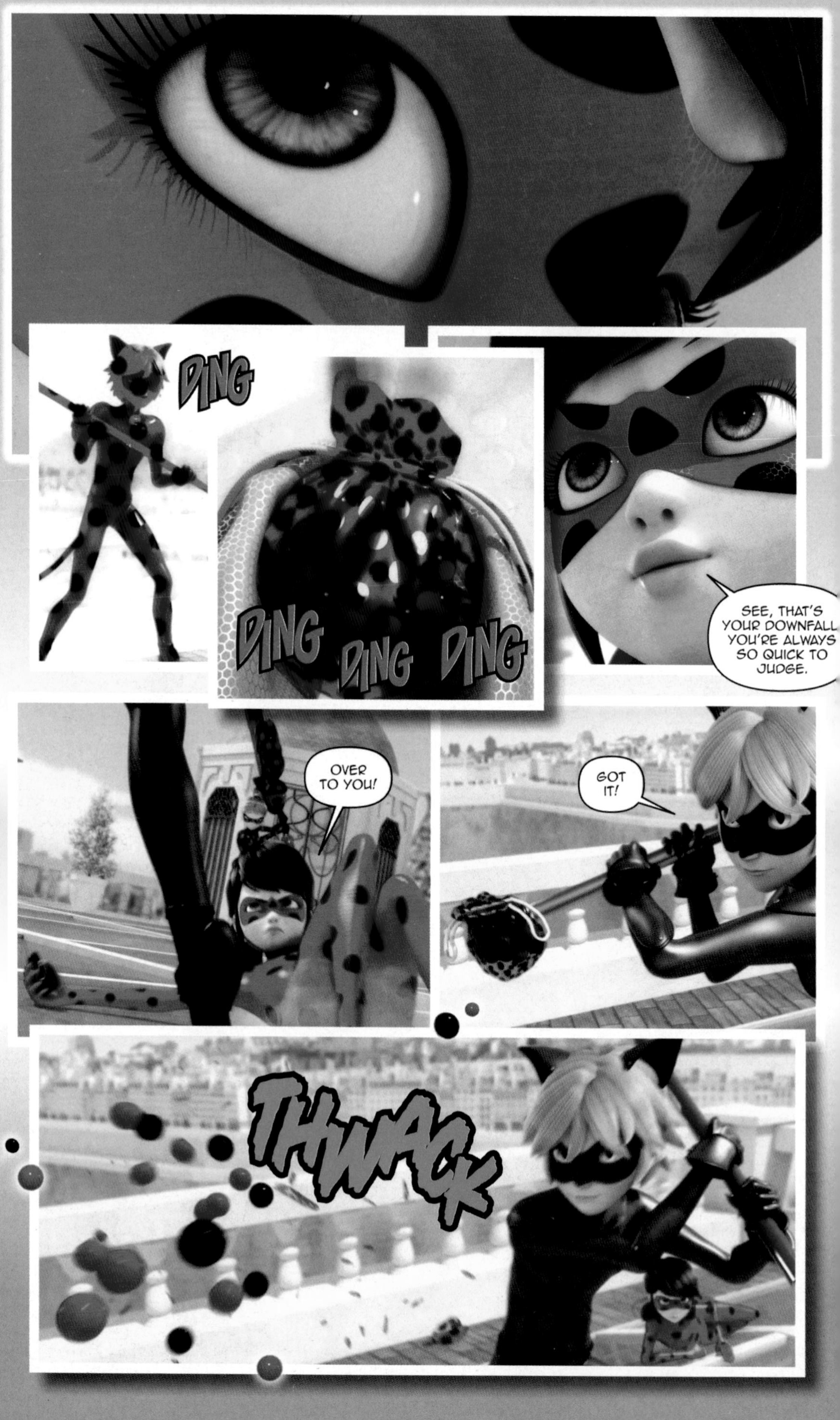
DING
DING DING DING
SEE, THAT'S YOUR DOWNFALL. YOU'RE ALWAYS SO QUICK TO JUDGE.
OVER TO YOU!
GOT IT!
THWACK

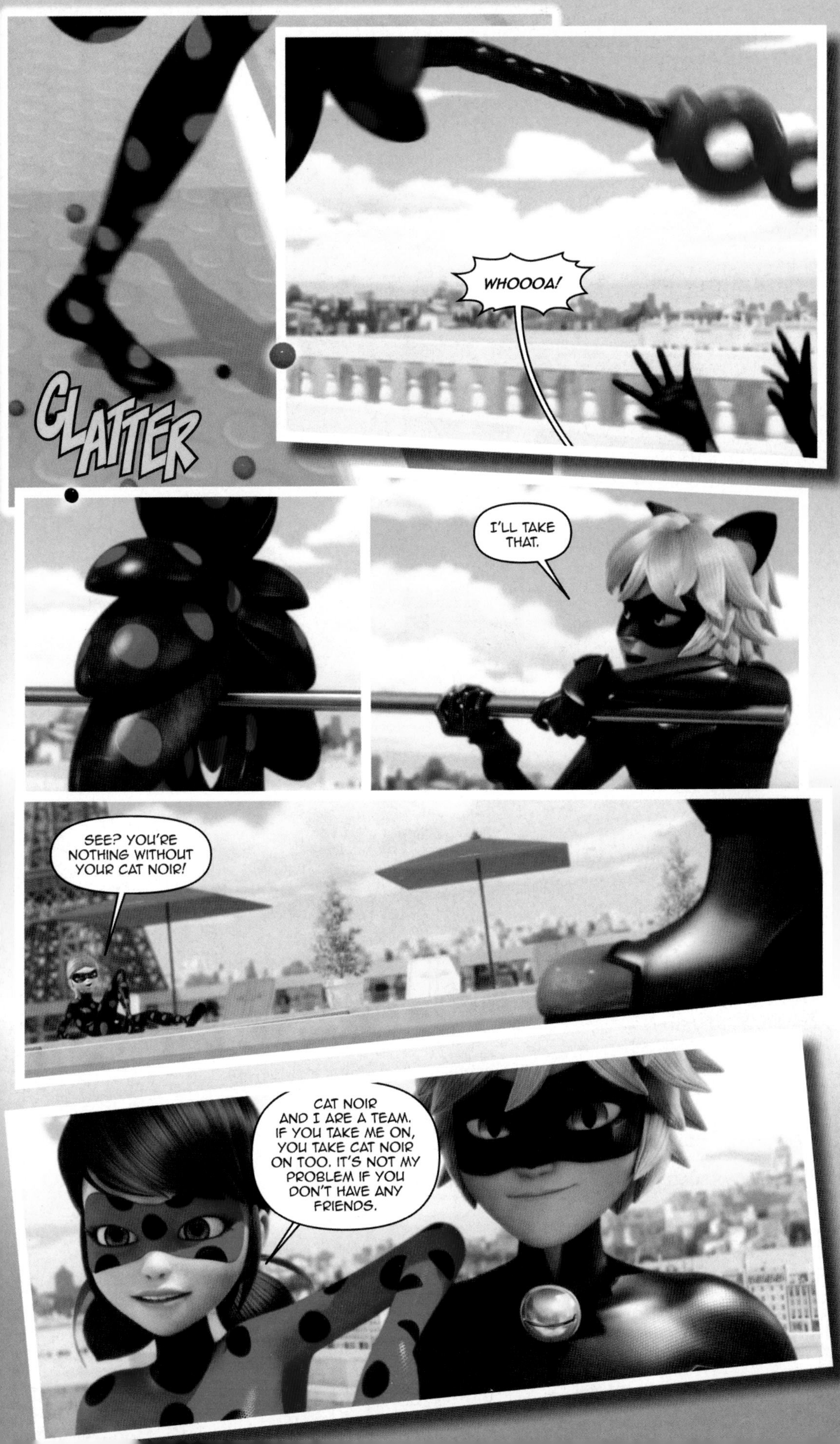

CLATTER
WHOOOA!
I'LL TAKE THAT.
SEE? YOU'RE NOTHING WITHOUT YOUR CAT NOIR!
CAT NOIR AND I ARE A TEAM. IF YOU TAKE ME ON, YOU TAKE CAT NOIR ON TOO. IT'S NOT MY PROBLEM IF YOU DON'T HAVE ANY FRIENDS.

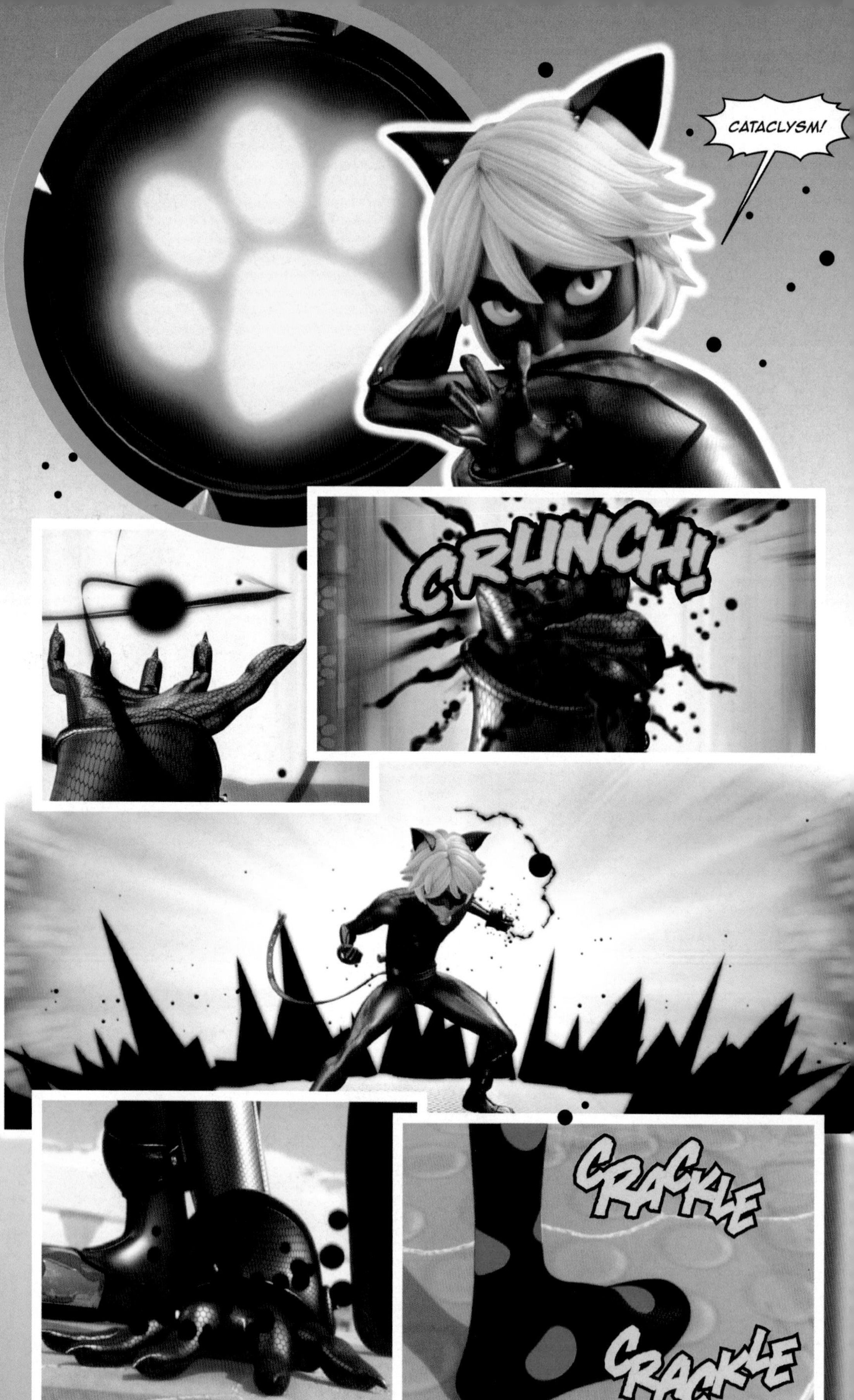
CATACLYSM!
CRUNCH!
CRACKLE
CRACKLE

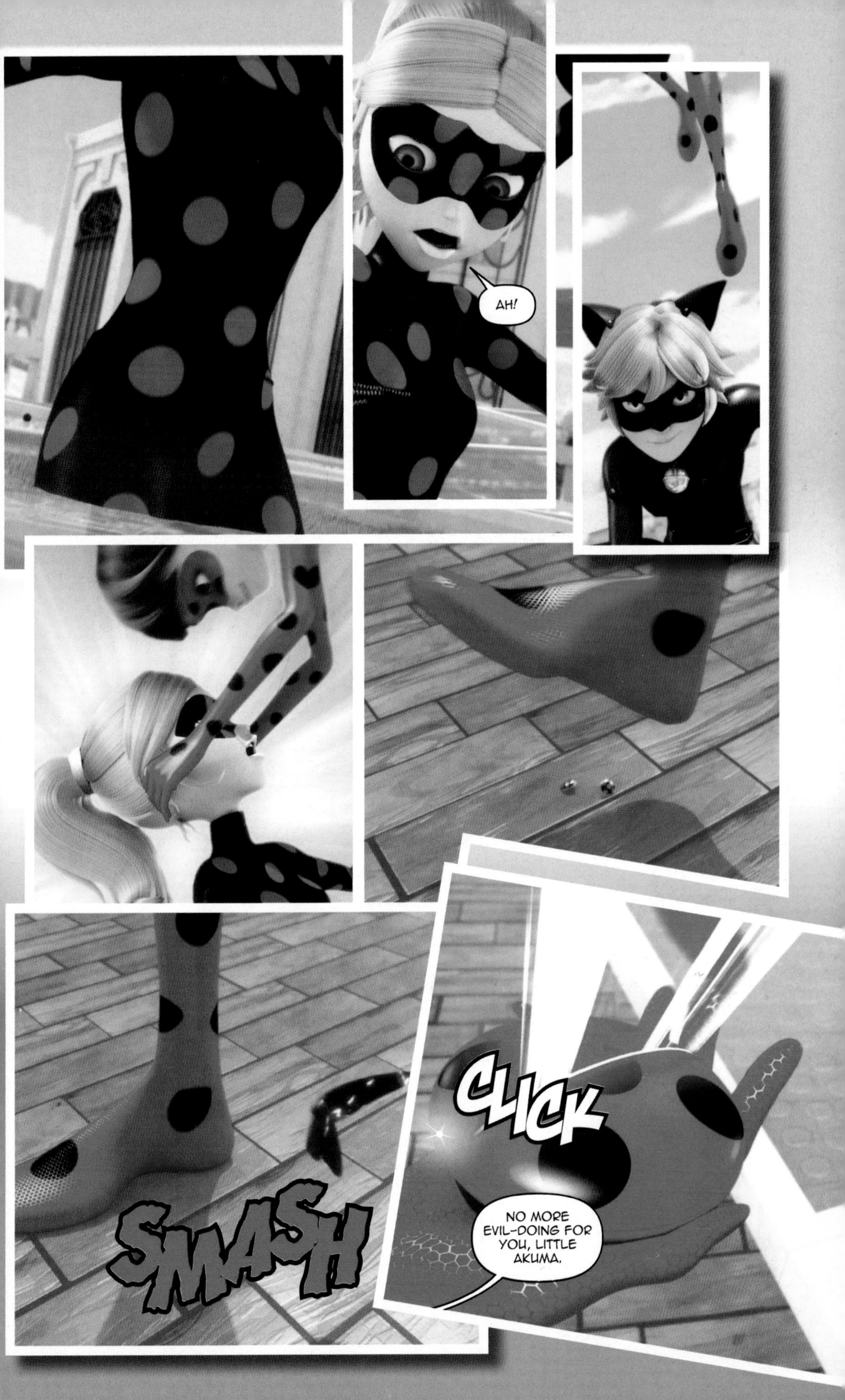
AH!
SMASH
CLICK
NO MORE EVIL-DOING FOR YOU, LITTLE AKUMA.

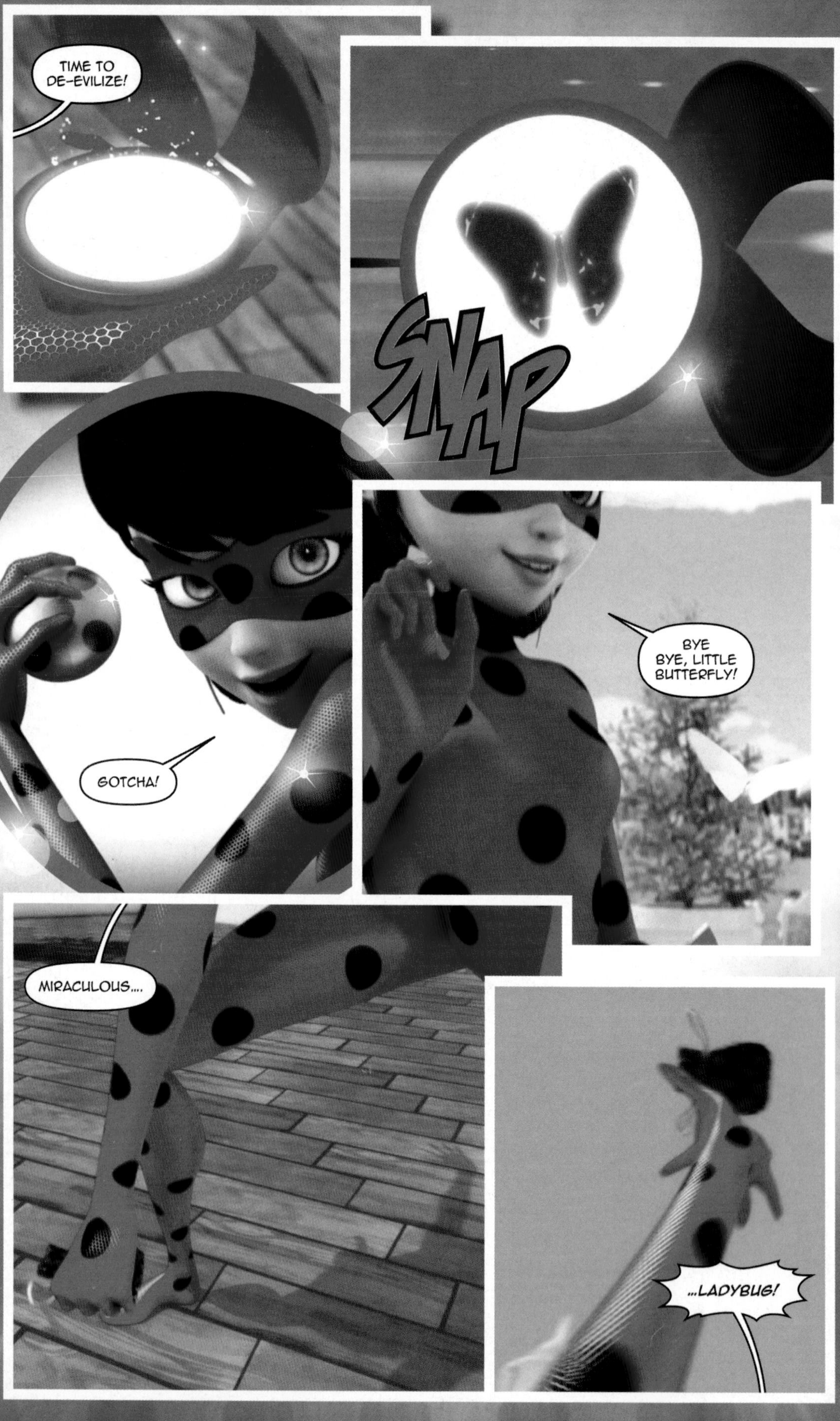
TIME TO DE-EVILIZE!
SNAP
GOTCHA!
BYE BYE, LITTLE BUTTERFLY!
MIRACULOUS....
...LADYBUG!

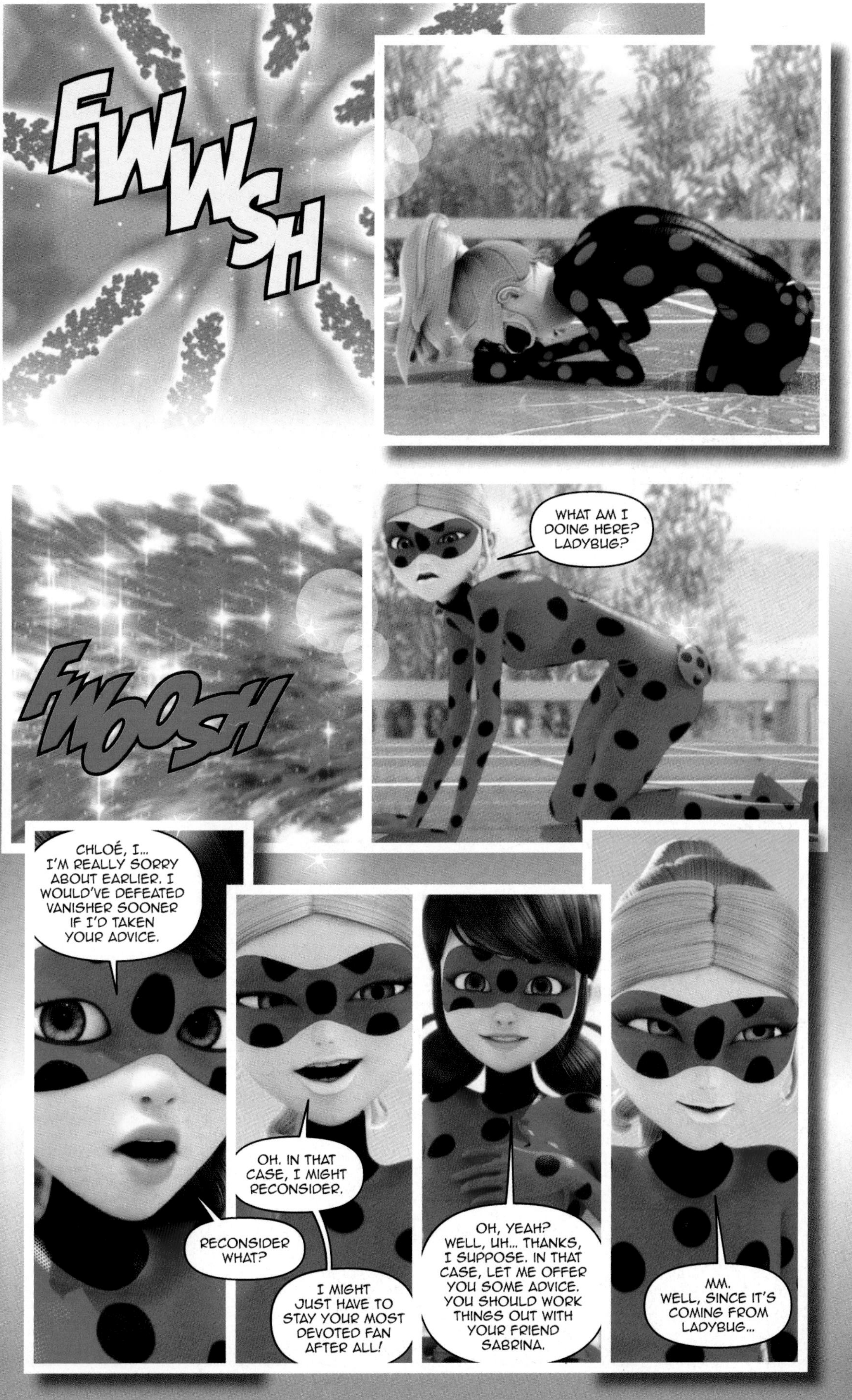
FWWSH
FWOOSH
WHAT AM I DOING HERE? LADYBUG?
CHLOÉ, I... I'M REALLY SORRY ABOUT EARLIER. I WOULD'VE DEFEATED VANISHER SOONER IF I'D TAKEN YOUR ADVICE.
OH. IN THAT CASE, I MIGHT RECONSIDER.
RECONSIDER WHAT?
I MIGHT JUST HAVE TO STAY YOUR MOST DEVOTED FAN AFTER ALL!
OH, YEAH? WELL, UH... THANKS, I SUPPOSE. IN THAT CASE, LET ME OFFER YOU SOME ADVICE. YOU SHOULD WORK THINGS OUT WITH YOUR FRIEND SABRINA.
MM. WELL, SINCE IT'S COMING FROM LADYBUG...

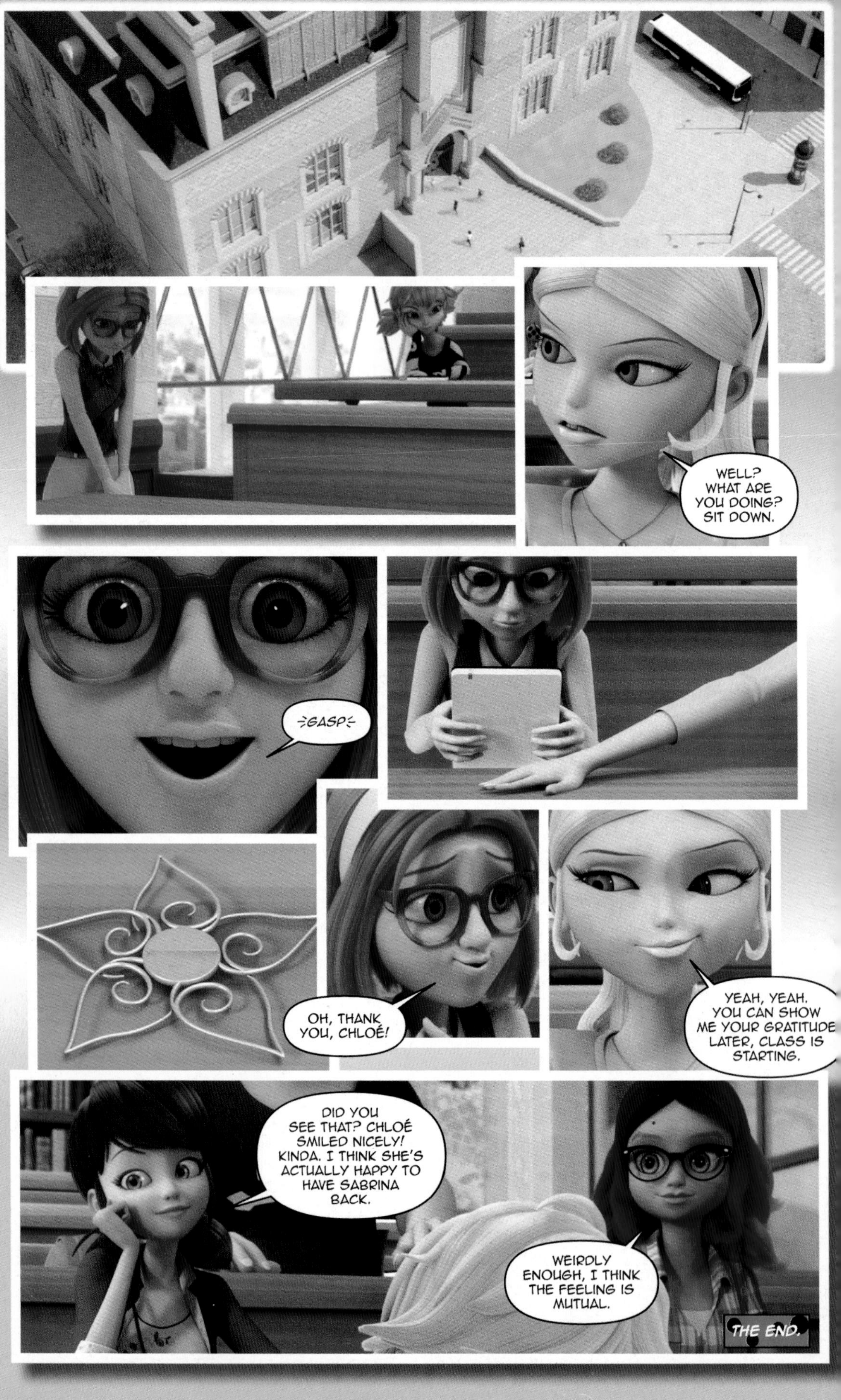
WELL? WHAT ARE YOU DOING? SIT DOWN.
GASP
OH, THANK YOU, CHLOÉ!
YEAH, YEAH. YOU CAN SHOW ME YOUR GRATITUDE LATER, CLASS IS STARTING.
DID YOU SEE THAT? CHLOÉ SMILED NICELY! KINDA. I THINK SHE'S ACTUALLY HAPPY TO HAVE SABRINA BACK.
WEIRDLY ENOUGH, I THINK THE FEELING IS MUTUAL.
THE END.

Volpina

Created by: Thomas Astruc
Comics adaptation by: Nicole D'Andria
Written by: Matthieu Choquet &
Léonie de Rudder
Art arranged by: Cheryl Black
Lettered by: Justin Birch

Bryan Seaton: Publisher/CEO
Shawn Gabborin: Editor In Chief
Jason Martin: Publisher-Danger Zone
Nicole D'Andria: Marketing Director/Editor
Danielle Davison: Executive Administrator
Chad Cicconi: Akumatized
Shawn Pryor: President of Creator Relations

YES, I'M BUSY. I WAS RIGHT IN THE MIDDLE OF SOMETHING VERY IMPORTANT. WHAT DO YOU WANT?

WHAT?!

THIS IS UNACCEPTABLE! THE SAMPLE GARMENT DOESN'T MATCH AT ALL!

ALL YOU HAD TO DO WAS FOLLOW A PATTERN.

IMBECILES!

ZAG

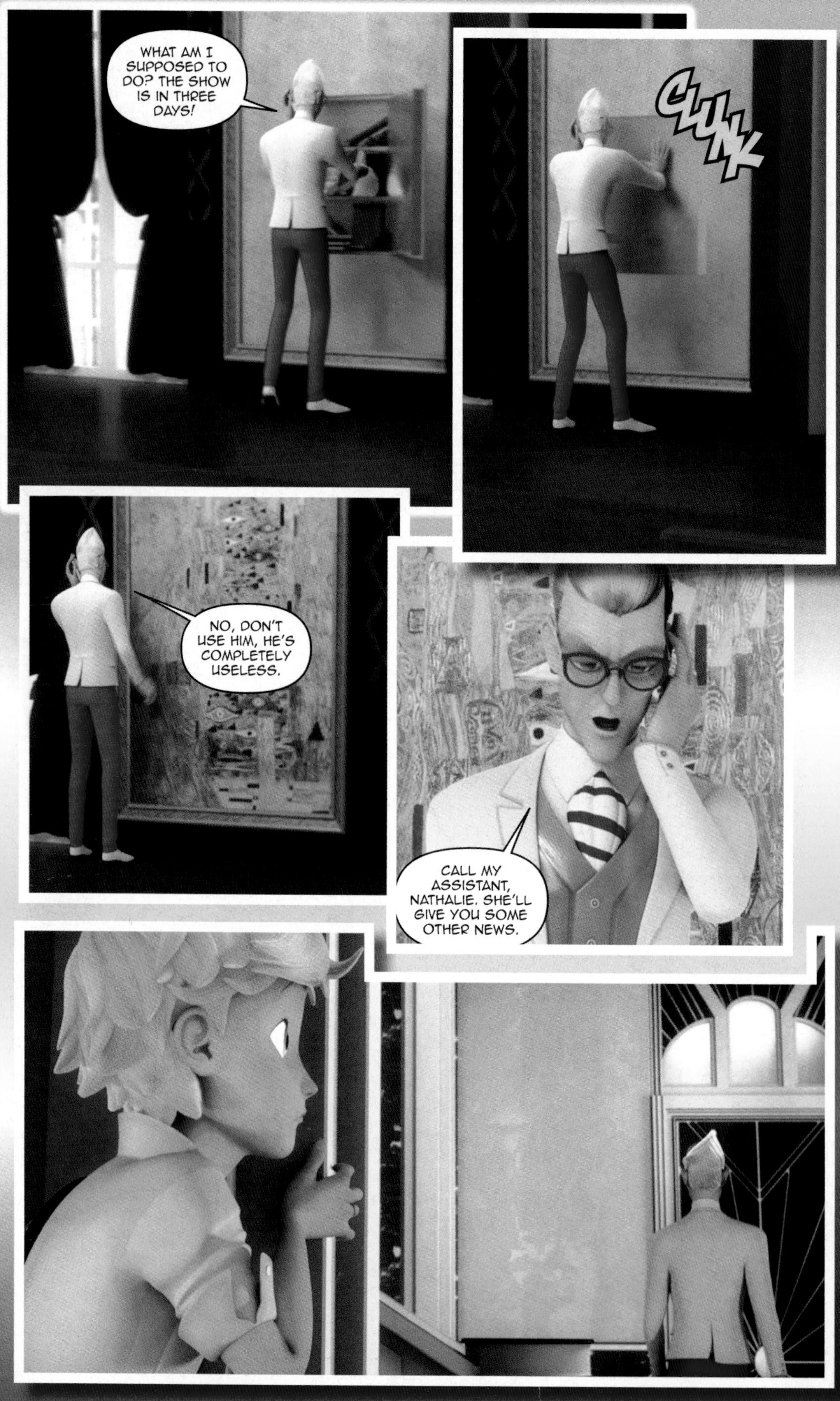
WHAT AM I SUPPOSED TO DO? THE SHOW IS IN THREE DAYS!
CLUNK
NO, DON'T USE HIM, HE'S COMPLETELY USELESS.
CALL MY ASSISTANT, NATHALIE. SHE'LL GIVE YOU SOME OTHER NEWS.

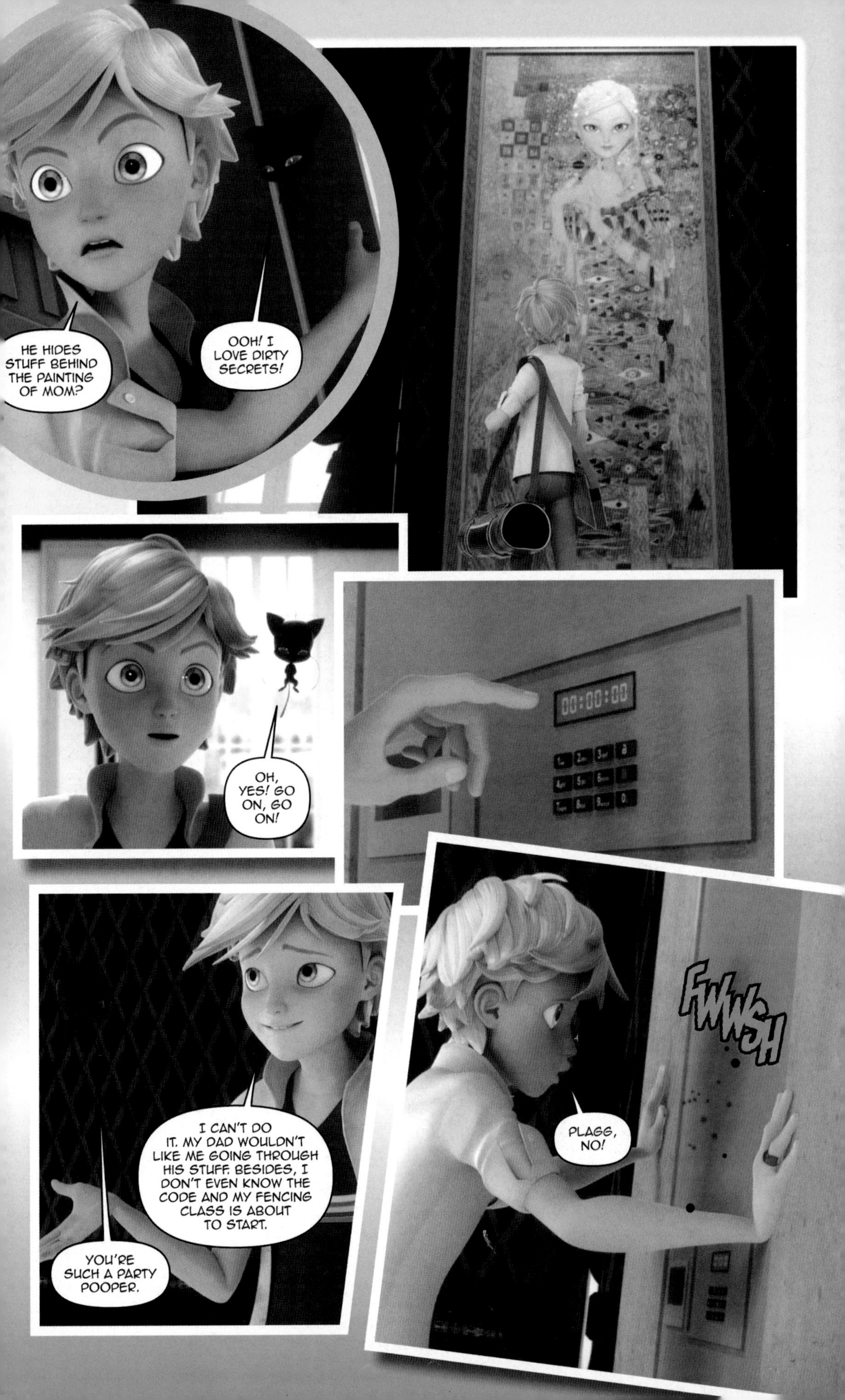
HE HIDES STUFF BEHIND THE PAINTING OF MOM?
OOH! I LOVE DIRTY SECRETS!
OH, YES! GO ON, GO ON!
00:00:00
I CAN'T DO IT. MY DAD WOULDN'T LIKE ME GOING THROUGH HIS STUFF. BESIDES, I DON'T EVEN KNOW THE CODE AND MY FENCING CLASS IS ABOUT TO START.
YOU'RE SUCH A PARTY POOPER.
FWWSH
PLAGG, NO!

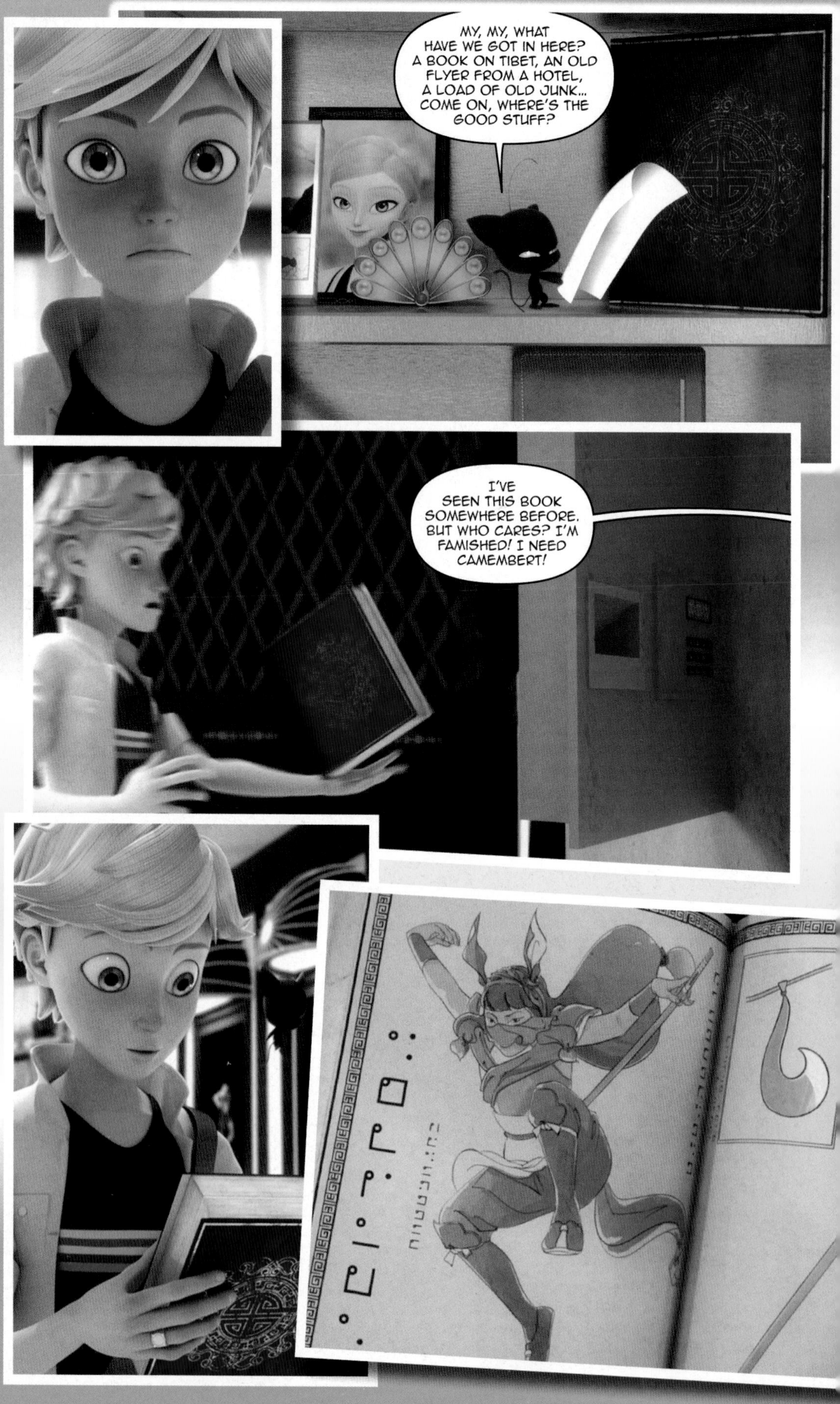
MY, MY, WHAT HAVE WE GOT IN HERE? A BOOK ON TIBET, AN OLD FLYER FROM A HOTEL, A LOAD OF OLD JUNK... COME ON, WHERE'S THE GOOD STUFF?
I'VE SEEN THIS BOOK SOMEWHERE BEFORE. BUT WHO CARES? I'M FAMISHED! I NEED CAMEMBERT!

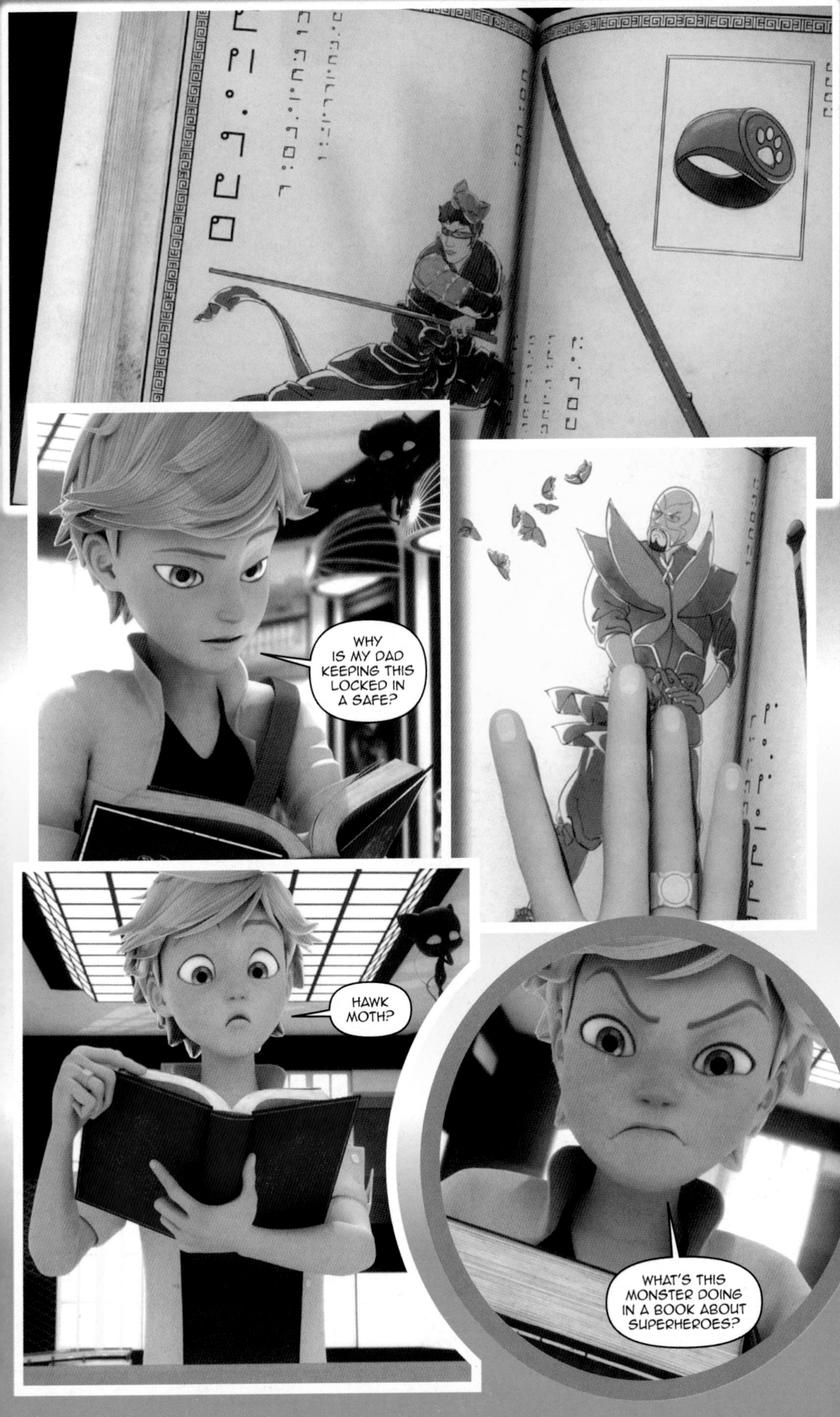
WHY IS MY DAD KEEPING THIS LOCKED IN A SAFE?
HAWK MOTH?
WHAT'S THIS MONSTER DOING IN A BOOK ABOUT SUPERHEROES?

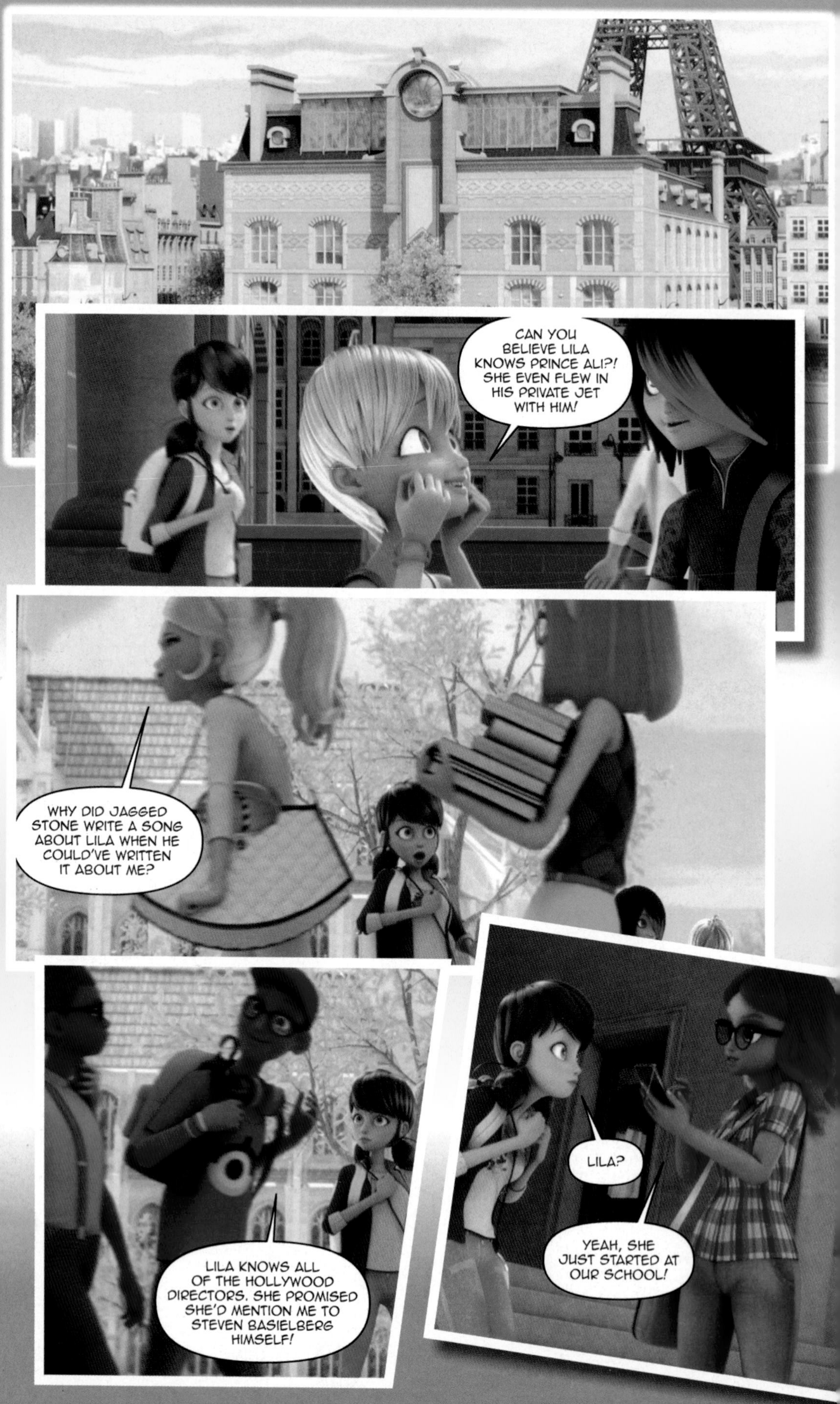
CAN YOU BELIEVE LILA KNOWS PRINCE ALI?! SHE EVEN FLEW IN HIS PRIVATE JET WITH HIM!
WHY DID JAGGED STONE WRITE A SONG ABOUT LILA WHEN HE COULD'VE WRITTEN IT ABOUT ME?
LILA KNOWS ALL OF THE HOLLYWOOD DIRECTORS. SHE PROMISED SHE'D MENTION ME TO STEVEN BASIELBERG HIMSELF!
LILA?
YEAH, SHE JUST STARTED AT OUR SCHOOL!

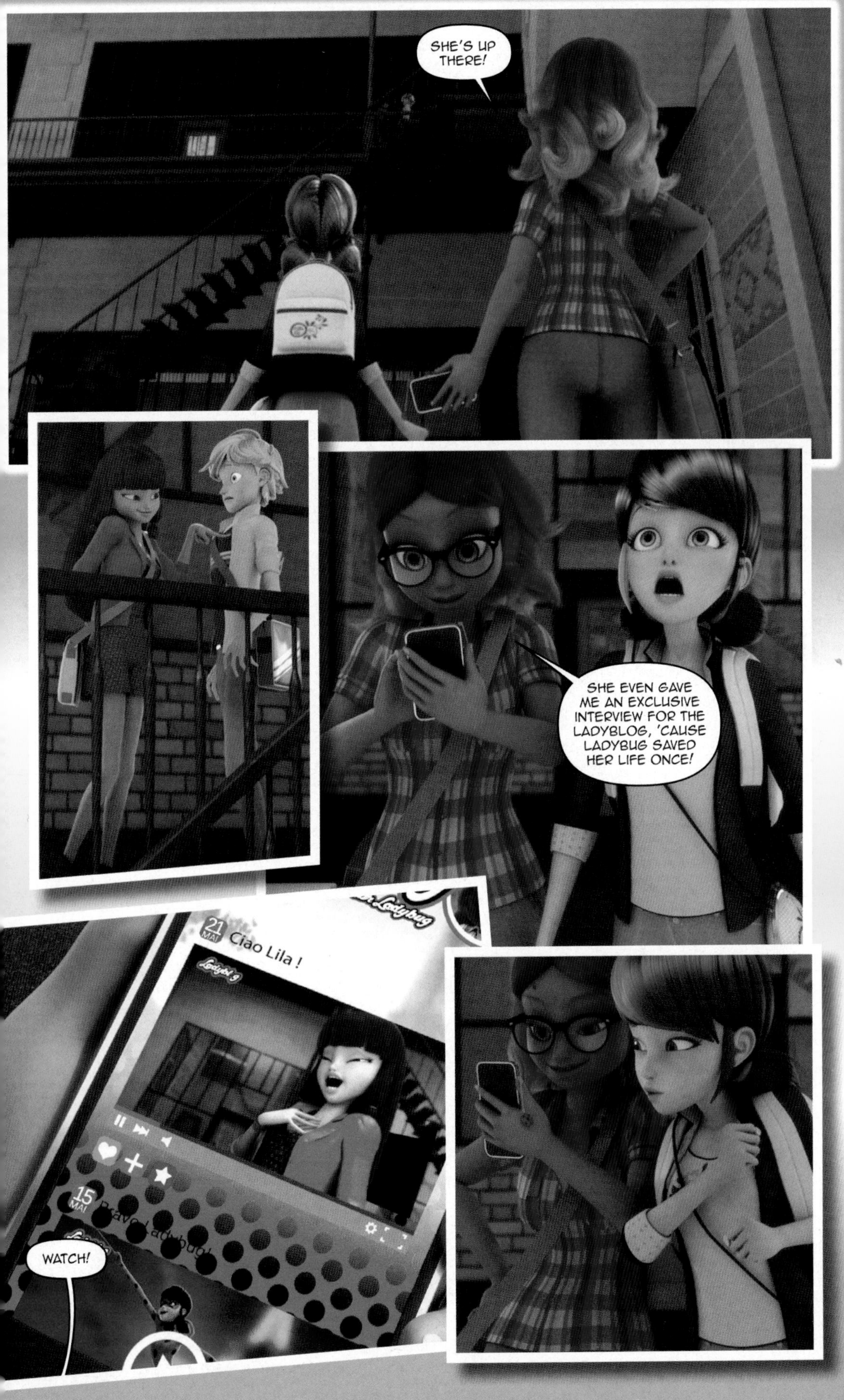
SHE'S UP THERE!
SHE EVEN GAVE ME AN EXCLUSIVE INTERVIEW FOR THE LADYBLOG, 'CAUSE LADYBUG SAVED HER LIFE ONCE!
21 MAI Ciao Lila !
WATCH!

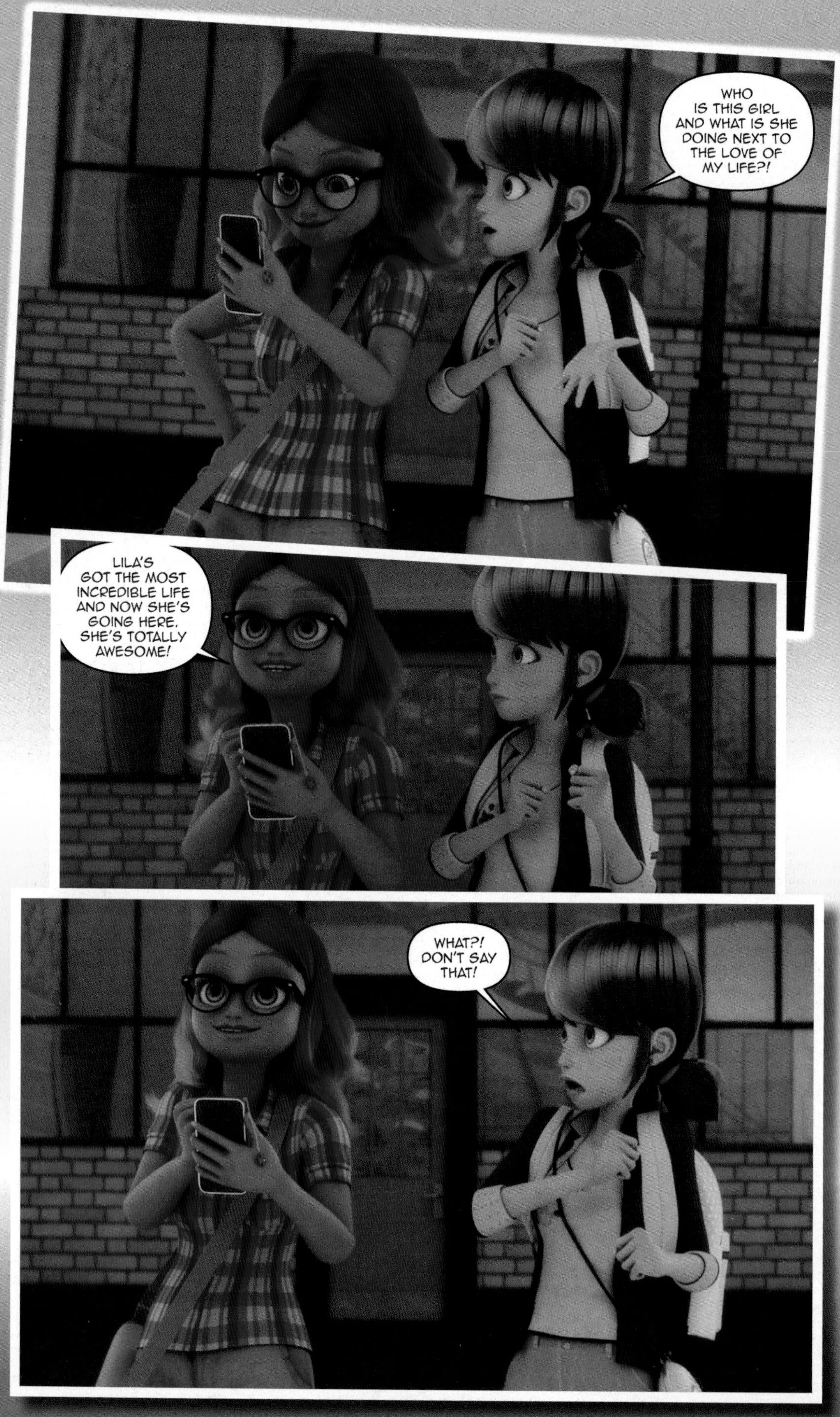
WHO IS THIS GIRL AND WHAT IS SHE DOING NEXT TO THE LOVE OF MY LIFE?!
LILA'S GOT THE MOST INCREDIBLE LIFE AND NOW SHE'S GOING HERE. SHE'S TOTALLY AWESOME!
WHAT?! DON'T SAY THAT!

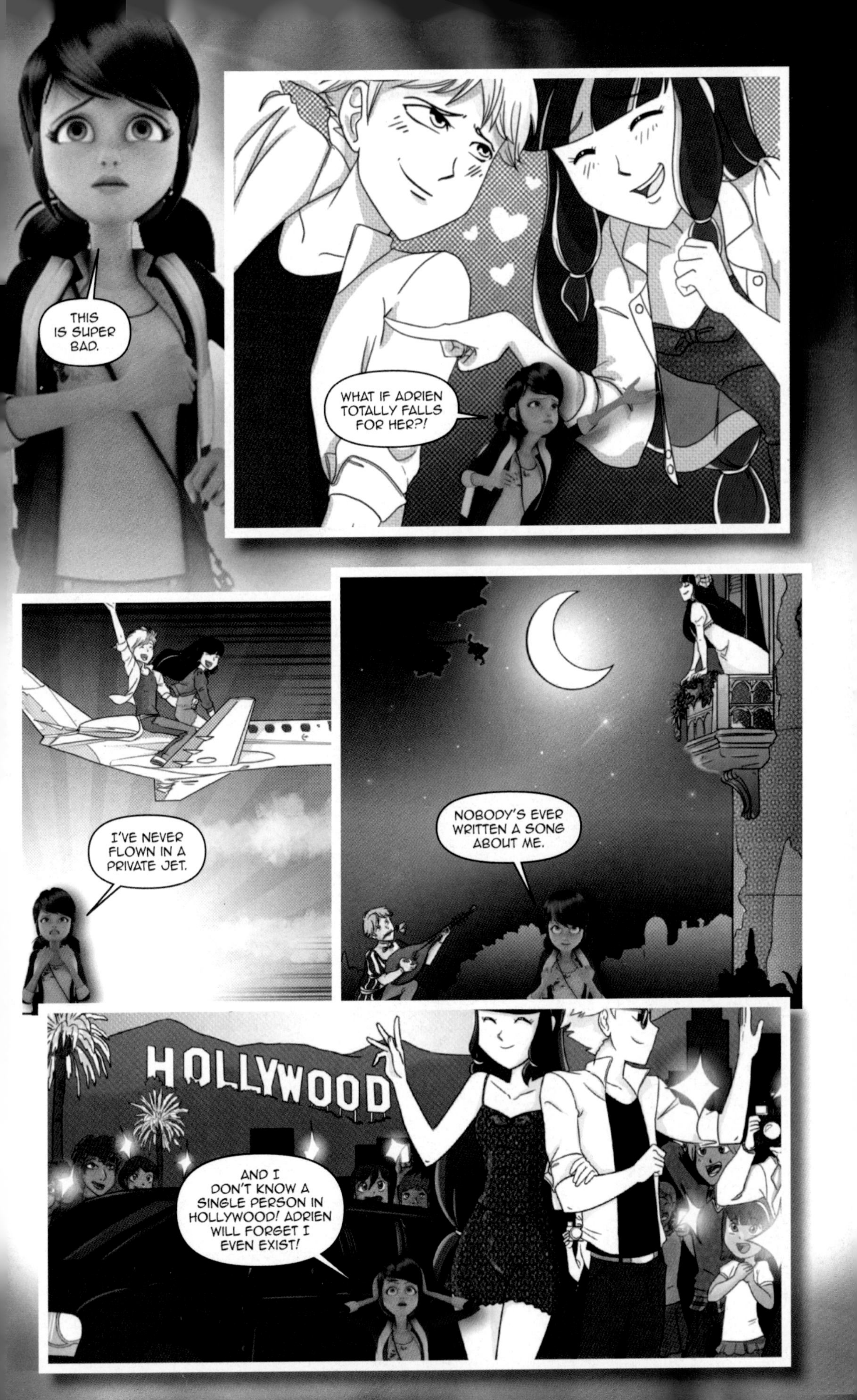
THIS IS SUPER BAD.
WHAT IF ADRIEN TOTALLY FALLS FOR HER?!
I'VE NEVER FLOWN IN A PRIVATE JET.
NOBODY'S EVER WRITTEN A SONG ABOUT ME.
HOLLYWOOD
AND I DON'T KNOW A SINGLE PERSON IN HOLLYWOOD! ADRIEN WILL FORGET I EVEN EXIST!

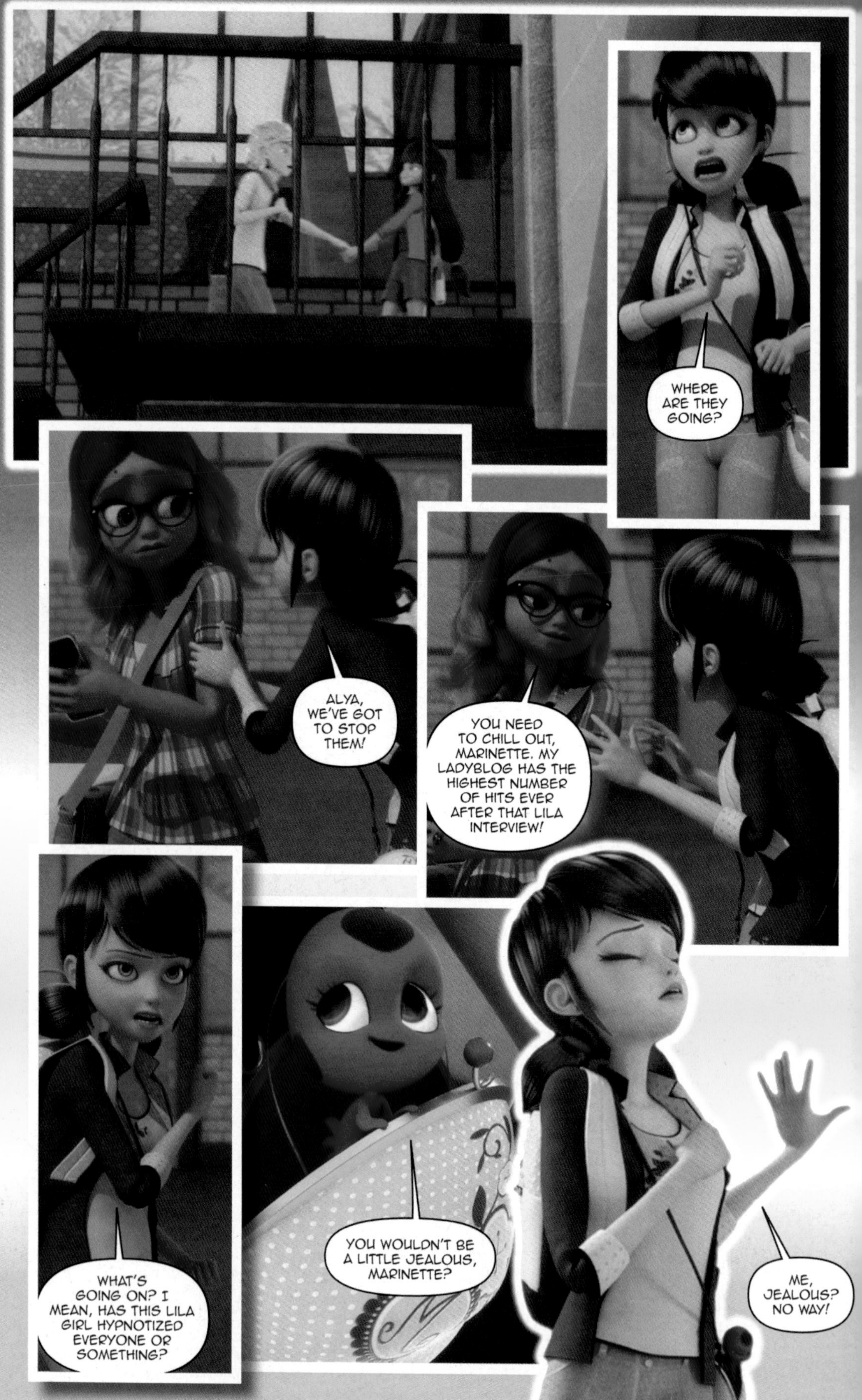
WHERE ARE THEY GOING?
ALYA, WE'VE GOT TO STOP THEM!
YOU NEED TO CHILL OUT, MARINETTE. MY LADYBLOG HAS THE HIGHEST NUMBER OF HITS EVER AFTER THAT LILA INTERVIEW!
WHAT'S GOING ON? I MEAN, HAS THIS LILA GIRL HYPNOTIZED EVERYONE OR SOMETHING?
YOU WOULDN'T BE A LITTLE JEALOUS, MARINETTE?
ME, JEALOUS? NO WAY!

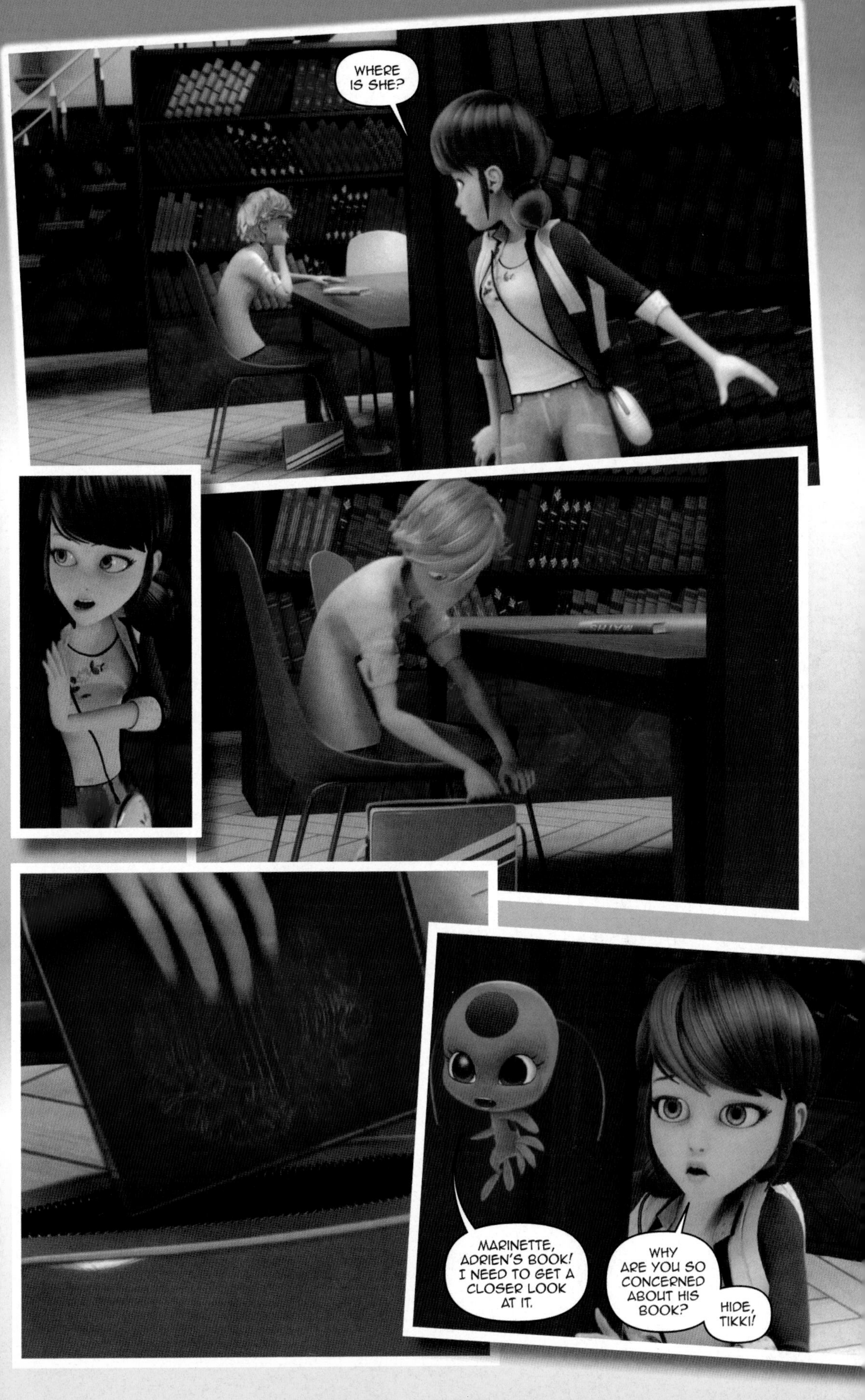
WHERE IS SHE?
MARINETTE, ADRIEN'S BOOK! I NEED TO GET A CLOSER LOOK AT IT.
WHY ARE YOU SO CONCERNED ABOUT HIS BOOK?
HIDE, TIKKI!

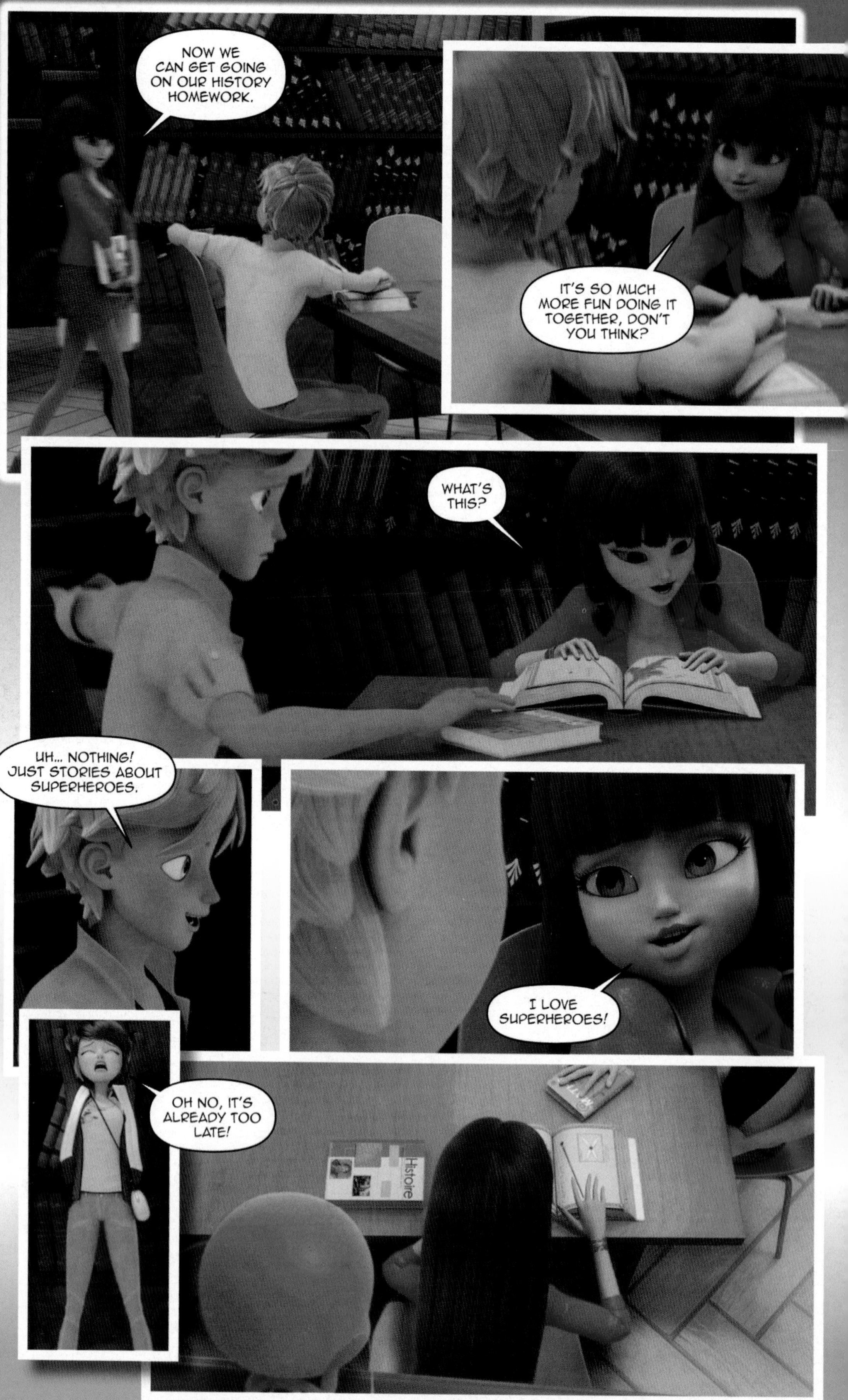
NOW WE CAN GET GOING ON OUR HISTORY HOMEWORK.
IT'S SO MUCH MORE FUN DOING IT TOGETHER, DON'T YOU THINK?
WHAT'S THIS?
UH... NOTHING! JUST STORIES ABOUT SUPERHEROES.
I LOVE SUPERHEROES!
OH NO, IT'S ALREADY TOO LATE!
Histoire

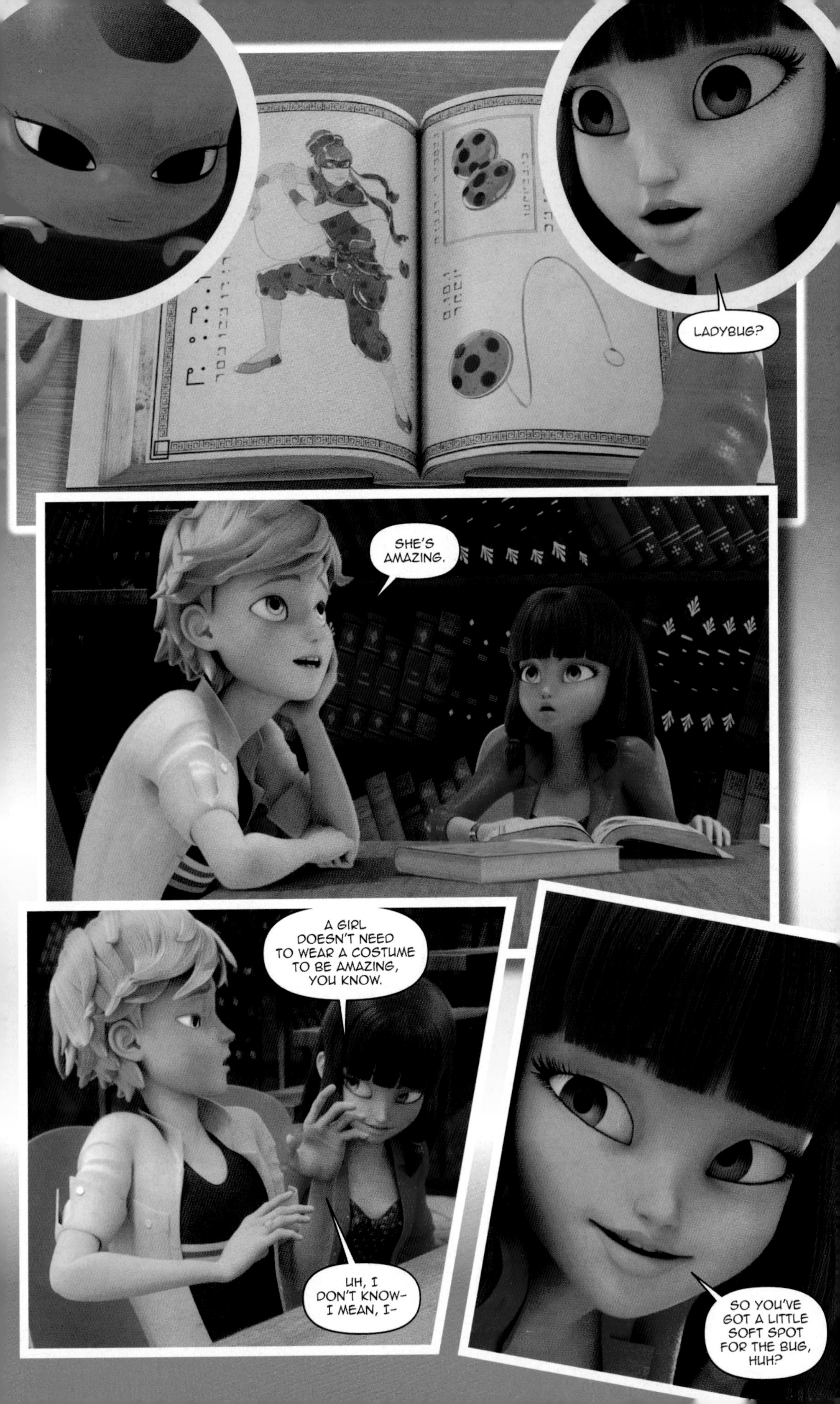
LADYBUG?
SHE'S AMAZING.
A GIRL DOESN'T NEED TO WEAR A COSTUME TO BE AMAZING, YOU KNOW.
UH, I DON'T KNOW- I MEAN, I-
SO YOU'VE GOT A LITTLE SOFT SPOT FOR THE BUG, HUH?

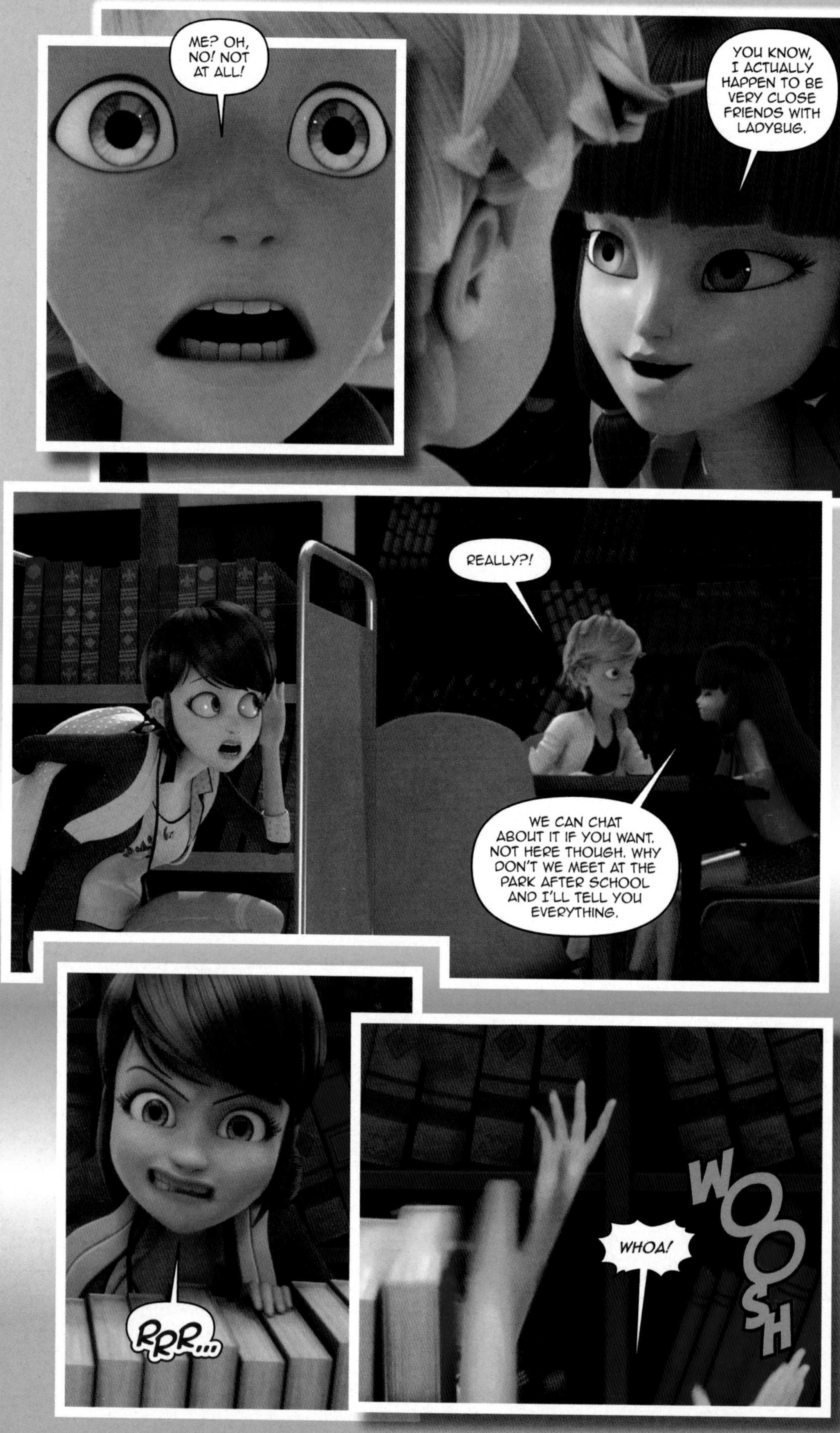
YOU KNOW, I ACTUALLY HAPPEN TO BE VERY CLOSE FRIENDS WITH LADYBUG.
ME? OH, NO! NOT AT ALL!
REALLY?!
WE CAN CHAT ABOUT IT IF YOU WANT. NOT HERE THOUGH. WHY DON'T WE MEET AT THE PARK AFTER SCHOOL AND I'LL TELL YOU EVERYTHING.
RRR...
WHOA!
WOOSH

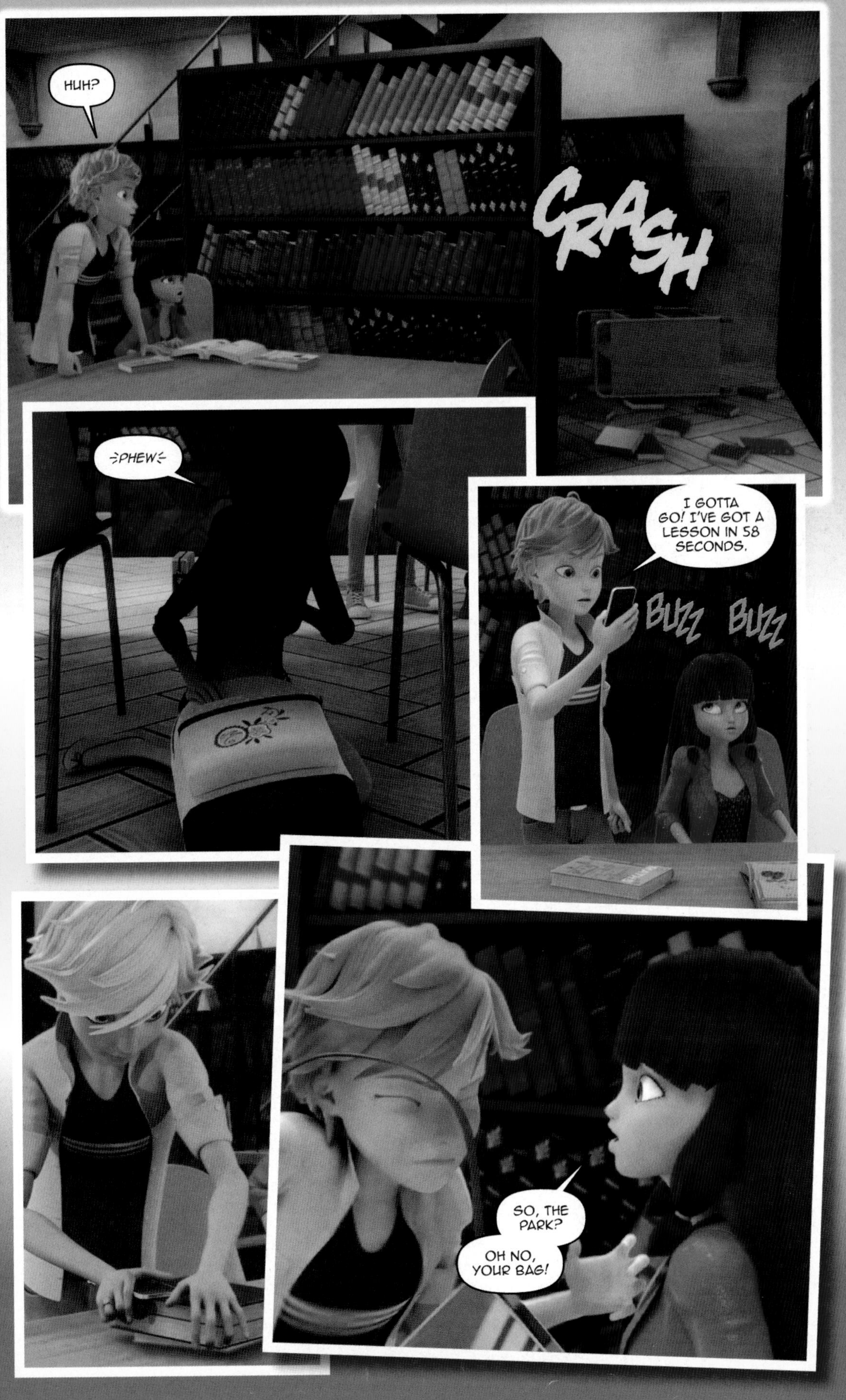
HUH?
CRASH
PHEW
I GOTTA GO! I'VE GOT A LESSON IN 58 SECONDS.
BUZZ BUZZ
SO, THE PARK?
OH NO, YOUR BAG!

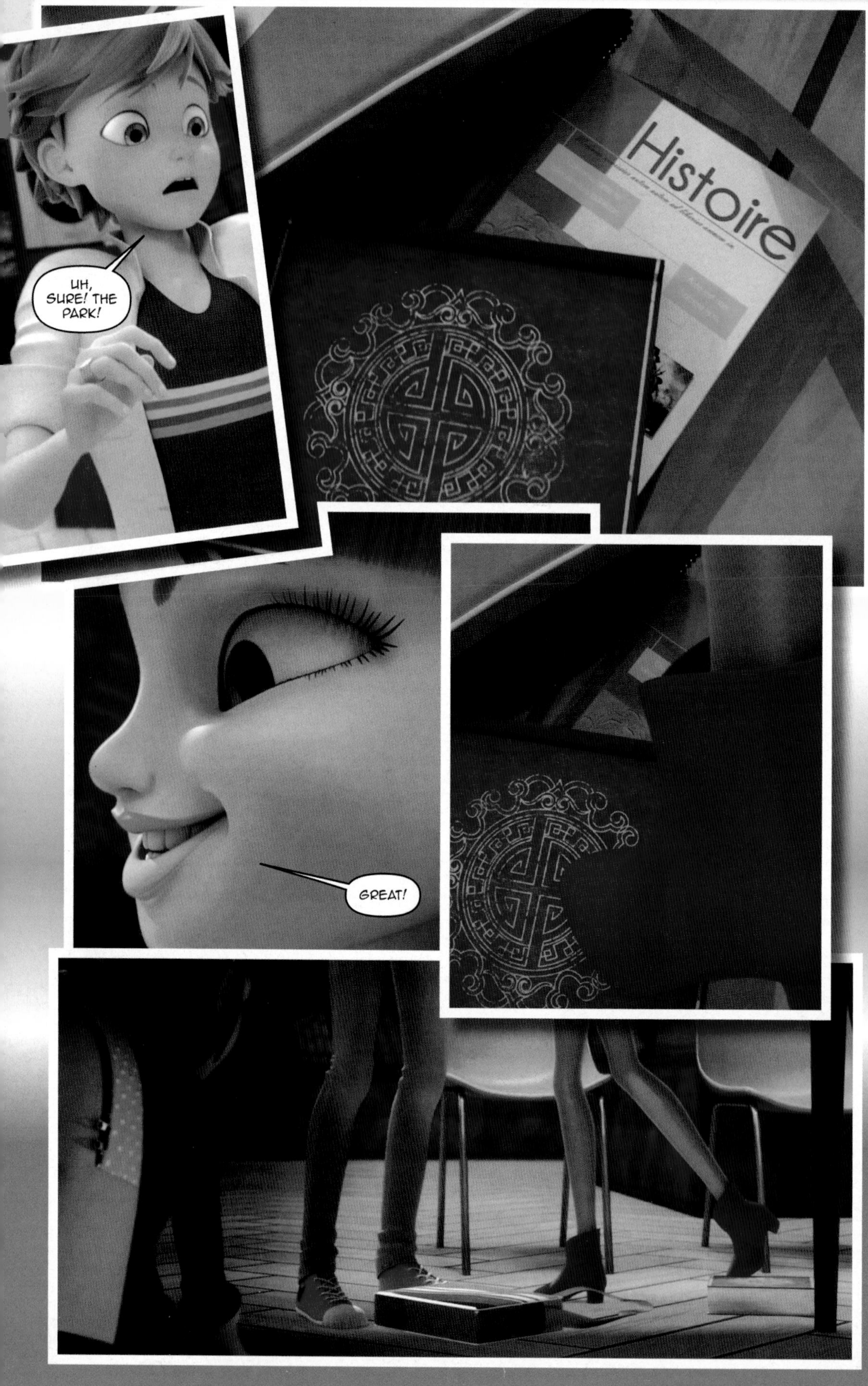
UH, SURE! THE PARK!
Histoire
GREAT!

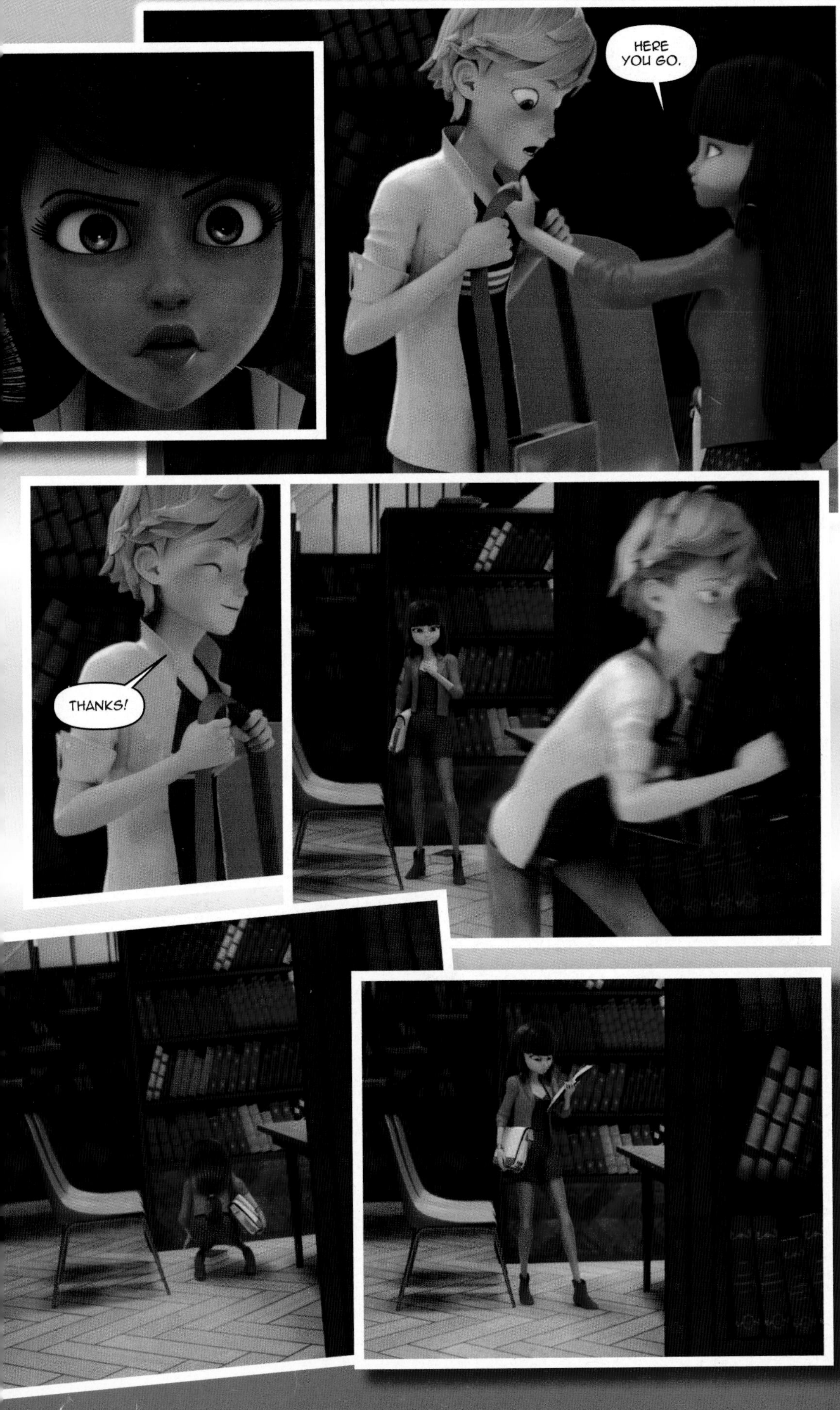
HERE YOU GO.
THANKS!

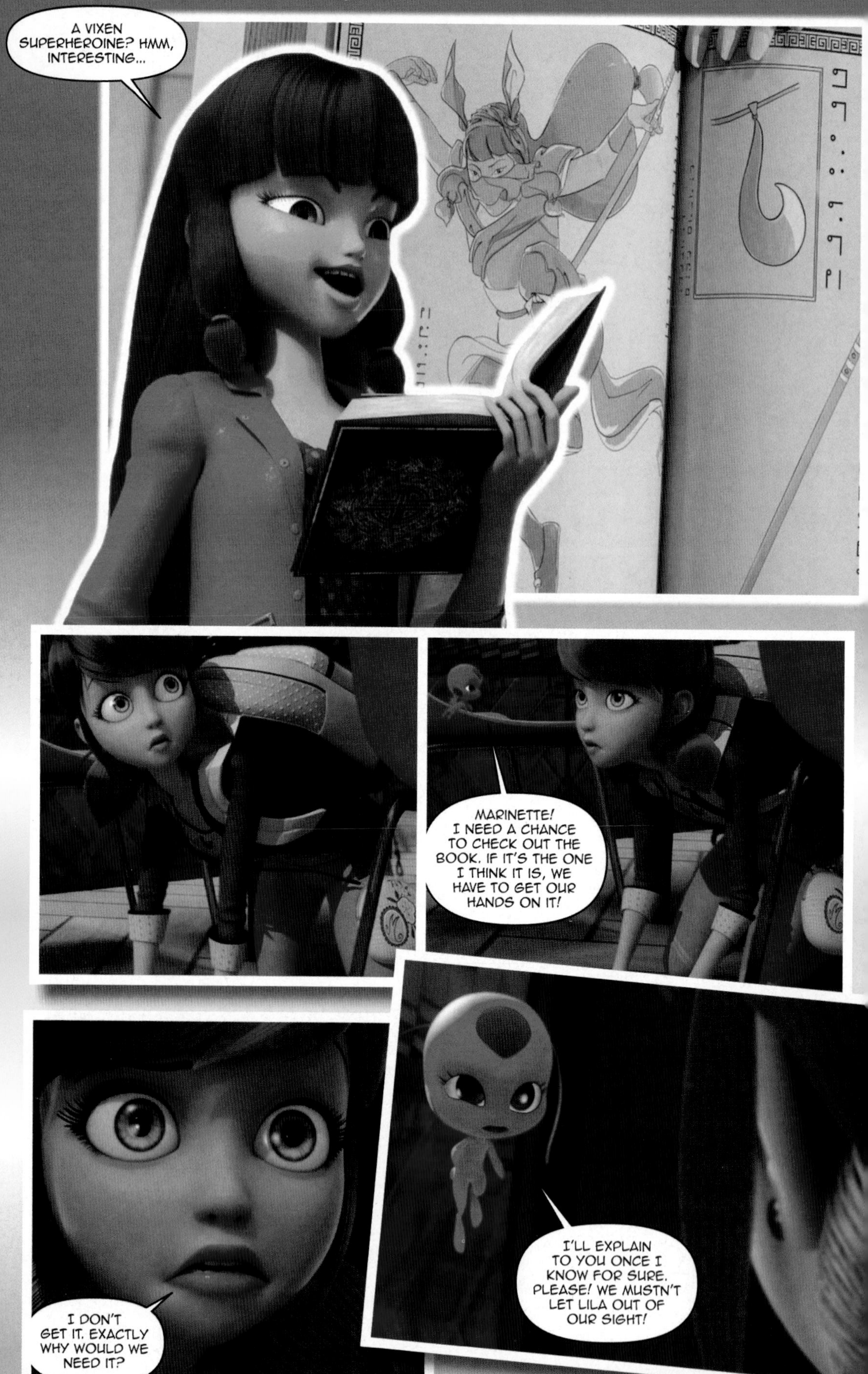
A VIXEN SUPERHEROINE? HMM, INTERESTING...
MARINETTE! I NEED A CHANCE TO CHECK OUT THE BOOK. IF IT'S THE ONE I THINK IT IS, WE HAVE TO GET OUR HANDS ON IT!
I DON'T GET IT. EXACTLY WHY WOULD WE NEED IT?
I'LL EXPLAIN TO YOU ONCE I KNOW FOR SURE. PLEASE! WE MUSTN'T LET LILA OUT OF OUR SIGHT!

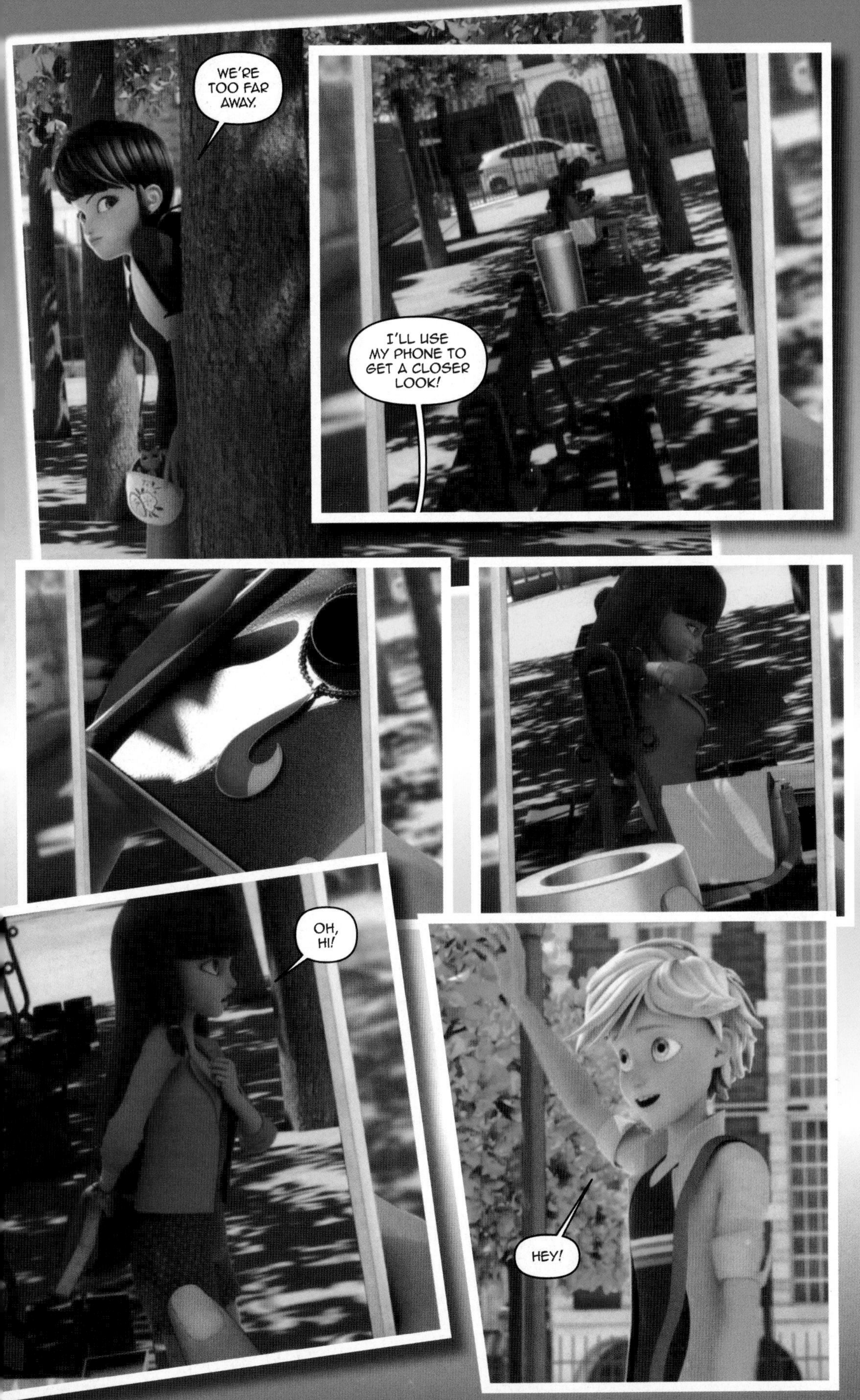
WE'RE TOO FAR AWAY.
I'LL USE MY PHONE TO GET A CLOSER LOOK!
OH, HI!
HEY!

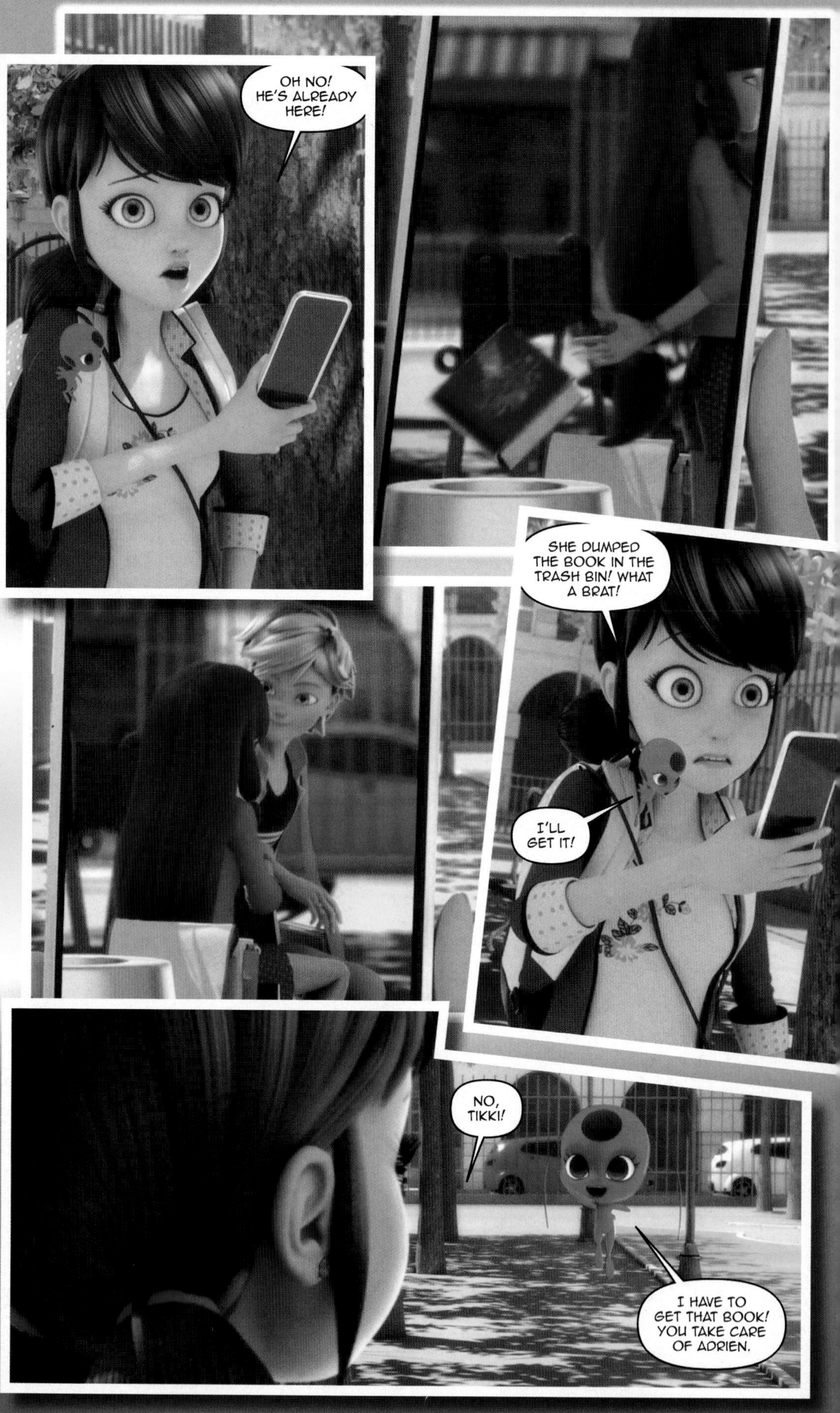
OH NO! HE'S ALREADY HERE!
SHE DUMPED THE BOOK IN THE TRASH BIN! WHAT A BRAT!
I'LL GET IT!
NO, TIKKI!
I HAVE TO GET THAT BOOK! YOU TAKE CARE OF ADRIEN.

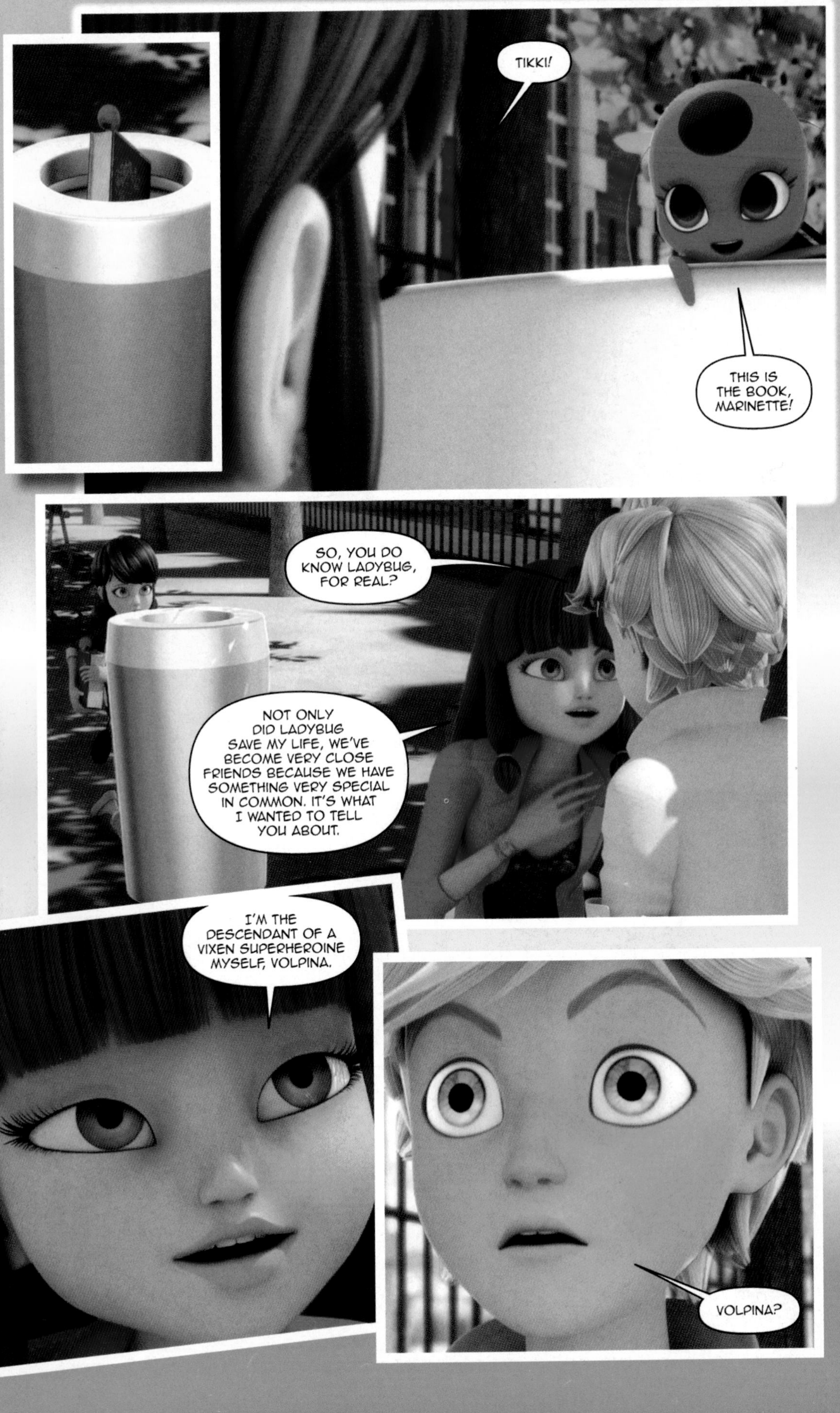
TIKKI!
THIS IS THE BOOK, MARINETTE!
SO, YOU DO KNOW LADYBUG, FOR REAL?
NOT ONLY DID LADYBUG SAVE MY LIFE, WE'VE BECOME VERY CLOSE FRIENDS BECAUSE WE HAVE SOMETHING VERY SPECIAL IN COMMON. IT'S WHAT I WANTED TO TELL YOU ABOUT.
I'M THE DESCENDANT OF A VIXEN SUPERHEROINE MYSELF, VOLPINA.
VOLPINA?

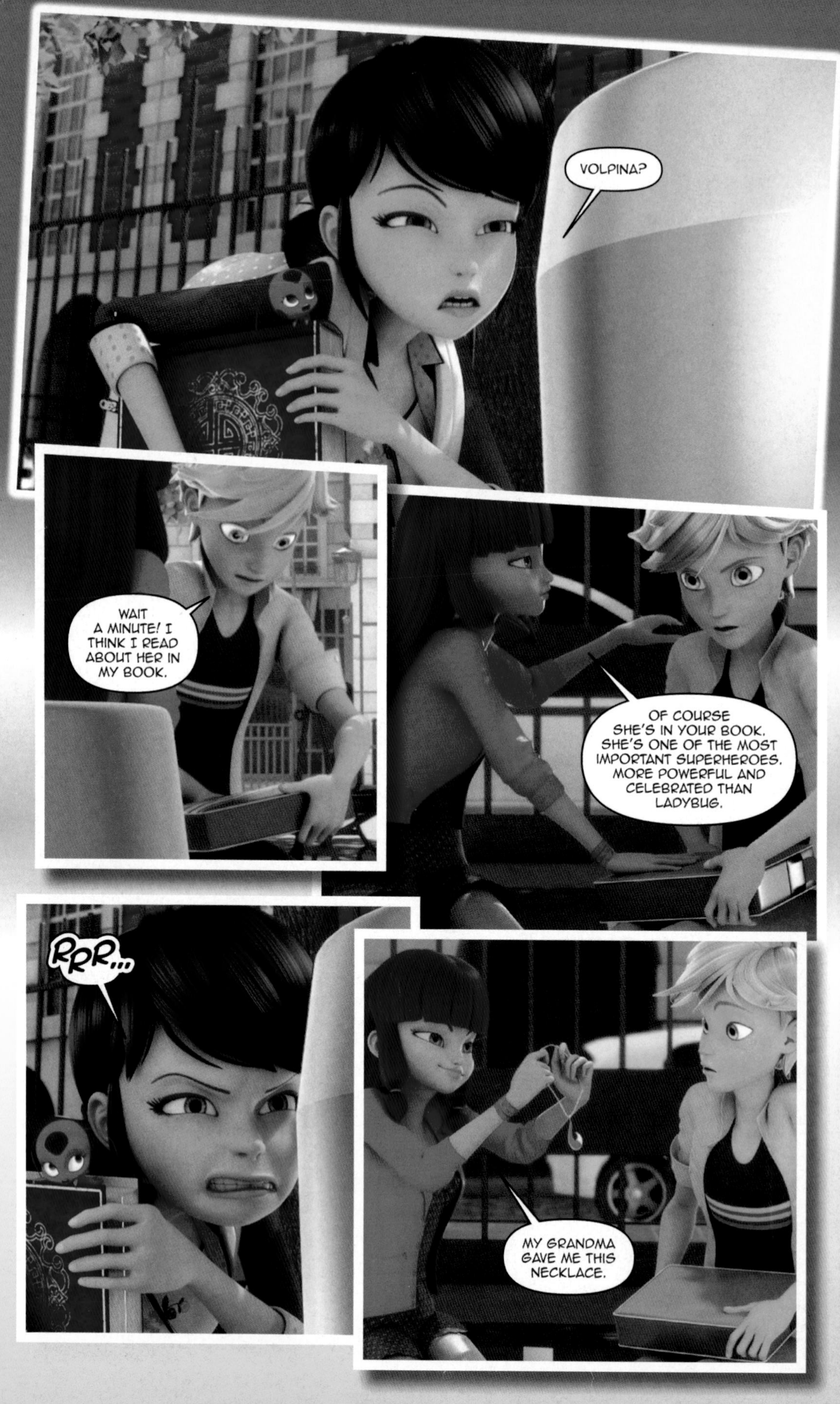

VOLPINA?
WAIT A MINUTE! I THINK I READ ABOUT HER IN MY BOOK.
OF COURSE SHE'S IN YOUR BOOK. SHE'S ONE OF THE MOST IMPORTANT SUPERHEROES. MORE POWERFUL AND CELEBRATED THAN LADYBUG.
RRR...
MY GRANDMA GAVE ME THIS NECKLACE.

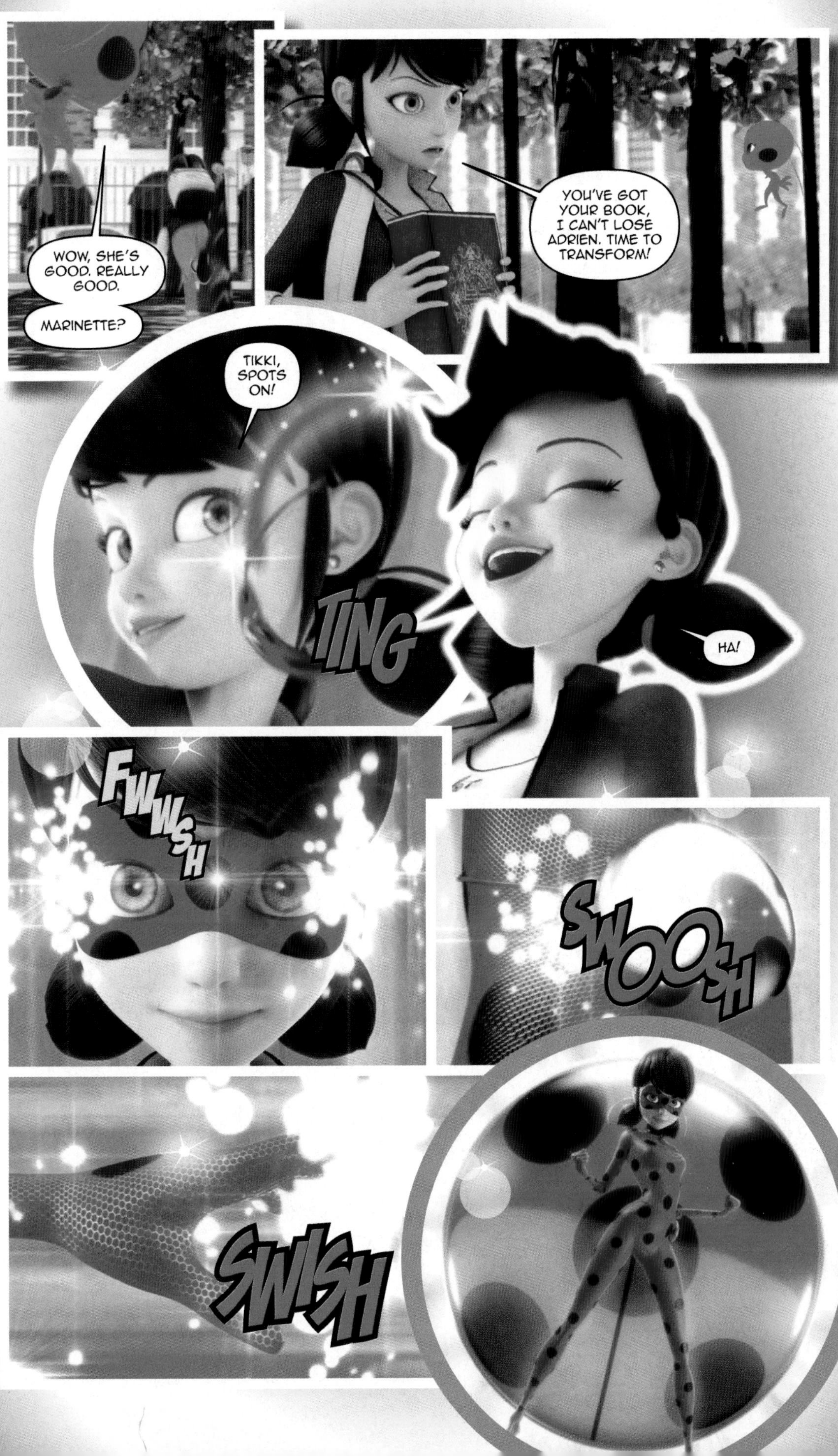
WOW, SHE'S GOOD. REALLY GOOD.
MARINETTE?
YOU'VE GOT YOUR BOOK, I CAN'T LOSE ADRIEN. TIME TO TRANSFORM!
TIKKI, SPOTS ON!
TING
HA!
FWWSH
SWOOSH
SWISH

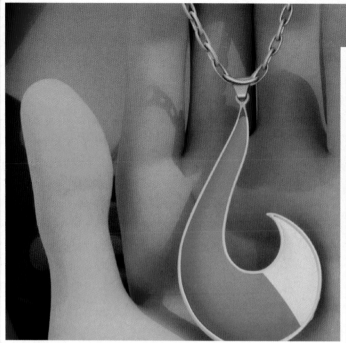

ARE YOU TELLING ME THIS IS A... MIRACULOUS?!

WELL HEY, LILA! HOW'S IT GOING? LONG TIME NO SEE. I SAW YOUR INTERVIEW ON THE LADYBLOG. AWESOME JOB!

OH SURE! I REMEMBER OUR INSTANT CONNECTION WHEN I SAVED YOUR LIFE, AND WE'VE BEEN REALLY GOOD FRIENDS EVER SINCE! PRACTICALLY BFF'S!

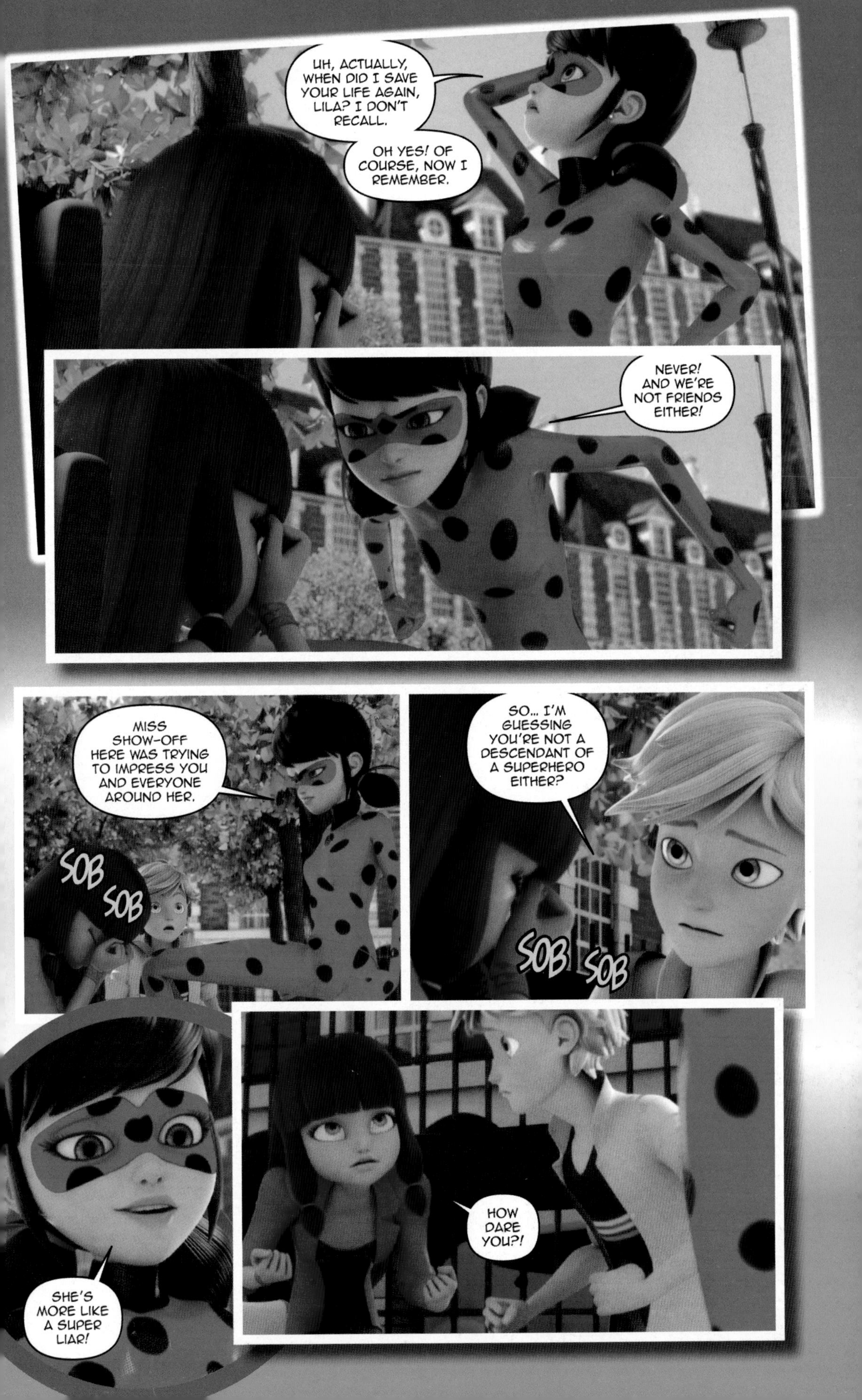
UH, ACTUALLY, WHEN DID I SAVE YOUR LIFE AGAIN, LILA? I DON'T RECALL.
OH YES! OF COURSE, NOW I REMEMBER.
NEVER! AND WE'RE NOT FRIENDS EITHER!
MISS SHOW-OFF HERE WAS TRYING TO IMPRESS YOU AND EVERYONE AROUND HER.
SOB
SOB
SO... I'M GUESSING YOU'RE NOT A DESCENDANT OF A SUPERHERO EITHER?
SOB
SOB
SHE'S MORE LIKE A SUPER LIAR!
HOW DARE YOU?!

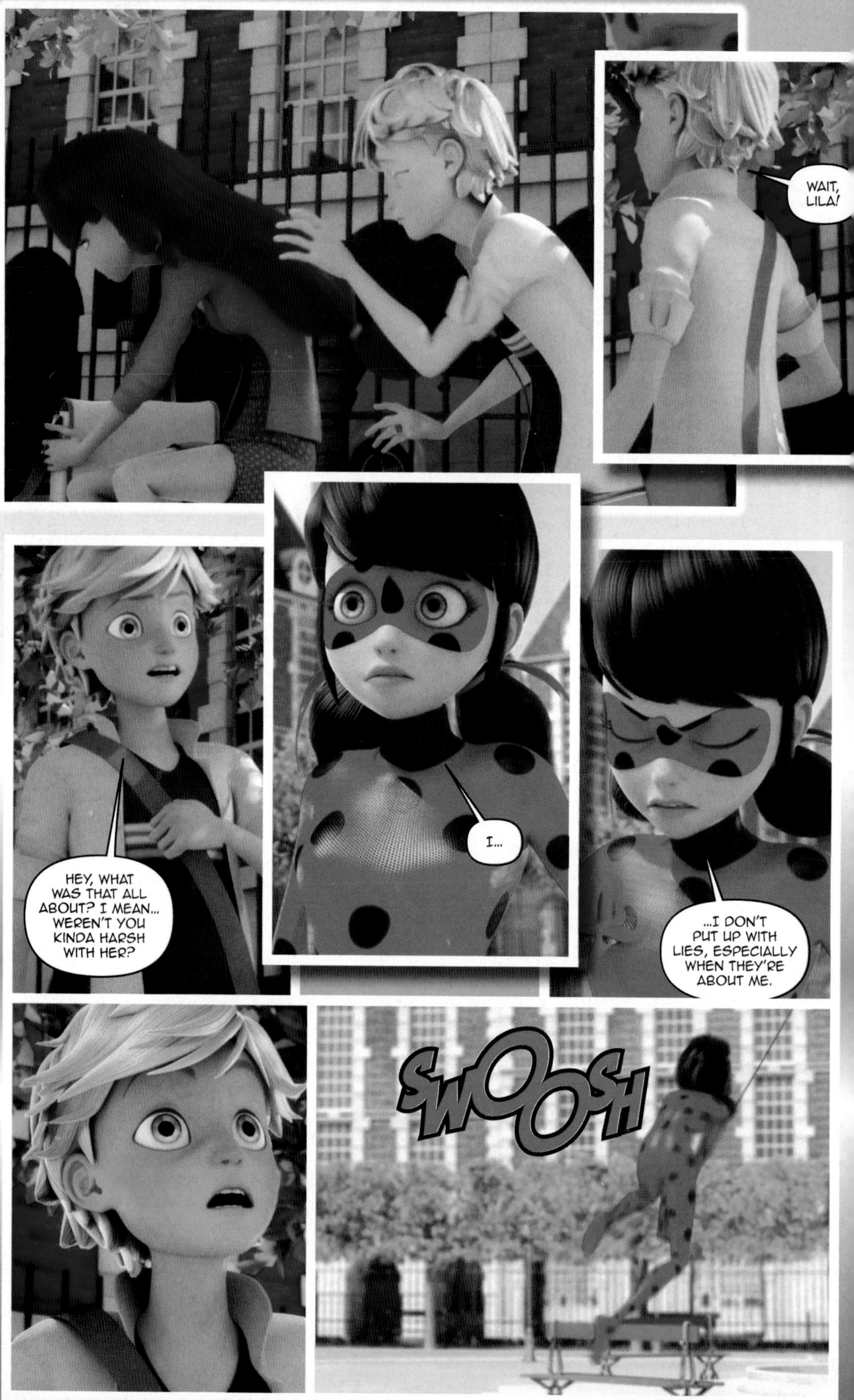
WAIT, LILA!
HEY, WHAT WAS THAT ALL ABOUT? I MEAN... WEREN'T YOU KINDA HARSH WITH HER?
I...
...I DON'T PUT UP WITH LIES, ESPECIALLY WHEN THEY'RE ABOUT ME.
SWOOSH

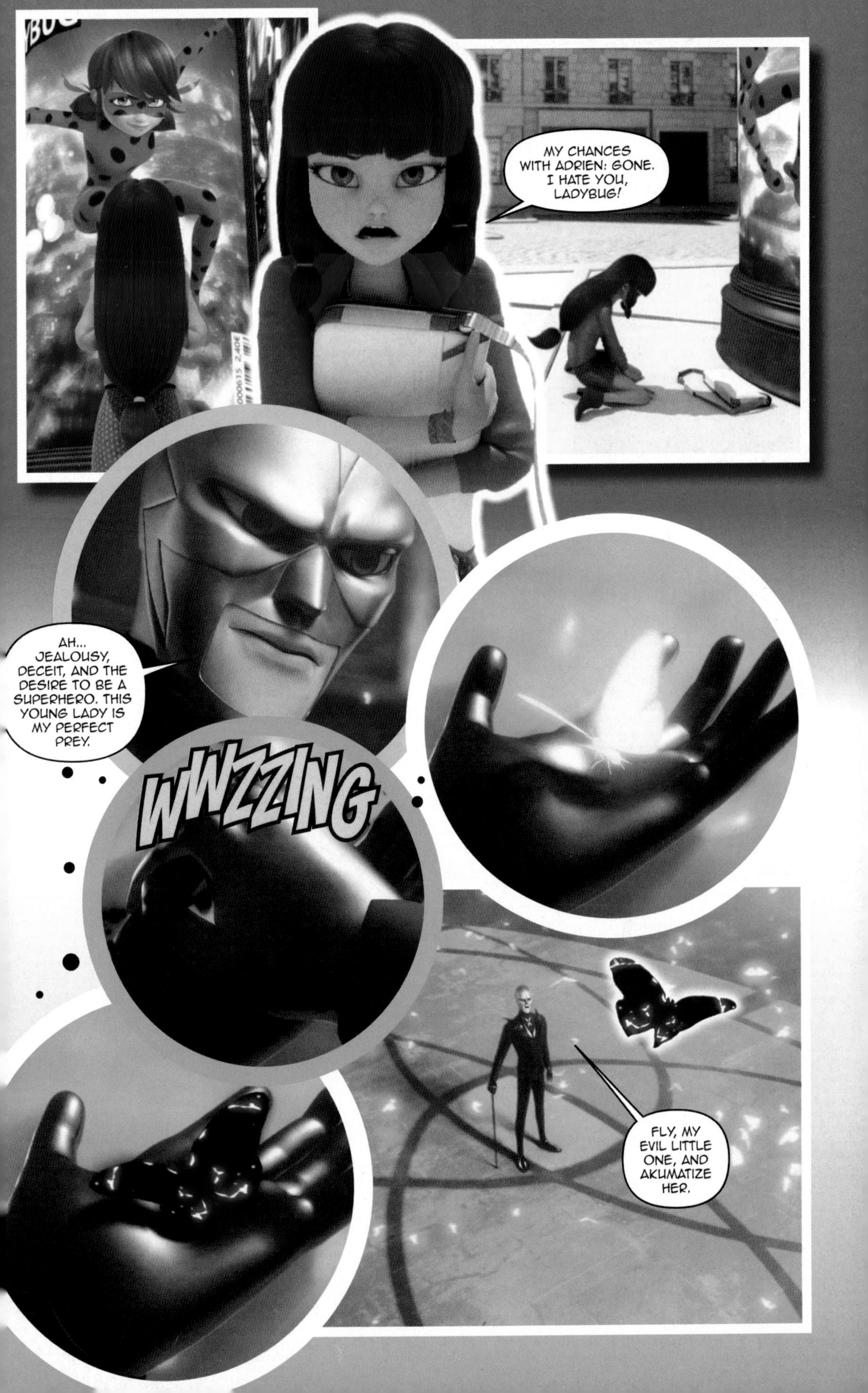
MY CHANCES WITH ADRIEN: GONE. I HATE YOU, LADYBUG!
AH... JEALOUSY, DECEIT, AND THE DESIRE TO BE A SUPERHERO. THIS YOUNG LADY IS MY PERFECT PREY.
WWZZING
FLY, MY EVIL LITTLE ONE, AND AKUMATIZE HER.

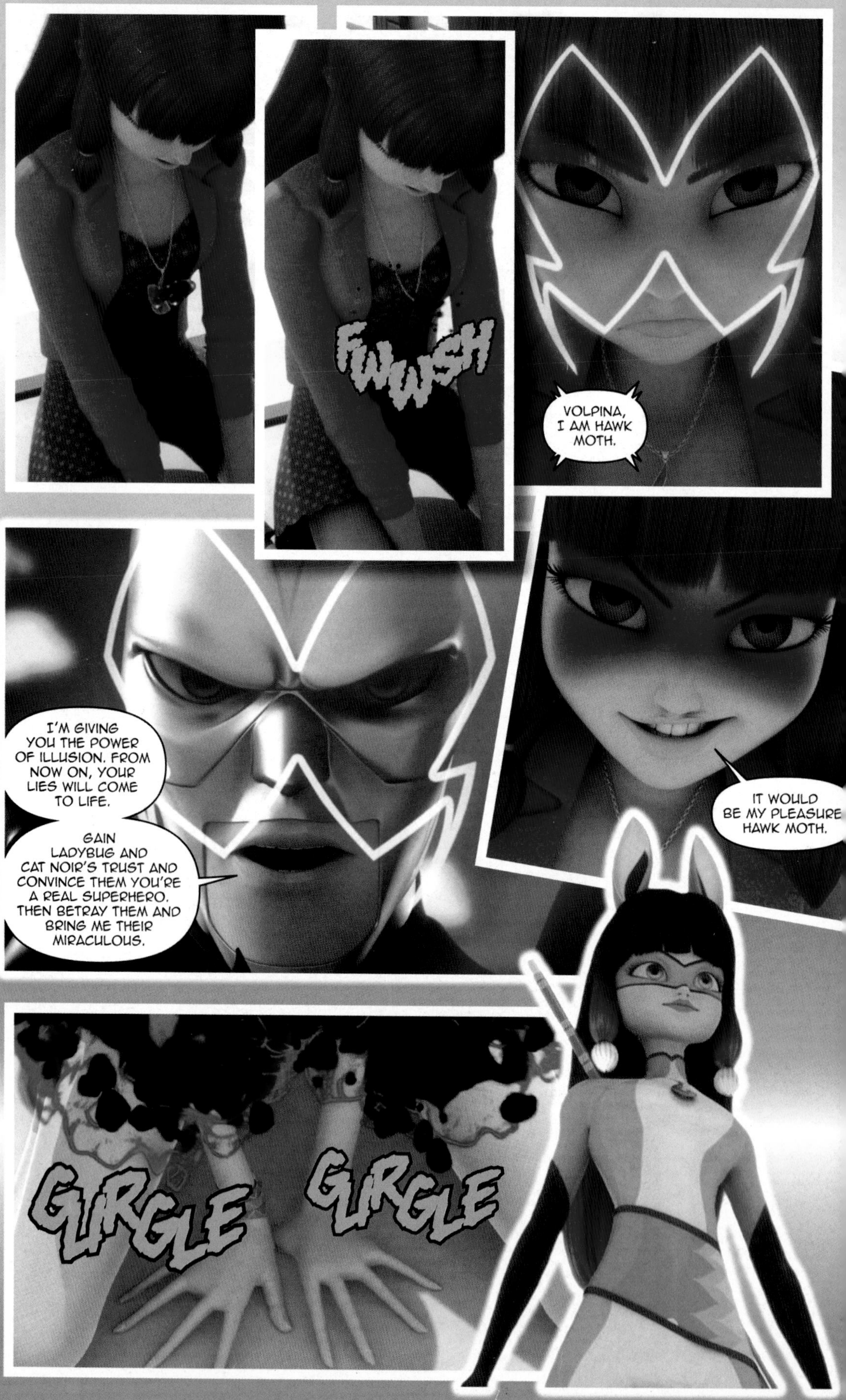
FWWSH
VOLPINA, I AM HAWK MOTH.
I'M GIVING YOU THE POWER OF ILLUSION. FROM NOW ON, YOUR LIES WILL COME TO LIFE.
GAIN LADYBUG AND CAT NOIR'S TRUST AND CONVINCE THEM YOU'RE A REAL SUPERHERO. THEN BETRAY THEM AND BRING ME THEIR MIRACULOUS.
IT WOULD BE MY PLEASURE HAWK MOTH.
GURGLE GURGLE

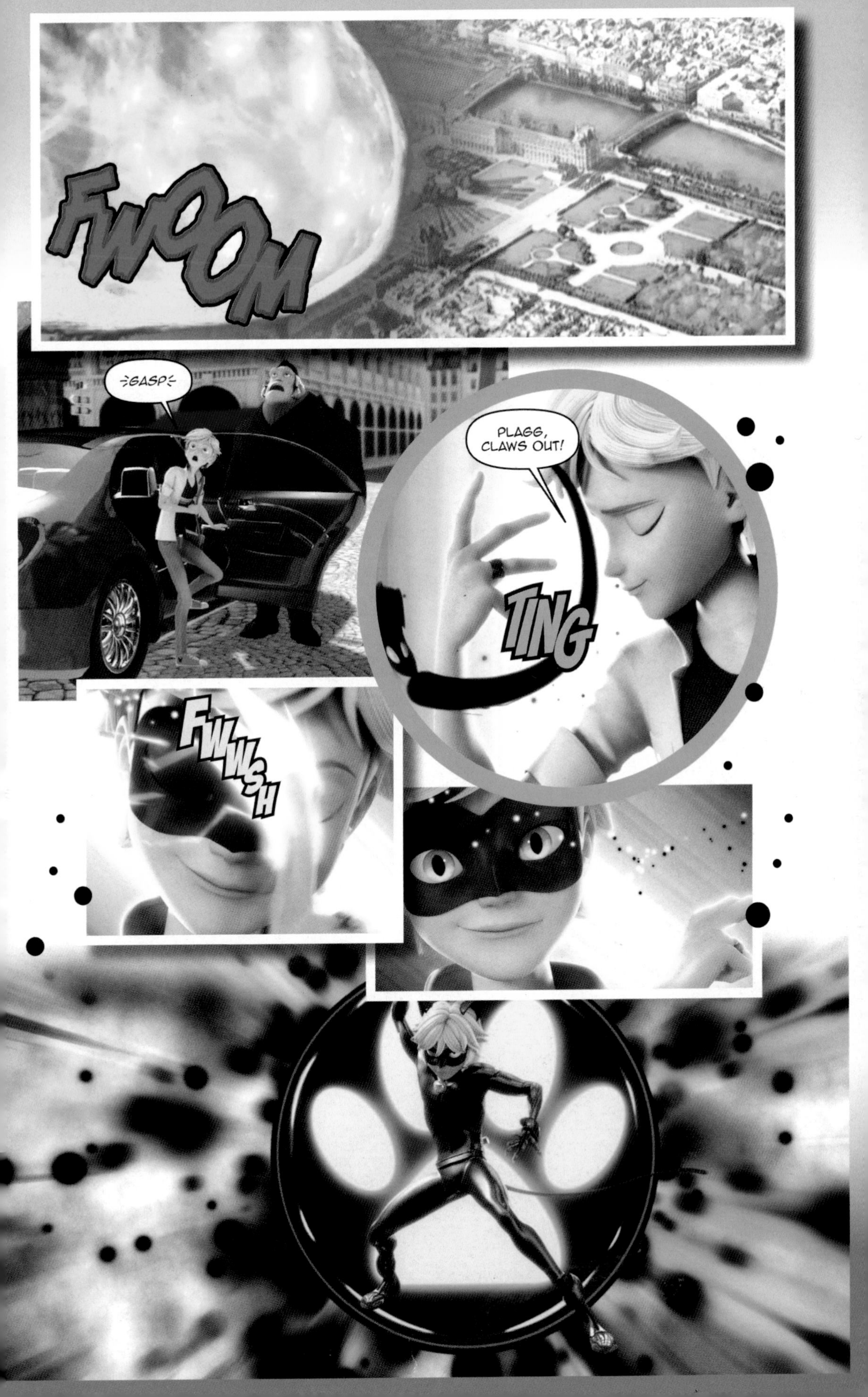
FWOOM
GASP
PLAGG, CLAWS OUT!
TING
FWWSH

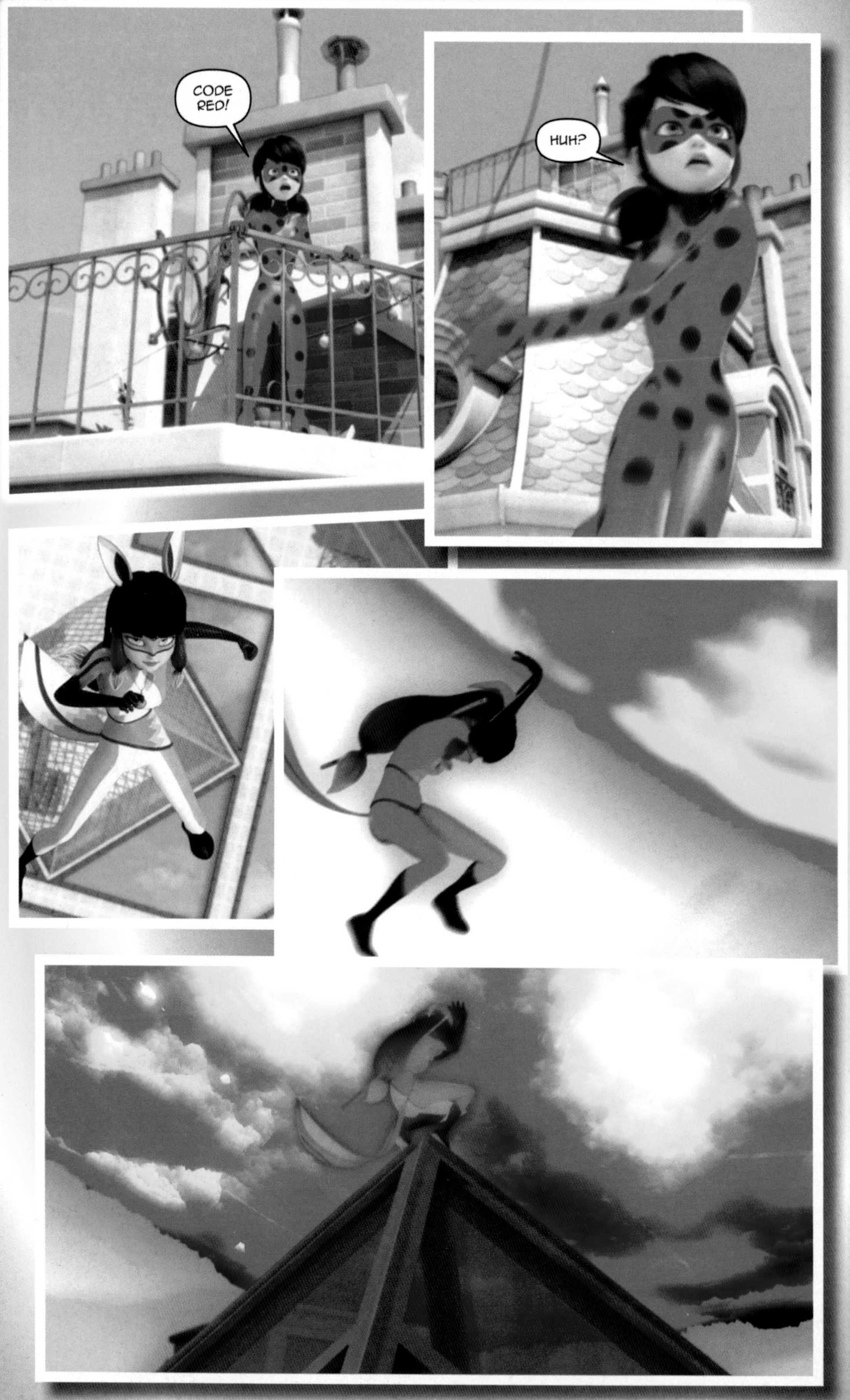
CODE RED!
HUH?

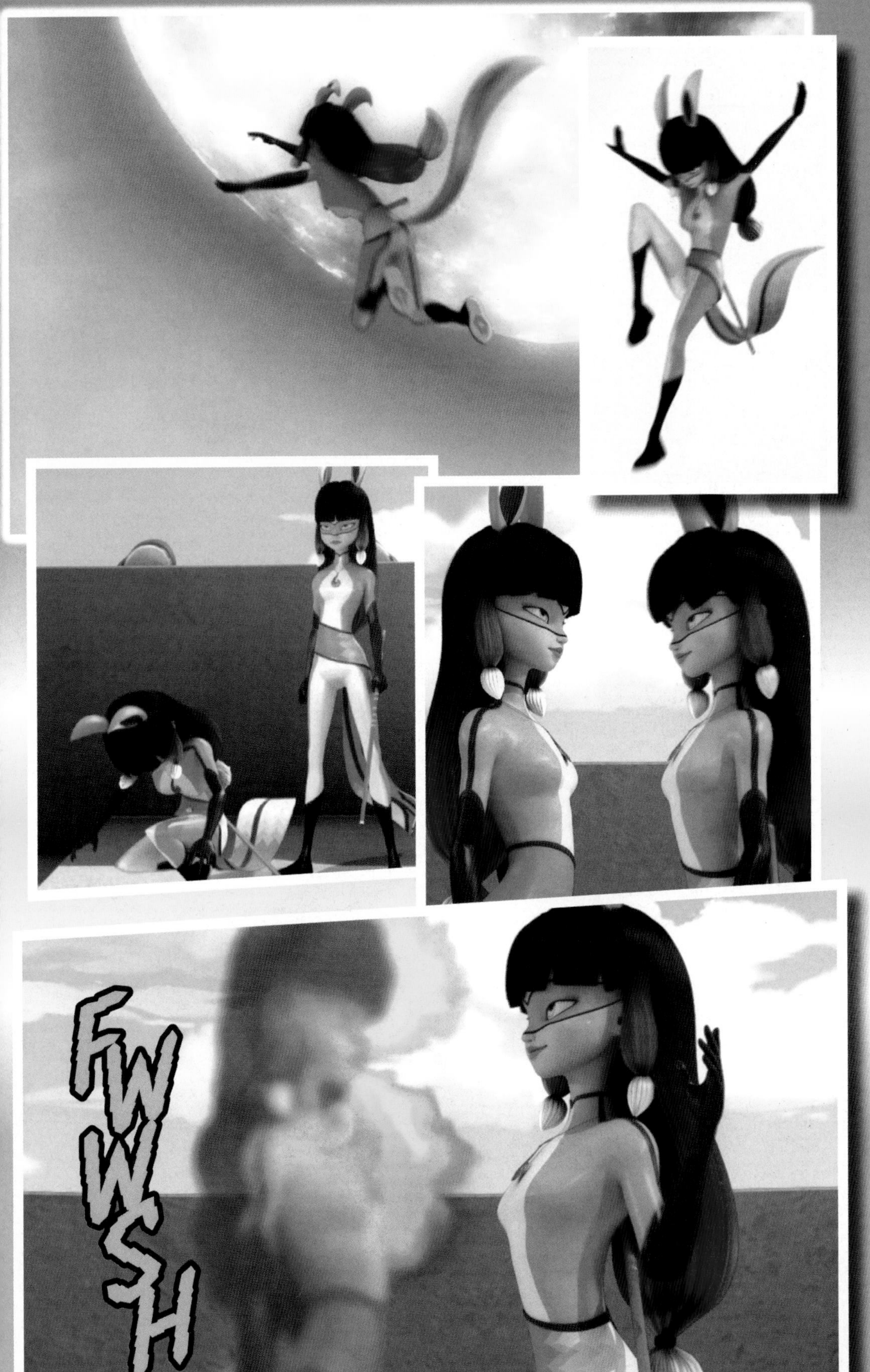
FWWSH

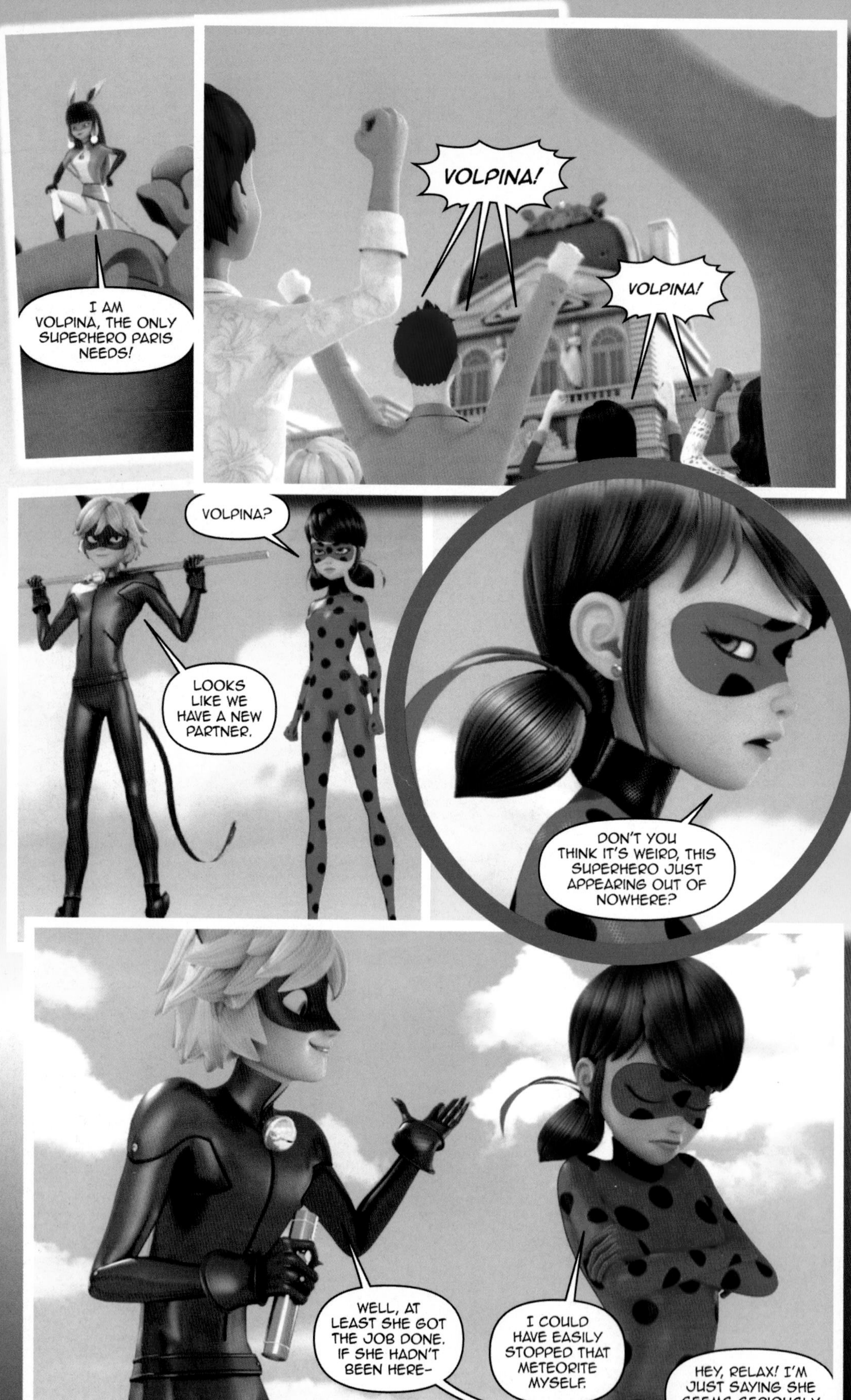

I AM VOLPINA, THE ONLY SUPERHERO PARIS NEEDS!
VOLPINA!
VOLPINA!
VOLPINA?
LOOKS LIKE WE HAVE A NEW PARTNER.
DON'T YOU THINK IT'S WEIRD, THIS SUPERHERO JUST APPEARING OUT OF NOWHERE?
WELL, AT LEAST SHE GOT THE JOB DONE. IF SHE HADN'T BEEN HERE-
I COULD HAVE EASILY STOPPED THAT METEORITE MYSELF.
HEY, RELAX! I'M JUST SAYING SHE SEEMS SERIOUSLY AWESOME.

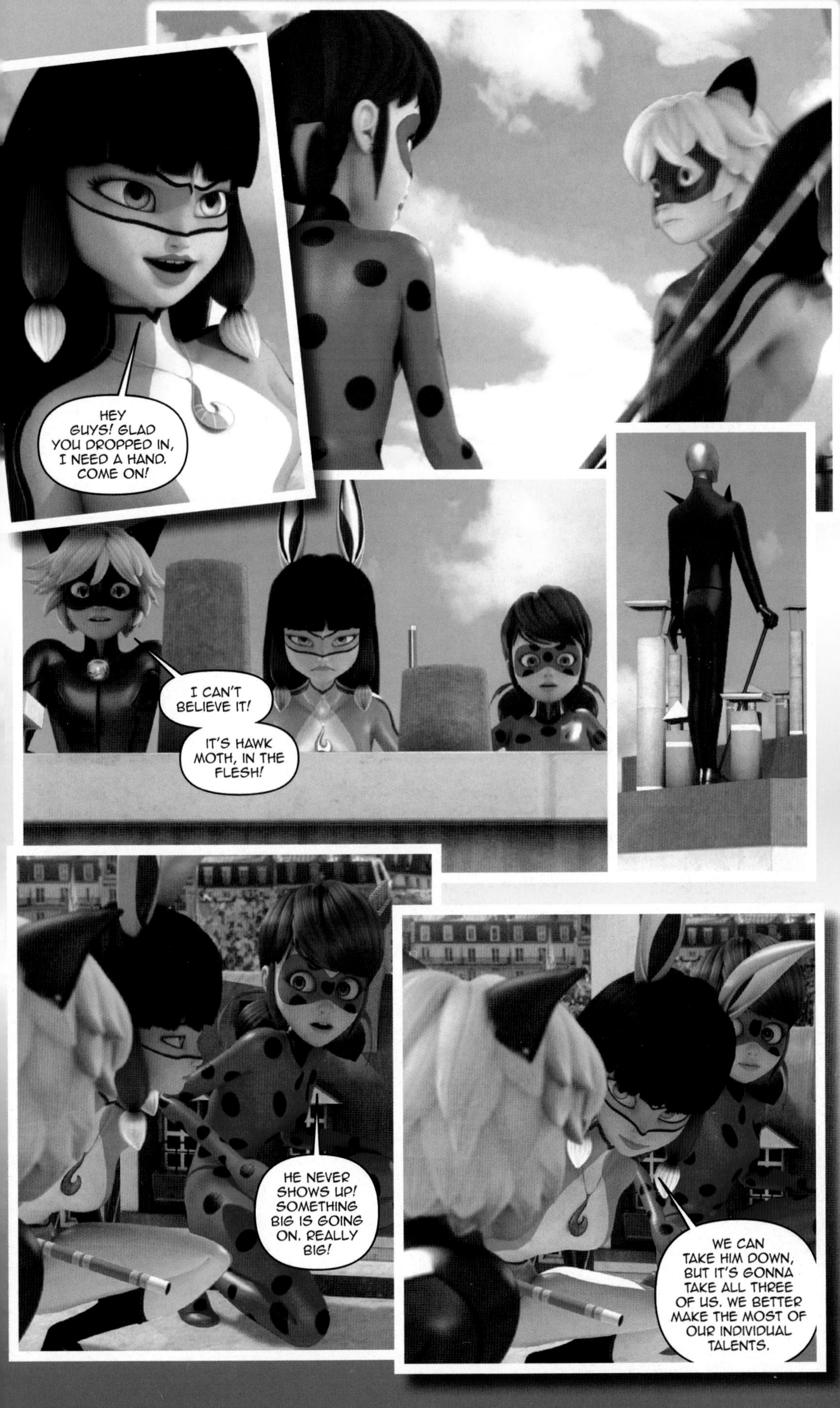
HEY GUYS! GLAD YOU DROPPED IN, I NEED A HAND. COME ON!
I CAN'T BELIEVE IT!
IT'S HAWK MOTH, IN THE FLESH!
HE NEVER SHOWS UP! SOMETHING BIG IS GOING ON. REALLY BIG!
WE CAN TAKE HIM DOWN, BUT IT'S GONNA TAKE ALL THREE OF US. WE BETTER MAKE THE MOST OF OUR INDIVIDUAL TALENTS.

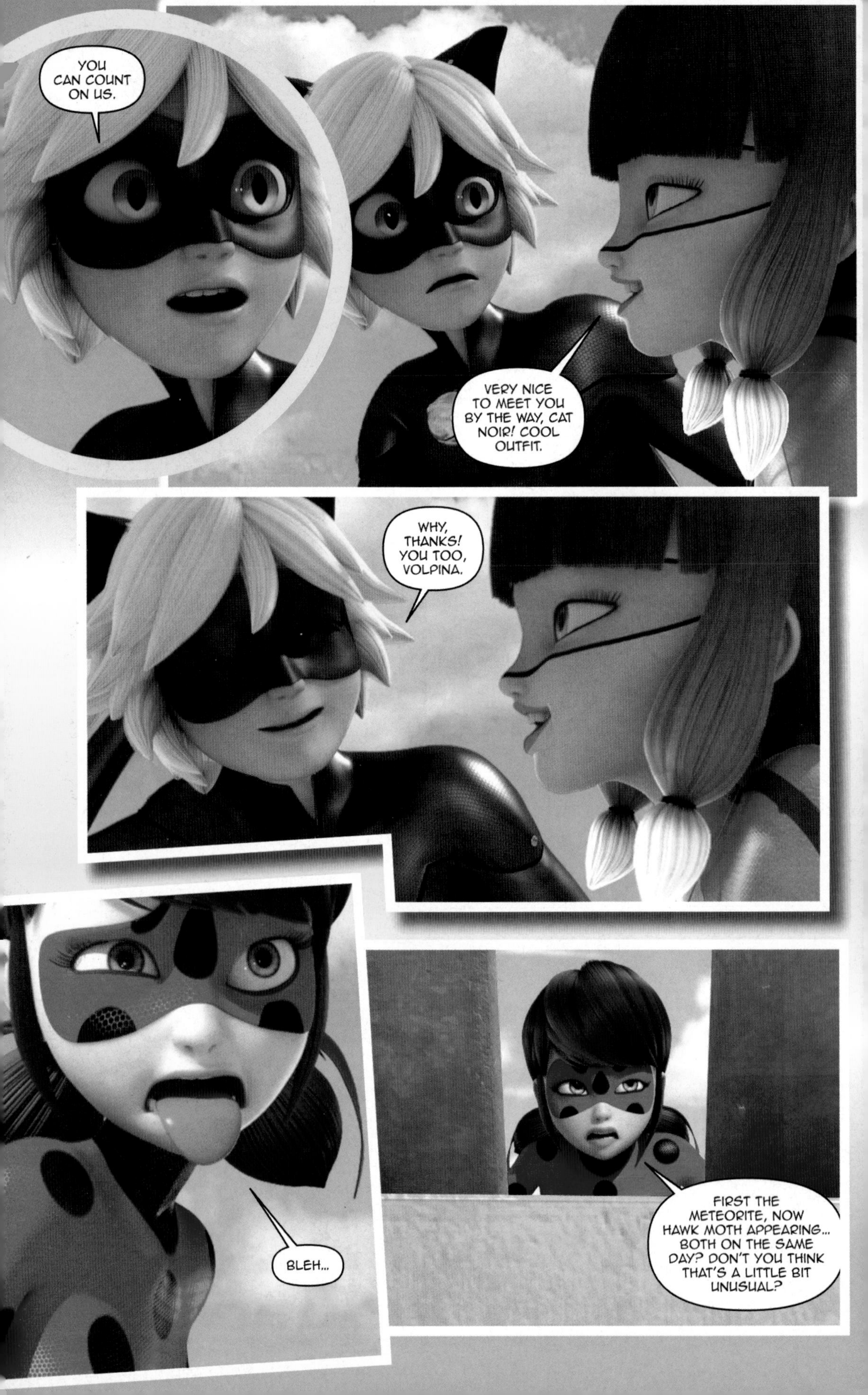
YOU CAN COUNT ON US.
VERY NICE TO MEET YOU BY THE WAY, CAT NOIR! COOL OUTFIT.
WHY, THANKS! YOU TOO, VOLPINA.
BLEH...
FIRST THE METEORITE, NOW HAWK MOTH APPEARING... BOTH ON THE SAME DAY? DON'T YOU THINK THAT'S A LITTLE BIT UNUSUAL?

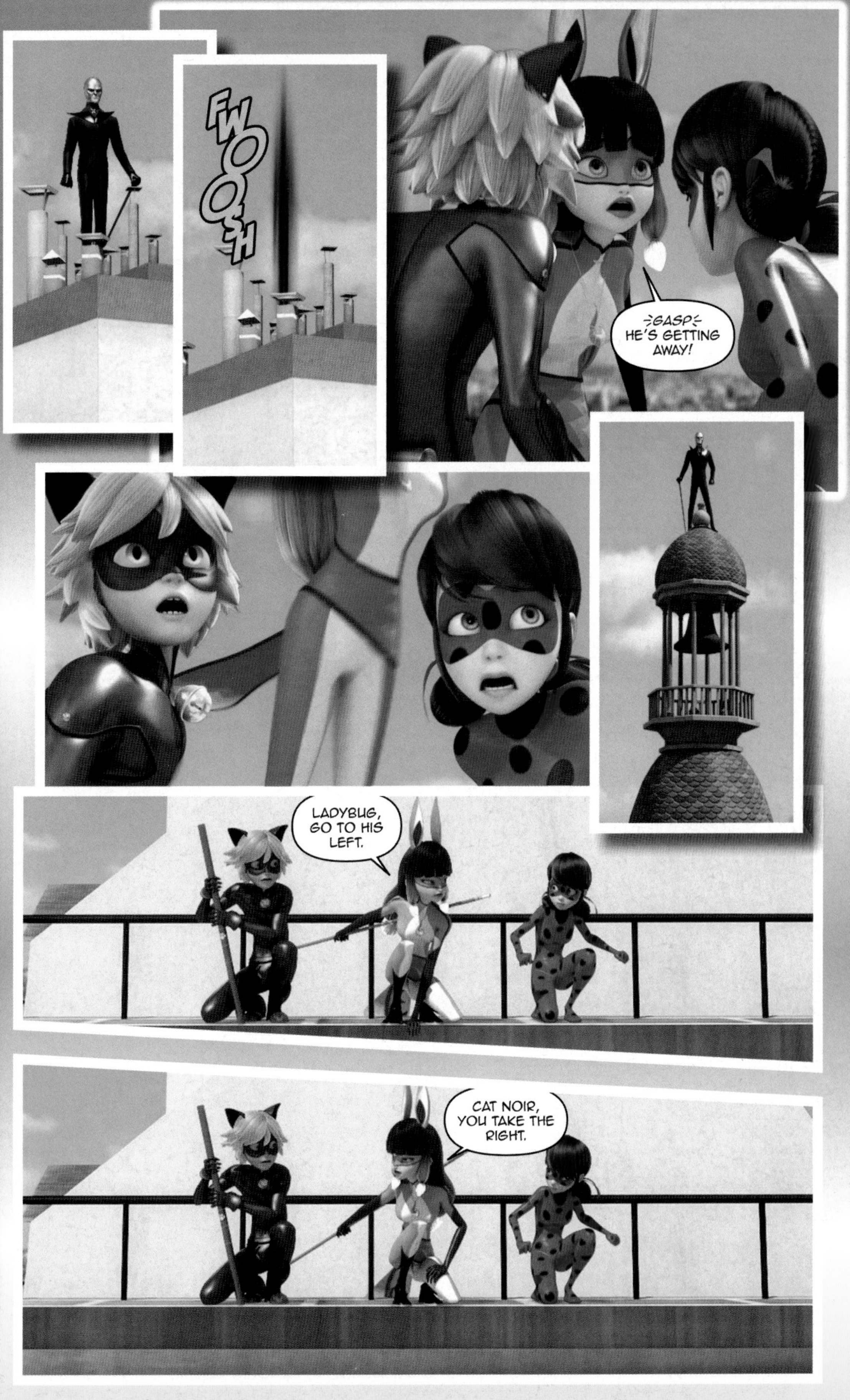
FWOOSH
⋟GASP⋞ HE'S GETTING AWAY!
LADYBUG, GO TO HIS LEFT.
CAT NOIR, YOU TAKE THE RIGHT.

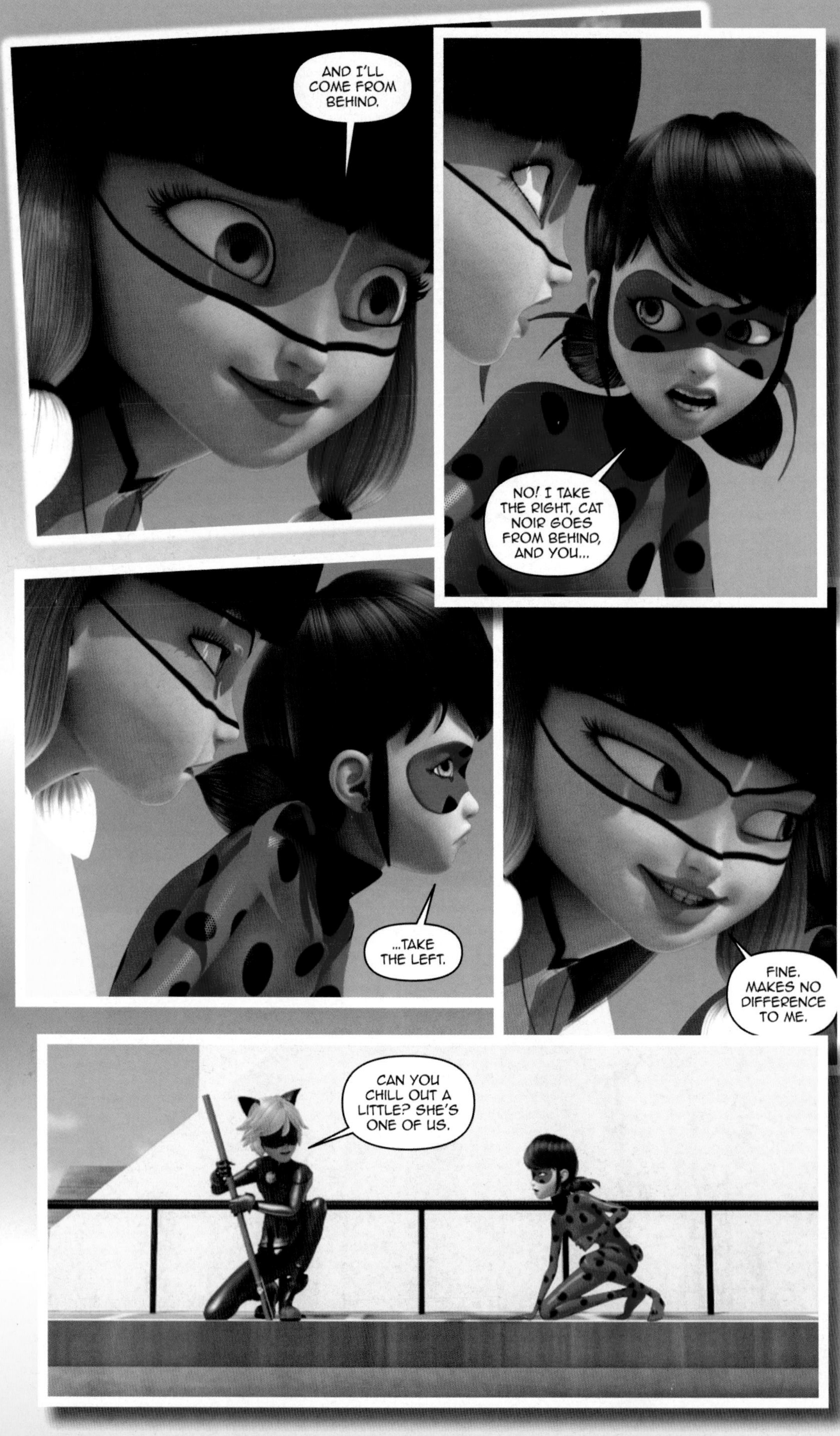
AND I'LL COME FROM BEHIND.
NO! I TAKE THE RIGHT, CAT NOIR GOES FROM BEHIND, AND YOU...
...TAKE THE LEFT.
FINE. MAKES NO DIFFERENCE TO ME.
CAN YOU CHILL OUT A LITTLE? SHE'S ONE OF US.

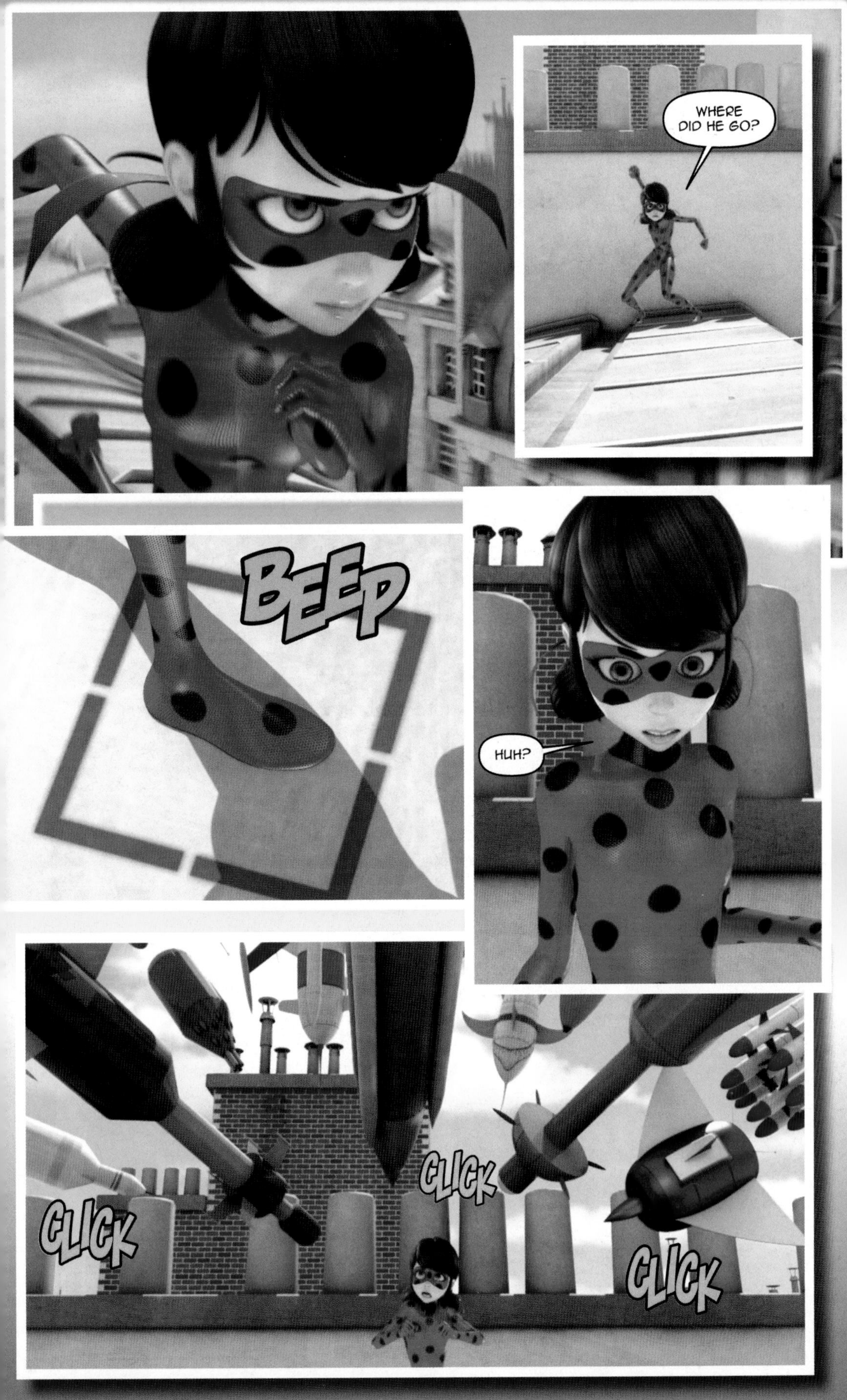
WHERE DID HE GO?
BEEP
HUH?
CLICK
CLICK
CLICK

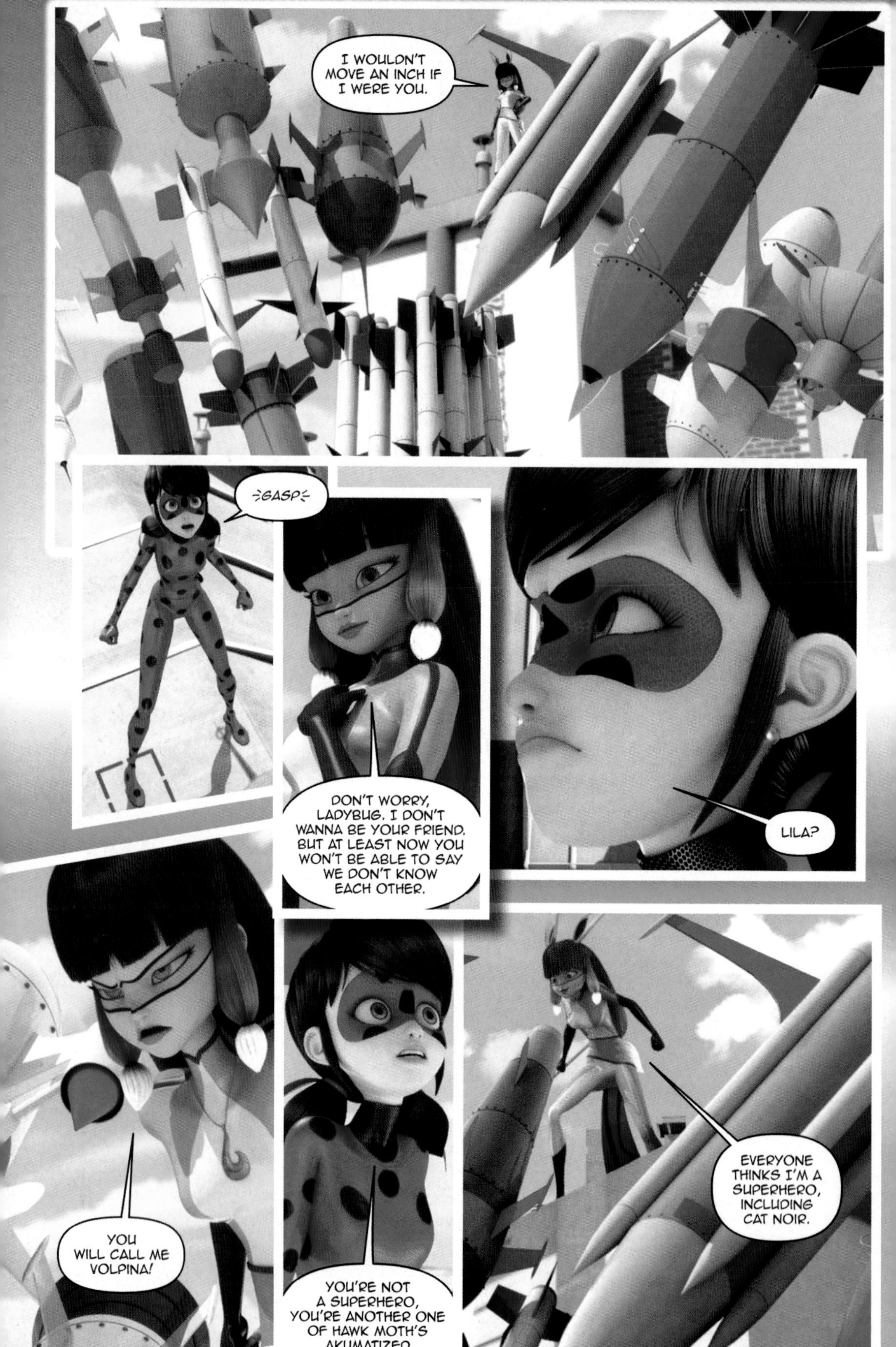
I WOULDN'T MOVE AN INCH IF I WERE YOU.
GASP
DON'T WORRY, LADYBUG. I DON'T WANNA BE YOUR FRIEND. BUT AT LEAST NOW YOU WON'T BE ABLE TO SAY WE DON'T KNOW EACH OTHER.
LILA?
YOU WILL CALL ME VOLPINA!
YOU'RE NOT A SUPERHERO, YOU'RE ANOTHER ONE OF HAWK MOTH'S AKUMATIZED VICTIMS!
EVERYONE THINKS I'M A SUPERHERO, INCLUDING CAT NOIR.

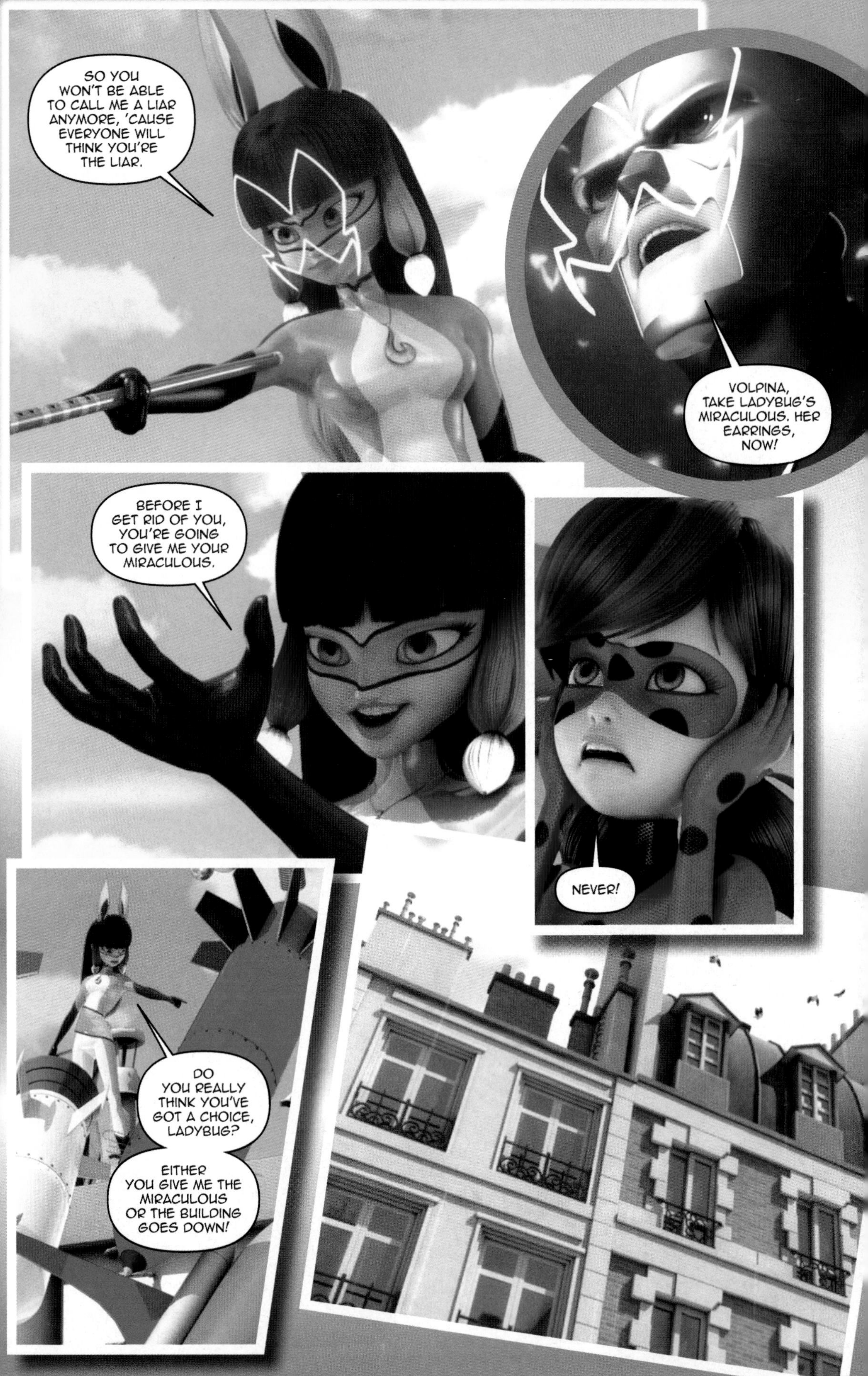
SO YOU WON'T BE ABLE TO CALL ME A LIAR ANYMORE, 'CAUSE EVERYONE WILL THINK YOU'RE THE LIAR.
VOLPINA, TAKE LADYBUG'S MIRACULOUS. HER EARRINGS, NOW!
BEFORE I GET RID OF YOU, YOU'RE GOING TO GIVE ME YOUR MIRACULOUS.
NEVER!
DO YOU REALLY THINK YOU'VE GOT A CHOICE, LADYBUG?
EITHER YOU GIVE ME THE MIRACULOUS OR THE BUILDING GOES DOWN!

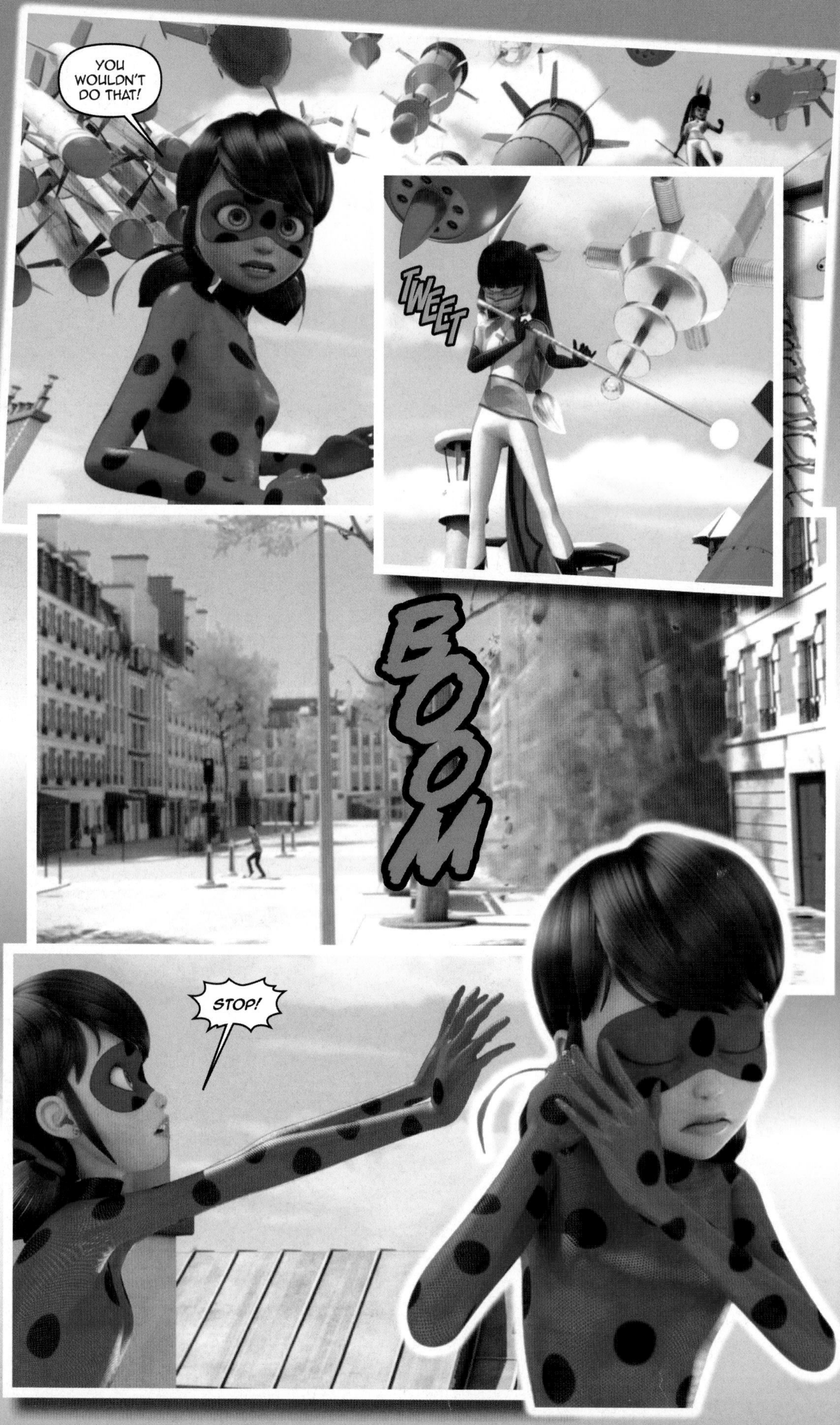
YOU WOULDN'T DO THAT!
TWEET
BOOM
STOP!

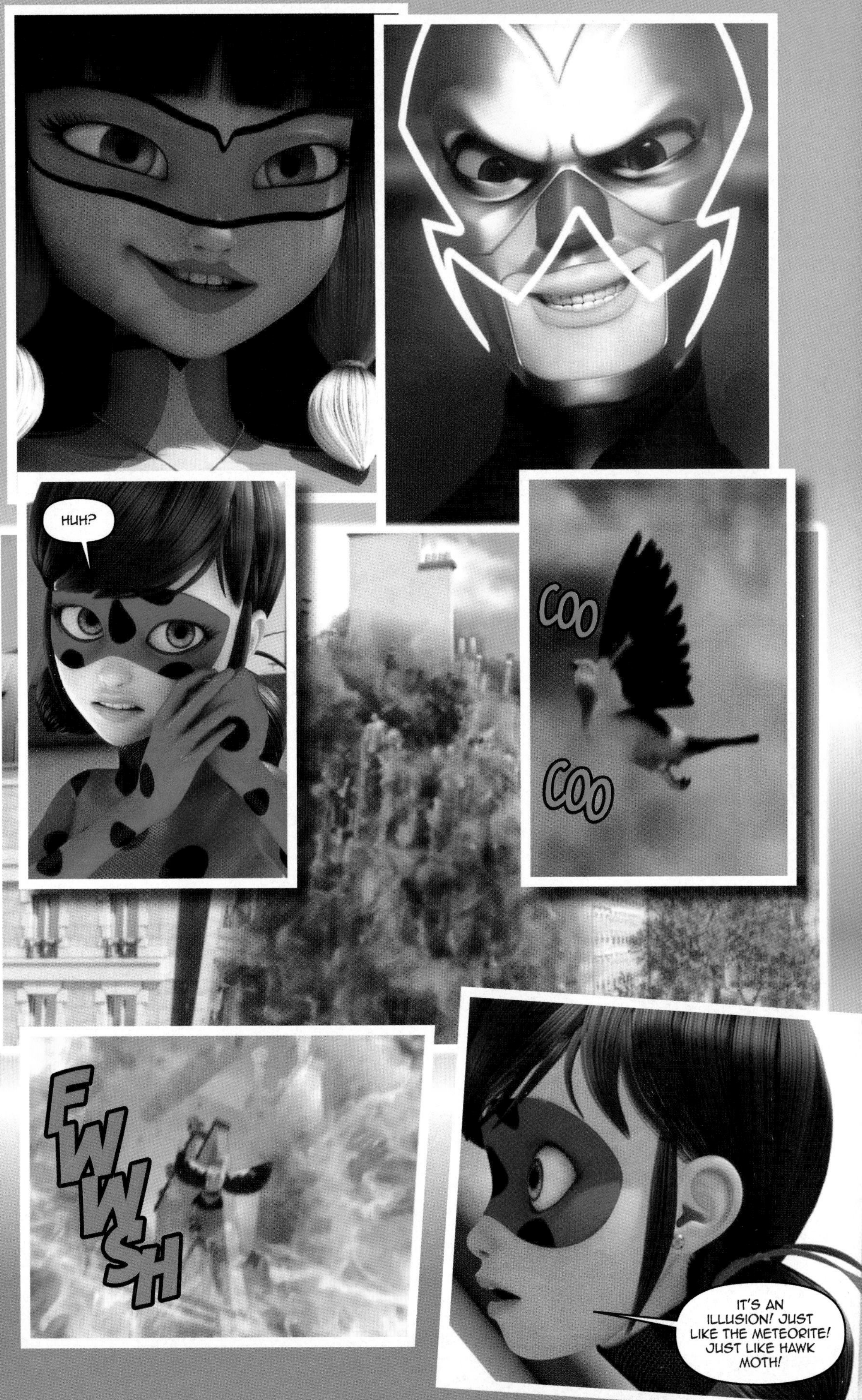
HUH?
COO
COO
FWWSH
IT'S AN ILLUSION! JUST LIKE THE METEORITE! JUST LIKE HAWK MOTH!

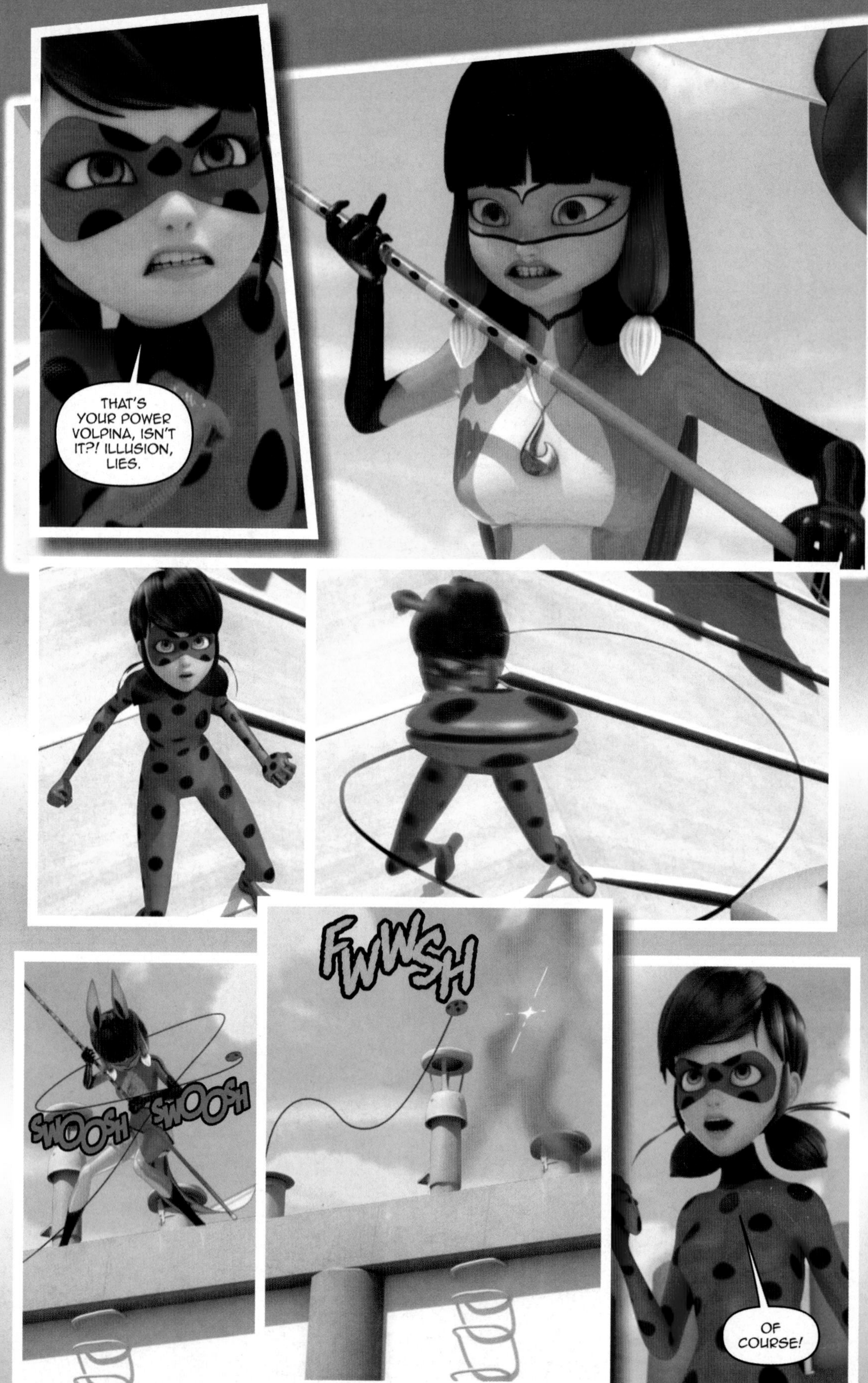
THAT'S YOUR POWER VOLPINA, ISN'T IT?! ILLUSION, LIES.
SWOOSH
SWOOSH
FWWSH
OF COURSE!

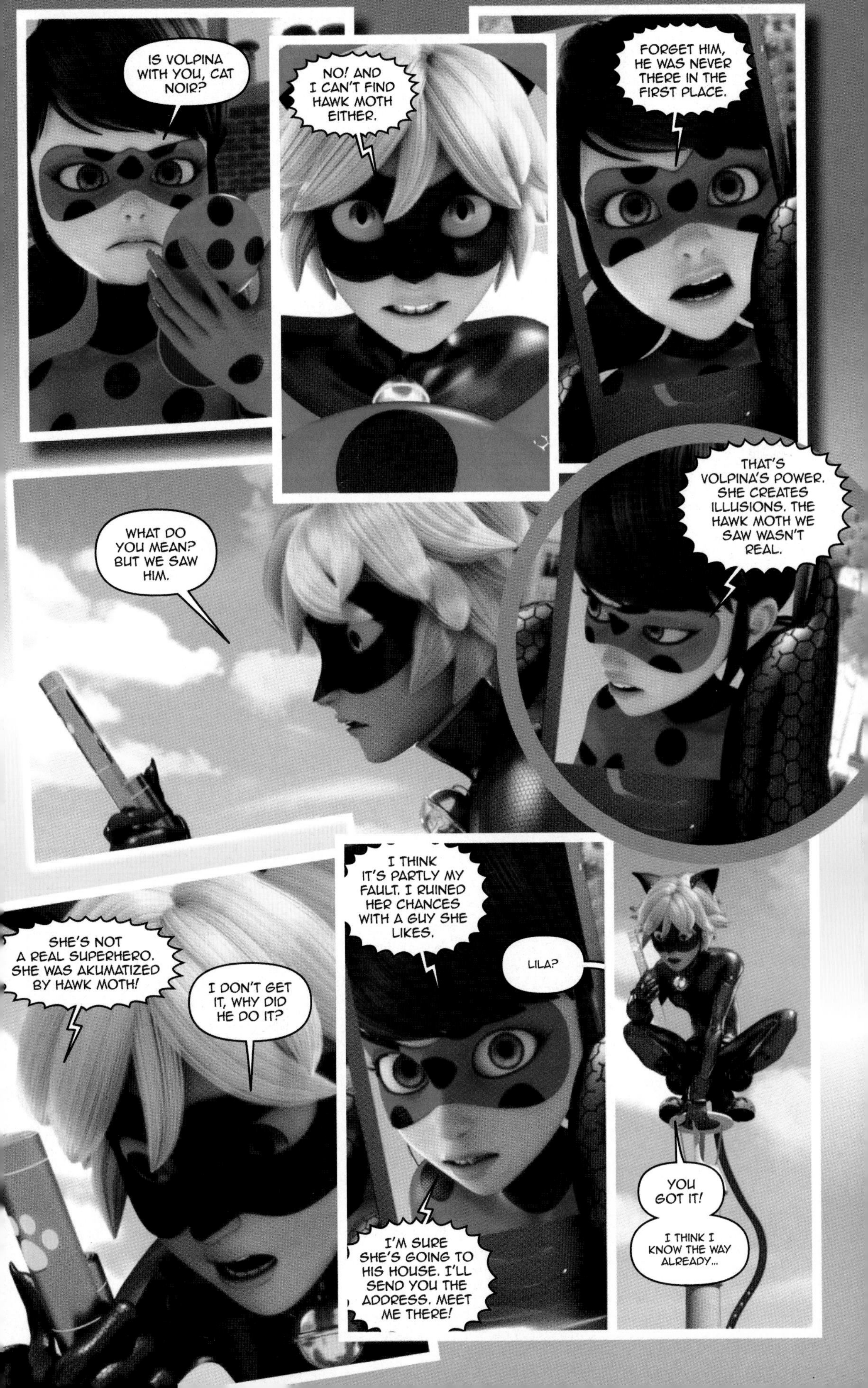

IS VOLPINA WITH YOU, CAT NOIR?
NO! AND I CAN'T FIND HAWK MOTH EITHER.
FORGET HIM, HE WAS NEVER THERE IN THE FIRST PLACE.
WHAT DO YOU MEAN? BUT WE SAW HIM.
THAT'S VOLPINA'S POWER. SHE CREATES ILLUSIONS. THE HAWK MOTH WE SAW WASN'T REAL.
SHE'S NOT A REAL SUPERHERO. SHE WAS AKUMATIZED BY HAWK MOTH!
I DON'T GET IT, WHY DID HE DO IT?
I THINK IT'S PARTLY MY FAULT. I RUINED HER CHANCES WITH A GUY SHE LIKES.
LILA?
I'M SURE SHE'S GOING TO HIS HOUSE. I'LL SEND YOU THE ADDRESS. MEET ME THERE!
YOU GOT IT!
I THINK I KNOW THE WAY ALREADY...

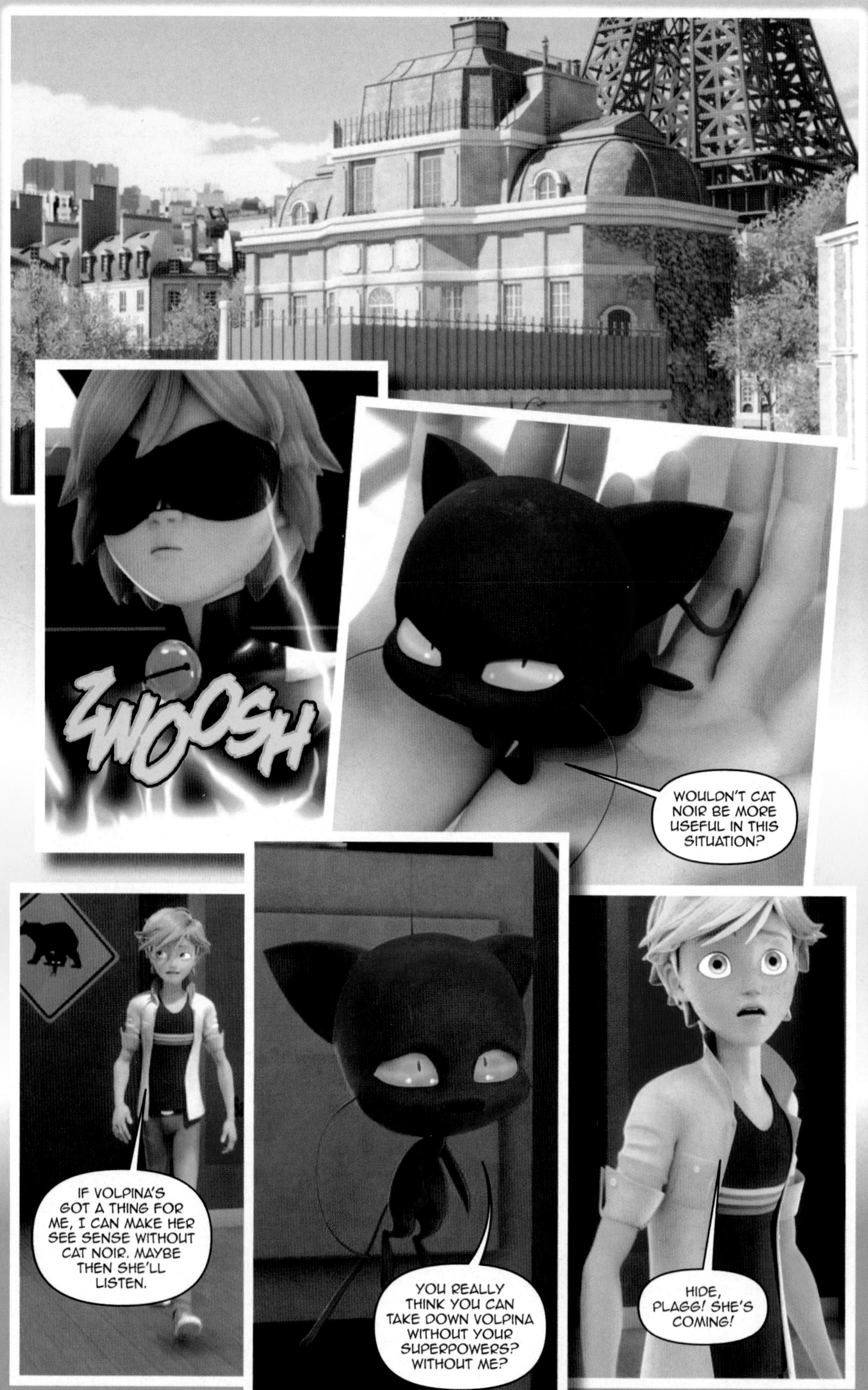
ZWOOSH
WOULDN'T CAT NOIR BE MORE USEFUL IN THIS SITUATION?
IF VOLPINA'S GOT A THING FOR ME, I CAN MAKE HER SEE SENSE WITHOUT CAT NOIR. MAYBE THEN SHE'LL LISTEN.
YOU REALLY THINK YOU CAN TAKE DOWN VOLPINA WITHOUT YOUR SUPERPOWERS? WITHOUT ME?
HIDE, PLAGG! SHE'S COMING!

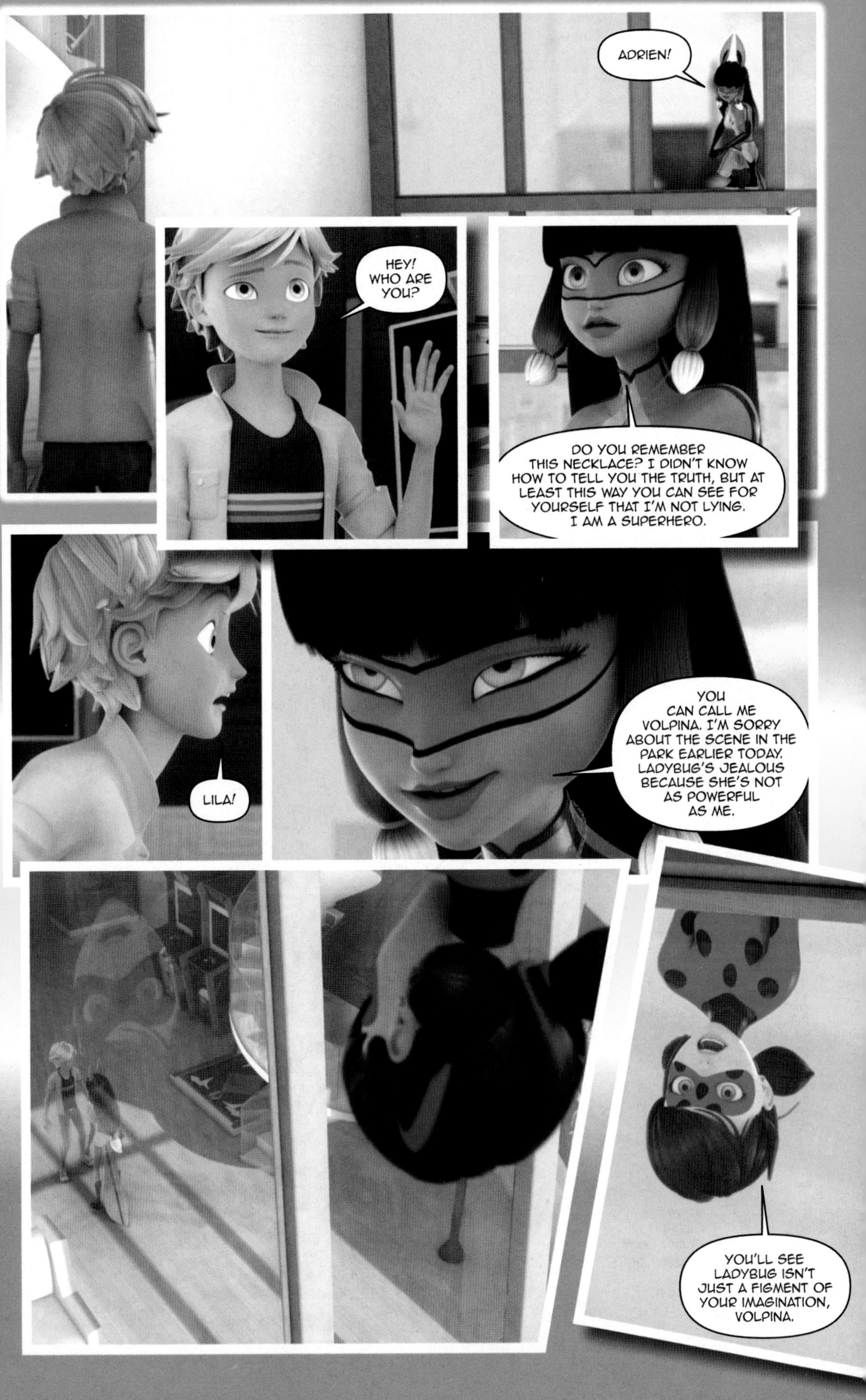
ADRIEN!
HEY! WHO ARE YOU?
DO YOU REMEMBER THIS NECKLACE? I DIDN'T KNOW HOW TO TELL YOU THE TRUTH, BUT AT LEAST THIS WAY YOU CAN SEE FOR YOURSELF THAT I'M NOT LYING. I AM A SUPERHERO.
LILA!
YOU CAN CALL ME VOLPINA. I'M SORRY ABOUT THE SCENE IN THE PARK EARLIER TODAY. LADYBUG'S JEALOUS BECAUSE SHE'S NOT AS POWERFUL AS ME.
YOU'LL SEE LADYBUG ISN'T JUST A FIGMENT OF YOUR IMAGINATION, VOLPINA.

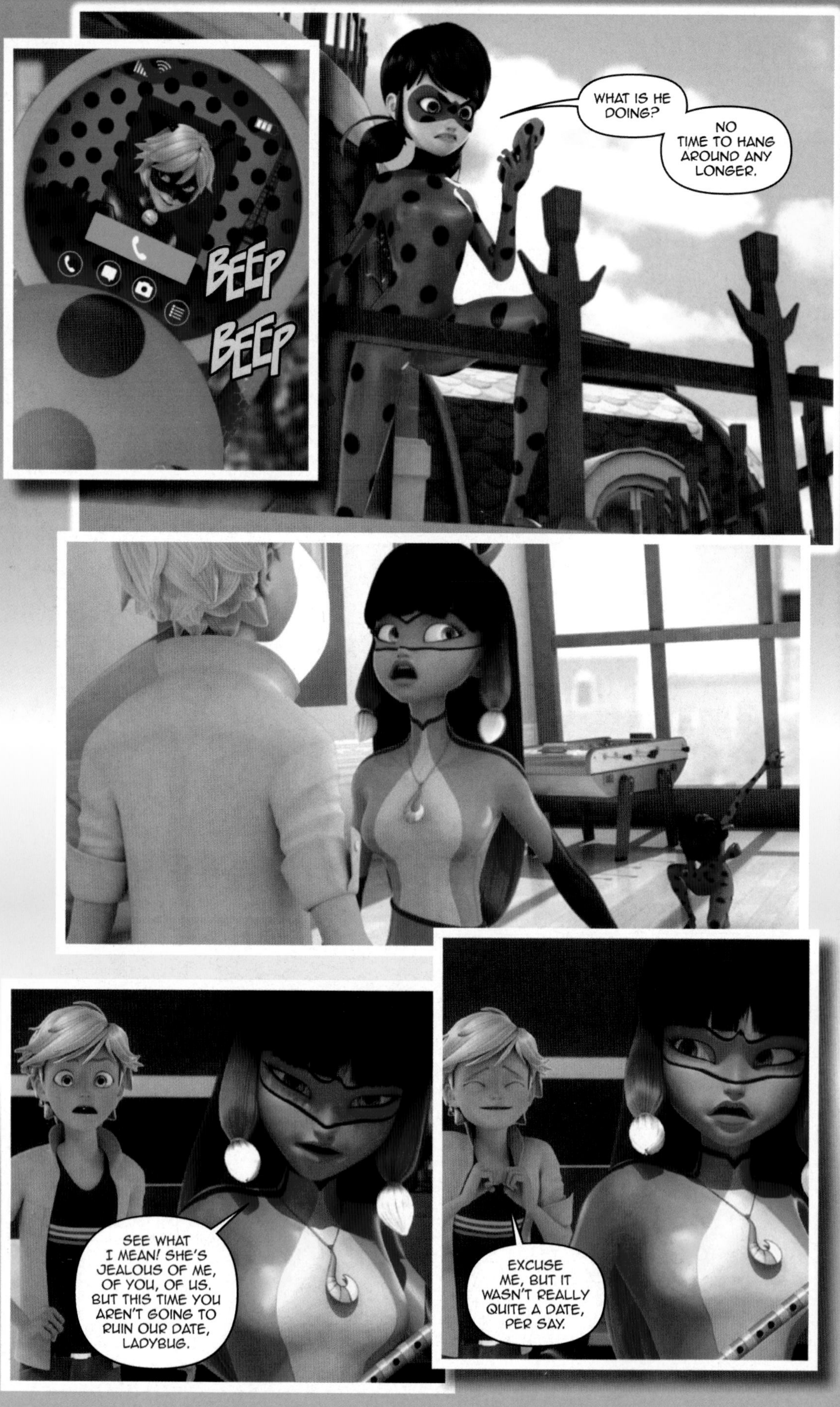
BEEP
BEEP
WHAT IS HE DOING?
NO TIME TO HANG AROUND ANY LONGER.
SEE WHAT I MEAN! SHE'S JEALOUS OF ME, OF YOU, OF US. BUT THIS TIME YOU AREN'T GOING TO RUIN OUR DATE, LADYBUG.
EXCUSE ME, BUT IT WASN'T REALLY QUITE A DATE, PER SAY.

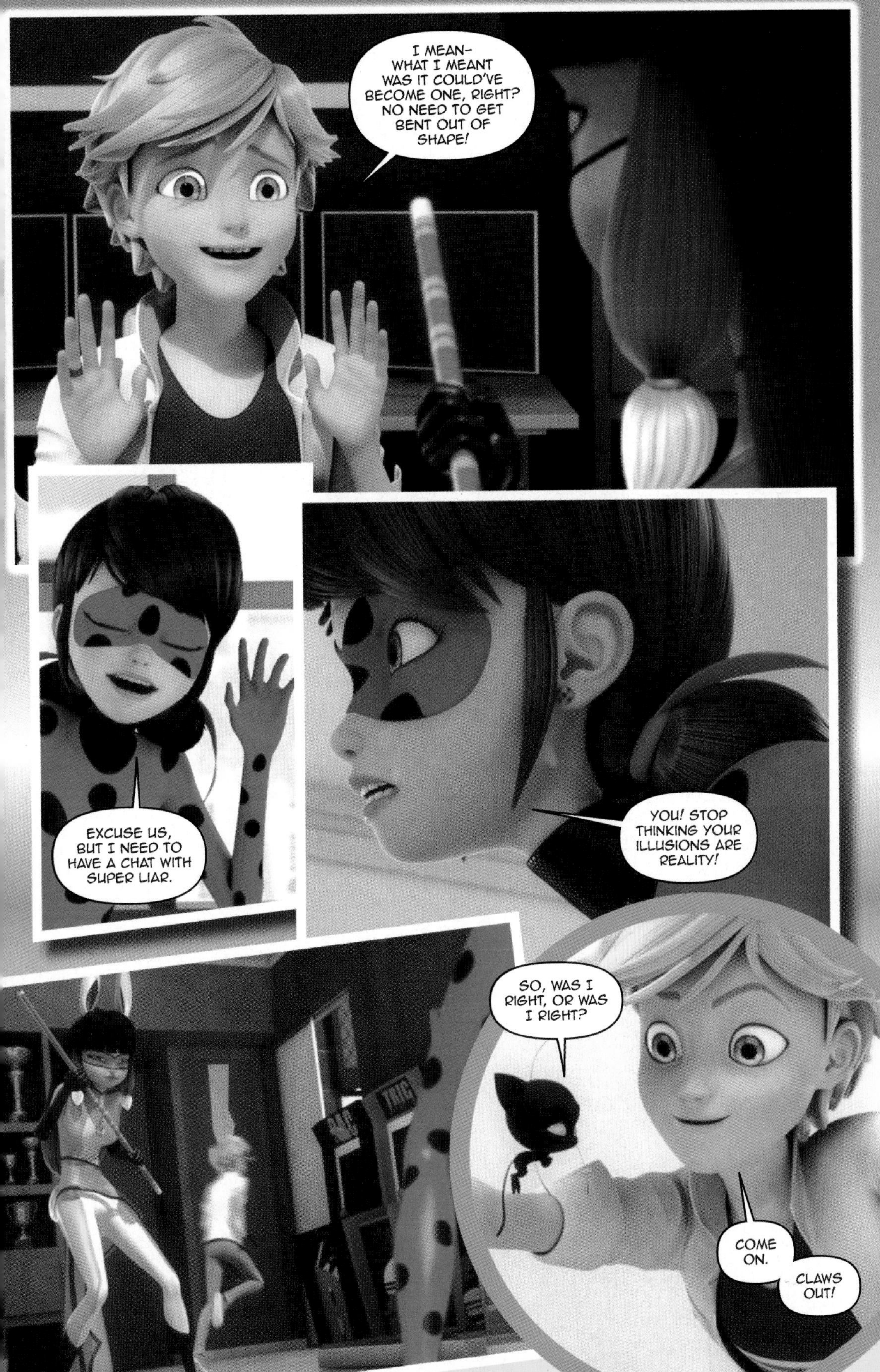
I MEAN–
WHAT I MEANT WAS IT COULD'VE BECOME ONE, RIGHT? NO NEED TO GET BENT OUT OF SHAPE!
EXCUSE US, BUT I NEED TO HAVE A CHAT WITH SUPER LIAR.
YOU! STOP THINKING YOUR ILLUSIONS ARE REALITY!
SO, WAS I RIGHT, OR WAS I RIGHT?
COME ON.
CLAWS OUT!

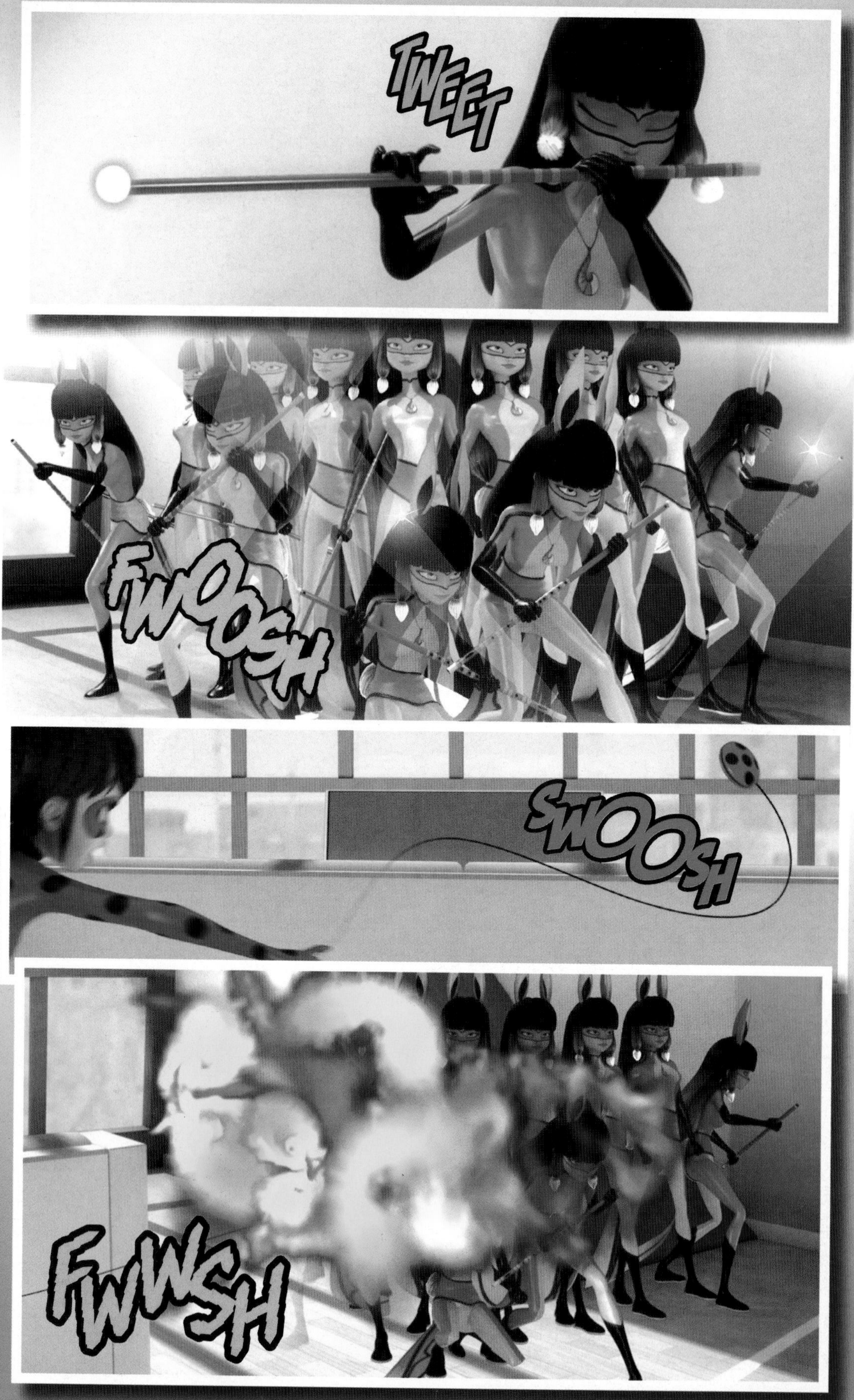
TWEET
FWOOSH
SWOOSH
FWWSH

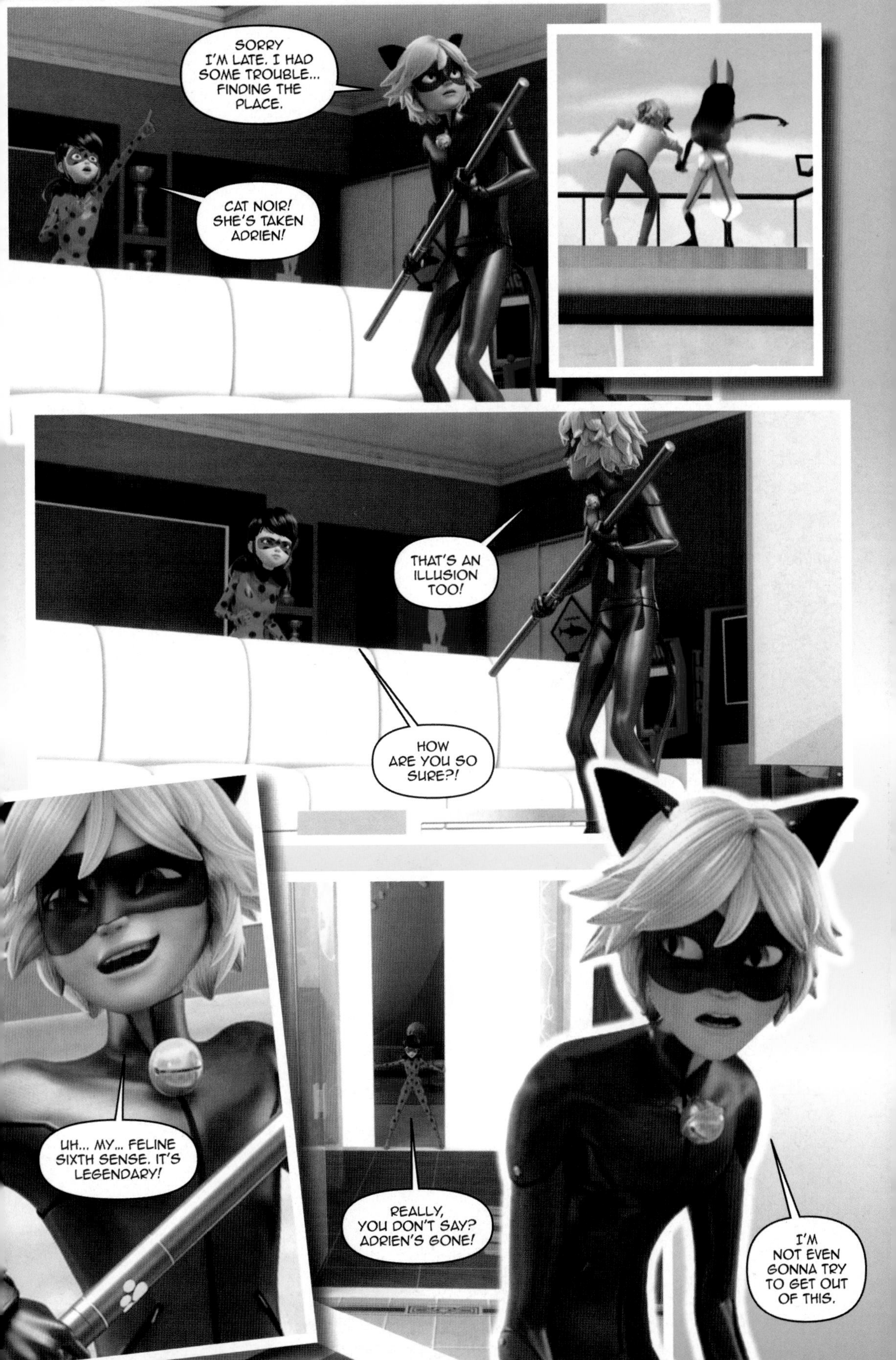

SORRY I'M LATE. I HAD SOME TROUBLE... FINDING THE PLACE.
CAT NOIR! SHE'S TAKEN ADRIEN!
THAT'S AN ILLUSION TOO!
HOW ARE YOU SO SURE?!
UH... MY... FELINE SIXTH SENSE. IT'S LEGENDARY!
REALLY, YOU DON'T SAY? ADRIEN'S GONE!
I'M NOT EVEN GONNA TRY TO GET OUT OF THIS.

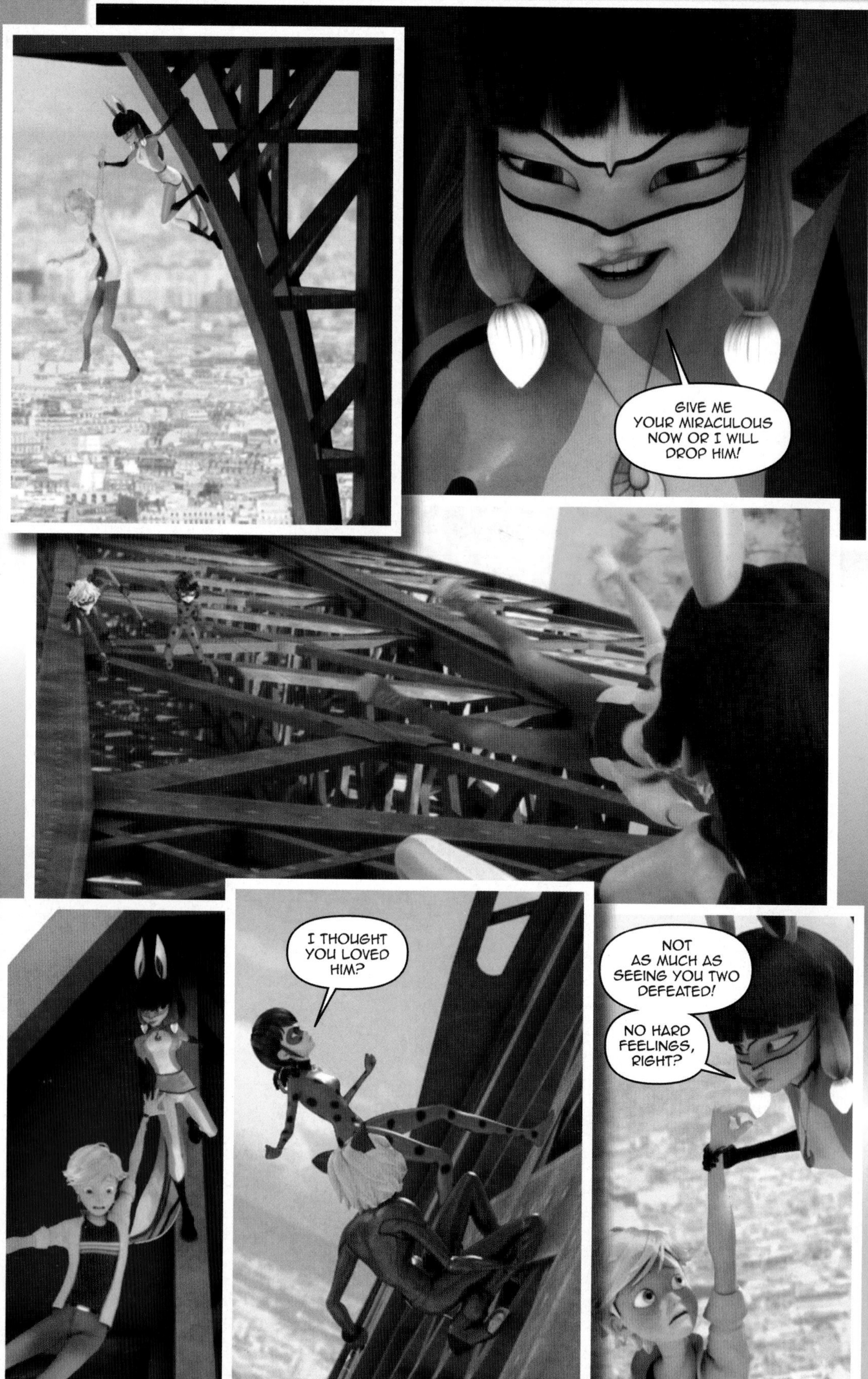
GIVE ME YOUR MIRACULOUS NOW OR I WILL DROP HIM!
I THOUGHT YOU LOVED HIM?
NOT AS MUCH AS SEEING YOU TWO DEFEATED!
NO HARD FEELINGS, RIGHT?

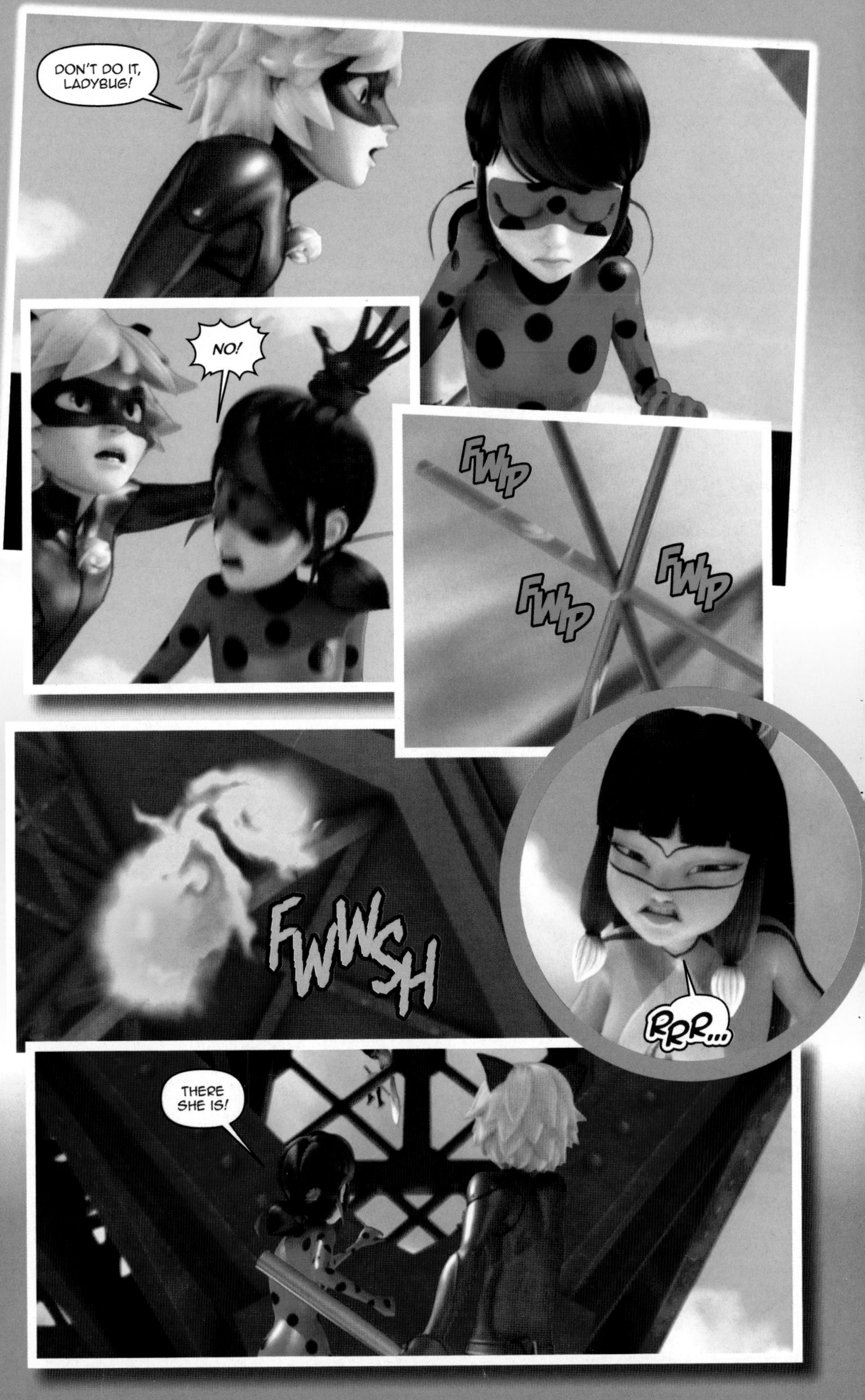

DON'T DO IT, LADYBUG!
NO!
FWIP
FWIP
FWIP
FWWSH
RRR...
THERE SHE IS!

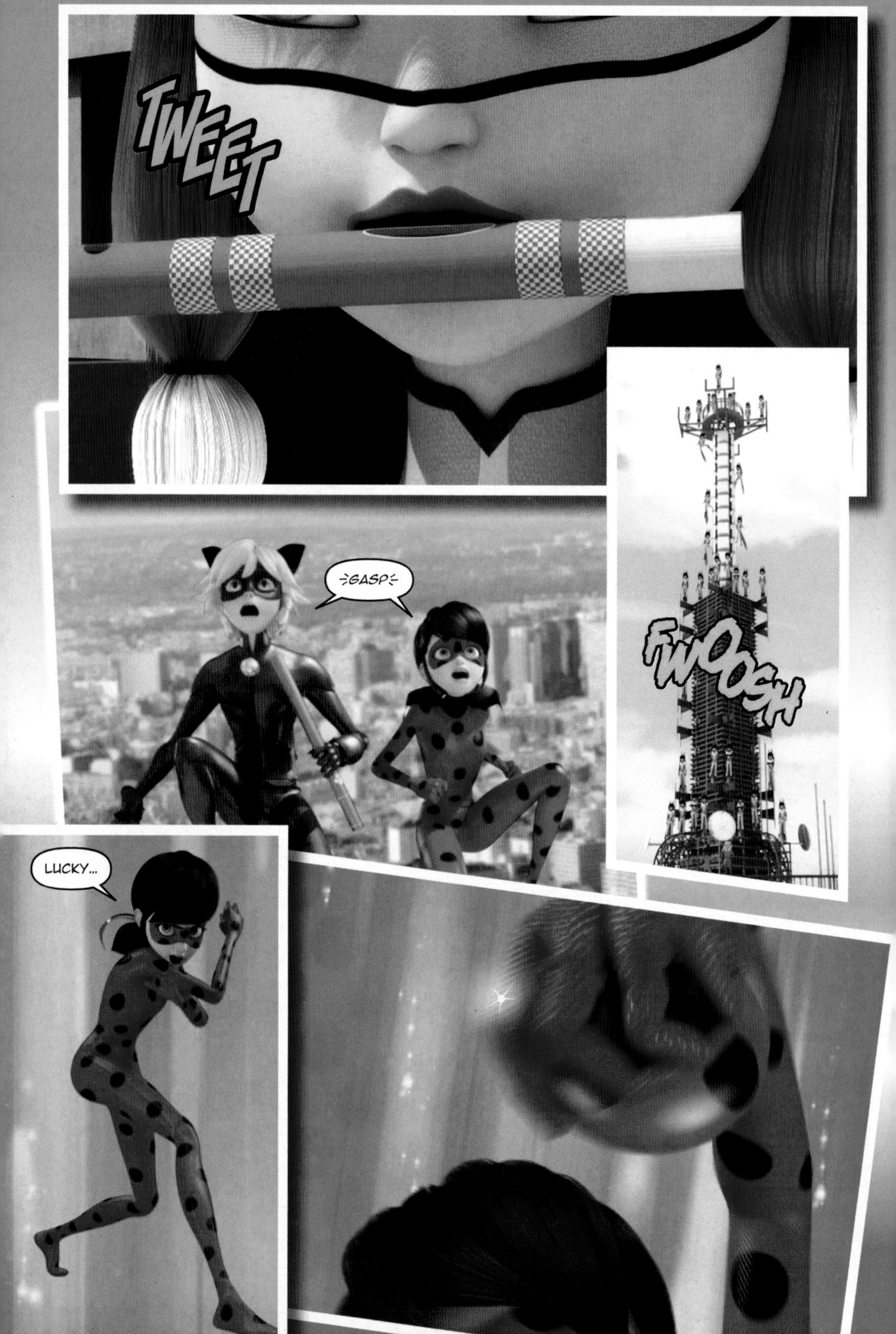
TWEET
GASP
FWOOSH
LUCKY...

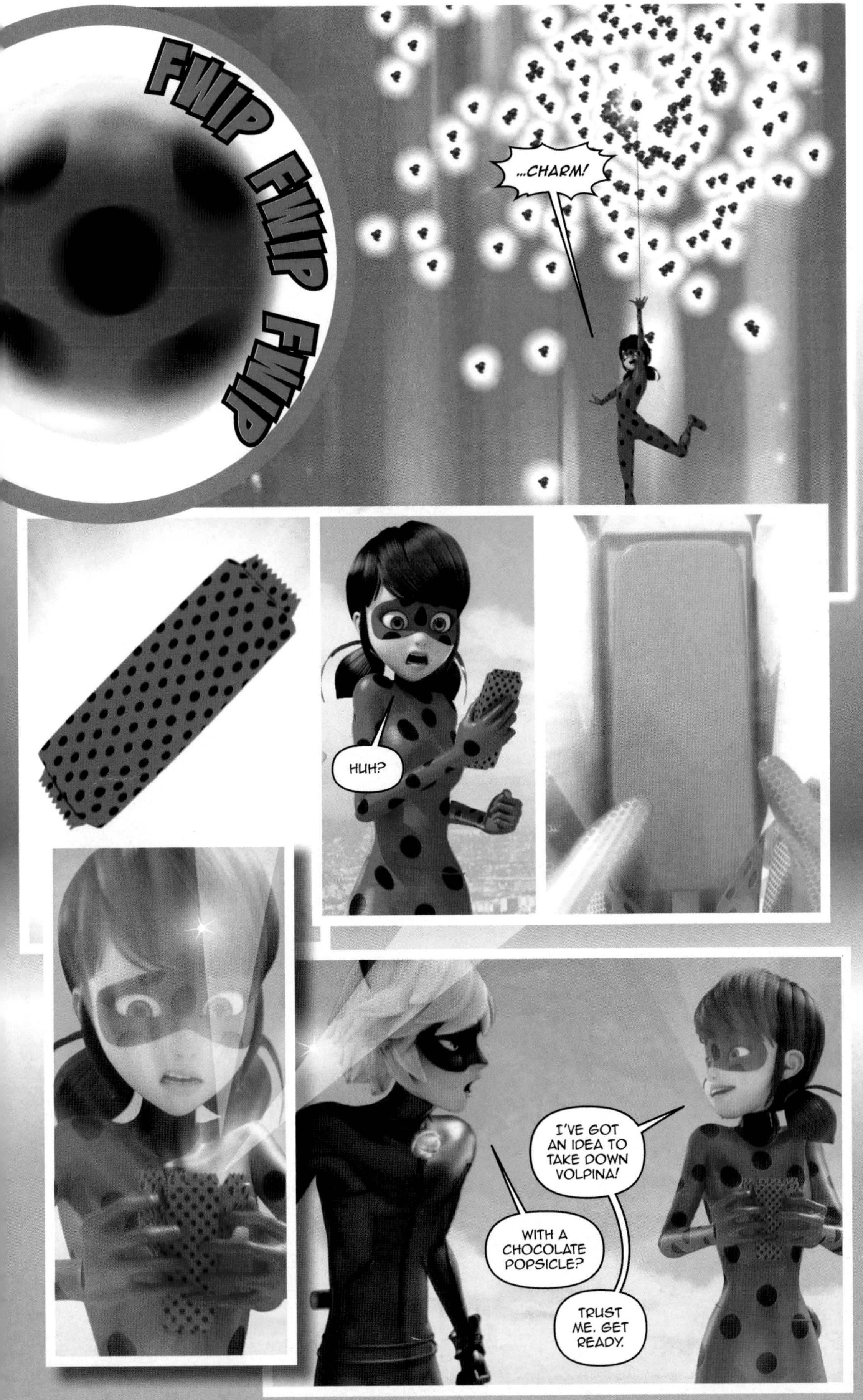
FWIP FWIP FWIP
...CHARM!
HUH?
I'VE GOT AN IDEA TO TAKE DOWN VOLPINA!
WITH A CHOCOLATE POPSICLE?
TRUST ME. GET READY.

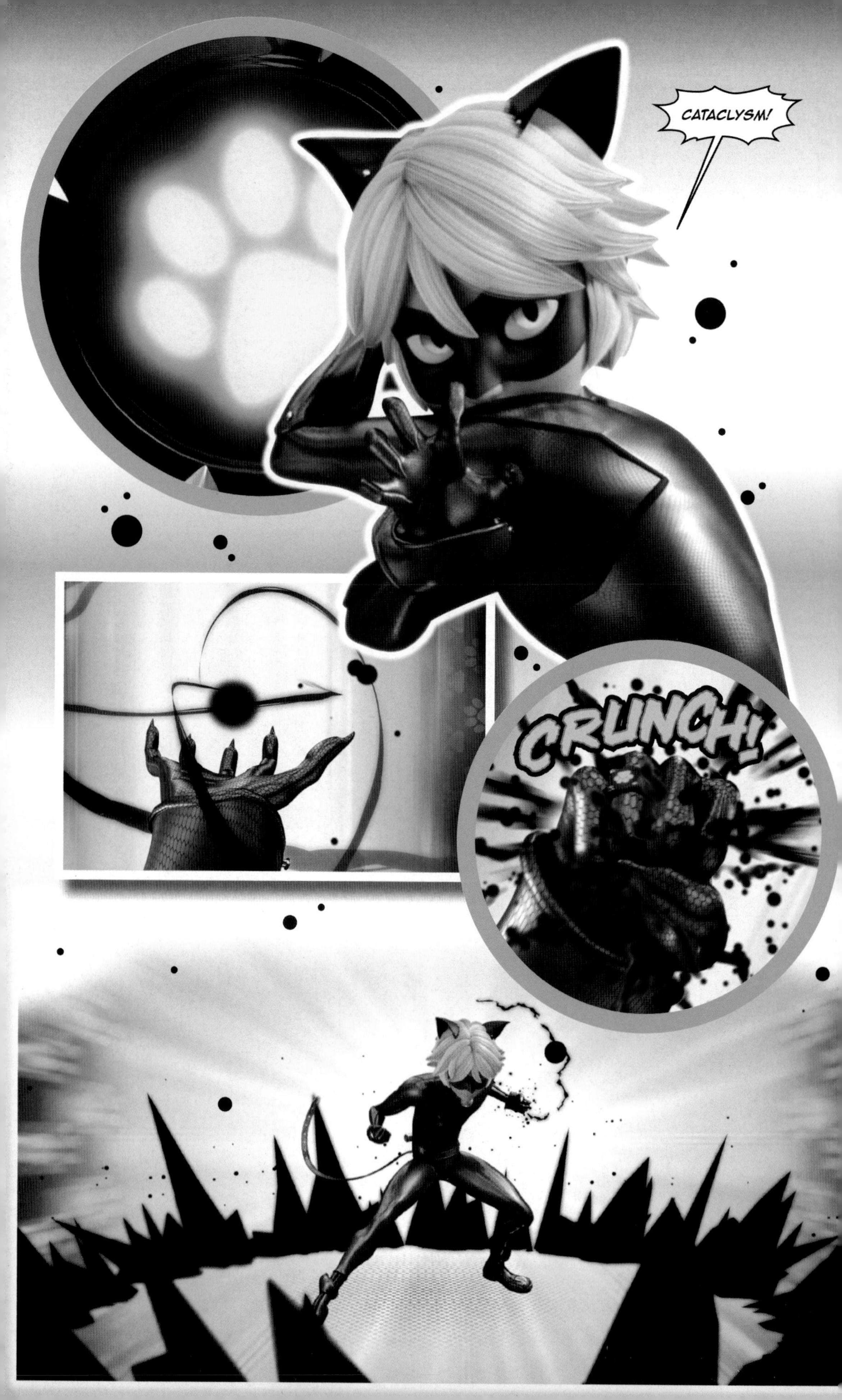
CATACLYSM!
CRUNCH!

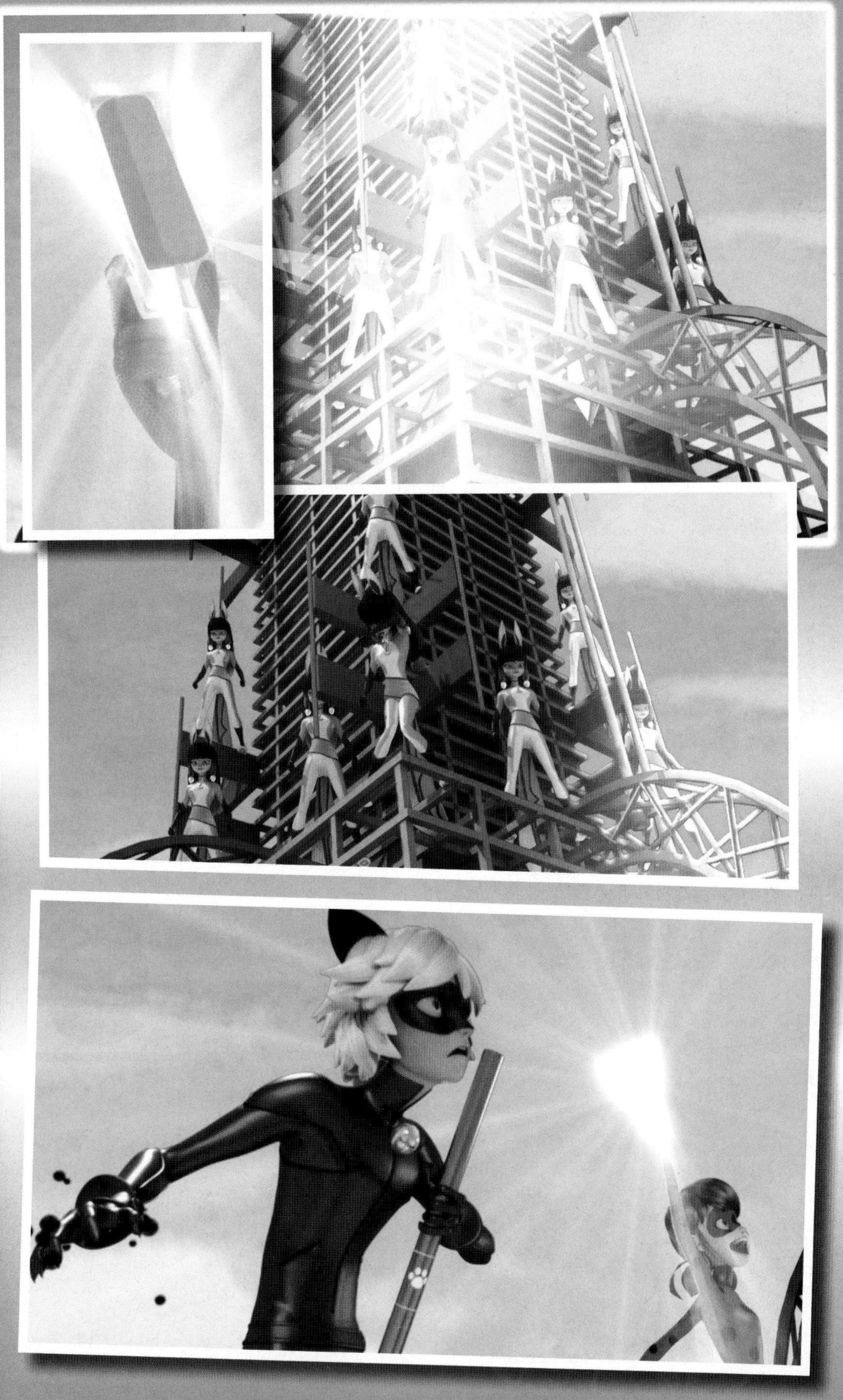

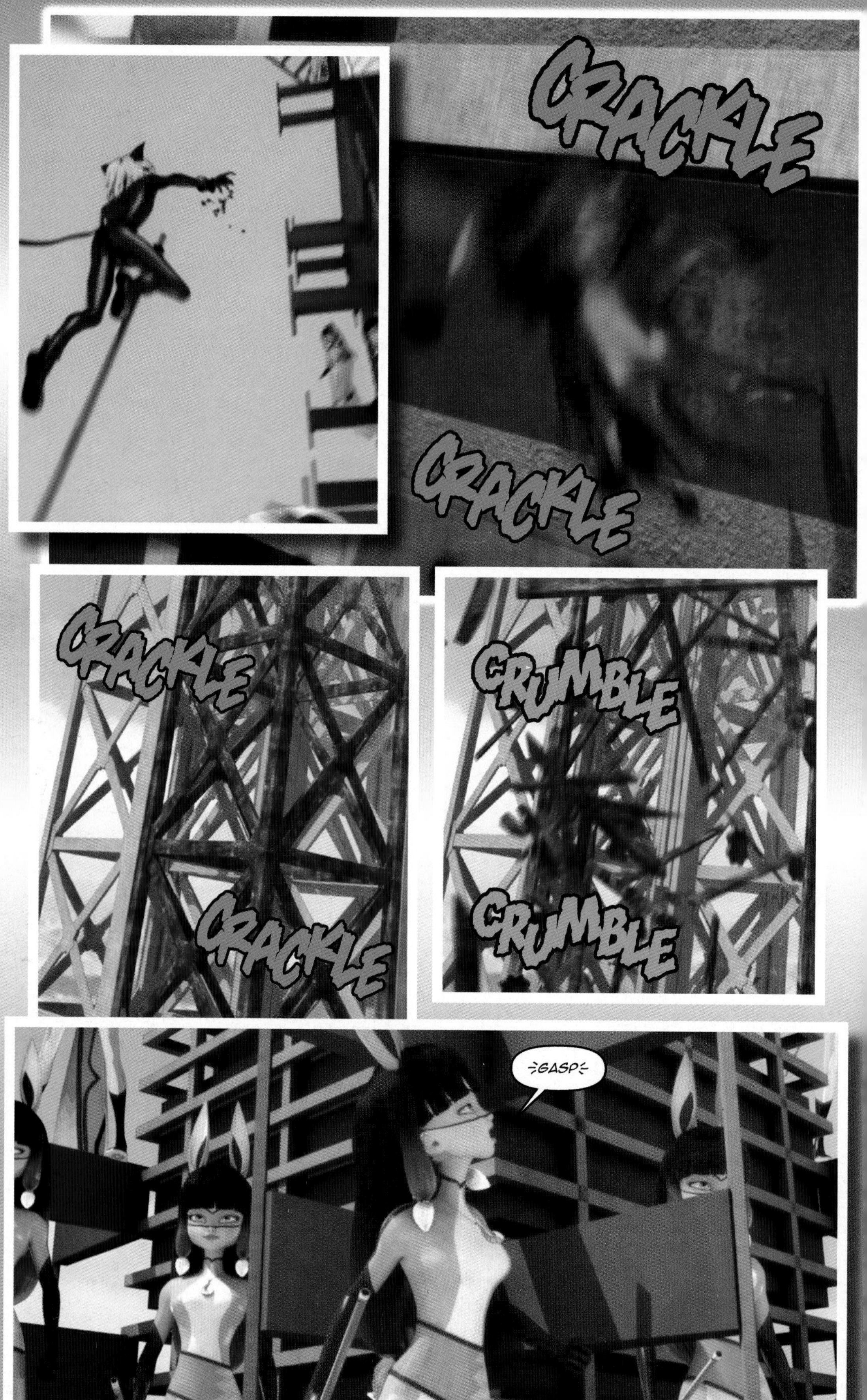
CRACKLE
CRACKLE
CRACKLE
CRACKLE
CRUMBLE
CRUMBLE
GASP

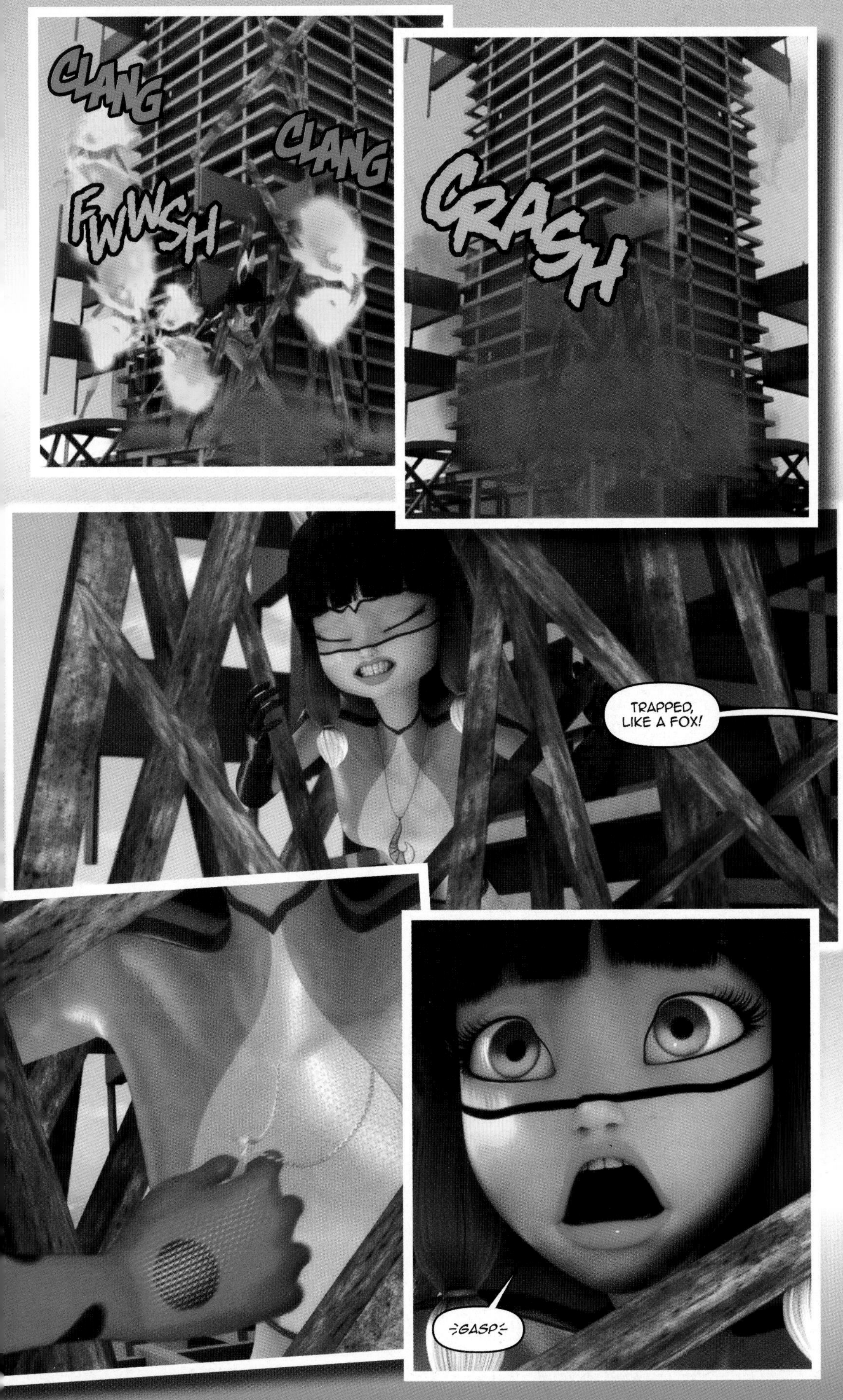
CLANG
CLANG
FWWSH
CRASH
TRAPPED, LIKE A FOX!
GASP

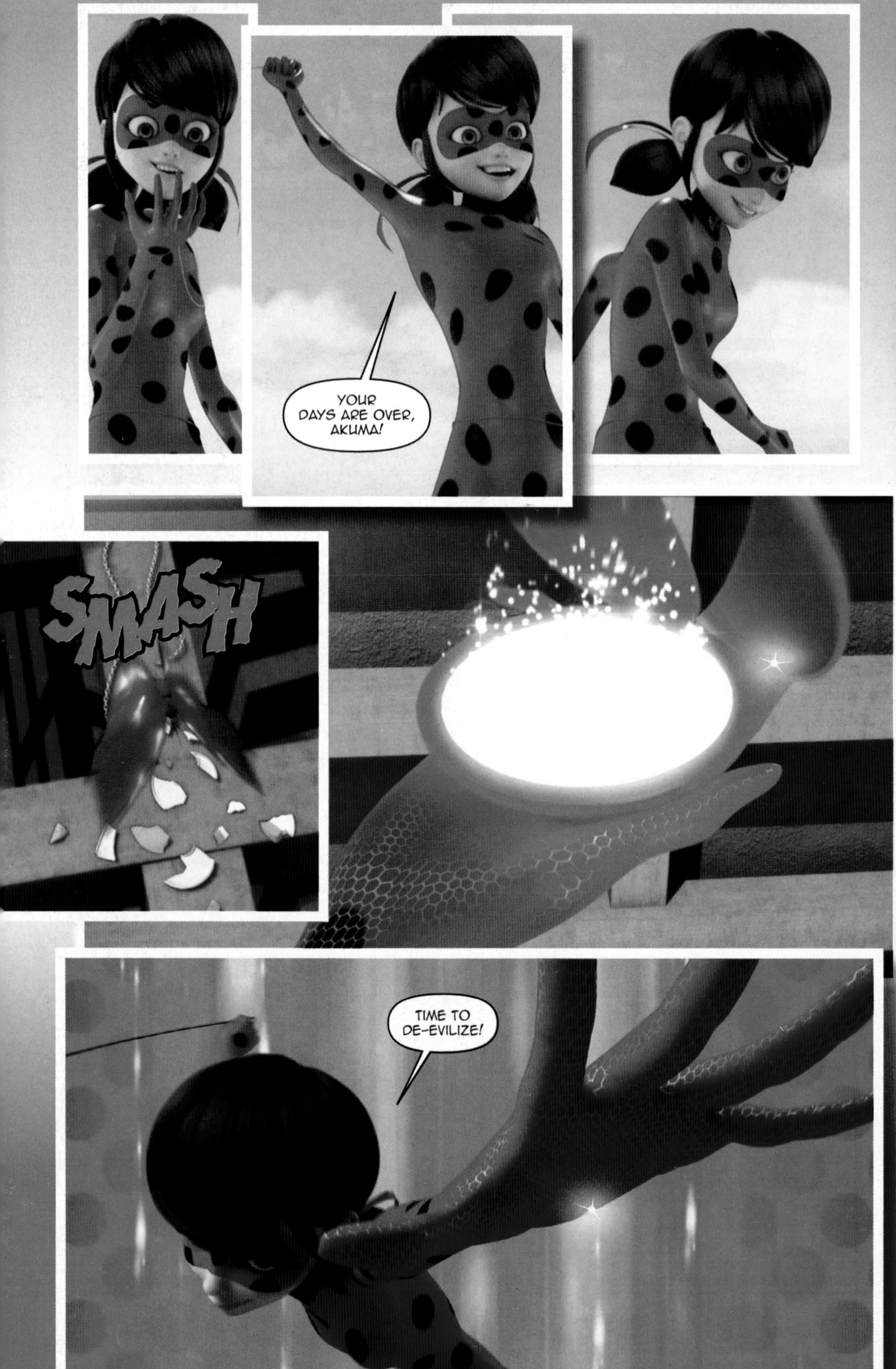
YOUR DAYS ARE OVER, AKUMA!
SMASH
TIME TO DE-EVILIZE!

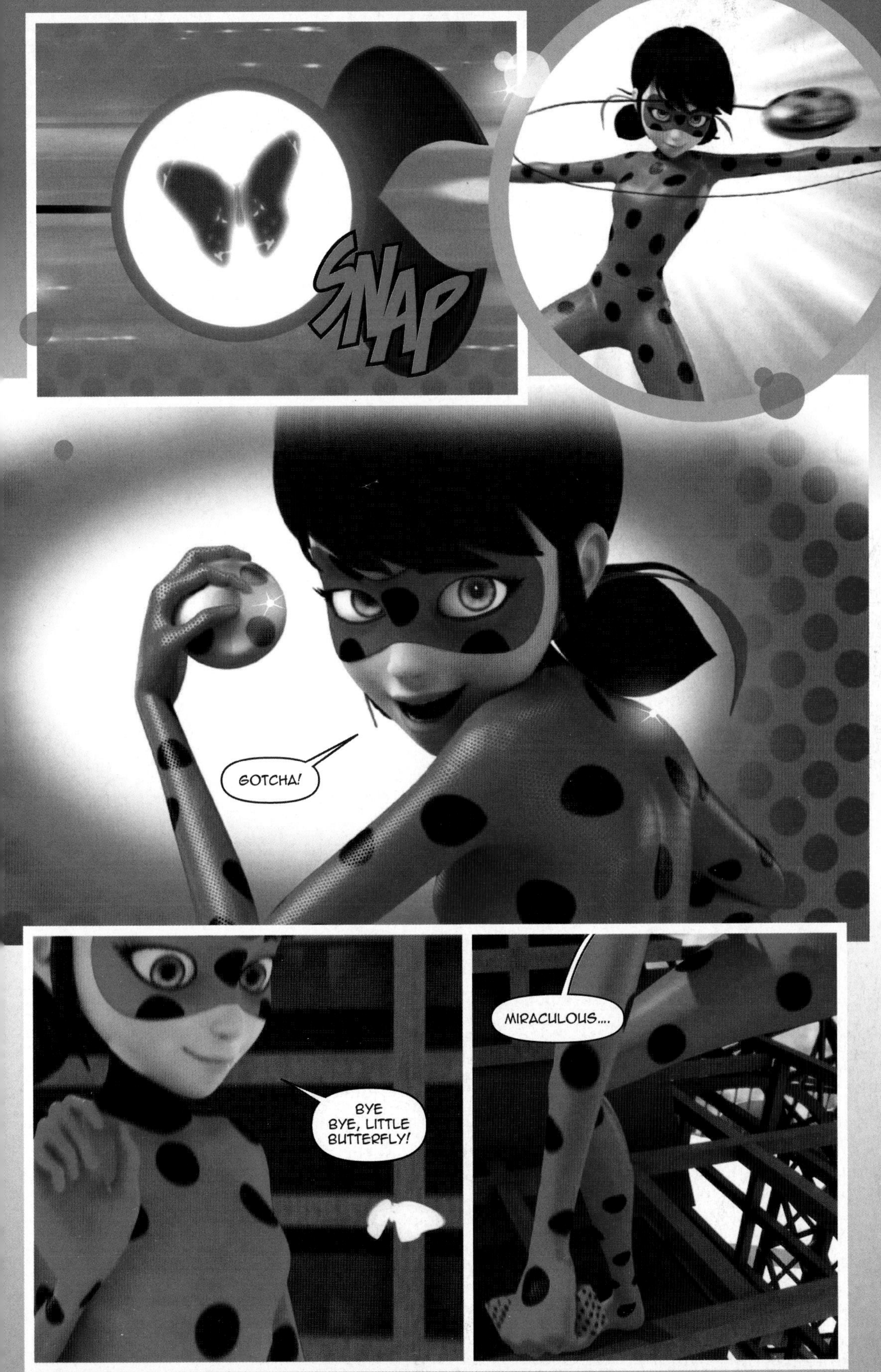
SNAP
GOTCHA!
BYE BYE, LITTLE BUTTERFLY!
MIRACULOUS....

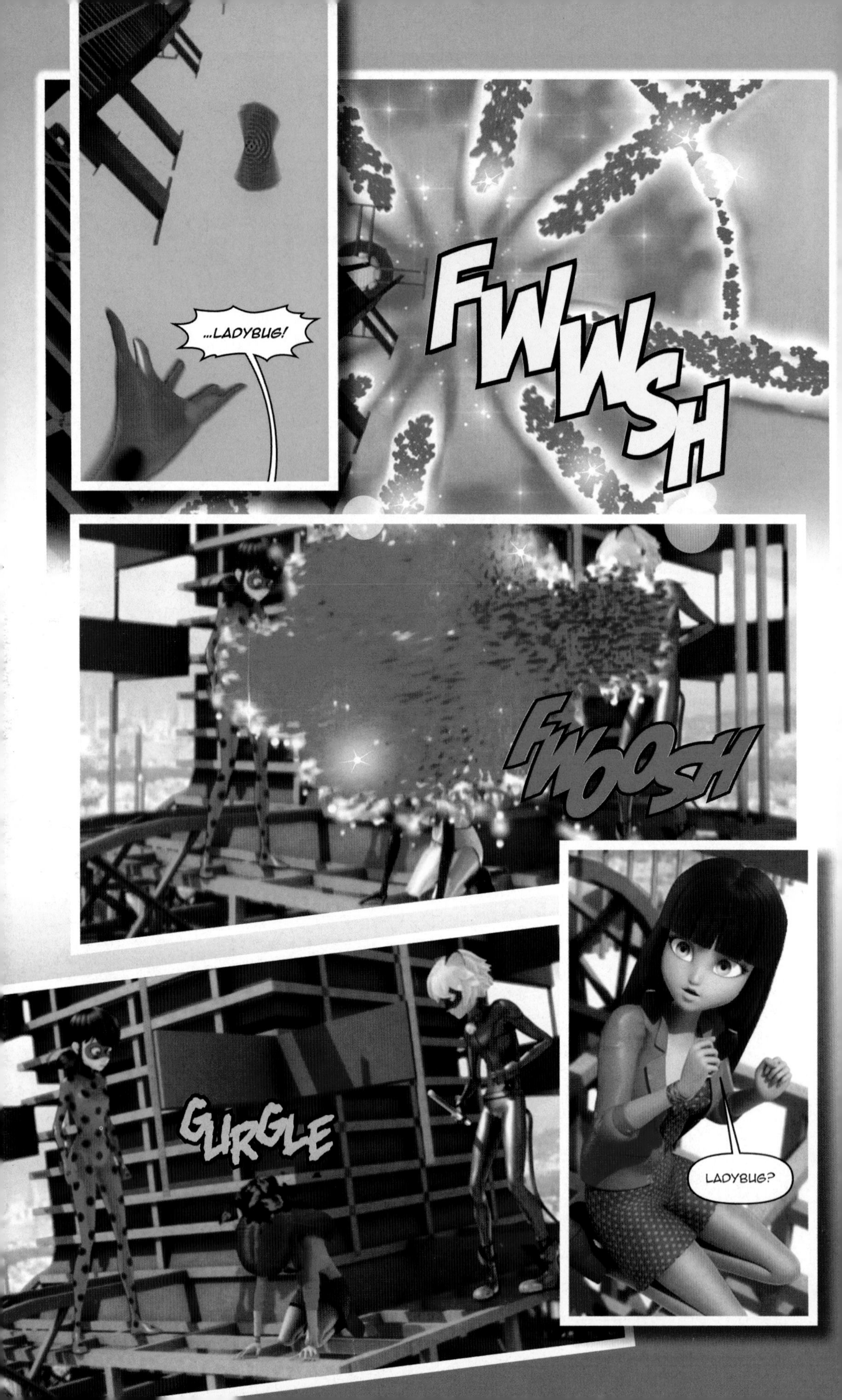
...LADYBUG!
FWWSH
FWOOSH
GURGLE
LADYBUG?

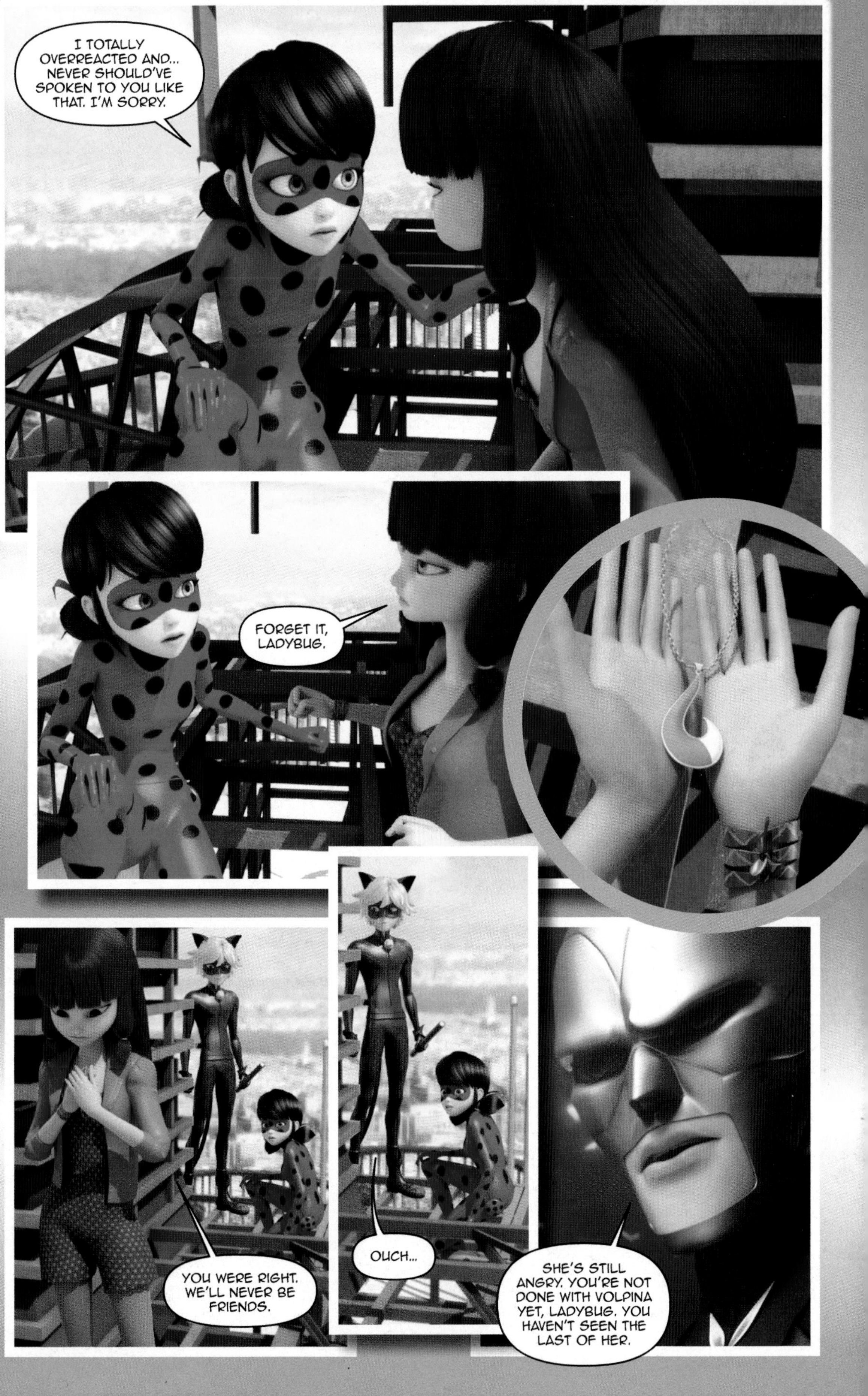
I TOTALLY OVERREACTED AND... NEVER SHOULD'VE SPOKEN TO YOU LIKE THAT. I'M SORRY.
FORGET IT, LADYBUG.
YOU WERE RIGHT. WE'LL NEVER BE FRIENDS.
OUCH...
SHE'S STILL ANGRY. YOU'RE NOT DONE WITH VOLPINA YET, LADYBUG. YOU HAVEN'T SEEN THE LAST OF HER.

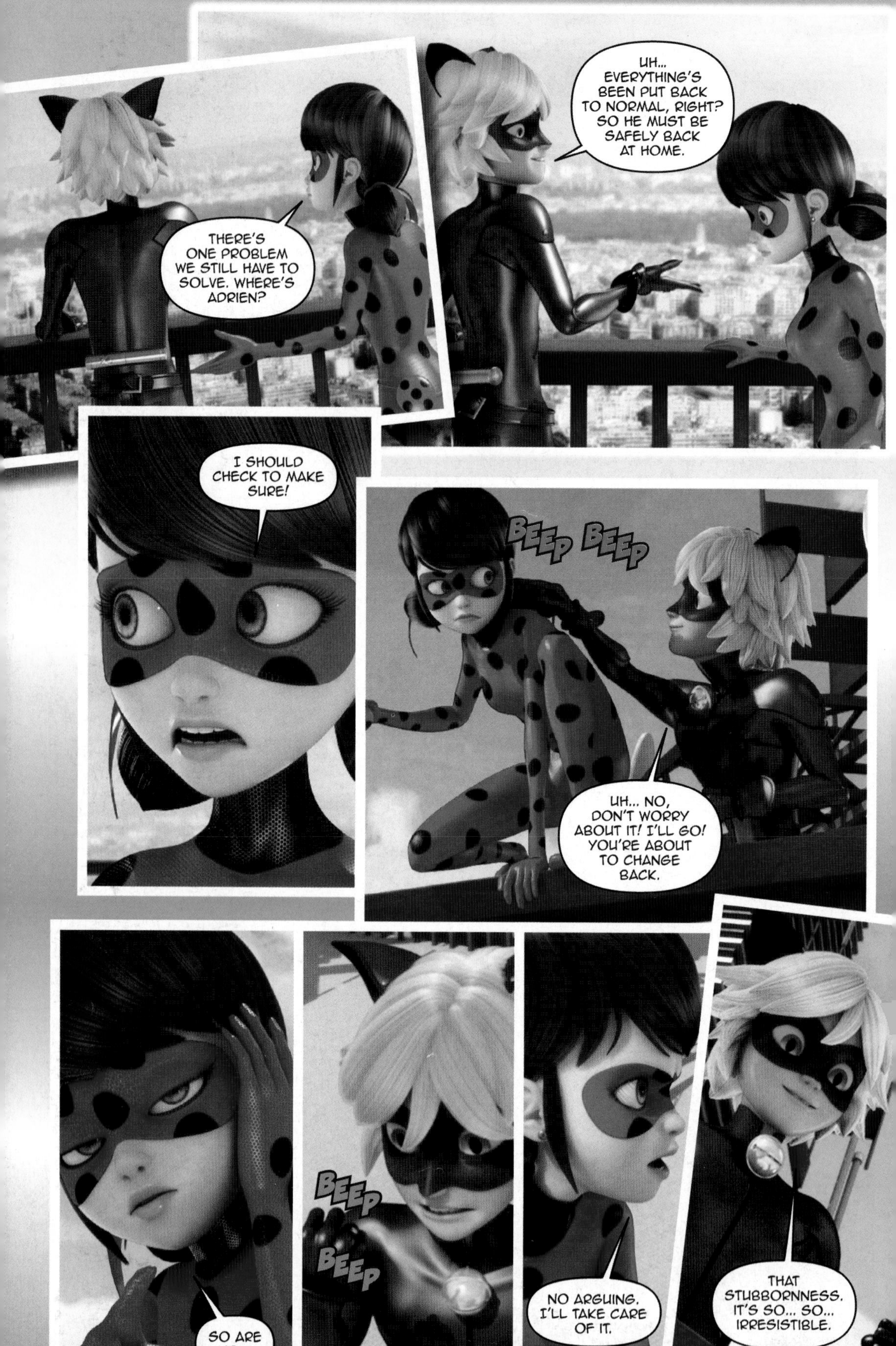

THERE'S ONE PROBLEM WE STILL HAVE TO SOLVE. WHERE'S ADRIEN?
UH... EVERYTHING'S BEEN PUT BACK TO NORMAL, RIGHT? SO HE MUST BE SAFELY BACK AT HOME.
I SHOULD CHECK TO MAKE SURE!
BEEP BEEP
UH... NO, DON'T WORRY ABOUT IT! I'LL GO! YOU'RE ABOUT TO CHANGE BACK.
SO ARE YOU.
BEEP
BEEP
NO ARGUING. I'LL TAKE CARE OF IT.
THAT STUBBORNNESS. IT'S SO... SO... IRRESISTIBLE.

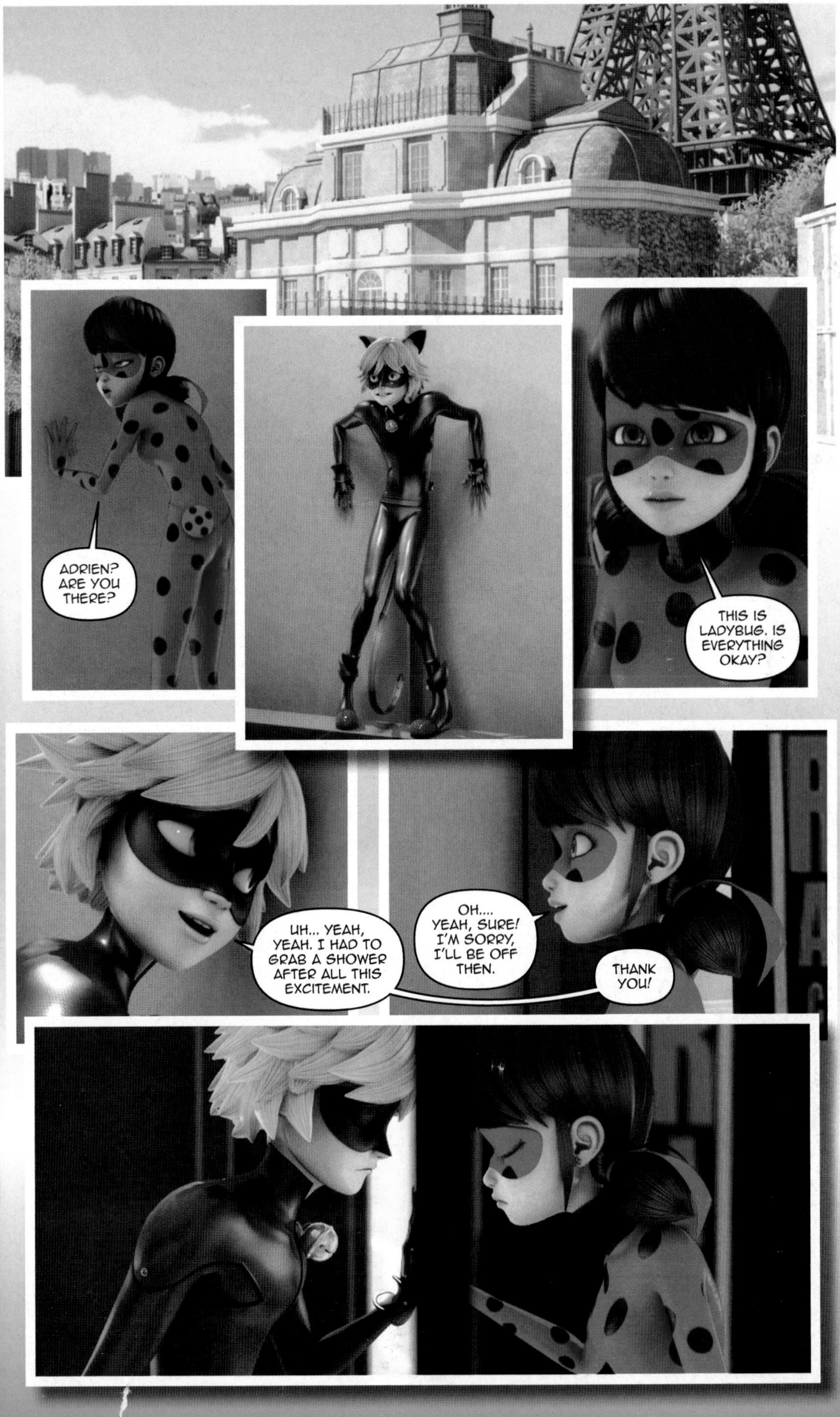
ADRIEN? ARE YOU THERE?
THIS IS LADYBUG. IS EVERYTHING OKAY?
UH... YEAH, YEAH. I HAD TO GRAB A SHOWER AFTER ALL THIS EXCITEMENT.
OH.... YEAH, SURE! I'M SORRY, I'LL BE OFF THEN.
THANK YOU!

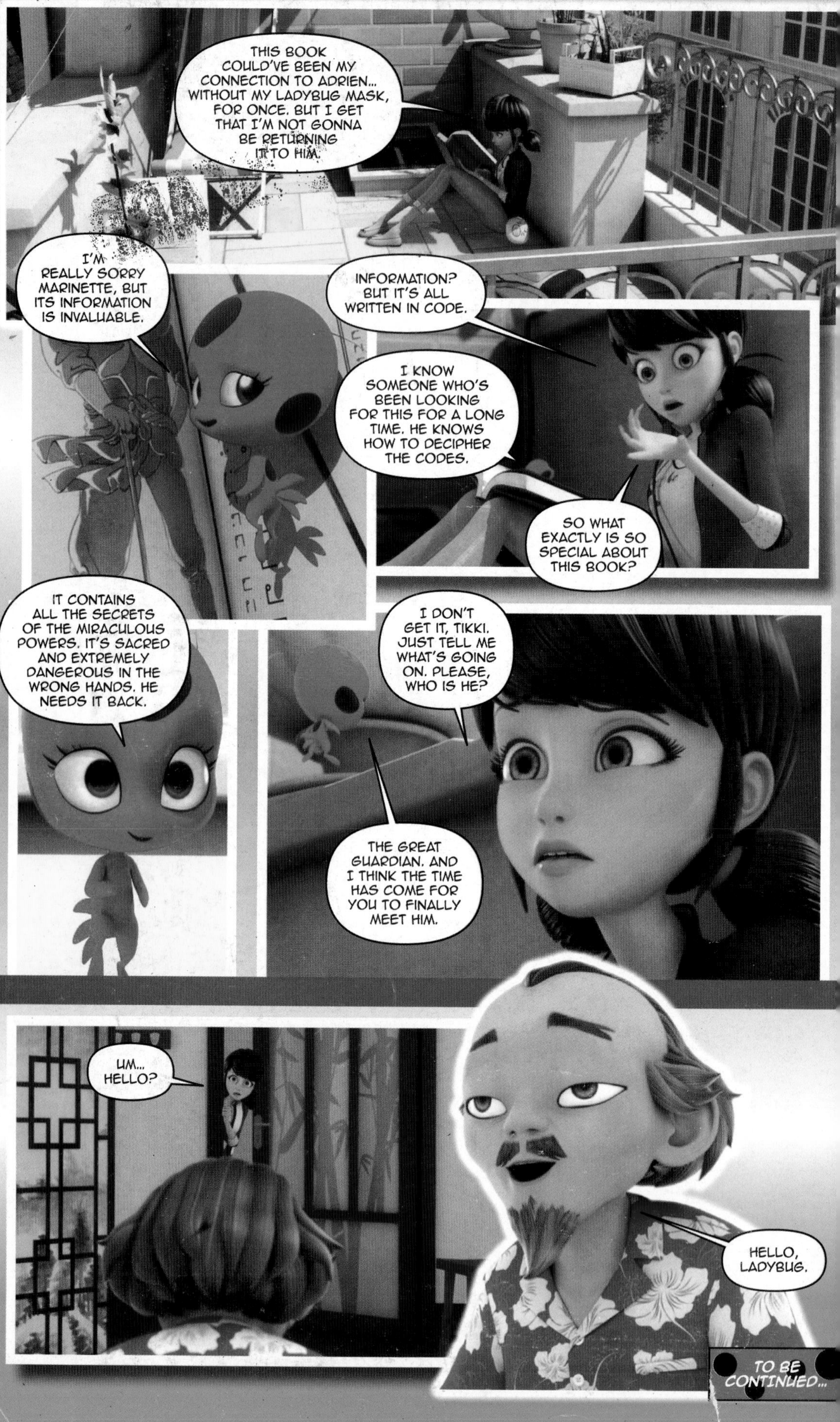
THIS BOOK COULD'VE BEEN MY CONNECTION TO ADRIEN... WITHOUT MY LADYBUG MASK, FOR ONCE. BUT I GET THAT I'M NOT GONNA BE RETURNING IT TO HIM.
I'M REALLY SORRY MARINETTE, BUT ITS INFORMATION IS INVALUABLE.
INFORMATION? BUT IT'S ALL WRITTEN IN CODE.
I KNOW SOMEONE WHO'S BEEN LOOKING FOR THIS FOR A LONG TIME. HE KNOWS HOW TO DECIPHER THE CODES.
SO WHAT EXACTLY IS SO SPECIAL ABOUT THIS BOOK?
IT CONTAINS ALL THE SECRETS OF THE MIRACULOUS POWERS. IT'S SACRED AND EXTREMELY DANGEROUS IN THE WRONG HANDS. HE NEEDS IT BACK.
I DON'T GET IT, TIKKI. JUST TELL ME WHAT'S GOING ON. PLEASE, WHO IS HE?
THE GREAT GUARDIAN. AND I THINK THE TIME HAS COME FOR YOU TO FINALLY MEET HIM.
UM... HELLO?
HELLO, LADYBUG.
TO BE CONTINUED...